BOOKS BY

REYNOLDS PRICE

KATE VAIDEN

REYNOLDS PRICE

KATE VAIDEN

NEW YORK

ATHENEUM

1986 *cp. 1*

Parts of this novel appeared, in earlier forms,
in TriQuarterly *and* Vanity Fair.

Library of Congress Cataloging-in-Publication Data

Price, Reynolds
    Kate Vaiden.

    I. Title.
PS3566.R54K3   1986   813'.54   85-48143
ISBN 0-689-11787-6

Published simultaneously in Canada by Collier Macmillan Canada, Inc.
Composition by Heritage Printers, Inc., Charlotte, North Carolina
Manufactured by Fairfield Graphics, Inc., Fairfield, Pennsylvania
Designed by Harry Ford
First Edition

FOR

DANIEL VOLL

KATE VAIDEN

O N E

THE BEST THING about my life up to here is, nobody believes it. I stopped trying to make people hear it long ago, and I'm nothing but a real middle-sized white woman that has kept on going with strong eyes and teeth for fifty-seven years. You can touch me; I answer. But it got to where I felt like the first woman landed from Pluto—people asking how I lasted through all I claimed and could still count to three, me telling the truth with an effort to smile and then watching them doubt it. So I've kept quiet for years.

Now I've changed my mind and will try again. Two big new reasons. Nobody in my family lives for long, and last week I found somebody I'd lost or thrown away. All he knows about me is the little he's heard. He hasn't laid eyes on me since he was a baby and I vanished while he was down for a nap. I may very well be the last thing he wants at this late date. I'm his natural mother; he's almost forty and has got on without me.

I was christened Kate Vaiden. The name had been ready before they conceived me—my father's mother's name, *Kate* not *Katherine*. He'd loved her so much, and she had died on him before he was grown. So what did that say I was meant to be? I still pause to wonder, though it's way too late. He had known my mother—my father Dan Vaiden—since he finished high school and met her at a grand celebration house-party up on the Roanoke River. She was Frances Bullock and was brought by another boy who soon passed out. They were well-chaperoned of course—1925—but according to Frances, they found time apart and in less than a whole day had bit down hard on a plan to marry. She had what she thought was the world's best reason— an orphan living at the mercy of her sister in Macon, N.C., the real deep country. Dan lived with his father and a single servant fifteen miles away in Henderson, a town—streets lined with water oaks and good dark homes. Neither family had money but Dan's had a Ford, and soon he was making that long trip to Frances on roads rough as gullies. It must have been worth it.

All I remember is Frances telling me about the one time he drove her to Raleigh on a Saturday night to hear *Gypsy Love*, the whole operetta. It was January and cold as igloos. Halfway home she was dying to pee; but of course in those days, you couldn't mention that. So when Dan stopped briefly to buy cigarettes, she raised up the floor-board of his Model T and cut loose, much to her relief. But then as they drove on and the car warmed up, thick waves of the smell of pee rolled up—she'd peed on the gear box or some crucial part, and it was near boiling.

Dan never knew the reason till the day he died. They were married in October, against his father's wishes. He'd been what his father had for so many years since the first Kate died. So he thought if he moved my mother to Henderson, the father would soon be cherishing her too; her eyes were famous in that part of the state.

It didn't go well. Dan would work with his father, dawn to dusk— they sold hail insurance to tobacco farmers—then they'd both drive home to find my mother, bathed and nervous as a hamster from reading since breakfast under unbroken glares from the Negro man-cook. She would laugh too much and show her wet gums, the one thing about her my father didn't like till just before he killed her.

I wasn't there to see any of it of course, their first married days. What I know comes to me in spells of recalling fall afternoons when my young mother would be blue as indigo, stretched on the sofa—me combing her hair and her rolling those few sad memories out for me to approve and eventually use. Not once did she say one word against my father. Dan was nearly God to her, which even so is less than what she was to him.

It scared me long before I guessed where they were headed. I used to have to leave some rooms they were in, just to find air to breathe. They would simply be talking, Sunday breakfast maybe. I would be looking back and forth to follow their words, feeling sleepy and safe. Then it would hit me *I'm not in this, this is all for them.* And their slow words about food or rain would switch into some secret language of love that left me a stranger, stranded dry by the road, wondering would they turn back and why they'd made me.

Frances swore they'd made me by plan, not chance. After nearly twelve months of misery in Henderson, Dan told her one cool night he'd found a way out. He'd got a wire that day, offering him a job just far enough west—Greensboro, ninety miles. Some insurance adjustor had commended Dan's smartness to the home office there. Would Frances mind moving? *Mind?*—she all but died of joy and that started me. Not the joy itself but the vow it triggered. Dan had told her he'd give her the child she wanted once he saw his way clear. Now he thought he saw it and kept his bargain. Frances told me that much the summer she died.

I've imagined the rest—him rolling down on her in the dark, smelling good. They were children themselves at the time, both lovely and gentle as breezes. Or so they thought. I always knew better. They were children all right, which is why I mostly call them Frances and Dan, but nothing like as gentle as they let themselves think.

Dan's father was understandably hurt by the news of them leaving. The new job didn't start till November 1st, and life in Henderson got grimmer fast. Dan made the quick choice to send Frances home to Macon with her family while he lived in one rented room in Greensboro, learning his job and hunting a house. They were parted eight weeks, and it may have ruined them both or started the process.

This year for the first time I read the letters they wrote every day in those weeks. I'd kept them buried in a trunk all the while but spared myself the knowledge. Since finally I was hoping to understand though, I made myself read them—a terrible effort. I couldn't bear more than one or two a night, and then I'd need gaps. No harsh revelations, just two people holding themselves toward each other at absolute white-heat, bound to fade or shatter. Frances may not have known she was pregnant when Dan left, but she's bound to have had proof by Thanksgiving week. It's not in the letters, not even in their little private hints and jokes. She must have kept it from him till he came at last to get her—Christmas week; they meant to start their new life on Christmas.

These are the last two letters they wrote before reuniting. To the best of my knowledge, they're the last happy words that survive from the rest of their lives. They lived more than eleven years longer, strong and talking; but they never agreed to part long enough to make letters useful.

December 18, 1926

Dearest Dan,

It's two in the morning. If it wasn't cold as scissors up here I'd be out on the stoop now dark as it is listening for the train. You don't leave there though for 46 hours and we have a hard frost still holding on outdoors and in. Yesterday at breakfast I told my sister you and I would be leaving on the 24th. She said "Suit yourself" and I said "Well I will" but she seemed relieved. It was Swift that scared me. He waited ten seconds, then shot up like a banner and said "You can leave people once too often, Fan." Sixteen years old and splotched on the face and hands with great red whelps like he'd get as a baby when I'd leave for school. I told him "Swift, you been knowing right along Dan was coming for me. You can visit us at Easter." But he wouldn't look at me. He marched out not making one scrap of noise. Quit a whole day's work and is still not home. I'm sitting up thinking he will be drunk and need some protection from his daddy. You know he wouldn't hurt me and Uncle Holt is scared of me now with you coming. He thinks you are rich. I don't dare tell him we will live in bare rooms for a year or so still. Did you find a bed?

I think we are rich as the caves of Peru and I know we are going to last as long. If you'll just hurry, Dan—

Hurry. Love. Eternal.
Frances

(Caroline was Mother's older sister, the one that raised her and later me. Holt was Caroline's husband and weak enough to get mean when anybody crossed him. Swift was Caroline's youngest boy, younger than my mother but her nephew. He's still alive and badly stove-in, no danger now.)

December 18, 1926

Only Girl,

It is almost three a.m. and why can't I rest? I tell myself every minute or so that I'm just worked up about seeing you soon but then I wonder if you're safe and well and asleep like you should be. I have strained not to bother you with what I know happens only in my head. But now that our separation is ending, I can say that one of the two cruelest things on me was my own mind when idle. I would have to press it to believe in you.

Why should you want me? Why should you hold true? I have to say truly that the only ease I have had since we parted is either when I'm working a specially hard day or when I'm here in the dark and we come together for some minutes in my head. Even those end sadly when the dream caves in and I'm me here alone.

If the human mind had any kind of power to invent mind-travel, this boy Dan Vaiden would have stretched against you every night of these weeks and known your loyalty by touch and smell.

I am fine. Don't let those funny thoughts throw you. Just wanted you to know one more time, darling, who is life's blood to me. He'll be by you soon as iron rails can bear him.

Eternally,
Yours

My childhood memories are the happiest of anyone's I know and the earliest. Most people start keeping back pictures and sounds at the age of three. But the first thing I *know* I remember is sky—just pure blue sky and straight warm light. There's a pad beneath me, a white cotton blanket; and there seems to be nobody else in the world but me and those quiet things. Since I was born the June after they moved to

Greensboro and since our house had a quilt-size yard of successful grass and sunbaths had come into style for babies, the memory must come from late summer, early fall. I wasn't more than five months old anyhow. Notice I'm alone. Was Frances near behind me or indoors checking through the window now and then? The Lindbergh baby was still years away, and my own memory of the scene is of *safety*. I am on my own and calm in the light. If my parents exist, they are calm and trustworthy.

I really think they were until the last three days; and they didn't come for eleven more years. I think I could prove it too, reeling off my memories. But I've generally felt people's childhood memories are like their nightly dreams, interesting to them but boring to us. Unless their childhood was somehow amazing for adventure or pain. Mine was normal as tapwater, up to a point; and I knew it at the time.

The one special thing was that, when I learned to read, I plowed through the small case of books at home. They were mostly Dan's—Frances and her people only read the paper and devotional pamphlets—so I got a good early bait of boys in danger: *Treasure Island* and one I've looked for ever since called *Brave Lads Victorious*. They would give me nightmares, but that was fine too since then Dan would either come and lie down beside me or Frances would lead me in to their bed between them. They could sleep with me there. I noticed that early. I would stay awake and think how happy we were, partly touching each other.

It went on like that, with just enough bad knocks to keep us from giving the world a blank check. I was two years old when the Great Depression struck. Dan's company suffered. Few people had anything left to insure, and some of the old hands were turned out to pasture. But who in the business of peddling a product as invisible as assurance would turn loose a boy with a grin good as Dan's? It seemed like the time was hard on his temper though. My main scare before I started to school was the way I could not predict his explosions. They were always aimed at Frances or at something she'd touched. I would suddenly be transparent as glass, stood off in a corner while he tore at her. Just words—I never saw him strike her unkindly. But a hot flow of words ran naturally in his family; and he could burn a broad strip off my mother from clear across the room, not meeting her eyes.

There was never a question, so far as I knew, of children after me. Now and then I would put a new baby in my prayers, sometimes wanting one and sometimes begging that I stay alone as the third to their two. I seldom felt lonesome. We lived on a street, so I had little friends. Some of their voices are still clear to me; but I've lost their faces—David Sumner, Grace Walker, six or eight more. We played in a long dream, summer and winter. And then we started school.

I can name every teacher I had in the ten years before I quit. They were mostly single women that seemed old and wise, though from here I can guess they were in their late twenties, mid-thirties at most. If the thought of men and marriage had creased their brains, they kept it from us. Catholics were scarce even in a town then, and we never thought our teachers were some brand of nun. But they were and the fact that I've made it this far upright is partly a tribute to their hard example that you get up each morning and *Take what comes*. If you have to scream, you sure don't ask the world to listen; you go in your own room (if they've given you one) and gnaw a dry towel.

That was what I learned—and my hunger to read anything in print, which is all they can give you beyond simple fractions and how to tell time. The only mean teacher I ever had was married, a face like a used bandsaw still spinning. Frances would walk to meet me every day of that year, bringing some small consolation in a napkin, like brownedge wafers to show I was back home or on the way at least.

She's still the big question from my own early past. Who was Frances Bullock Vaiden? Besides my son, she's the one human being I hope still to know. It will have to be in whatever life comes next. What I knew till I tracked down Swift last week was little more than what I've told here above, with these additions. Her parents died when she was eight years old. Her father got what was then called galloping consumption. All her brothers and sisters were grown and gone; so her mother had to nurse him through to the end, then caught it herself. It took her like dry brush; in six weeks she was gone.

Frances's oldest sister Caroline lived thirty miles east with her husband Holt and three sons not much younger than Frances. Holt would make a nice profit in timber once a year and then not work. They all moved to Macon to watch the mother die, then stayed on to raise Frances. In those days either your family took you in or you went to the orphanage—brown smocks and soupbowl haircuts—or you tied your red bandanna to a stick and tramped on the road.

Years later *I* more or less chose to tramp. But young as she was, Frances sat there in her parents' cool rambling house under wide old oaks and watched her place be taken by others, even if they were kin. In her mind she knew Caroline was goodhearted, and she welcomed the boys for company (though loud). It was Caroline's husband that poisoned things. Holt Porter had his mysterious job, occasional deals in huge stands of timber that would give him just enough money to rest for two or three months; then trouble would start. As with most men then, trouble came in glass bottles. He would drink and turn mean and, as we said, "Kick the dog"—take his miseries out on whoever came to hand, mostly a child. In time, it did him in—liver trouble and arthritis—but by the time I knew him, they had seasoned him some. Or softened him at least, and I got to like him. He was good to me. The tragedy of Frances and Dan seemed to finish some process of breaking him; then his kindness could flow. But when Frances was a girl, he bore down on her steady and hard—more than once with a strap. It gave her that wild claw of hunger that would seize her. *Something* gave it to her anyhow. It struck from outside her. Her own heart believed it was satisfied with Dan.

The June I was eleven and in the fifth grade, Aunt Caroline's middle son Taswell was killed in a motorcycle wreck. He had been my favorite member of the family since I'd started going to Macon every summer and spending a month. He had tight brown curls and had already gone through a wife and two babies, still grinning white as daylight. Anyhow that Thursday we were eating supper in the kitchen; the dining-room ceiling had fallen in the night a week before for no known cause. The phone rang and it was Uncle Holt with the sad news; the funeral would be on Saturday morning. Frances had answered. I saw her go pale and just seek Dan's face in the air like a port. She only said "Holt, tell Caroline I'll be there" and "How is Swift?" Then she hung up and sat down, ate a bite of ham, and told us dry-eyed.

Dan watched but never touched her hand that was near him on the table. Finally he said "I promised to work late Friday night. You and Kate drive on. I'll stay here and have waffles for you Sunday night." (Frances had learned to drive as a child, and Dan cooked hash and waffles every Sunday night.)

Frances knew he had little use for her people, the men anyhow. But this was the first death she'd faced since her parents'. She took back the hand that had stayed near Dan.

I knew what that meant, plain as any inscription. By then my eyes had filled up for Taswell.

She watched me awhile; then said "Thank you, Kate" and raked one finger deep through my eyebrows. I used to remember that as her last words, but sadly they were not. She didn't speak another word to Dan, at least till I'd gone to sleep. She stood up silent and cleared the table, food still on our plates, and began to fill the sink.

Dan asked me did I want to take a walk with him?

Any other night, before or after in my life, I'd have said yes fast. But my mother's straight back at the sink kept me home.

He went on his own—went somewhere far enough to keep him out late, though he went and came back entirely on foot.

Frances moved through the time like the air was stiff. She said just the few words to get me started packing. She packed in her room and ironed a few clothes, but she never stepped over to my room again.

When I'd shut my bag (that had been Dan's father's, a worn country-satchel), I was too excited to play or sleep, much less do homework. I sat on my bed and silently named all the friends of my whole life, my age or grown; there were dozens then or so I believed. That put me to sleep, fully dressed, propped up. A hundred other nights I'd done the same thing and waked up next morning undressed and carefully tucked in by Frances. But that night I woke to my own bed lamp.

My hair was soaked and I heard raised voices, strange as thieves. I was terrified a way I'd never been before, in absolute earnest, sure this was real. I couldn't move to hunt my parents though.

I thought these voices had already killed them. It was maybe three minutes before I knew the words were theirs. I've said Dan would suddenly fly out furious when no one had touched him—but mostly at things, the car or a wheel—and that Frances was subject to blues and craving. But this was the worst discovery I'd made in a life that naturally seemed long to me. I'll be writing down other conversations later that I couldn't swear a Bible oath are word-faithful, but here I feel responsible only to what I'm reasonably sure I heard.

Dan said "I left my home for you and broke my father like a dry stick."

Frances said "I never asked that from you."

He said "You're a lie. You *begged* it every day. And when I gave in and Kate landed on us, you made her love your people—turned her against my few last kin."

Frances said "You hate your aunts and they well know it. But take her there tonight if you're so hot to have her love them—good luck."

Dan said "Everybody that's ever known me knows all I feel, one minute to the next. I've never been sure of you for one clear second."

Frances waited a long time. Then she told him "That's the saddest thing I ever heard."

Dan said "That is not the same as saying I'm wrong."

Beyond that, I don't remember the night. They may have said or done more that I've mislaid. Just lately I've wondered if I *did* see things, that night and before, that I buried too deep. I'm told that children can forget the worst—with what I recall though, what could have been worse? What happened surely is that, young as I was, the fear eventually put me to sleep.

What I know next is, Frances woke me early and said to dress quick; we were catching the train. I asked her "Where to?" and she said I knew. I did. I saw it as the rest of my life, and I saw it as hard. But most children see that several times a month. Someone had stripped me to my underwear; so I washed my eyes, dressed, and went to the front room. No trace of Dan and the place quiet as rocks.

Frances sat in the awful straight chair by the door, and a Negro taxi was waiting at the curb. I'd never been in any car but ours. The newness and the bright day—and skipping Friday school—had me half cheered-up by the time we were moving. I never asked a question and Frances looked calm.

She said almost nothing till we were on the train. Then she said "This is going to end very soon. Dan'll see he's wrong before the day's out."

What I recall from the rest of the trip is buying a small glass bear full of candy (of which I never ate one piece) and then deciding to pretend I was a boy. My neighbor David Sumner and I had swapped clothes one day when we were five, but I knew we were playing. I hadn't ever tried to *be* a boy before. Dan had always told me that, if you kissed your elbow, you turned into your opposite—boy or girl. It had taken me a few tries to know he was joking.

And now I didn't pull any silly contortions. I sat stock-still on the seat by Frances and slowly turned into a boy named Marcus. He was red-headed, taller than me but thin; and he had elaborate braces on his teeth (I'd always wanted braces, though my teeth were straight as walls—braces seemed like a complicated hobby you could run). He owned a gray pony, wanted no friends, but was envied by all for eyes so pale blue they barely appeared. Nobody on earth had ever hurt his feelings, though many had tried. And he often took long thirsty hikes in the hills with only dry rations, never writing to his parents who were forced to wait and pray. My body was nearly a boy's in any case. I didn't have even the nubs of bosoms but was finished smooth and lean as the back of a good country-fiddle from neck to groin. There I was split of course but also still smooth. Yet my whole body now was Marcus in the ways I'd seen boys were different. I had their bitter smell on the skin of my arms. Dan had walked past me naked hundreds of times, but I didn't think of my sexual parts. It was nearly sufficient to catch quick whiffs of my new odor in the train's loud fan and imagine my patience.

Frances gave no sign of noticing, even when I spoke in a voice like Marcus to tell her we were there.

*   *   *

Swift met us at the depot. He was Caroline and Holt's youngest boy, two years younger than Frances but her nephew. He'd always had a face so alive you couldn't watch it long—slanted green eyes and cinnamon hair that looked warm as bricks in the August road. Any fool, any age, could see straight off he was shaking you down for all you'd give from heart, liver, lights, purse—anything you owned. Most people refused him *because* he was so hungry (Holt had been hard on him in his early childhood, long sessions with a strap). But my young mother was built to understand; *No* was a thought she'd seldom had, much less expressed.

And he met us in tears. The first thing he said, once he got us in the car, was straight to Frances. "I never cried a drop till I heard your train, Fan."

Frances said "Well, I'm here" and cupped her left palm to the back of his neck.

I noticed nobody had mentioned me. But that was all right, the way I felt. Something had told me during the trip "You are grown from now on. Start acting brave." In my later life I never tried turning back into Marcus; but he may have told me that, which is why I recall him.

The Second World War was still a year off, and nobody close to my family had died since I could remember; so Taswell's funeral was the first I attended. We got there Friday afternoon at four-thirty, and the rest of the evening and Saturday morning were normal for funerals. The only difference was a kind of steady silent whistle in the air like the cry of bats. I felt it from the moment I entered the room where Taswell lay, and it wasn't till my own mother's funeral on the Monday that I guessed the sound was a natural companion to early wasteful death. The years since have proved me right.

The men in the house were the ones that seemed crushed. Caroline was back in the kitchen when we came in, helping black Adelaide cook supper. The whole town of course had brought in food enough for starving Armenia, but Caroline wanted us to have *her* food.

Frances went straight over to the stove and hugged her. That was the first time Frances cried.

But Caroline stepped back politely, faced me, and said "Where's your daddy?"

I said "At home" and pointed wherever I thought Greensboro was.

She smiled—I remember thinking "Look, she can smile"—and said "*This* is home," pointing toward her own floor.

I didn't know how right she was, and I couldn't stop thinking of Dan's hot words to Frances last night—that she had kept me from knowing his people. So I took his side. I said "I live in Greensboro on South Elm Street."

Caroline made a frown but then smiled again.

Frances said "Dan's boss couldn't let him go. He sent you much love."

Caroline still spoke to me. "That's always welcome."

Swift was behind my mother and me. He hooked a finger in the back of her belt and said "See Taswell."

Frances turned to go with him.

Caroline said to me "You stay here, Kate."

I looked to Frances but she wasn't watching me, so I disobeyed Caroline's order and followed Frances and Swift. They were magnets. Or Frances was. Up to that minute I'd never understood her pull on others. It was hid all in her short kind good-smelling body, strong as a riptide.

Taswell and the coffin were in the dining room. When Swift led us in, I saw right away that the place was nothing but men. Uncle Holt was sitting beside the bank of flowers, and four or five others were standing round him. Even I knew every face from my visits; they'd been the main features of my mother's life here before she met Dan. Some hugged her; some nodded and fired off short smiles. But every set of eyes tried to sweep her body without Frances knowing. She seemed not to; I caught every one. Uncle Holt strained to rise, but she rushed to press him down and bent to kiss his scalp. I knew what that cost her. She looked to a boy at Holt's side and asked "Did Walter come yet?" I'd never heard her voice so clear and deep. The boy went blank and froze.

Holt shook his head and the biggest tears I'd seen dragged down his cheeks like white corn-syrup. I'd liked him till then. (Walter was his oldest boy, my first cousin. He'd fought with Holt some years before and left home for Norfolk, not looking back except to send his mother nice checks at Christmas. Frances also got money from him every birthday; but I'd never seen him, just a cheerful picture.)

Swift said "Walter sent the pall. Come on and see it." He took my mother's shoulders in his big hands and kissed her neck.

She leaned back against him. Then she reached for me—first time she'd touched me since we left the train.

I let her steer me to the coffin. Swift lifted me. Most people I've met speak of the shock when they first saw a corpse. The first thing I felt there, tight in Swift's arms, was "Why can't all statues be this real?" I'd only seen a few streaky green ones, old stout men and soldiers. I wondered why they didn't have him up in a chair—anything that neat and carefully colored.

Swift said "You can touch him" and jogged me once.

Frances said "No, darling."

But I did anyhow, on the back of his hand. There'd been a birth-mark there that I'd always liked, a tan map of Spain. They'd tried to paint over it, but I knew where to touch. It was tender and cool like he'd always been. Then I suddenly knew I was still a child. A wave of tiredness swept up in me, and before Swift had hardly set me down I was asleep. Why of all things in childhood is that the one blessing invariably lost, that chance of dropping down a hole with no warning into sleep black as closets till a kind friend wakes you? So I slept from five on Friday afternoon, not a bite to eat, till six the next morning.

Caroline woke me. She was sitting by me on the bed I shared with Frances, and she held a small bowl. The other hand was gripping my ankle through the sheet. When I finally looked she held up a finger—let Frances sleep—and then she spooned baked apple to me, smiling. I thought "She must not have really loved Tas," but I swallowed gladly and followed her out.

Frances slept on like a child herself till nearly nine. Then Caroline told me to wake her and Swift; they had gone for a ride to the river last night. Swift's room was right off the kitchen, easy reach. But waking him was always like rousing a tree.

Frances came to, the instant I touched her chin. She thrust it up against my finger and said *"I'm* sorry."

I thought she meant her laziness. I'd never known her to sleep past me before. I told her she needed it. That seemed to relieve her, and I helped her dress.

All my life I had loved to watch her dress. I'd hang around her half a day on the chance she might get a sudden mood to bathe and change. I think at first I was fascinated simply by the complicated strangeness—hooks-and-eyes, frail straps, green garter-rolls, her powder. Then I heard school rumors of how babies came; and I'd dread but seek any glimpse of a place I'd passed through, helpless and blind. And just that spring I'd felt the start of a truth that's never left me— a grown woman's lovely strength and mercy. I still knew Frances wasn't much more than pretty, but now I could stare at the full under-sling of her upper arm or the start of a pale blue crease just south of her big dark navel and pray I would one day earn such gifts and use them as gently.

This morning she said very little but sponged herself (the house didn't have running water for years yet). When she had on her black silk stockings and the black dress she'd borrowed from a Greensboro neighbor, she came and sat beside me on the bed. She looked at my eyes a good long while, then again dug a finger almost hurtfully deep through my thin brows.

I let her finish. Then I pressed her arm away. My eyes must have filled.

She said "I didn't *hurt* you."

I said "Almost."

She was looking toward the yard through the low open window. Men's voices had started to mutter on the porch. Then she recollected me and kissed where she'd dug.

I bowed to her warm neck.

She said "I didn't hurt you" two more times.

I suddenly knew, after these two days, a vow I'd break before many years; but I made it then to Frances. I said into her bosom "I'll never be a mother."

Frances waited, then surprised me terribly by laughing. "Oh darling, that'll barely be your choice to make." She stood like a spring and went to the kitchen where Swift was being fed in striped pajamas.

Everybody held up through the funeral but Holt who sobbed right along, making yips in his nose. I didn't understand he'd been drinking since the death. Even Taswell's widow appeared at the church with his two little boys and claimed a front pew but watched, dry as Egypt, and kept the boys solemn. We were back at the house and the big meal by noon. I ate an unusual lot for me, and Frances took that as one more sign I was not myself. So while the other women were washing dishes and the other children playing Giant Step in the field by the house, my mother called me to her; and even when I told her I felt all right, she said "Let me show you something pretty you can have all your life." She went to the living room where Caroline had kept back three sprays of flowers to break the sadness, and I was on her heels.

But I asked no questions. I watched Frances slowly choose a mass of fine blooms—carnations, glads, roses—and I followed as she went out the back way, still silent and in her black dress. We went almost out of sight of the house, past a high privet hedge, down near Holt's garden.

Frances stopped at the foot of a hickory tree, studied the ground, then crouched and began to pinch her blooms off their stems very carefully. Midway, she looked up and said "Step there to the shed, and see if there's not some glass in the back. Find the cleanest piece and bring it here please. Try not to cut yourself."

I knew about the glass. Holt warned me every summer. But I told myself this place belonged to my mother more than him. So I found the best piece and took it toward her. All the way I watched her through it. The dust and the bubbles in the surface made her seem in a whole different world—gone from me already but working hard, not stopped like Tas. I paused in my tracks and wanted her to stop.

But she said "Come on. This is for you." With just her hand she'd already scooped out a bowl in the ground at the foot of the hickory and was lining it with flowers.

I'd had pretty nearly my fill of flowers in these two days, but I knew not to say so. She was deep in the job. This was really for her.

When she had the blooms perfect, she took the glass from me and brushed it with her hand. I knew if the mourning dress had been hers, she'd have used it as a rag. Then she set the pane flat like a window on the deep bowl and scraped soft dirt all back across it. When she'd finished she stood up and staggered from dizziness.

I couldn't have sworn she'd worked there an instant. The ground looked completely undisturbed.

Frances said "Now give me a penny please." She knew several men at the funeral had slipped me small pieces of change.

I liked money simply for the weight and smell. I seldom spent it. But something stopped me now. I said "Please don't scare me again."

I could see that hurt her feelings briefly. But she laughed. "Tightwad! Just give me the penny. I've made you something magic." Her hand was out, dirty.

So I stepped forward and gave her the coin.

She pulled me down to squat beside her. Then with that same hand she swept back the loose dirt over the glass. There underground was a tight nest of flowers so fresh they already were breathing on the glass. I knew of course it was what she'd made a minute ago; but through the old pane and so far out of place, it looked like a miracle. I expected it to move and offer me something. When it didn't I knew it was time to thank Frances and ask her its name.

She said "My mother called it Buried Garden. I think she invented it. But once I was orphaned, I called it Penny Show and tried to earn my way out of here."

I said "It worked." I could hear the other children yelling in the front yard. I was worried they'd find us and want to share. Nothing here seemed final to me, but it did seem special. And like most only children, I had a limited appreciation of noise and roughness.

Frances said "What if we stayed on here awhile?"

I said "I'd get behind in school." I had a horror of that and, to this day, still dream about it.

Frances said "There's a school here; *I'm* not a dunce, am I?" She'd graduated here and could sing the French national anthem in French.

I said "Where would Dan be?"

She stood up again and looked toward the house. "He would make his own choice." She started walking then.

She didn't know I'd heard him say he hated this place. That your parents could go separate ways like dogs was something I knew of from stories and the radio, but till then my cousin Taswell was the only near example. It seemed to have killed him. So when I'd covered up my mother's buried garden, I thought "I will die if we break off from Dan." In my mind he was mostly Dan, a friend not all that much older than me who mattered like the world. But I followed Frances back to that house she'd been born in. Up till then I'd loved it.

By late afternoon the place was empty of all but immediate family. I'd considered picking up some more change by showing the garden, but then I decided to keep it a secret. When Frances went to our room for a nap, I went along and told her I planned to keep it private; but could she and I uncover it again just before we went home?

She said "Yes, if it's still there by then."

I knew not to press any harder now. She was down to her white slip and lying on her back. I undressed too and stretched beside her, keeping my dry body separate from hers but close enough to feel her heat through the space. In a minute she was breathing like genuine sleep but I didn't try. I was used to much more peace than I'd had in the past three days, and I saw this as a chance to think about troubles that had stacked up behind me. Despite the funeral, death really wasn't one. I've said I liked Tas, but I never leaned on him. I naturally worried about my parents.

The worst ache though was knowing I was *grown*, in my mind at least, and how little that helped me change awful things. Nothing told me my mother would be dead in four hours and my young father with her. But I felt, like an icepick thrust in my side, that safety had ended— my personal safety, guaranteed by people who made me their duty. I was now the one to protect myself. Surprise and pain and being captured were my fears. Gentle as I was, I couldn't imagine steady days of defending myself. The only girl I'd read about who went on her own was Joan of Arc, and they killed her horribly before she left her teens. I didn't shut an eye, but I flat forgot Frances. When the door opened silently an hour later (nobody knocked here and no lock worked), I knew it was something coming *at* me—my first public trial.

It was Swift. Even dim as the room was now, he didn't look that much older than boys in my grade who'd failed once or twice. He caught my eye and whispered "Is she tired?"

I nodded in the pillow.

But he came on anyhow and stood two feet from my side of the bed.

I hated him suddenly. There was no present reason (except the way his hair shingled out from his neck like a stiff cheap wig), but I'd heard Dan say a lot against him through the years. He held down a job clerking men's clothes in Warrenton; but he still lived at home and used Caroline his mother like a servant—though he always had some ignorant girl slung around his neck, pretty as babyteeth. He'd ride them to Raleigh just to eat chow mein or wrap them in flowers for some summer dance and then get so drunk he'd come home without them or sleep by the road. But my mother had always taken up for him. I hope it was pity. He had the hands of a fine pianist, long and bony; but his eyes were weak and subject to tears. Here now they were brimming as he looked past me toward Frances's back. I said "You leave her alone. She's sad."

Swift looked at me a long time, blank as a sheet. Then he took the last steps and sat by my legs. Right to my face he whispered "I loved her years before you came."

I couldn't smell liquor but I thought he was drunk. I was scared anyhow and froze in place.

He leaned, pressing heavy on the calves of my legs, and set his hand on Frances's hip (she was turned away). He shook her and said "Fan, I need you. Get up."

She rolled back, saw him, and studied him a minute. She never looked at me or asked me a word. Then she got up quicker than I'd ever seen her move. She craved sleep and dreams.

Swift sat while she dressed, gazing at the pulled windowshade like it was still noon outside and sunny. When they went through the door, she smiled back and said "Go play while it's light."

I remember thinking clearly "It'll be night soon" and that somehow Frances was acting too happy. Then I heard the car leave. So I went through the dim house to find Caroline. I promised myself I would not raise a question. Uncle Holt was snoozing in their room when I passed, but the house was empty.

Caroline heard me though. She was out in the evening, in the wide porch-swing. She called clearly "Somebody's waiting for you."

I thought "At least there's one voice left to want me and say so," and I went straight toward her.

An hour later it was seven o'clock and still not night. Holt had somehow roused himself and joined us, mostly silent, in his shirt-sleeves. I had lain in Caroline's lap the whole time while she told me the stories of my mother's own childhood that never ceased to hold me—how Frances built a little store and sold snuff and starch to Negroes, how she'd dress like a boy and take trips to Norfolk to visit Walter (Caroline mentioned Walter free as if he'd never left or was due home tomorrow).

I could always do two things at once with Caroline—hear every word and still dedicate time to thinking of her kindness. This evening I wondered where she'd stored up the sorrow of losing another son, this one to death. And how was she able to sit here calm as the distant ocean and focus on me, a normal child? I didn't see myself as any replacement. I was nearly consoled.

Then Holt, who had been there scratching his head, stood bolt upright and gave a deep grunt.

Caroline said "Leave now while you can, whoever it is."

He scuttled for the door and vanished inside.

I was mystified and craned up to see. A car was slowing to turn in on us. It had raised a long tunnel of dust so thick it looked like a tail or a train. That kept me from recognizing who it was till the car had pulled up under the oak by Holt's Chevrolet.

Caroline spoke first. "Lord—" Then she pushed me up from her lap.

It was Dan. He usually left a car almost before it stopped, but I still ran to meet him.

When I'd got to the foot of the porchsteps, twenty yards from him, he hadn't climbed out or even looked toward me. So I waited in place.

Caroline came up behind me and looped both arms round my neck. When he still hadn't moved, she said clearly "Won't you land here, stranger?" I didn't think it then; but he was on some kind of perishing boat or raw in the pounding waves, just his body.

He finally looked out to throw down a cigarette. Then he looked to Caroline; his face was white as rice. He said "I'm sorry you have to bear this."

Like me, she thought he meant Taswell's death. Dan may have thought so too. She thanked him and said "You're bound to be starved."

He seemed to consider that. He said "No ma'm, I'm burning my *lean* meat." Then he saw me at last. He hadn't spoken to me since supper two nights ago. He didn't smile but said "Hey, Duchess, you're *growing*." I knew I hadn't grown a hair's breadth since Thursday. Still I said "Will you love me if my bubbies don't come?" (A bosom was fondly called a *bubby* by us, to rhyme with *chubby*, and he'd sometimes chafe my chest with his palms and say "Any day now! We got to make em welcome!")

That cheered him enough to get him on his feet. He staggered three steps and I thought he was drunk too. He seldom took a drink. But then he put both arms straight out like eagle wings to steady himself and finally smiled. He told me "Your goldfish sent you a kiss" and made a stiff fish-kiss in the air. When I ran to him though and hugged his hips, he didn't bend for me.

Caroline was already walking to the house, planning his supper. Halfway, she looked back and asked us to join her. "Keep me company, why don't you?"

Dan said "Isn't Frances there in the house?"

I knew not to answer but Caroline had to. She pointed east as if that could help. "Frances has gone back down to the cemetery. Swift drove her, Dan. To check on the flowers. They'll be back directly."

I said "Let me show you a beautiful secret." I meant the Buried Garden. I'd stopped holding Dan but was rubbing the cloth of his pants in my fingers, a light gabardine he'd bought that spring.

He said "No, I'll ride down and pay my respects."

Caroline said "You'll meet them coming back." If she felt any worry, she kept it from showing.

I said "Can I go?"

Dan touched my hair. I've always wondered if he meant to say yes.

But Caroline said "You come help me. It's snakey down there once the light gets thin."

When I was that age, all women gave orders to anybody's children; and the children obeyed or saw blue stars. I turned to Dan for a sign he'd contradict her.

He was already in the car, looking back to leave.

As he rolled I stood there, watching him long as he offered a sight. I thought no other child known to me had a father that fine-looking or that completely ready to say he was wrong and beg people's pardon. I was terribly mistaken in part of that. He had driven up here, yes, tired as he was. But why did I think that was his way of saying he took back the hardness of Thursday night and that we would drive home like tame lambs tomorrow? Why did I think I was part of a thing that weighed enough in his mind and heart to gentle him now? All my life I've run like a shot dog to similar conclusions. I live on hope the way most humans do on air and coffee. He did have the finest neck on earth, and it was the last I saw of him alive till more red dust roared up and took him.

We fixed him a bountiful plate of food and made new tea. But an hour later nobody was back, and night was on us. One of my only big virtues is promptness, since I learned to tell time. I was nervous pretty quickly and was picking the red surface off of the oilcloth that covered the table.

Caroline noticed the beginnings of damage, reached for a flashlight, and handed it to me. She said "Frances said you made a Penny Show. I'll give you a dime to let me see it." There was no dime in view, and again I felt like keeping it private, but I knew she was trying to help me wait. So I led her out through the yard that was already clanging with crickets. My own attempt to hide the garden had been as good as Frances's; and even knowing where it was, it took awhile to find it. I can feel right now the thrill in my fingers—very much like fright—when they first scraped the cool pane under the dirt. By then Caroline was holding the flashlight. I told her sternly to turn it off, and in pitchdark I swept the glass clear. Still dark I said "Now where is my dime?"

She said "You'll have to trust me. I'll get it from Holt."

I said "I'll never trust anybody else." I knew it was a fact that instant; and it's stayed so, I'm sad to say.

In the dark Caroline leaned over neatly and laid the flashlight by my foot. Then she turned and started back to the house.

Among all the shocks of that weekend, her leaving was the most unexpected by far. She was loyal as your skin and patient as the floor.

When I could barely see her outline, I said "I'm sorry. Look one time free. Nobody but you." That didn't even slow her step. She'd left me alone in the dark because of meanness. I'd stay here then till I starved and died and made them miserable the rest of their days. Or they'd come and rescue me and say they were wrong.

She let me stay out there a long time. Looking back, I can see I was in no danger. Macon was generally peaceful as a fern. But it's strange to this day that a person as gentle as my Aunt Caroline left a girl child alone in the black night air. I can't imagine how long I sat there, propped on the tree. I know that I left the flashlight on and that well before they came to tell me, it had worn out.

I've been in some fairly black alleys since then, but none of them matched this hour for pure thick hopelessness. It poured up against my lips like tar till I doubted every breath, but I held my ground. It would be good to say my mother's little garden was a consolation; I never thought of it once Caroline left, not till late the next day after so much else. What got me through it—that time in the yard—was knowing I hadn't deserved such treatment, not this or any of the badness since Thursday. I meant to last it out and be free.

Then I could hear more than one set of footsteps on the back porch. I calculated it was Dan and Frances, coming to find me. I even dreaded them now, I'd got so sufficient to myself in the dark. But a silent wait followed and then a voice I didn't know at first. It was Caroline, all changed by her message.

She said my name twice and, when I didn't answer, said "Don't fail me, Sugar."

So I said "Yes ma'm."

And she said "Wave your light."

I said "It's dead" but I tried it and found it had recuperated slightly. It gave a weak glow.

She said "Come toward me. I'll meet you halfway."

Just her strangeness made me go. She kept her promise and met me by the stack of old iron Holt collected from ditches when his back let him move. I thought I could smell its strong flaky rust, but I couldn't see more than a kind of cloud where Caroline's hair must have been.

She said "Kate, the worst thing in the world has happened." Speaking for herself, her family, and me, she was telling only the minimum truth.

She hadn't touched me yet, so I had to ask "What?"

She said "Come on in the house right now" and turned to go, then remembered who she was enough to step back and take my shoulder and lead me.

At no time later in my full life could I have walked that far in that much silence without demanding the truth, head-on. But for fifty yards of deep wet grass, I was dumb as the blooms in my Penny Show. I just kept thinking two things that both seemed equally bad—I'd left the show uncovered, free for all, and Frances and Dan were someway dead.

In the kitchen Swift was standing by the icebox; Holt was at the table, straighter in a chair than I'd ever seen him. When they saw me they both glanced quick to the window. It was aimed toward the cemetery, always had been. But nothing showed now except our own reflections. Holt said "Katie, sit here and drink some cool water." He motioned for Caroline to dip me a glass and she obeyed. I saw how tame she was, a curious exception where Holt was concerned.

When she handed me my favorite glass (an old chipped blue one), she looked round suddenly on Swift and told him "Tell Kate now and then go call the Law."

I saw she was stronger than anything else here. That far, I was safe.

But she should have told me. Nothing could have made the news any worse, but taking it from lips I hated was almost too hard a test.

Swift stayed where he was. All his skin had splotched red like pictures of lepers. His left hand was flat on the top of the icebox, fine old oak. He had to face the floor to tell me, but he got it out. "Frances and I went to see Tas's flowers. Most of them were ruined, but the pall Walter sent was fresh as this morning. Six dozen carnations red as your heart. Frances said 'Swift, we ought to have brought a jar of water. If I sprinkled these now, they'd last through the night and help ease Caroline's visit tomorrow.' I told her I had an empty can in the car and that we could walk down to the creek for water. She said that was fine and took off her shoes and stockings at the car since I guess she remembered the path down was steep—we'd used it a thousand times before. She took me there the first time when I could barely walk, to show me the quicksand where a pony smothered. She led the way tonight like always; and by the time I scrambled down, she was sitting on a rock with her feet in the water. It was darker than up by the grave, and I wanted to head out fast. But Frances asked me to sit down a minute and remember Tas. She'd known him even better than me, being nearer his age. They'd driven a Model T to Warrenton once to get Dr. Peete in the night for Mother when neither one of them could see above the dashboard. More stories like that. We must have been laughing. Then Frances spun around. I hadn't heard a thing. A man was loping down the hill, not a sound. I didn't recognize him, even when he faced us. I could see he was white, nice clothes, bareheaded. But Frances stood up on the rock and said 'Daniel.' I never had heard he was any more than *Dan*. He looked so changed, she had to call him *something*. I stood up too but he never met my eyes. I couldn't swear he even knew who I was. But he said 'Leave me here alone with my wife.' I called his name then; he still didn't look. So I said to Frances 'I'll wait at the car.' She smiled 'Please. You've got my shoes.' I knew I was leaving something private, and a bigger fool than me would've seen Dan was wild, but I waited up by the car like I promised. Tas's flowers never got sprinkled. I was too far away to hear their voices, and Aunt Hazey Hargrove passed in the road and called me over to hear a long tale about Eleanor Roosevelt and a nigger child that needed false teeth and got them by mail from the White House, postpaid. So maybe fifteen minutes went by, and Hazey had staggered on round the curve, when the first shot fired. I told myself it was some boy killing rats at the dump. But then a low scream—more like a deep bellow—came out of the woods and I went cold. It had to be Dan. Before I could think to move either way, came the second shot. Just the two, then a quiet like I never hope to hear again. Dan's car was stopped right up against mine, but I went to mine and cranked up and sat there, facing the woods for another ten minutes. Nobody came out and no more noise. I didn't know anything to do but come here."

Holt said "You did right."

Caroline had come up behind me by then. She stroked a little circle at the crown of my head and said to Swift "Now go get the Law."

Holt said "I can't go down there with you, too dark and my leg—"

Caroline said "Your leg could take you to the nearest liquor jar if it stood in *Asia*. Swift, go get the sheriff." There was no telephone in the house. He would have to drive five miles to Warrenton and find him.

He took a step toward me and held out a hand. I wasn't feeling anything by then and I froze, but Caroline brushed him away before he touched me. He said "You've always got a home, long as I'm alive."

Caroline told him "This house is mine. Kate's safe here with me. You better start begging Christ to keep you out of jail."

Swift went to the kitchen door and looked back at her. "I haven't done a single thing I can't *tell* Christ."

Caroline said "Then tell Him in the car. Just spare us now."

I stayed awake for at least another hour. Holt brought out his good checkerboard, not the one he kept for children; and he and I played quiet games in the kitchen. Caroline went off somewhere in the house. I could hear little motions occasionally to prove she was there; but whether she was shut up back in a wardrobe gnawing rags for pain or praying on her bed or staring at the night, I never knew. And I didn't question Holt. For the first time I knew that my old dread was right. My parents were someway dead, lying now in the cool night air not a mile from this game I was almost winning. It made me still and serious.

When Caroline came back calm again, she didn't speak either except to say "Take this dose of paregoric." Then she led me to my bedroom and undressed me gently as a china doll. She sat on the bed and said "Now say your prayers."

I tried to say silent prayers; my mind wouldn't work. But I kept my eyes shut to show my intention. Then I said "Amen" and she stood up to go. I let her get all the way to the door before I told her "Dan and Frances are dead."

She thought that over. I was scared she'd lie. But she said "I'm very much afraid that's the truth."

I'm prepared to swear she went out then. She'd left a light on. Before the paregoric struck I thought "She's lost as much as me." I was probably wrong but it put me under.

She woke me up early, washed my face, and put me back in yesterday's dress. It was not clean enough, but it was navy blue, and I guessed it was needed. Then she said "There's a man here wants to speak to you."

I said "All right" but I didn't ask why.

He was out on the porch, talking quietly to Holt. But Caroline brought him in the front room to me. I'd guessed it was the sheriff—though until I actually saw his face, I let myself think this might be a joke. Dan loved practical jokes and would go to great lengths. Were he and Frances set to burst in on me? If something bad had happened, why were people not already driving in with food?

The man was in clean wash-clothes but not a uniform; and he'd left his gun somewhere, in courtesy. He was short as a girl and empty in the face as a hoop. He stopped in the door with Caroline behind him. His glasses were thick and he took awhile to find me. I was standing by the radio, a tall old Philco. Caroline said "Kate, this is Mr. Rooker. You sit down there and talk to him a minute." She guided Mr. Rooker to a straight chair near me. Then she came and sat on a stool by my knees.

Mr. Rooker's face went suddenly bright and gave a broad smile. It turned out later that was all it could do. He wouldn't meet my eyes, and his voice was high and hoarse. "I don't aim to put you through a whole lot more, but maybe you can help me."

I must have nodded.

Caroline took my ankle and heated it up in her palm.

He said "Had your mama and daddy been happy?"

I said "About what?"

"Being together. Any money troubles, either one of them drinking or shirking the other?"

I figured if anybody knew, he did. So I asked him "Are Dan and Frances dead?"

He smiled again. "You call them by their name?"

I said they'd told me to.

Then he looked at Caroline for help.

She just faced the floor.

So he said "Yes, darling"; and tears big as peas sprang up and streaked the smile.

I said "Who killed them?"

He said "Your daddy."

I said "Then what have you done with Swift?"

Caroline said "He's asleep now, Sugar. He was up all night."

I said "He caused it."

Mr. Rooker dried his cheeks and drew out a pencil from deep in his hip. It was one of those old kind, thick as a cigar and with no eraser. Dan had once told me they were only meant for people who never made mistakes.

I expected Caroline at least to say "Hush," but she just carefully adjusted my anklets.

Mr. Rooker didn't seem to have any paper. He asked me "How do you mean what you said?"

Then I knew I didn't know. Grown as I'd felt these past three days, I didn't even know enough to guess what I meant. I was sure, to the marrow of my strong bones, that Swift Porter set Dan wild against

Frances and then against himself. But I couldn't say why, not till years too late. I sat there dumb.

Mr. Rooker said "You mean to say he shot them?"

I said "No sir."

He said "Were you with them?"

I said "Yes sir" and believed it at the moment.

Mr. Rooker fell forward like a folding hinge. His chin was all but meeting his knees. Then he licked his pencil tip.

Caroline said "Sheriff, we've got her confused. She was here with me and Holt every minute last night."

I said "You left me alone in the yard. You don't know all."

She said "Sheriff, this child never left the lot."

He suddenly stood up and looked at the door. Nobody had come. He turned back to me. "You've got a grand home anyhow, Sweetheart. That's one sure thing." Then he thanked Caroline and said he should leave.

She asked "Is it settled now?"

He said "Pray Jesus, Mrs. Porter. I hope so."

It turned out it was. They took people's word then, especially white men's. Nobody knew Dan. Swift's story prevailed. The coroner, a cotton-gin owner, glimpsed the bodies and passed them for burial—a murder and a suicide. Dan was sent off to Henderson to lie by his parents; none of us went to that. We buried Frances at her own mother's feet on the Sunday afternoon. She'd been dead eighteen hours. I never saw her body. She was not displayed and the funeral was just a quick graveside thing with the Porters and me, Mr. Rooker and his blind wife, and two or three more that felt like they knew us well enough not to be trespassing. Everybody was very quiet with me, very gentle and polite like I was an elderly lady with money. I partly enjoyed it.

Nobody followed us home except the preacher, and he left soon after hugging me longer than the tragedy called for. I changed my dress then and went down the yard to my mother's secret garden. I thought it would be cooked dry from the day. But even though I'd left it uncovered to the sun, it was fresh as she'd made it. That was when I could finally cry. Far as I know, no human being saw me.

And that night asleep I started what I kept up for years. In dreams I'd make good on what I told the sheriff. I'd be down there at the creek with Swift and Frances. Or I'd ride down with Dan. Or run on my own. Sometimes I would just stand quiet while he shot her one time through the chest (I'd overheard the nature of her wounds). Or I'd scream for them to stop and listen to me. Then I'd say they had no right on earth to start my life like a small thriving business and then one night just abandon me to fail or work on alone, all streaked with their blood. More than once in the first weeks, Caroline would hear me struggling through sleep and come in to wake me and stay there till day. But I never told one scene of what haunted me.

Swift had been planning a week's vacation at Nag's Head the following Saturday. He changed plans, drove Caroline and me to Greensboro; and they spent four days clearing the house. To ease my feelings they farmed me out to neighbors on the weekend and let me go back to my old school one last time on Monday. The news from Macon hadn't traveled that far, so Swift got to tell his story again in shortened form when he came to get me. My teacher was of course an old maid, Miss Limer; but I thought she looked like Loretta Young, and I worshipped her tracks. I'd memorized her clothes and could prophesy the day she'd wear which dress. Right to this minute I can smell her rich hair that was dark as good loam. When she'd heard Swift out—I was still at my desk—she didn't say a word but took her own stationery (blue with rough edges) and wrote a short letter in her beautiful hand.

To Whom It May Concern:

Kate Vaiden has been my outstanding pupil this entire year in the whole fifth grade. She excels in reading, drawing, and music. She is also kind to her classmates, friends, and appropriate elders. The one small failing is common to her age, a tendency to talk.

I commend her to any other teacher's close attention. She is rarely deserving of meticulous care.

Rosalind Limer, eighteen years a teacher

She put it in an envelope and gave it to Swift. Then she finally looked at me.

I couldn't help smiling and she stood up and came forward to me, those long legs whispering sweet secrets in their stockings. I could see what she had in her hand but couldn't believe it. All year I'd admired her paperweight, a glass rectangle with a real seahorse inside laid on cotton. I had asked her more than once where she got it; but she never had said, just laughed me off.

When she got to my desk that last day though, she said "You used to be interested in this; do you think you are still?"

I told her "Yes ma'm."

So she laid it in front of me—the little brown creature facing off to my right through his dry eye-socket. I didn't know whether to touch it or not.

Miss Limer said "That was sent to me by a boy I loved, from the port where he sailed off to fight the World War."

The word *love* in her dignified mouth shocked me almost more than the whole last week. But it thrilled me too. She had opened me a tunnel onto some distant light. I believed for the first time I'd be loved again, someday if I lasted.

Swift said "Thank her, Kate." I wished he would blow away.

Miss Limer said "That would be premature." She shot him one of her blistering looks. Then like he really had vanished, she said "You take this from me now and go." She touched me, the first time she'd ever touched a student in my presence.

I cherished the spot, on my left collarbone, till I grew and it faded. And more times than one in the years to come, I'd stare at her seahorse or reread her letter and try to remind myself I should live. (There was another letter that didn't reach me for forty-six years—thank God, I guess. Swift found it on Dan and Frances's bed and hid it from me— Dan's conditional farewell, in case the worst happened. I'll put it in later, if I can stand to.)

So they sold more than half of our household goods. There was nothing that was fine; but Caroline shipped a few pieces to Macon—most of them my own, to ease the move. Dan had met an old cabinetmaker in the country and had him build me a narrow walnut-bed. It has a round carving on the high headboard that's meant to be me at nine years old, my profile aimed west. I never could recognize it as me, but a number of people have admired it through the years and envied me having a bed that personal. I say "If a bed can't be, what can?" I'd sleep in it now if I knew where it was; it's still long enough.

They carted that to Macon with my small yellow radio and what few toys I selected to keep. I sent the three dolls to the Salvation Army. Dan had lavished them on me, and I'd played like I loved them. But I couldn't truly care for things that cold and quiet—pressed sawdust and paint and eyes you could ruin with a poking finger.

The main things I kept were books and a beadweaving loom with a million loose beads. The books were *Tales from the Arabian Nights, A Girl of the Limberlost, Doctor Doolittle,* and my row of Nancy Drews. The nearest library was five miles from Macon, so I knew them pretty well by heart before they finally came to pieces in my hands. The loom was the last thing Frances gave me, to make headbands and decorate moccasins in Indian-style. I wove some days till it all but smoked; and I turned out miles of straight beading for gifts—in mostly white and blue, the colors that soothe me.

I had always enjoyed my visits to Macon. But living there was a different proposition. First, it was tiny—not two hundred people, more than half of them black. No entertainment but summer revivals at the two white churches, Methodist and Baptist; and once or twice a year, a fishfry or Brunswick stew. Otherwise, you *talked* to the people you lived with and let *them* talk. Food and family were the only two legal subjects for the women. Men could talk about cotton, tobacco, Negroes, sex, Roosevelt, and money. I hung around men whenever they let me and spent long drowned weeks of time by myself.

They had a two-story brick school with kind teachers, and children were bused in from way in the sticks. But after the first week I got past being a public martyr, and they started asking me awful questions and offering their own little homegrown versions of what had gone wrong down by the dark creek. They meant real harm, don't tell me they didn't; but I seldom showed a bruise. So they mostly lost interest and let me be. And then I began to reach out for friends.

*   *   *

Up to now I've stressed a lot of early hard luck; and I may have sounded too much like the Little Match Girl, a starving orphan in the Christmas snow. That's not a true impression, and I'll try to correct it. Till I was eleven I was loved, maybe too much, by young parents vivid in their lives as fresh paint. Then they died for their own secret reasons, suddenly and dreadfully but out of my sight. I naturally grieved long after the shock; but from then on, the troubles I had were normal. Caroline raised me the way she did everything, like the smallest chance for courtesy mattered and must be fulfilled. Swift got married the Thanksgiving after I moved to Macon. He and his wife lived just across the road, but he kept a distance from me ever after and that suited fine.

Holt was no more pathetic than a number of husbands; and though he'd been famous for ruling his own sons and Frances with iron, he'd mostly given up by the time I arrived. Anyhow he mellowed a lot in my sight.

My main memories of him are poetry. In his boyhood up by the river with a one-armed Confederate-major-father, he learned half the poetry in English by heart. He would sit me in the swing and recite Scott's *Lady of the Lake*, start to finish, and I'd willingly listen. Or Byron's *Bride of Abydos*. Useless as he was in most everything else, he literally never faltered in verse. My mind still owes him thanks for lines that come to me now when I least know why—

> *The winds are high on Helle's wave,*
> *As on that night of stormy water*
> *When Love, who sent, forgot to save*
> *The young, the beautiful, the brave,*
> *The lonely hope of Sestos' daughter.*

Or the ones that seemed his absolute favorite—

> *'Tis time this heart should be unmoved,*
> *Since others it hath ceased to move:*
> *Yet, though I cannot be beloved,*
> *Still let me love!*

In that first year, I instinctively didn't try to love or be loved by anybody. I think my heart was taking a much-needed rest in the country. What kept it from going permanently cold was the new cook that came soon after I did.

She was Noony Patrick, nineteen years old and six feet tall. She'd been cooking from birth, was excellent at it, washed white curtains on her own initiative, and kept the back end of the house more cheerful than it had ever been. I clung to her every chance I got; she would talk on endlessly about the great mysteries a child sees dimly and not expect me to join in or answer. She had a sick husband, nearly eighty years old; and the reasons she was with him and the lunges she made at younger men and freedom were her main subject. Sundays and Mondays she and I would seek times alone together so she could let off the steam she'd boiled up on Saturday night at The Hall in Warrenton. That was a big high warehouse on stilts, all unpainted pine. One match would have barbecued everybody in it; and according to Noony, there would be hundreds dancing their black woes away and taking sweet pauses in the brush out back.

The summer I was twelve, I was helping her set up curtain stretchers in the backyard sun. Noony looked around grinning, to check for spies, and beckoned me to her. Then she hauled up a red cord that hung between her breasts; and there was a pearlhandled razor, her weapon. She could flick it open—four inches of straight steel—and cut up a rival before they could focus an eye to flee. That was the day I realized the question that had been building in me all year while she rambled. I asked it right out, in the sizzling day. "Is any of this any *fun* to you?"

She laughed. "Only fun there is but church."

I told her I'd never liked church that much and sure didn't need any boy pounding on me.

She waited till we were almost indoors. Then she took my shoulder and said it as solemn as a horse in harness. "When you needing that, Kate, you warn Noony, hear? I got *advice*."

* * *

I had already started getting advice. The previous winter, halfway through the sixth grade, a girl in my class brought a dirty poem to school. She claimed she'd found it in her father's drawer and had snatched odd hours at considerable danger to copy it out and share it with us. In view of her dumbness and backhanded script, it must have taken her days of application. But when word got out that something this secret was available at last, children got to school well before nine and waited their turn to read it in the cloakroom, two by two. You'd have thought it was flung from on-high in gold flames. I was one of the first in line; and though I'd read more than most country children (including *Anthony Adverse*), it was still revelation—pure and strong as grabbing a live wire and not letting go. The title was "Rhonda's Road to Womanhood," and it took a poor typist from the farm to the city and a fast string of bosses. They ranged from old and fat to young and lean, every one as overheated as a pigeon in a park. Despite her girlhood among pigs and chickens, Rhonda didn't understand and left the men gasping with their pants at halfmast. Then the last boss's son graduated from college, joined the firm in June, and succeeded— at great length in rhymed lines—in showing poor Rhonda the road to adult bliss. I remember exactly how the last lines looked on the ruled dingy page and the trouble that poured up through me when I read them—

> *She whispered "Hank, I love you!" and he moaned*
> *"My lamb, what luck!"*
> *He'd carried her to paradise and taught her how to fuck.*

For many nights after that, I'd lie in my dark room and guess what it meant. Not the physical act—I accepted that as something your parents did to make you, and of course I'd seen dogs locked together and helpless. The main word everybody used was *seed*—"He gives her the seed." Nobody my age could tell me what the seed was. The best guess seemed to be, the man peed in you; and that was the seed. But then there were all the times they didn't want babies but still sought it out. What troubled me to wonder was *Why people do it when they don't want babies?* Why chase it down through pain and shame and public laughter? I already understood pleasure in my body. My hand had discovered my own facilities years before; but though such private moments felt fine and helped me sleep, they seemed like a shut room with no door for anyone but me to enter. How they could ever open out on feelings of mutual joy and protection, I failed to see. But I figured I'd wait. Noony and most everything else around me seemed to be saying more clearly each day "You *wait*. Your life is coming toward you." I prayed it would hurry.

Prayer took a big share of my time then. I've said I didn't enjoy church a lot, though I went with Caroline twice a month when the circuit rider passed. What I really had was long talks with God, Christ, angels, trees, the Devil, birds, and dogs. Anything seemed liable to turn sacred on me, and I'd worship it freely till it faded off. I don't much recall what I talked about, but I do know it sometimes worried me that I wasn't asking *pardon* more often than I did. I saw that this awful bad luck had struck me. Church told me that a good deal of fun was sinful and that children could sin just as easily as others. I knew for instance that touching my body, to honor and please it, was officially one brand of idol-worship. So I kept on thinking I should be more repentant. Maybe I just couldn't bear that extra pain. Or maybe I heard God had vowed to love me, whoever I was, and was leaning on that. Even this late, I doubt I was wrong.

I plunged on into the joys I could find. They mostly came from a distant cousin named Fob Foster. He was in his early fifties and had never got married. A young black man kept house for him just down the road from us; and though he owned great stretches of land and woods and must have been rich from tobacco and pulpwood, he dressed and lived as simply as a saint. His work consisted of roaming the county in a truck, with his man Tot beside him, overseeing his farms (which mostly meant *looking*; he had honest tenants). His time-off consisted of talking in Mr. Russell's store by the depot, buying grape drinks for children that passed and could call his funny name, and occasional foxhunts with his many hounds.

With no explanation he drove up to get me one Saturday dawn, my second fall in Macon. Caroline came to wake me and said "Fob Foster wants to take you foxhunting. Do you want to go?" I was upright and in the only pants I owned, tan corduroy overalls, before she paused for breath. I'd known him forever but hadn't thought he liked me. He waited in the kitchen while Noony cooked my breakfast (Tot stood in the corner, still as a pillar; Noony despised him). The few words he said were to Caroline—they'd have me home by supper. No, there'd be no drinking. Who did she think he *was*? He laughed just to say it.

We were out in the cool light, bumping down a gully in some distant woods, before Fob spoke again except to give directions. Tot was driving; we were all three close in the truck, me of course in the middle. Fob turned to my face and said "Kate, I want to love you. *Amount* to something, hear?"

I could feel Tot grinning on my other side, but I stayed calm enough to speak an honest reply. I said "Thank you, sir. What I need now is *money*."

There was one long silence. Then they both broke down into helpless laughs.

I knew they'd be describing my brass for years to come. So I blushed and then joined them.

To his eternal credit, in my books at least, the next thing Fob said was "I can see to that, if you keep your mouth shut." He leaned and looked to Tot. "Yours too, Tot. Shut."

Tot nodded, still laughing.

By then we had leveled off in sight of the river; and there was Mr. Stegall and his son, who kept Fob's dogs, waiting for us by a fire. They were cooking more breakfast—bacon and boiled coffee—and the dogs were toiling and grumbling in a truck with sides.

Mr. Stegall greeted me as mildly as if I was natural, a regular fixture in this part of his life, and called me "Little lady" till I told him I was Kate or nothing else please.

He nodded acceptance but his son yelled "Katie!" His name was Gaston, two grades beyond me with the smutty beginnings of a mustache already and that lightly oiled look boys get when they're ready and don't know it yet.

I told myself I hated him, but the day proved different. For now though, he just ate and talked to nothing but the dogs, very gently, and never met my eyes. There were no horses present, which relieved and disappointed me. *Relieved* because I'd never ridden and was scared to fail in public but *disappointed* because, like most girls my age, I'd read a lot of horse books and more or less worshipped their shape and smell. They seemed the main animal, along with certain dogs, that you could confide in and they would understand, even if they couldn't help.

It turned out we weren't really going anywhere. A local foxhunt bore no resemblance to the ones I'd read about—red suits, jumping horses, and a merry chase—except both hoped to end in a balked fox, torn by dogs. After everybody drank more coffee than they needed, Mr. Stegall and Gaston let the hounds loose. For all their complaining, they came out slow and almost delicate. You'd have thought their feet were too tender for dirt. Then Gaston gave them the scent—an old foxtail—and that got their interest. They spread out quick as a stain in cloth, each one sniffing hard at the ground. Then a young bitch over by the edge of the woods gave a short high yell. The whole pack rallied and followed her down into thicket so dense we lost sight of them in a matter of seconds.

That was pretty much it. The dogs bayed deeper and deeper in the trees, and we five humans stood near the fire and listened. Every now and then, Mr. Stegall would say "That's Bucket or Nasty"—naming a hound by its faroff voice. Two or three times Fob blew his foxhorn to keep the dogs posted on where we were.

I was glad to be present but also bored when, after an hour, Gaston asked if I wanted to see the river. I of course said yes but looked at Fob to see if he objected.

He first said "I hoped you were happy with *me*," and I almost felt relieved. But before I could blush, he laughed and said "Just listen to my horn and come back before noon."

It was something past nine. I figured we wouldn't be gone twenty minutes.

Mr. Stegall didn't say a word to Gaston, and Gaston didn't really wait for me. He headed off on a narrow downhill track, so I ran to catch up. But when he never turned to see me or talk, I slacked off and let him move on out of sight. Something told me (in a chill, not words) that I was rounding a critical bend. I stopped to pray but not for protection—just that I know how to act and not shame myself. I doubt I even called God by name; I was talking to the woods. Then I went on downward—there was no curve to turn—and in another fifty yards the Roanoke River, brown in the climbing sun, struck me broadside. Its name had always been a favorite word of mine; I would say it to myself some nights like a secret that might yet open to long repetition.

It looked so fine (this was long before they dammed it) that I stood there, watching it slide on by and forgetting Gaston. But then a moan that wasn't the dogs rose from nearby. I looked to my left; and there half back in the bushes was Gaston, studying himself. His pants were open and he held his penis like a wingshot quail and explored its considerable length with a finger from his other hand. I had seen Dan naked a thousand times, and sometimes he'd joke with his thing— stretch it thin and strum it like a banjo and yodel "You Are My Sunshine" to Frances and me.

But this was no joke. Gaston didn't look at me, though he must have heard. He kept on staring down like he had a problem; and by then it was staring back, solemn as him.

I was twenty feet off, but I thought I should speak. I said "Is something the matter with you?"

He waited as long as a doctor at bedside. Then he said "With *this*" and aimed it out toward me.

At first I was scared that it might close the distance between us and touch me. But it stayed there, nodding. So I said "Is it sick?" It looked blind and feverish like something just born that might not survive.

He said "Come here and see what you think."

I went. He was quite a bit taller than me and was standing on a knoll, so I didn't have to bend. The first, and last, thing I thought was *It's fine.* It seemed like something you would win as a prize—a live handy pet with elaborate features, rising up in black curls. So I said "Have you named it?"

Gaston said "He hurts me."

I said "How did you figure out it's a boy?" I stepped back a little.

But he said "Oh *don't*. You can help me out."

With all its faults, my family were not known for turning down pleas that deep from the heart. I moved back closer than I'd been before and said "Show me how."

I'm not sure he knew or maybe he felt too shy to say or give a demonstration. Anyhow he stood there, looking at the river and pressing his thing down with one long finger like a pointer in school.

I followed the point. We were still there alone with the sliding river and a few lazy birds. I could barely hear the dogs. I somehow felt more peaceful than I'd felt since Frances and I ever left Greensboro. Somebody'd finally asked me for something that seemed more important than the date of Cortez or to fetch a brown egg. I suddenly thought of the poem in school—what Rhonda realized she'd known all her life, from living in a dairy—and took the last step and milked Gaston dry.

In maybe twenty seconds the job was over. I'd brought a bandanna and cleaned myself, though I liked the smell and imagined it for days. By then he had got his legs still again, but his eyes were closed. I knew the answer but I said "Did it help?"

I thought I'd lost him. He leaned back against a sapling and rolled his head to the sky. The high sun made him look clean and good, but his eyes stayed closed.

That was when I wondered if I'd somehow stumbled on what killed my parents. It started to scare me.

But then Gaston looked down and met my eyes. He'd stayed as solemn as he'd been all morning, but he said "Helped a good deal. Yes ma'm, it did."

"It was me," I said. "My name is Kate."

So he laughed once—"Kate, oh Kay"—and touched my hair.

I felt amply repaid, especially since what I'd done was both easy and a kind of fun. Understand though that I'd really believed him. I thought he was having a bad attack of something which only hit boys his age. Girls then used to idolize nurses, maybe since that was almost all you could be but a teacher or a strumpet (if you meant to work farther off than the stove). I thought I'd nursed Gaston Stegall through a crisis, and I guessed he'd never forget my aid.

But he seemed to, once we were back with the others. Fob asked if we'd seen anything special. When Gaston said "No," I said "Just the river"; and Fob said "That'll last all your life." I wondered if he meant the memory of the river or the river itself. They both have, clearly. But the lasting results of the day were double, and both came from men. Fob had wanted me with him; Gaston begged for my help. I honestly think the course of my life set, then and there, before my body really understood the use of men or needed their presence.

Fob stood up then and said "They've lost it."

Mr. Stegall said "He lost *them*, Fob. I told you you were making me feed em too much."

Fob laughed. "Well, a day like today helps trim em down." He looked at me. "Shall we run em next week—same time, same station?"

I said "I'll be ready."

Fob said "Then it's certain. Gaston, call the boys in." He called the hounds *boys*, though many were bitches.

Gaston had his own horn, not as grand as Fob's. Fob's came off a Texas longhorn bull and had *San Antonio* scratched in its length. Gaston's came off some local steer and was stubby. But when he lifted it and blew long wails, I knew without question this next week could not move fast enough for me.

That night when I had my flannel gown on, I went to the wash-stand mirror in my room and studied my face. I never had been that interested in it; and since my mother had used this mirror the day she died, I'd been a little nervous of what it might show. But now I stood still and tried to be honest. *How good did I look?* My standards were based on the memory of Frances and the movies we'd seen and who she'd praised. She thought Kay Francis was the perfect beauty—dark and sleepy-eyed. Loretta Young was second. She thought Barbara Stan-wyck was a little pinched and trashy but really had "It."

I decided that was me or was going to be. I knew what Gaston and I had done was some kind of hanging around the edges of being grown and babies and eternal troth. I couldn't imagine what the center would be or whether it would suddenly *be here*, uncalled, like Gaston had been or whether I'd have to learn skills and hunt it. But I thought for the first time, that chilly night, the idea that's been my main lifeboat through frequent high seas—*You have already lasted, with all your teeth, through something far worse than most people get. You can last through the rest.* I was twelve years and five months old and was right, to date anyhow.

As if to confirm me, the next morning once Caroline and I set off alone to church, she told me her own news from yesterday's mail. Walter, her oldest son that had left home years ago in a fight with Holt, had written her to ask would he be welcome Thanksgiving if he got time off? We were in plain view of the church, and people gathering, when she stopped me on the path and looked behind us. Nobody was coming but she'd gone sick-pale; I thought she might faint. Then she said "Kate, I don't know whether I can stand it."

I said "I'll lead you back. Lean on me." Home was not a quarter-mile.

She shook her head hard—her stiff blue hat—and said "Can we bring Walter here in peace, you think?"

I knew very little about why he'd left, but I said "What does Holt say?"

She said "I haven't told him."

Something made me say "You want me to?—after church? He likes me."

She walked a few steps with me close beside her. Then she said "Let me think. But thank you for now."

Half an hour later while they took up the collection and Ray Batts sang like a frog in a well, she whispered in my ear "Be thinking of a way, this afternoon."

All I said was "Yes ma'm"; but I felt proud and noticed that my legs had grown in the month since we sat here before—my skirt was too short, nearly up to my knees.

Sunday was normally Noony's day off unless we had company, so I would always clear and wash dishes after midday dinner. But this day when Holt got up and headed for the radio, Caroline waved me on to follow him. He loved good music—the first human being I knew who did—and Sunday afternoon was his chance to hear it. He could spend hours happily adjusting the dial one hairsbreadth to find some staticky patches of Toscanini or the Longines Symphonette. When I came in and sat on the hassock three feet away, he turned down the volume and smiled at me. "Never rains but pours."

I asked "How's that?"

He said "A good dinner, sweet music on the air, a visit from you."

"With a new poem," I said. That year my teacher was hell on poems. We memorized two a week, reciting them in unison.

Holt took out his watch. "Well, we've got five minutes before Paderewski cranks up the Steinway."

So over some panel discussion of Catholics, I recited "A Victory Ball" by Alfred Noyes. I seem to be the last one above ground who knows it now. We learned so many poems from World War I, and I remember them all. But the end of this one can rattle me still.

> *Victory! Victory! On with the dance!*
> *Back to the jungle the new beasts prance!*
> *Gods, how the dead men grin by the walls,*
> *Watching the fun of the victory balls!*

It obviously touched Holt. His eyes were full. He dug in his pocket, pulled out a quarter, and held it toward me. I shut his hand on it and gently pushed it back. But he said "Kate, in two years you've shown me more pleasure than my boys in their whole lives."

I said "Then you ought to had a girl a lot sooner."

He said "I tried. I tried till she stopped me, cut me off at the well."

"She loved what she got," I said. "She misses Walter."

Holt said "*I* miss Walter. Never think I don't. It tore my heart out to have him leave here."

I said "Then you can mend it now—your heart, I mean."

"How so?"

"Call him home," I said. "He's asking to come."

Holt fell back in his chair. "Where have you seen Walter?"

For one hot minute I imagined I *had*—had run off to Norfolk and

roomed with him or looked up and seen Walter walk in my school-
room and call my name to take me with him. But I finally said "We
just got a letter. Walter asks can he come here and see us Thanksgiving?"

Holt said "Who is *we?*"

"Aunt Caroline," I said. I never called her *aunt.*

When I looked up at him then, he'd somehow gone flat. Air and
life had leaked out, and he seemed old as he'd ever be. His Paderewski
concert was starting on the radio; he didn't rise to it. Finally he said
"Have you seen this letter? She show it to you?"

I said "She told me on the way to church."

"And begged you to tell me?"

I can remember another real wait. I was still there beside him, at
his feet in fact. But in my mind I was way up high, well above the
yard oaks. I wasn't feeling proud or judging anything. I was asking myself a whole new question that, with all my past, I'd never asked before. *Why in the world do people do this?* I meant, gaze at each other
hypnotized like frogs, then marry, make children, set them loose on
the ground, and most of them wind up hating each other under one
hot roof or running to Norfolk. But I told Holt "No sir. I asked her to
let me. I thought you'd like the news and like me for bringing it." It
was just half a lie.

He began to rally. He propped up and dialed in better on his music.
It was Chopin and fast. Then he looked down at me, solemn as a
plate. I expected him to cry—he kept tears ready any hour of the day—
but he stayed dry now. He said "Walter Porter is my son, Kate. I'll
write him a letter myself tonight."

"And tell him to come?"

Holt still didn't smile. All he said was "Don't you lose any sleep."

I didn't know whether I'd won or lost, but I knew not to ask.

The women in the house didn't know for ten days. I told Caroline
exactly what happened, and she said "Then we'll wait. Don't mention
it again." I knew when Caroline had put her foot down, and this time

it was *flat*. Whether she also wrote to Walter, I never knew. Noony would always walk to town after breakfast to get the first mail. But now school was on, I couldn't go with her and had to rely on quizzing her later—not too satisfactory since her reading skill was spotty. But the middle of the next week when I got home, Noony held off till she and I had gone for the eggs. She had her hand under the old mean hen when she looked back at me and said "They got it."

By then my curiosity had flagged. I had to ask who and what.

She pointed toward the house. "Them yonder—that letter. Norfolk, Virginia."

"How do you know?"

Noony drew back her hand—a big white egg on the cocoa-butter palm—and said "This hand know what it *does*. Holding a egg right now, you can see. This morning it brought that Norfolk letter here."

"You sure?" I said.

"Fool, can't I read *Virginia?* My sister named Virginia—oldest one, long gone. Said *Virginia* on the outside; said *Mr. and Mrs. Porter.*"

I said "Both of them?"

"And both of em read it."

"What did they tell you?"

Noony had three eggs now and brought them to my basket. "Miss Caroline asked me could she count on me Thanksgiving."

"What did you say?"

Noony frowned. "Where'm I going, Miss Skinny? This is my *location.*"

So I broke out right there and told her what I'd kept in—Gaston and me that morning by the river. I told everything.

When she'd heard, she stepped forward, took the basket herself, and set it on the ground. Then she took my right hand and studied it, both sides. It looked like it always looked to me, but Noony shut it finally and said "I could have told." Then she laughed once and said "Now ain't you a *sport?* Did his knees start buckling and his eyes roll back?"

I said "His eyes were shut."

"You didn't get it on you?—nowhere on your body."

I said "My hand. You said you could tell."

Noony said "On your privates. Keep it *way* off them; one drop of that stuff is good as a carload."

"For what?"

"Babies, fool." But she said it kindly.

I'd suspected as much and, as I've said, heard rumors at school; so I let Noony tell me all she knew. Even then I guessed she knew very little but the bedrock basics. Caroline had warned me, when I had scarlet fever, against believing too much of Noony's science. Young as she was, she had a big store of charms and cures. You couldn't mention any trouble she couldn't help. Tell her "I've got cancer," she'd say "Lick the spot every time you can. Your slobber dry it *up*." At the end that day, after warning me always to sponge down with vinegar before and after boys, she took a step back and beamed at me. "It was fun, though—won't it?"

I could tell her oh it was. And that was the main help she always provided—a listener to hear how good things were, that other people scorned. But she had her own limits. There was stuff she wouldn't tell me, wide strips of discretion. As we aimed back toward the house with the eggs, I tried to ask what had gone wrong with Walter and Holt long ago.

She just said "I heard some mess but God won't let me tell it."

I knew not to push. She was strong as a door.

I didn't push Caroline or Holt at supper either, and we ate without mentioning Walter or a letter. When Noony had left, and Caroline and I were alone in the kitchen, I said "Are we having any company Thanksgiving?"

Caroline was drying forks, every tine individually. Then she looked up at me. Though she'd raised my own mother, she was not an old woman—fifty-seven years old, my age now as I sit here recalling her. Her hair was still brown as a pecan shell, with the same streaks of deeper brown and very little gray. But I thought she was ancient and wondered when all this family pain would kill her and where that would leave me. She said "I've been trying to find a way to thank you."

I'd lost myself in watching her. I had to ask "For what?"

"Walter's coming. You did it."

So I said "Don't ever leave me." I meant, don't leave if you really mean *thanks*.

She kept her place and finished drying the forks; but she said "You've got my written guarantee, if the Lord gives me breath." Then she finally smiled, on the new gold tooth Holt had made her buy. It still shamed her mouth (back then gold teeth were the pride of young Negroes and Bible salesmen). She never put the promise in writing of course, but she kept it in ways she never foresaw and as long as she breathed.

The next two weeks I nearly stifled on excitement. You have to understand how small Macon was, how seldom any new face entered our door. I think too, for me, there was all the thrill of mystery—why this poor boy had left his home and mother—and the thought that Walter Porter would be the only adult close to me who'd had no first-hand share in the grief surrounding my parents. He'd sent flowers again for Frances's grave and a twenty-five dollar check for me—riches then. I reported it at school, and my classmates barely listened; but one Miss Murdoch that taught world history stopped me in the hall and asked "Is it true Walter Porter's coming home?" She had stiff whiskers and was taller than any man I knew.

I managed to nod and say "Yes ma'm."

She said "I hope he'll have the grace to come alone."

I didn't understand but must have mumbled yes.

And she loped off, saying "A shame in this world."

But that didn't faze me. I prayed he'd be handsome, and I'd be his favorite child.

Handsome he wasn't. I could tell that before he touched ground from the train. In the years since the young snapshots I'd seen, he'd taken on thirty pounds and lost some hair. Whatever his troubles with Holt had been, he'd now become a Porter—in looks at least. Except for the eyes. They were Caroline's, hot and steady as hers. And he smiled at me first as he stood by his bag. He later said his parents had aged so much, he barely knew them but that I was the image of my mother as a girl (nobody else had said it and it fascinated me). I strode out to meet him, but Holt took me gently and pressed me back—"Let his mother get him first."

There was plenty for us all. He was no Gary Cooper, but he had love to give. Where other people would nod and smile, Walter would rise up from where he was reading and cross the room to touch you. Nothing gummy or bad, just a tap on the neck or waist—just warmth like a dog's, that constant but drier. And he'd brought us all presents, which he passed round soon as we got him to the house. There was one too many—Swift hadn't come to meet him—but he'd even found out somehow about Noony, who was new since his time, and had brought her two pairs of orange silk step-ins. I got a white clipper-ship in a bottle. I kept it by my seahorse and studied it for years, both lovely and trapped.

The day went fine, far as I could see. Holt dressed himself up and was sober right through. Caroline had a lot of food to oversee, but whenever she appeared she seemed relieved and called Walter "Goose" every time he squeezed her.

It was well after we'd had the big turkey dinner that Walter asked in general where Swift might be. Caroline told what was partly true—that he'd gone to his wife's home in Weldon for the day but would visit tomorrow. So Walter turned to me. We were crouched by the radio while Holt heard the news; the war in Europe was just underway and to me seemed distant as the new moon through trees but was urgent to Holt. Walter said "Kate, get your hat. Let's walk off the feast."

Holt offered us the car, claiming exercise had stopped more hearts than bullets.

But Caroline said "Hush. They want open air"—the first firm thing she'd said in three weeks.

So I knew we were free to go; and once outdoors, if Walter said "Flap your arms hard now and let's fly to Cairo," I'd have flapped them and flown. As it was, he led us up to the road and turned left, moving at the fast clip I like. I figured he'd be pointing out spots from his boyhood and telling me stories. I always enjoyed that when older people did it, since (like most children) I thought the idea that the world had existed and *worked* before me was incredible but funny. All he talked about was me though—what my life now was like, my teachers, my friends. I'd never had an adult interested in my news for more than ten seconds, so I rattled along as pleased as a jay and had almost brought myself to the point of telling him the secret of Gaston and me when he stopped and turned my face up to his.

His eyes were brimming tears, and I thought I'd done wrong or he'd guessed about Gaston. But he said "Will it hurt if I take you to the graves?"

Of course it would but I said "I'm used to it. We go once a month."

Walter said "Is it too far to walk in the cold?"

The afternoon was clear but a cool wind had come up. I'd have headed into blank walls of snow to be with Walter. I said "In case of frostbite we can stop in at Fob's."

Walter asked if I saw very much of Fob.

"He likes me," I said. "He gives me money." Twice since I'd asked for help, Fob had met me by the church on my way home from school and slipped me five dollars, folded tight as a pill. They were hid in my room.

Walter said "He's *got* it, way past a millionaire and lives like a dog."

"Don't worry," I said. "He and Tot are real happy."

Walter said "Lord God, is Tot still with him? Last thing I knew, he was young and bound for prison."

I said "He's out now and takes Fob everywhere. They ride all day, sometimes late in the night."

Walter said "Let's see them then, before they wear out. But on our way home." He ran forward ten yards, waddling at the hips.

There was nobody down at the graves but us, and the handful of holly Caroline had brought last time was still sharp and green over Tas and Frances. They were side by side like husband and wife (there was room at Tas's feet for his real separated wife if she ever wanted it). I fiddled with the holly and worked not to think how my mother's face looked now, so close there below me.

Walter said "Where is Dan?"

I figured he'd heard. "By his mother in Henderson. Her name was Kate too."

"Who made that decision?—to part him from Frances."

I had to say I didn't know; I'd never seen his grave.

Walter suddenly dropped to his knees beside me. "You want to go see him now? I'll get the car and take you." He was almost whispering and his eyes had filled again.

I realized that Dan's grave was about the only place I wouldn't go with him. I said "You asked about *hurt* awhile ago; that's a trip that would hurt."

Walter said "Don't hate him, Kate. Dan did what he had to."

I'd overheard a good many words about Dan, but these were the first that showed him any mercy. At once I knew two things—I'd love Walter Porter for the rest of my life (and so I have), and I'd ask him the question I'd swallowed in dread for seventeen months. I looked in his wet eyes and said "Why did he do it?"

Walter shook his head and scratched the grass on Frances's grave. "I wasn't here, Kate. When I knew him, he was nothing but a handsome boy."

"Somebody must've told you. My daddy wasn't crazy."

Walter nodded. "I doubt it. No, something made him see they had to stop *here*. You can't keep living just because your body wants to."

I didn't understand two words of that, not then anyhow; but somebody kin to me had finally said something new about the big thing. I figured when I got a little older I could ask him more and then understand.

Walter said "When Frances was a girl and I knew her, she was better to me than anyone alive. Never said a harsh word, never judged me once." Then he said "You can come to me anytime."

I knew he meant to Norfolk—I'd dreamed that already—and I knew I'd heard a promise I could save for some future need. But I also knew he was stranger than me; he would say what he meant quick as I would say "Bread." And that scared me a little, reminding me of Dan. I thanked him simply and said I was cold.

Walter said "In that case, we'll thaw you at Fob's." Then he bowed in one clean sweep and pressed his mouth to the ground above Frances.

* * *

You always entered Fob's house through the kitchen. The front latch had broken years before, and he'd nailed the door shut to keep out dogs (he said raccoons but dogs were more common). First you'd pass through a short back-hall dark as night, with long dry gourds on the wall and the skins of animals he'd caught and tanned and hung up to forget. Then you'd break out on a kitchen the size of some towns. Fob was standing by the sink, eating cold turkey-dressing with a butcher knife. When he saw us he said "Tot brought me this last night. He's home with his mammy. Give him two days a year off, but he still feeds me."

I suspected right away that he didn't know Walter.

But Walter said "Fob, you haven't changed a wart in—what?— twelve years."

Fob said "Thank you kindly. *You've* changed past recognition. Sit down and finish this." He extended the dressing in an old black pan.

Walter's mouth fell open but he laughed and gave a little curtsey from the knees. "Great God, Fob, it's *Walter*—your long-lost cousin."

Fob looked at me in genuine puzzlement. "It ain't."

I grinned that it was and said "Holt invited him."

Fob set down the knife and buttoned his collar. "Least I can do is put on a tie." He hadn't smiled yet but I knew he was pleased.

Walter said "The age of miracles returns." He stepped forward then and gave Fob a long hug.

Fob's eyes watched me through the whole transaction and eventually winked. But he said "I meant it—dressing's all I got. I told Tot I planned to fast today."

Walter said "What for? I'm the great family sinner, and I've just eaten turkey and ham."

I said "And mincemeat."

Fob said "Worst mistake either one of you's made. Sit down here and talk it off. You're both too fat." Walter was a little plump; I was thin as a file.

We sat down carefully (the chairs were old wrecks). Fob set out a new jar of artichoke pickles and that cold dressing, and he chewed on and asked Walter questions about his job and life in Norfolk.

Walter said "I love it. God knows it's not Macon."

Fob thought that over, then said the next to me. "No, and bound to be a lot less like Macon once we go to war."

War had crossed my mind of course, from Holt's news programs; but I'd never heard a grown man say we'd be in it. I sat up to listen.

Walter said "Mr. Roosevelt'll keep us out. He won't want all those sons of his shot."

Fob said "Mr. Roosevelt's a Dutchman, you notice. Dutchmen'll *scrap*."

Walter laughed. "War would do a world of good for Norfolk business."

Fob stood up and opened the back door a crack. I could feel the chill at once. Then he sat down again, chewed another artichoke, and told me "He's forgot I served in France. He's forgot I was gassed and my cousin Clyde killed."

Walter said "No, I hadn't. I thought you enjoyed it. You used to tell stories about killing cooties and crapping your pants when shells dropped near you; you'd laugh like you loved it."

Fob still spoke to me. "Yes, I very well might have. He was just a child then."

I said "I'm one now. Will there really be a war?"

Fob nodded. "Time for one. People praying for a war."

Walter said "Not I. I'd be drafted, first pop."

Fob waited again and I dreaded his voice. But he leaned over suddenly and patted Walter's hand that was drumming the table. Then he said "No, Walter. Rest easy; eat up. You're not what they need. Just tell em when they ask you."

Walter said "Fob, how come you never got married?"

I knew enough to guess I was watching a fight. I wanted to run.

But Fob said "Kate, you coming with me Saturday? The dogs asked about you."

I said "Oh yes."

Then he looked back at Walter. "—Same reason as you, I'd estimate."

I had no notion of what had gone wrong—why they were clawing each other with *war*—but I knew it'd been my idea to come here, so I took on my old job of clearing the air. I said "I'm cold as a cabbage leaf." Where I got that from, I never could guess; but it struck them both the same way, crazy and funny. And when they laughed, to keep the air gentle, I ate an artichoke with awful frowns (*Jerusalem* artichokes, the old hot kind, not the new sweet green ones)—I'd have rather licked an iron.

Fob got up and shut the outside door. Then he came back and said "How you like this girl?" He was speaking to Walter, and he probed my ear.

Back then they saw no reason on earth to lie to a child just to help her grow up. They would tell you the flat hard absolute truth from the day you could breathe—"You'll swing from the gallows before you can dance"—so I sat there chewing my stinging cold pickle and waited in dread for the final sentence. I trusted them so much, I'd have borne what they gave.

And Walter thought it through, no joke to him either. His oval white face fogged over, and his eyes shut down to black slots. Then he said "I loved her mother like a sister."

Fob said "You get no credit for that. Her mother was *Frances*. This is *Kate*, here now." He was still there behind me, touching my shoulder.

Walter thought again—I was ready to bolt—and said it to me. "I've already told her she can come live with me."

Nobody had smiled but I hoped that was praise, though milder than I dreamed of.

Fob suddenly clamped both hands round my neck, not tight but firm. "You love her at a distance awhile longer please—just mail her nice presents. We need her here now."

Walter said "This town has hurt her already."

Fob said "Say how."

Walter chucked his chin back toward the cemetery. "It killed Dan and Frances."

Fob still held my neck. "Dan and Frances killed themselves."

Walter nodded, to mean "We've gone far enough. We're abusing her now."

But I realized I was hungry for this—two grown men taking me as seriously as war. I didn't say a word but stared out the window at a far-off horse I hadn't seen before. It was steaming at the nose and looked so bright in the hard dark day that I thought it might be the ghost of a horse. I tried to imagine I also saw fire. I was guessing I still might *matter* on earth, if they would say so.

But Walter pulled back. He followed my gaze to the smoking horse and asked me "You ever ride him? He looks rough."

Fob said "It's a mare. I got her for you."

At first I understood he meant for *Walter*, and I almost laughed— Walter Porter on a horse was a hard thought to manage. But then I missed Fob's hands on my neck, and I turned back to see.

He had stepped well back and was by the sink again with a window behind him. All the light of the gray day touched his broad body and shone at his boundaries like personal radiance. He was past middle-age and would never look better, but his eyes had filled, and I suddenly wanted to spare him pain.

I said "I live here, Fob, and you know it."

He nodded toward the door. "Go name your horse, Kate."

I called her Rosalind, for the Greensboro teacher who had given me a seahorse; and from that first day, I joined onto her like the first local centaur. And with her full permission—she took me like a gift she needed and could use. Walter and Fob stood and watched me mount her. I'd never had more than pony rides at the fair, so nobody knew whether I would stay or fall. I remember thinking that as I slung myself up—"For all these men know, they're watching me die in the next five minutes" (a girl in my school had been thrown and killed by a horse she'd loved and tended for years). But the day was going so much better than I'd hoped that I saw the risk they were putting me through as one more means of silent care. They meant me to prosper; who was I to fail?

I never learned technical words for riding or the parts of horses— I was a grown woman and Fob was dead before I knew such a language existed (and then it seemed meant for television shows of the Princess of England, straight as a board). So I can't describe Roz any better than to say she was middlesized, six years old, light gray, with eyes that God had to envy for wisdom. You could travel on her eyes a lot farther than her feet. Once up, the first time, I looked down to Fob and said "Where shall I go?"

He said "That's your problem."

I said "But come back? You want me back?"

Fob said "Someday."

And Walter said "Soon. I'm leaving on Sunday." He looked a little trumped, a little small for his clothes. He'd meant himself to be the day's great news.

But I tore on off. Or walked a few yards; then she chose a hard trot that rattled my bones till I finally said "You're aging me fast. You'll be alone soon." With no further signal from me, she shifted to a hydraulic lope, smooth as skin in oil; and we toured the gigantic edge of that field like a low lovely glider. I could touch tree trunks as we passed and name them (I was in a naming mood). At one point I thought we were headed for an overgrown logging trail, and I pictured myself smashed off by a limb or caught by the hair like Absalom and hung, but I didn't try to stop her. She veered off though and kept the circle perfect.

When I could see Fob and Walter still standing in the cold up ahead, I told myself what I suddenly thought," You are safe, Kate. These grown men are waiting on nothing but you. Now turn out good." I was less than half-right, and I turned out stranger than they could have dreamed, but that one moment got me through many others less happy and free.

Walter left on the Sunday. By then I was wondering if I'd let him down badly, dividing my feelings between him and a horse and a cousin of his that had never left home, much less returned as the prodigal forgiven. But he took it in good grace with frequent jokes—"Here I brought her a prince, but she wants the frog." He meant Fob of course. But Saturday evening, when it was even colder, he walked down to meet me at Fob's at dusk.

Tot was back on the job and had been out with me all afternoon, showing me how to think like a horse but faster. Fob had gone off to try to find a sober well-digger (they needed new water).

Tot was on Roz behind me and saw him first. He whispered "Here come poor Walter. We running?"

I said "No and what's so poor about Walter? He makes better money than anybody here" (Fob was land-poor, precious little cash on hand).

Tot said "Money won't buy what Walter's after."

I didn't understand but I said "Norfolk sells everything people want." I was dumb but right.

So Tot turned Roz and we ambled toward the gate. There was just enough light to make out shapes; and Walter was the biggest, a grin like a baby's. When we got close to him, Tot said "Here, Walter, you lift Kate down." With Tot up behind me, getting down was awkward.

Walter said "Oh Jesus, she's too big for me."

That was back before people said "Jesus" every minute, and I was as thrilled as if we stood at the bar in a Pecos saloon. I started trying to work my right leg over Roz's head.

But too slow for Tot. He said "Take her. I got this horse to feed, then supper to cook. Mr. Fob be here soon."

I knew I was causing Tot extra work, and anyhow I was worn out and cold, so I opened my arms and just fell on Walter.

He yelled but caught me—I was no small package—and we headed home, me laughing and Walter moaning for his back that he claimed I'd broke. It was full dark by then, and we could see Caroline's kitchen light, but he stopped me by a broad cherry tree near the railroad track and said "Can you see me?"

I could sense he was there, but no I couldn't see any of him but the paleness of his face and hands. I said "No sir."

That seemed to ruin whatever plan he had. For maybe a minute he sighed and drew breaths, but he didn't move on. Finally he found my chin with his hand and turned me toward him, then stroked my neck on both sides gently.

I was old enough to think "Lord, he's going to get funny" (I'd heard a lot at school about amorous brothers, fathers, uncles, inlaws).

But he just stroked in-place—people love to touch children, the skin is so fine—so I waited calmly.

Finally Walter said "You've been through some Hell, Kate; far more than you'll ever earn in this life. I can't tell you now—you can't use my full story yet awhile—but Hell is a place I've served time in. *I'm on your side.*" He stopped there, waiting for word from me.

I guessed he meant my Hell was Dan and Frances, and it had been rough. But at no point had I felt held-down and tortured, by them or God. And these last months, my appetite was rising for a whole run at life. I could only say "Thank you."

That made him clamp me to him, his black overcoat. And with me half-smothered, he said "Don't thank me. Just know I'm there, right up these rails, on Bruges Avenue in Norfolk, Virginia. Stay here long as you can and are happy. My mother is a saint, but she's wearing out fast. Then come on to Walter."

Right then I couldn't imagine leaving Macon—least of all to go live with this big strange cousin, wilder than me. But I told him I would. I said "I think it'll be in five years" (I was wrong by a year).

Walter suddenly turned me loose and stepped back. I heard him stumble but he stayed upright and said "All right. If the world's still here, and I'm alive *in* it, I'll have your room ready."

I could hear, by the tight high quiver in his voice, that he meant every word. I thought it was funny, and thought it was strange, and thought no human had ever bet more on me than Walter Porter. I was right, all round. And when we saw him off on the Sunday morning train, both he and I wept.

Swift had never showed up. We knew they had to be home from their trip, but he never so much as displayed his face. And nobody mentioned him until Walter stepped up to board the train. He said to Caroline "Tell Swift his living brother hated to miss him" and Caroline nodded.

That night after supper she and I were in the kitchen. She'd already seen how much I liked Walter; and I knew that pleased her, though I'd kept secret all the oddness about me coming to Norfolk when I was unhappy. I'd heard Walter say she was wearing out, and I'd studied her closely to see what he meant. Looking through Walter's eyes, and compared to old pictures, I saw how she'd shrunk in recent years; how her smile had thinned to a line you almost dreaded to cause on her lean face. But I also knew she could answer the question these days had asked—why did Walter ever leave and stay so long, and why did so many people speak meanness of him? She had sent Noony home, and we were drying forks as carefully as scalpels. I said "Am I big enough to ask you something?"

Caroline said "Just ask and I'll be the judge." She faced me and smiled.

I almost stopped but I had my nerve up. "What's wrong with Walter?"

She didn't look at me. "Not a thing, to my knowledge. He's put on flesh but that's everybody's right."

I knew I would hurt her, but I saw no way round it. I said "Then why do people round here hate him?"

Caroline said "That's news to his mother." But she didn't ask for names.

I said "Did he do something bad before he left here?"

We'd finished the forks and I'd put them away. We were both standing idle, but she still hadn't faced me. She said to the window "He treated every human soul as gentle as pups. That may have made some people mad but not me."

It's the first big thing in my life I'm ashamed of, but I gave her the list—"Miss Murdoch at school, Fob and Tot, his own brother."

She turned on me then, her face calm as wax and both eyes dry. But she said "Kate, I'd think—with the parents you had—you'd want to try to hold down spite in your heart."

I said "Yes ma'm" and felt like the filthy dog I was. In another few minutes I went to my room, asked God's forgiveness (a good deal easier to ask than Caroline's), and then concentrated on the internal movie of Roz I had already started making—Roz and I alone in an empty world and none the worse for it, Roz and I rescuing each other daily while we learned each other's language. My light was out.

I'd finally thawed enough territory in the icy sheets to think about sleep and was passing out when I heard soft steps in the hall coming toward me. I knew one of two things was bearing down—Caroline had something even worse to say or she'd beg my pardon. Either one seemed more than I could handle in the dark. So I sat bolt upright and switched on my lamp.

She was not a big woman, but she filled the whole doorframe. She'd put on her gown and robe and let down her hair that was strong and waistlength. She knew I liked to plait it, and I hoped she'd come for that—the one long loose plait she wore every night. But she met my eyes and said "I don't need *light*."

For an instant I thought "This is what Frances saw, last thing, with Dan." But I switched off the light and slid to the far frozen side of the bed to give her room (right after I moved there, she came in most nights and lay down beside me, telling tales from her stoneage girlhood that I loved).

Now though she sat on the edge of the mattress, next to my feet, and touched me nowhere.

She waited a long time in absolute silence, long enough for my eyes to open in the dark and make the mistake they've made ever since— thinking that something which looks benign can do no harm. I had my mouth open to start my apology.

But she said "Kate, I'd have better drunk lye than said what I said to you just now."

I said "You were fair."

She said "*Fair*'s nothing to be proud of; plenty animals are fair."

I said "It was my fault."

She said "It was not. You rubbed on a raw place. It was me that chose to strike."

I said "Then let's don't remember this tomorrow."

She was able to laugh—not bitterly, I could hear. Then she lay on top of the cover beside me and said "Let's try."

I said "I'm wiping my mind clean now." I had this idea I could stare at my mind in the cold pitchdark and see it as a blackboard and wash it clean (at school we'd beg for the right to wash a blackboard, a perfect result from very little labor in the burnt smell of chalkdust). And I could clear my mind for months, even years—I thought of Dan and Frances seldom by then—but of course the only memories I've really erased are of short happy minutes, harmless as wrens. All the others fly in like bats any time.

She gave me a minute to finish the job. Then she said "If anything happened to me—"

I rolled right to her and said "No," loud. I wouldn't have another person near me die.

So Caroline touched me finally, on the hip. But she kept on-course. "I hope to see you grown, and I'm trying to last. It's not my choice though, and you'd go to Walter if I passed on."

I didn't say he'd already offered more than once to take me in. I said "I'm happy right now with you and Roz. We don't have to plan past here—the war and all."

Caroline said "War can come if it needs to. It won't come here; they won't want Macon. But Norfolk'll be hot as cinders—ships and boys. And Walter's railroad'll do fast business. So you might need this; I guess you're old enough."

She'd been propped at the head of the bed. Now she lay down flat and turned over toward me. I could feel her breath like a plume on my eyes. As always, it had no odor whatever.

She said "Walter Porter was born out of me the very same thing he is today—funny and harmless as April leaves and as different from every other boy in Macon as butter from lard. He couldn't hit a baseball broad as this house, and more than once he asked me to buy him dolls. When Holt wouldn't let me, Walter carved his own and dressed it in scraps and hid it in the smokehouse under old sacking—I found it years later. He wasn't ever lonesome though. Other children loved him because he'd give away everything he had; they just needed to smile. And his own brothers thought he was good news *daily*. They laughed through whole years of boyhood with him, not a grievance in sight. Then he started to grow—sixteen, seventeen—and other people, up and down the road, started noticing what I'd seen for years. He wasn't going to live the life people live—flocks of children and a woman, ninety million meals to buy. I'd seen he wasn't *meant* to, but I never told him or Holt or anybody but God in prayers. I'd had an uncle like him, that finally hung himself shortly after Appomattox. But Walter struggled on a few more years and then just left—rode off from here one Sunday morning with Douglas Lee and stayed gone all these years. Three of them, I didn't even know where he was." She thought she was finished.

I was alert and waited for the rest.

But she lay on quiet, turned to her back again, and smoothed the cold pillow as if she planned to stay.

At first I thought "That's surely no help." I decided to give her a minute and then ask what it meant and how in the world it was anything I needed. But several minutes went by, and Caroline's breathing plainly slid into sleep. I was mad till I realized how that much at least meant she bore me no grudge and trusted my body. She'd left me wide awake though, so I picked closely at her story for secret passageways to something I could spy on till more years passed and gave me understanding. I couldn't find so much as a seam to rip. Young as I was, I might well have guessed everything she said. Why would anybody vanish from home and his mother just to ward off children and a wife at the stove? I'd decided, just lately, to be single myself. I had scads of examples—nine-tenths of my schoolteachers, Fob, and some animals. Any blind girl could see they were clearly better off; it had caused them no pain, surely left none of them in a state like Walter. I never thought to ask who Douglas Lee was, not then anyhow nor until I saw his face. *That* was news might have helped me change my whole life, the part that soon was to turn round Douglas like a ferris wheel lit with live flames and no brakes. But I can't regret that; silence was my nature then. Like most healthy children I figured big mysteries were still my lot till some magic day when one smarter human would switch on the last light or lift the last veil on full disclosure. Poor kind Walter Porter, all gifts and tears, was not the main lion in my little path.

The official start of being a woman was no threat either. Enough girls had started their monthlies before me to give fair warning of what to expect. I even prayed for it just to *commence*, as a badge of something (having slim information on any connection between my blood and babies). Late that winter the Lord obliged.

It was the second week in March, a Saturday so warm and fine you wanted to fall down and eat the dead grass to clear way for green. I'd been down at Fob's to talk to Roz. Something told me not to ride her that afternoon and she seemed glad. She stayed close by me while I walked round the field and told her my woes of the past two days, normal schoolchild woes. Once I shut up and took two silent steps, she stopped in her tracks on the piney south-side and left me to stumble back by myself. I whistled and called but she wouldn't budge. I laughed and left her, and she watched me go. I was tired in the legs, but I felt very light. Fob was not at home; and Tot was on the back porch, scalding milk pans. So I waved at him and kept on going.

As I got near the tracks, I heard a train whistle, an unscheduled freight coming through from the west. I had nothing but time—and a penny in my pocket. I ran forward, laid it on one shiny rail, and stood close enough to feel the freight's strong wind as it swayed on past— some two dozen cars, long for those days. Then I bent to find my penny, squashed to the size of a half-dollar with Lincoln stretched out like a funhouse face. I recall thinking what I always thought after pressing a penny, "Keep this up and one day you'll wreck a train." I pictured myself in the Woman's Penitentiary, girls on all sides telling me secrets most people never hear.

When I stood up and took the flat copper in my mouth (I liked the bite of copper), I knew I had changed. As quick as that. But I didn't know how. There were no streaks of blood crawling down my legs, like you see in movies. No pounding, no sickness. But I felt very much the way I'd felt that time on the train from Greensboro when I turned myself into Marcus, the redheaded boy with braces. I was somebody else, I was utterly at peace, and I had a new odor. Nobody but me or a delicate animal would ever have noticed. As I climbed our steps, I wondered if Roz had smelled it and refused me.

Caroline and Holt had gone to Roanoke Rapids for a corset-fitting (his dreadful lumbago). But Noony was making slaw in the kitchen. From the front-door sill I could hear cabbage grating, and something in me broke. Again it was nothing you could bandage or stitch. I had just stood up, or settled down, through some old ceiling or floor that had bound and protected me till now. As slow as if I was bearing a full cup, I went toward the kitchen and Noony—not a sound. Halfway down the hall, clearer than I'd ever been Marcus the boy, I saw myself as a grayhaired woman in a blue crepe dress stood up near a tall window staring at a cold road, empty as the sky. She was waiting and didn't even know what for, but her name was Kate, and she had to be me. By the time Noony saw me—I stopped in the door—tears were rolling down. I couldn't say a word.

Noony said "She throwed you." She took it as a fact; she resented Roz and the time I spent having fun with Tot.

I shook my head.

She went back to her cabbage. "You ain't broke nothing if you walked that far."

I meant to say "Help," but it came out a sob.

Seeing me cry was as scarce a sight as snow. But Noony held her ground. "That nigger ain't touched you, is he? Tell me if he did." She was whispering by then and wiping her hands.

I knew she meant Tot, and that was as likely as me touching some mole on Tyrone Power's back. So I laughed once and that set me free to move. I wanted to fold deep in somebody's arms and be cherished blindly, but Noony was not a regular hugger (the one time I grabbed her, she was like a tall thicket of polished broomsticks). Still I went as close as I thought was safe. She was in easy reach.

And she did touch my forehead, testing for fever. Then she stepped back and studied me. Then she did something I'd never seen—she moved over quick and shut the door that opened on the hall. I'll bet it hadn't been shut since they hung it. There was no other human in a quarter-mile. Then she came back and said "Step out of your britches and hand em here."

I thought she was crazy, but I didn't stop to say it. Maybe she still knew a remedy for me. I had on a wornout plaid schooldress (I hadn't worn my trousers, not intending to ride). So I shucked my underpants in two easy steps and handed them over.

Noony turned her back to me, went to the window, and inspected them slowly. Finally she brought them an inch from her nose. Then she turned and said "When did you turn twelve?"

A birthday seemed like a foreign event in some other life. But I said "June the third. I'm twelve and nine months."

Noony wadded my pants to a ball in her palm and said "You *late*. Come on here with me."

I said "Late for what?" but followed her. We were in the far corner of Caroline's room, and Noony was scrabbling in the back of the wardrobe for something hidden, before it dawned on me—"Great God, I've started." I think I was pleased, though a little embarrassed I hadn't understood maybe half an hour sooner. It was also the first of many times when I knew I was glad my father was gone and would not have to learn.

As she helped me on with the regulation outfit worn in those days (more straps than a parachute and less fun to rig), Noony broke down at last and laughed to herself.

So I said "This is something natural, I thought."

She nodded and met my eyes to beg pardon. "Yes, Lord Jesus. You in *business* now."

I apparently was but other business outside seemed more pressing. Hitler had taken Poland in the fall. By spring he was ready for Norway, Denmark, Belgium, and Holland. Every evening at six I'd sit on a hassock by Holt's big chair, and he and I would listen to the radio news. Anyone watching would have thought, from our faces, that we'd been somewhere in the world and understood what this meant—Queen Wilhelmina's grand voice leaving her land, quislings and commandoes. (Holt had been too old for World War I, and I just knew the road from Greensboro to Macon.) What I did understand was, *it made life important.* I felt good knowing Holt wanted me by him through the daily bad news. And even when he'd finally switch off H. V. Kaltenborn or Gabriel Heatter and say "Oh Katie, we'll be in it soon," I would feel scared first and then so stirred I'd lie awake late and guess my futures.

Nobody, least of all an untraveled girl, could say then that war wouldn't land square on us. Mr. Roosevelt himself never promised we were safe. So I'd see bombs dropping and waves of refugees—handcarts stacked with bedsprings, roosters, and big-eyed children no stronger than me. Or Hitler would postpone invading us long enough for me to study nursing and be a real help to the wounded and lost before I was either dead or a heroine. Or I would love a pilot and be wearing his ring when he flew out one day and never came back, so I couldn't feel free again to turn elsewhere but would dress severely and be envied by others for my sacrifice and beauty.

I was also noticing that beauty might settle on me soon now. My room had a tall mahogany wash-stand with a four-foot mirror you could tilt back and forth. By my thirteenth birthday, as the Germans ruined France, I was spending long minutes watching my face. I'd never been a pretty child, and no one had lied and claimed I was. But they hadn't winced or fled. It didn't bother me. I may have even thought a round plain face on compact bones would be the best way not to share my mother's luck. Nobody would crave me enough to turn wild.

Now though, I'd catch a slow change round my eyes or along my jaw. In later years I met several men who'd confess doing more with a mirror than me—kissing and other strange home-theatricals. I never so much as touched the glass but would stand and look and tilt the frame to shift the light. A nearly transparent but powerful smoke was drifting from some low fire down in me; and by the spring of 1940, it had marked me so several others also noticed.

Boys in the seventh grade were generally behind me and most other girls in growing up. We were swelling and flushing and oiling round the nose while they were still scuffling each other on the ground. I remembered my morning with Gaston by the river, his plea for help. But he was in the ninth grade, which might have been China for grand air and distance. The rare times he'd pass in the hall, I'd try to burn signals at him—*Just look. You remember.* They flew past or bounced off like birds on a car. He never seemed to know me.

Then late that May in the last week of school, I was out on the school steps dusting erasers (do they still have those old blackboard erasers in blue and gray felt that you slap together to beat out the chalk?). I heard boys laughing and here came the baseball team back from practice in striped uniforms. I went cold as sherbet and turned to run in, but then some senior boys swung out of line and there was Gaston. He walked in a sealed-off lonesome pocket of completely clear air like no one could reach him with word or deed. Something made me wait to see what would happen. I just expected shame. My arms were all chalkdust halfway to the elbow and dropped at my sides like belly-up fish. The line of older boys passed by, not a look. But Gaston slowed down as he got near the steps and stopped on the first one. I was four steps above him. He looked at me long enough to map me like a country. Then he said "You're dying from the fingers up."

I held out my corpse-arms but couldn't speak.

Gaston said "Summer's here. You'll come back to life."

I said "I hope to."

He said "Daddy told me they got you a mare."

I must have nodded yes.

He looked back out toward the baseball diamond hidden in pines, and he said "They let you take her out by yourself?"

I lied and said "Yes." The one condition Caroline had made was for me to ride always in sight of Fob or Tot. But Tot was already tired of watching.

Gaston's profile and neck were still slick with sweat that looked cool now. And he did shiver slightly as he turned back and looked square up at my eyes. With both broad hands he wiped his face hard. Then he said "I could show you the old lumbermill. You never seen that."

He was right. And stunned as I was, I thought it could hardly be much to see—old iron and sawdust. But I said "O.K." (Caroline hated "O.K." so much she'd nearly fired Noony for saying it once).

He finally smiled—something he did seldom enough to make it like the blast when you throw phosphorus off a bridge, which I did later.

I knew I'd follow him anywhere on earth. It scared me—I wouldn't turn thirteen for nearly two weeks—and I said "Gaston, I got to go in. Miss Finch'll kill me." That was the first time I said his name.

He said "Nobody's going to kill you now. Meet me Saturday right after dinner at the graves."

* * *

Dinner meant *lunch* as it still does in most farm areas, I hope. But the rest of that week I was tight as a harpstring, wondering when "right after dinner" meant. That bothered me much more than meeting in the cemetery; Frances's small grave didn't hurt me now. I even asked Noony if everybody ate at the same time as us. She said "All over the world. When else?"

So Saturday morning I woke up at six but lay still, letting the early sun find me. I'd left the shade on my east window up; and in half an hour, yellow light took my feet. Morning was one of my main times for prayers. But this one morning I was at a real loss. I didn't know what I wanted to do or would be asked for. And that meant I didn't know what *not* to do, what to ask strength against. So I just sang "Jesus Loves Me" in my head, and by then my feet were cooking. I heard Caroline and Holt get up. Then Noony came in and started their breakfast. I either played possum or napped an hour longer, hoping they'd head in for next week's groceries without calling me.

But a little past eight, while I was dreaming, Caroline stopped at the foot of my bed. She already had her old hat on, a brown stiff sailor with three red cherries. She was smiling and she sang a line of "Lazy Bones." Then she said "Holt is having that tooth pulled today; and knowing Dr. Taylor, it may take till night and cost him some blood. He's scared to death. I'll have to stay with him."

I'd known but, in my excitement, forgotten they'd be gone maybe longer than usual. I said I'd be fine, not mentioning Roz (so as not to be warned).

Caroline took the long pin out of her hat to reset it absolutely level to the ground. Then for reasons neither of us ever understood or talked about, she said "You have already brought me more than any son I had." It sounded like Swift and Walter were dead.

I said "You mean happiness?"

She said "I do."

If she'd flung a spear through me, it wouldn't have hurt worse. I must not have shown it.

She went on smiling.

So I said "I may not can keep that up."

She said "I know that" and then she was gone.

The strange thing was that I turned to watch her and, well before she was out of sight, I knew two things—that I'd love her all my life and I'd meet Gaston Stegall after dinner and do all he asked till he called time to quit.

The rest of the morning I sat on the back porch, away from the road, and read my favorite childhood book—*Arabian Nights*—more than halfway through. Noony cleaned indoors. Off and on the whole time, I wanted to tell her. I couldn't though. I figured I'd save her for afterward, in case something failed or proved too strange. But nervous as I was, I ate the big hot meal she gave me at twelve. Then I told her I'd be going down to ride awhile.

Noony pretended she hadn't heard that and went on heating water for the dishes.

So when I was ready, I stepped close behind her, thanked her for my dinner, and said I'd see her by suppertime.

She shook her head hard.

I said "Won't you be here?"

She never turned but said "Kate, I warned you before—don't never say what you *will* and *won't* do. Tuck your butt and say 'Noony, I'll see you if the Lord be willing and you and me both ain't dead or down by suppertime.' "

I laughed and thought I was humoring her when I said it back like a memorized poem.

I didn't go to Fob's. I'd decided in a dream after Caroline left that, whatever happened, I wouldn't ask a kind strong animal to help me. (Even right now, with everything I've done, I can't be myself if an animal's watching—anything bigger than a spider on the wall. I respect them that much and fear their judgment.) I struck out straight for the cemetery and passed nobody but an owl asleep and old black Pap in his ox-cart. He always thought I was Frances my mother and called me "Fancy." I didn't stop but smiled; he'd keep you till dark and, though he sold soap, give you nothing for your time. I was scared half-blind.

But of no human being. Just of the way my legs drew me on, not stumbling once.

Gaston Stegall was already there. I'd known, if he showed up, he'd be at our graves and start asking questions. But no, he was standing by the tall marble blasted tree-trunk that marked Ned Thornton—a boy killed by lightning on a clear afternoon. He was facing the road; but if he saw me, he gave no sign.

I went up to him and did, right off, what I'd vowed not to—I mentioned dead people. I said "Was Ned Thornton kin to you?" And I knew the answer. Thorntons owned half the world round Macon when Stegalls were sleeping in gunnysacks and gnawing pine-pitch.

He said "I'm kin to everybody, dead or live."

It turned out later, when I had sense to ask, that he meant *related through Adam and Eve.* But there in that sun, I'd have nodded if he said he *was* everybody (much less their cousin). How can one plain body drive a whole mind foolish at three feet distance?

I said "I've got no family at all." I know it was the first time I'd mentioned my parents to anyone but Caroline, Holt, and Walter. And I thought "Now I've handed him the ticket to that." I was glad. I wanted to tell him, first one. Everybody knew what nobody'd yet had the gall to say—my story, what I knew about Frances and Dan, was the big thing young Kate Vaiden had to offer. Or so I thought.

Gaston thought otherwise, if he thought about me. He may have just been in a state like mine, led on through this spring afternoon like a sleepwalker drowned but hearing a voice—*Come on, come on.* He said "All right." I never knew to what.

I said "I didn't get to bring my horse."

He said "All right" again and looked round behind him.

I'd been facing that way but hadn't seen a small rusty mare in the shade, hitched to a tree. I asked was she his?

He gave a big grin, at nothing I could see, and said "She's mine long enough to carry *us.*"

I said "Where we going?"

"Lake Michigan," he said.

At first I thought he was serious. I planned to say no.

But he grinned again. "Lord, how far is that?"

I said "Too far to get me home by supper. What happened to the sawmill? You advertised that."

"—Or the quicksand," he said. "You ever see any?"

I said I'd heard about it.

So Gaston said "Choose."

It didn't dawn on me what a funny pair of sights he was offering. If you weren't interested in natural wonders or burnt-out houses, you might as well shut your eyes around Macon. I said "Quicksand." Then I asked was it safe?

Gaston said "You already picked. Come on." He was moving out.

We were both on the mare, in a hard army-saddle, before I realized the way we were headed—down through woods to the same creek-bottom where Dan and Frances died. As I said, I had dreamed of being down there but had never felt ready. I was in front of Gaston; he was holding the reins. I started just to take his hands and pull back to stop. If he asked why, I'd tell him—and tell the whole story. But then I wondered if he understood. Did he have any clear idea where it happened? (it had been two years). Or was he testing me one more way? I decided to see. See his plan, that is. I knew I could shut my actual eyes if we passed anything I shouldn't remember.

It of course looked like any creek in the woods, back then anyhow. No old plastic garbage, no suds in the stream. Sometimes in my life I've been flat certain that places—especially places made of rock—can choose to sieve out strong acts and hold them a few years, maybe even longer, for others to feel.

But we rode down a slow mile of that creek and surely crossed my parents' last steps; and I felt almost nothing, barely blinked my eyes. There'd been heavy rain toward the end of winter. There were still signs of flooding underfoot, and I thought "Any blood that lasted this long is gone." That stopped my last fear; and I'll say this for Gaston, he never spoke a word till we got to where he aimed. And he held me no tighter than he had to, to guide us.

The quicksand was part of the edge of the creek. Gaston pulled up the mare (I think her name was Trudge) at ten yards' distance and finally proved he still had a voice. He said "Swing your leg. I'll set you down." I obeyed. He took me under each arm, and I gave him my weight till he had me safe down. Then he came down himself in a strange backward vault over poor Trudge's tail, too fast to get kicked. I didn't know whether he was showing off or acting the way he generally did so I didn't comment. But I didn't move either. There was hard ground under me; I didn't know where it ended.

Gaston bent down, found a rock the size of a potato, and chucked it toward the shoal of damp gray sand. It sat on the surface for maybe three seconds; and then it sank quickly, no trace whatever. Gaston said "My daddy lost a whole circus-pony and a fine studded harness in this same spot twenty-five years ago."

I said "When did your daddy quit the circus?"

He chucked another rock. "You're getting off the subject. *His* daddy bought the pony at an auction in Littleton and loved it like a baby. It had just retired and knew worlds of tricks. My daddy and some other boys stole it one Sunday, when they ought to been quiet, and sunk it in here. They didn't mean to. They saved the red cart that come with the sale; we still got that."

I mostly believed him, though the ribs of sand were no more than five feet wide and smooth as concrete. How far down were those pony bones now? I said "We could get a stick and see if we feel it."

Gaston said "I tried that years ago. Like to got lost too."

So I said "Maybe we better get out of here."

He thought about that. Then he took a step away to see me better and said "Where we going?"

I studied him slowly, hoping to guess what people saw in love. I liked Gaston's eyes and the fact he'd gone on and outgrown me. He stood a head taller; and though he wasn't shaving yet, his voice had loosened in his throat and deepened. When he spoke, it always took me a second to find him—he sounded so grown. I'd struck out on my own and followed him just because he asked me. But nothing in sight now justified the big dare of being down here.

He seemed lost too and stepped back to Trudge and started mumbling to her.

So I threw a rock myself. Mine was big as Gaston's; but mine didn't sink, just sat there at home. I took it as the sign I'd hoped for all day. I said "You can ask me anything you want to." I thought I meant the story of Dan and Frances.

Gaston kissed Trudge's nose and laughed and looked up. "And then what?" he said.

I said "Beg your pardon?"

He said "I ask and then you do what?"

I said "I answer if it's in my power." I sounded strange to my own ears and no doubt to the trees—not thirteen for three more weeks and speaking like a person with judgment and duties to fill every day.

He said "Well, who invented steam?"

I said "Robert Fulton" and we both got to laugh. When he calmed down I saw he couldn't think what next. All I knew was, he had to keep asking for things or I'd need to run. I said "Other things got killed down here besides a pony." I pointed behind us. "You want me to tell you."

He shook his head. "No ma'm."

He knew what I meant and refused the offer; I saw that at last. He had asked just me, for his own secret sake. So I said "That thing that was hurting you before—you know, by the river—is it hurting you now?"

He nodded. "Bout to kill me." His face didn't show the blank pain it had before.

Still I chose to believe him. I said "I could try to help you again." Helen Keller would have noticed he was up and ready. I took a step toward him.

But he flagged a hand to stop me. Then he flat ransacked my face with his eyes and finally said "Ain't you hurting yet, nowhere at all?"

I was not. I was happy. But I lied and said "Yes" to keep this going. So he beckoned me to him.

I wanted to wait and make him come get me, but then I saw he didn't understand the procedure any better than me. And I took the few steps till I could smell his hair, strong as a fox.

He said "Is it warm enough for you to get naked?"

I nodded. "I saw the first lizard last week." (They had a local saying that you couldn't go barefoot till you'd seen the first lizard.) Then I started on my buttons. But it turned out Gaston didn't want us to strip.

He said "There's a kind of moss farm back in here." He pointed deeper inward and followed the point.

I said "Won't Trudge wander off?" (I meant *follow us*).

Gaston didn't look back. He said "Trudge knows who cuts her hay." Then he told her to wait here till she heard her name.

Moss *farm* was not the right word. It was like the world-center for all breeds of moss. You climbed a high bank above the creek; and just beyond that was an outbreak of rocks, then another little valley in thick beech-shade. It was long and narrow, the size of a boxcar. Every inch of earth was padded with moss—green so clear it seemed more like a whistle than a color, rust-yellow, brown. It even climbed halfway up the trees and lit our skin till we looked like creatures from the backend of caves. Gaston stopped in the absolute middle and stood, looking up. I chose the spot. It was at the east end, the farthest from Macon (though Macon was no part of my mind now)—a valley in the valley, a trough that was easy as down to lie on and just wide enough to reach across if you spread both arms and stretched your fingers.

Gaston watched, then silently agreed, and walked over. He said the one last thing I needed to hear. "I don't know a thing about where we're headed."

I told him that just made two of us, and then he knelt down. This was some years before bosoms came into their own, mine or anybody else's (and since mine were hardly more than bee-stings by then, it was lucky for me). But he'd heard about kisses, I'll have to say. And I'd seen enough at movies to meet him halfway.

Adam and Eve (that were our connection) couldn't have understood less than us—the first time anyhow, and they were born grown. Gaston never mentioned *naked* again. Maybe it was still too cool for him. But he made a liberal allowance for buttons (boys still buttoned their pants shut then, and girls hid well behind squads of buttons). And though his hands were callused as antlers, they felt smooth and kind and in no big hurry.

After three or four minutes, I wondered to myself what we thought we were doing. As I've said, after Dan and Frances died, I tried to guess what people craved in each other if they didn't want babies. And babies shot through my mind there and then. For about one instant. I knew the vague road between where we were headed and a house full of children, but there on that ground I could no more picture myself as a mother than as General Pershing at Belleau Wood. Nor Gaston as a father. I knew less than naught about care and prevention; and when Gaston said he didn't have a rubber, I swear I wondered what he needed to erase.

After that, in spite of no small pain, I saw in my head as clear as a vision the thing I was doing (I didn't speak for Gaston). *I was being as good to myself as I could.* Better than anybody else had been. I was giving myself this long steady gift. The gift wasn't Gaston exactly or the feeling but the whole bright day, well-made as a gold watch and much less predictable. And I pictured my face overhead in beech leaves—normal size and nobody's raving beauty but a firm open face that could meet you unblinking with a likable smile. It said *You will never be gladder than now if you live to be ninety.*

I'm thirty-three years from ninety still, but the face didn't lie. I won't claim the day was the peak of my life. With all my badness I've enjoyed myself. But right to this day, I can see us there in that mossy furrow—every mole on the patches of skin we showed. And I feel Gaston Stegall toiling gently as a hot boy could. Three separate times he told me to tell him when anything hurt. I never said a word—pain is not the same as hurt—and both of us felt so relieved when it ended (so proud and surprised), we dozed off for some few minutes right in place. I've since heard that girls mostly lie there awake and think back through it. I was too tired for that; I'd been thinking all week. Just before I slept I wondered if I'd dream of my parents someway and be punished at once. But no, I didn't. Pure cool healing rest.

Gaston woke up first and said my name. Or *Kay*—from then on he called me Kay. He said we still had time for the sawmill.

Neither one of us owned any sort of clock, and the sky was mostly hid by greenery. But I guessed it had to be past three o'clock, and I thought I owed it to God or somebody to stop off and touch Roz at least once by dark. I said "We could maybe do that next time."

He said "Next time?" with a face straight as rails.

I thought he was mad so I said "—In case you ever want to."

He kept on staring like I'd turned into some wild surprise on his hands and might turn again. Then he launched the best smile I've seen to this day. It spun through the short space between us like a top made of some precious metal but light as air. And he said "You just got to name your day."

Nobody back then had any big plans. Children didn't take dancing lessons after school or join sports clubs to pretend they were grown. If their parents didn't farm, they had scads of time. But I said "I'll have to go home and decide." That seemed more polite than saying "Seven days from now."

Gaston said "If it's longer than a week, I'll die."

I told him not to worry, I'd try to help him last.

The only strange thing was, the horse had left us. When we'd straightened ourselves and walked to the creek, Trudge had disappeared. I thought she was lost and we'd have to hunt her up, or that now she was under that sand with the pony, but Gaston just said "She gets bored a lot. She'll be home by night." It may have been the first time I heard the word *bored*. In general, people didn't get bored in those days.

Then I told him goodbye. We hadn't touched again. When he went his way, on past my mother's grave, I saw him for an instant as a soldier in the war—half the earth against him, aimed at his back. It made me want him more.

The war of course obliged us. Through June the Germans were swarming on France, and Holt and I waited every night for news they'd crashed on to Britain and ruined her too. That came in late summer when the bombs hit London. The shortwave broadcasts reached Macon like they had swum the whole ocean—wavy and sometimes drowned in the spray—but once I'd heard the cheerful high voice of

Princess Elizabeth greeting other children and saying "Be brave," I was genuinely scared. She was just one year older than me, her palace had been hit, that meant we were all in actual danger. To me anyhow. Nobody in Macon or on the radio ever denied what I was scared to ask—couldn't German bombers find us as easily as England and shatter our homes, not to mention our skulls? Everybody I'd ever known in my life had British ancestors, including half the blacks. Others—like the Jews who sold clothes in Warrenton, the Greeks who ran a cafe—seemed like polite visitors in that little world. So even the men at Russell's store, who never mentioned anything but cotton and tobacco, were always mentioning Liverpool or Coventry like towns down the road and were acting extra brave. I kept my tears in and stepped up the prayers.

Gaston Stegall was glad. The summer of '40, he was sixteen (he'd lost a year of school with a case of pneumonia). We could seldom meet without him saying the war had to last till he could enlist. I didn't let on I thought he was crazy, that he ought to start running this minute to the moon and take me with him. But I did try saying we were not *in* the war—it was all overseas. He grinned and said "Wait. Just wait. They got boats." We met two or three times a month that summer.

He was working in tobacco with Fob and his father. When he had time to spare, he'd leave me notes in a blue Mason jar in a hole he'd scooped in the railroad bank. I'd go whenever I could leave without signaling Caroline or Noony. Always to the same moss we'd found the first day.

Since Noony and Caroline divided the housework, nobody expected anything from me but courtesy and smiles. They thought I was a child and left me to play. There was not another white girl my age in Macon. The schoolgirls I liked lived deeper in the country and worked with their families hard in the summer, so I'd wake up every morning with nothing but a hot empty day before me. I'd read every book in the house ten times, and the bookmobile just came once a week (what I liked by then were historical novels where men moved mountains with bare bloody hands to win some girl that waited, fully dressed).

So naturally I thought about love, dawn to dark. Or Gaston—I doubt I called it *love*. To me it was nothing but the way he looked and the gaps he'd leave for me to fill in with hopes and guesses. I didn't go wild, inside or out. Nobody else seemed to notice I knew him. But you could have counted on a new baby's hand the minutes of the day I didn't think about him and wish he was there. That may be as much of love as I ever understood—to this day, I mean—but it brought me to life, fast, in ways I never planned.

It made me the kind of spy I've been since then. Nothing sinister or mean, just a set of eyes that hunted out secrets in the world and saved them up. I had never for instance cared much about nature; and once Frances made that last Penny Show, I hadn't meant to touch another flower again. But after knowing Gaston, I saw leaves and creatures a whole new way—they were signs about him. And mostly they were good. I'd check a rosebud in Caroline's garden and tell myself if it opened by breakfast, I'd have a note from Gaston. I don't remember any bird or flower misleading me.

Gaston didn't either. Of all the souls I've known in my life, he and my aunt Caroline were the two that never lied—not even to spare me. He never mentioned love or plans for a life or any kind of future beyond the great day when he could enlist. He liked me, then and there, and could take all I gave. We were too young to know any special tricks to do, and back then every newsstand didn't offer you instructional pictures. In fact there was no newsstand for sixty miles (Raleigh must have had one). We stuck to the basic original idea, which was easing Gaston's body. It was like a new, slightly dangerous pet that I had to keep calm. And I seemed to know how. That was my main reward, mostly in my head. I thought it was sufficient. Looking back, I still do. We were nice gentle children.

By fall, when they started the national draft and began taking boys twenty-one and over, Gaston had his driver's license and could borrow his father's pickup most Friday nights. I'd dreaded the change. I thought it meant he would want public dates. I knew I was young for that and figured Holt and Caroline would throw big fits. But months went by and we kept to the moss and traveled on foot. I still hadn't seen the inside of that truck. I was beginning to wonder who had.

By then girls in my class had started talking about boys, a hot whispery rumor-service about who had seen who with who doing what. I knew it was pathetic, but I had to keep listening for fear Gaston's name would turn up tied to some girl his age. It never did. They'd say he was cute but stuckup. Stuckup was about the grandest thing you could be in Macon. That didn't do a lot to ease my fears. I just realized more every day how big a secret he and I had kept, and I had to wonder what others he was nursing.

But around Thanksgiving, when it got too cold to lie outdoors, Gaston stopped me in the hall as I walked into school one Monday morning and said "Let's go to the show Friday night." The *show* meant the movies in Warrenton; we couldn't walk to there.

I was one scared rabbit but happy as a bird. I looked all round us to see who had heard—nobody close enough. So I said "Oh Lord, I'll have to ask my aunt."

Gaston said "She's not your mother, remember."

I knew it was the first time he'd mentioned Frances. That was one more shock, and I almost got mad. Then it dawned on me he had cut me loose. I was free in the world. He hadn't said who would feed and clothe a free child, but that didn't cross my mind. Still I said I'd tell him after I went home to lunch.

He said "I think you ought to tell me now."

I said "All right" and was suddenly calm as gravel in the road. He walked me to my class door and said he'd see me Friday—like five long days didn't stretch out between us.

Late that afternoon I got alone with Noony and asked her opinion of me telling Caroline.

Noony said "Got to tell her. Can't just step out of here in the dark with her not knowing. She been struck time and time again. Next time might kill her."

I said "I'm near-grown and she's not my mother."

Noony raised her hand to hit me, then took a step back. "You *grown*," she said. "You could have six babies nine months from today. And yes, your mama's stretched flat in cold dirt. But who going to stuff your hungry mouth but Miss Caroline? And who slipping her the money to keep you but poor Mr. Holt?"

I said "I've got three hundred dollars left from selling Dan's car."

Noony said "Then *go*. See how far you get. But don't come howling back here next month. We all be busy having Santy Claus."

"So will Walter," I said. "He wants me anytime."

Noony said "Walter Porter don't want no girl, whatever he say."

I went off to pout, but at bedtime I called Caroline to my room. I said "Gaston Stegall wants me to ride in to town with him Friday and go to the show." She and Holt hadn't seen ten movies between them.

She waited. Then she started smoothing my bed like the king of England was due for the night. Then she sat at the foot and met my eyes. She said "How many more children will he take?"

I thought "She doesn't understand this a bit." But I said "Just me."

Then she smiled, the main surprise of the day, and said "You guess you'll be old enough by Friday?"

I said "I'm *moving*."

And she said "I can see." But she didn't say no or recall my mother or give any warning. To the last day I saw her, some years after that, she still hadn't mentioned my body or its dangers by so much as a word. It might have been smoke.

So I thought it was safe as a good new boat and was mine to sail.

It plowed on more or less fine through the full next year and a half. The Second War was fun, never doubt it, if you didn't get shot at. Many soldiers loved it too, especially Macon boys. It was far more to-do than they'd ever seen before—rushing round on trains so stuffed they'd have to hoist excess girls onto luggage racks to sleep, and getting paid to fire guns they'd fired in their cradles, and endless food, and the hope of seeing maybe one town in the world that offered more than pinewoods and Sunday school. After Pearl Harbor and so many drowned sailors, things sobered up some. But nobody born after 1940 will ever know the meaning of excitement in America. Korea and Vietnam and all the smaller mudfights were gruesome and hateful; the Second War though was like a long houseparty by a big stretch of water—every guest helped out, people took turns sleeping in limited cots; and the only hitch was, every few days a boy would drift off at night and be washed up dead.

Nobody died from Macon for the whole first year, and that hot crossroads finally felt like it mattered; it was *helping* things. Boys were out scouring sheds for scrap iron, making balls of tinfoil from cigarette packs, and collecting newspapers. Women were saving their bacon grease for bullets and knitting drab scarfs (the Army wore the ugliest color on earth; another reason most of my friends joined the Navy). Men were spelling each other in a little raw shack behind the post office, spotting planes that flew over, trying to name them from a silhouette chart, and then phoning Norfolk to say what they'd seen.

I'd help Fob with that when his stint came; he couldn't tell a bomber from a trainer without me (Tot had been drafted and Fob was lost). Otherwise my daily life didn't change. Swift and Walter were exempt from service—one for weak eyes, one for asthma. All the other men I knew were way too old, except of course Gaston.

After the first rash of swearing to join-up the first day he could, he barely ever said *war* again. His big brother Whitley was on a destroyer in the Mediterranean, running interference. He sent Gaston word to be sure to join the Navy since "In the Army they shoot at you; in the Navy they shoot at the boats." Gaston told me that much, then shut up on the subject. So I stayed quiet too, when we were together. I knew his family were wrapped up in war news. I figured he wanted one place in his life that stayed the same and caused him no fears. I volunteered to be that, though I never said as much; and he never mentioned it.

But he acted grateful. He'd always been gentle; and while he could farm and mend any engine ever made and pitch lovely baseball, he'd always admit in private he was helpless. Any time we were off alone, he'd spend the first half-hour, firm as a general plotting our march. Then when we'd settled in at his destination, there'd come a quiet minute; and the wind would turn. We could be in the woods or the hot theater or the freezing car, but he'd turn and face me. He wouldn't speak or usually even smile. I'd hear him plainly though, and I never heard wrong; he never complained. *He needed everything I had.* I was too young to ask him why on earth, or how he would mean to use it for years—my slim supply of human traits. What I'd mainly hear was my name in his plea. He wanted *me*, no other girl in sight. There were twenty more girls near Macon as ready and pretty as Kate but Gaston needed Kate. Kate was glad to serve, in the time she could spare from school and home duties without being caught.

Nobody caught us, far as we knew. A few other girls might see us at the show and ask me teasing questions; I'd lie through my teeth. Caroline would say "Ten o'clock" everytime we left on a date, and we both obeyed her to the letter of the law—the only law she gave.

Noony understood surely but she never fished for secrets and never embarrassed me in Caroline's presence. After maybe a month of the Saturday dates, Noony asked me one day as we took down sheets stiff with ice from the line "—That Stegall child taking wise precautions?"

I didn't have the slightest idea what she meant, but I laughed and said "Wise way beyond his years."

She said "It ain't his *years* I'm worried about." But she left it at that.

I figured she was making some reference to babies (remember, every magazine back in those days didn't show monthly pictures of sperms and eggs, not to mention whole bodies laid out like cans of tuna). I'd assumed that Gaston was seeing to that, but next time I said "Noony asked me were you careful." He thought and said "Careful as a hummingbird in daylight."

I knew even less about what *that* meant. I laughed though and didn't stop to worry again. Gaston was no more taking precautions than a year-old dog, but I didn't know that and trouble never struck. It was years before I wondered if maybe he might have been sterile. If so it was more or less all he lacked. He was long dead by then.

Nearly three years passed and seemed like a month. The world outside us was racketing loud but more or less cheerfully, from where we stood. In the midst of my mind, like a hard abcess, I knew the war would not end soon. In the early days there was no guarantee our side would win; and sure God, no guarantee that Gaston wouldn't yet have to help. My prayers were that he'd be passed over somehow. Some secret flaw the eye couldn't see would leave him unfit for service but safe for Kate. That was *all* I prayed. I'm glad to say I never felt an instant of shame or once asked God to pardon all we did. We were happy, I thought, and knew how to stay happy. I didn't even notice if I changed inside. I felt like I'd always felt—the same person but honored at last in the ways I'd dreamed.

So we got to the spring of 1943 in what I thought was good shape. I was finishing the tenth grade; Gaston was graduating. He'd turned eighteen back in the winter and had had to register for the draft, but we still never talked about it. Sometimes alone I'd tell myself to brace for the day he'd be called up (they let you finish school). I'd walk around feeling pitiful and brave for an hour or so, but the fear wasn't real. Maybe in the four years since Dan and Frances died, I'd pulled a thick curtain on even the *idea* that people could swear they needed you one night, then vanish by morning. I'd started believing people meant all they said. And even with my history, I still mostly do— which is why I'm a fool the size of Montana but can smile now and then.

The last Sunday in May was Commencement. I'd of course hoped to go, but Gaston hadn't mentioned it, and I got scared by late in the week. I'd spent six dollars on a gold keychain; and now it looked like I might not get to give it, in private anyhow. The previous Saturday night he'd acted normal; and all through our friendship, there had come blank stretches when he'd pull back and just be a smiler in the hall for two or three weeks. I'd lose a pound or two. But his graduation was bound to be special—I was fairly amazed he'd made it to the end.

So Thursday afternoon when I left school, he and Selby Kenyon were standing by a tree that I had to pass or take a wide detour. I tried for the straight route, but then dread swamped me—a sickening trap that clamps onto children and says "You're *here* and can't ever leave."

I swung out to detour, watching the ground. Before I'd gone fifty yards, Gaston blocked me—solemn in the path. I tried to dodge round him; he grabbed my arm. I dropped my books, wrenched loose, and struck him hard on the mouth. I can still feel his teeth on the tips of my fingers. At once there was blood, but he held his ground. I was frozen in place, praying not to cry. Gaston was the only boy I've known who always had a clean handkerchief on him.

He unfolded it carefully as a nun's bridal veil and touched his lip. Then he folded it over and handed it to me.

I said "I'm all right" and tried to refuse it.

He smiled. "—Know you are. Just thought you'd want this souvenir of the first blood you drew."

I wish I'd strangled before speaking next. But I said "I drew blood long before you."

He was good enough to wait. Then he said "Well, it's over. I got the car Sunday. Can we have a picnic?"

I said "With who else?" I'd never known a picnic for just two people.

Gaston laughed. "You're chairman of the entertainment. Invite who you want."

I said "What are you?—in the plans, I mean."

"The watcher," he said. "I'll watch you till dark."

I couldn't make myself ask what would happen then; but I kept the handkerchief and must have it still, somewhere in my things.

You can bet I didn't invite anybody. But Noony helped me fix it, food enough for ten orphans. Gaston drove up after church; and for the first time in all those months, Holt walked with us out through the yard to the car. Since he'd let Caroline run my social life, it never crossed my mind he'd chime in now. Nobody thought he'd had a drink since Dan and Frances died. But when Gaston had already started the engine, Holt leaned into my door and spoke right across me—"We're counting on you, Son." Right then I wanted to ask him "For *what*?" He could have meant anything from gang-rape to marriage. I froze up again though, and Gaston said "Yes sir. Lean on me." I stared straight at Gaston till he backed out and left. We were halfway to Warrenton before I could ask what I had to know—"Have you passed a single word with my Uncle Holt that I haven't heard?"

Gaston said "No ma'm."

I said "Don't lie."

And for the first time, Gaston looked at me harshly. "Remember this and prize it years from now—Gaston Stegall is one boy that can't lie to you."

Considering what happened, not in years but months, I'm glad to say I thanked him.

He bowed toward the road and said "You ever seen Annie Lee's grave?"

"No," I said. "Who's she?"

It turned out Annie was General Lee's favorite daughter. Halfway through the War Between the States, she and her mother had to leave Virginia when the guns got close. They came to a mineral-spring resort in the country near us, and there poor Annie caught typhoid and died. General Lee understandably had his hands full and missed the funeral but came down years later, right before his own death, to visit the grave.

It was one of the farthest trips we'd taken—maybe thirty miles roundtrip, a lot of rationed gas—and the whole way there, Gaston talked solid history. He knew more about the Lees than they'd known themselves. It shocked me and, after a while, began to scare me. To think I'd known Gaston nearly three years and trusted him with what little I had to give, and still he'd kept this big hunger secret—he loved the dead past. Back then I wouldn't give a nickel for yesterday. But I didn't try to hush him; he had a low voice.

When we got there it was drowned in briars and weeds. Nothing to see but the fenced-off graves of the family who'd owned the place and offered Annie room. The gate was broken. We trudged through the wilderness that far in silence. Then as Gaston moved to enter the gate, I pulled back on him and said "There's got to be snakes in there. You've already seen it."

He didn't turn to me but said "No, Kay. I know it from books." He went on forward to the ten-foot monument they'd piled on Annie.

I was flat scared then, though the day was fine. Who on earth had I loved, and where was he bound? I stayed at the gate.

When he got to her grave, he circled it once. Then he stopped at Annie Lee's feet and faced the ground. His back was to me. In his natural voice, that always seemed like it carried to Georgia, he said

> *"Perfect and true are all His ways*
> *Whom heaven adores and earth obeys."*

By the end he was halfway singing the words. The local birds stopped.

I hadn't thought Gaston knew the difference between a poem and a hoe. So I laughed and clapped twice.

He turned on me once more, eyes bright as tin. But he waited to speak till he'd got his control. "That's the song she asked them to sing while she died. Her mother and sisters stood round her and sang it too. They were that strong."

We might as well have gone fifteen thousand miles and been deep in Burma. I was just that lost. So I waited a minute and asked was he hungry. Those deviled eggs were spoiling in the car.

Gaston said "Not till after we've gone in the house."

So we got in the car and drove to the house—the old hotel. It was about a mile back toward the paved road and was pitiful. The porch had been ripped off completely, and what hadn't been carted away was strewn to the edge of the woods and beyond. There were great stretches where planks were gone from the sides, and the uprights showed like bones in a hand. I said "I doubt the floor would even bear us, if it's still got a floor."

But Gaston took my fingers, and we picked a dangerous path through junk toward the wide front door. The steps of course were gone, and the open door hung five feet in the air. Gaston cupped his hands and bent; I was meant to step in and be hoisted up. But I said "Is there anything in there you need?"

He said "Oh yes" but not to me.

So I said "I never lost a thing out here. I'll wait in the car."

He stood back up, opened his empty hands, and held them up at me. I was dreading what he'd say, but he suddenly turned and scrambled up the dista..ce through that old door and vanished completely.

For a minute or two, I could hear his hollow footsteps; but then it was quiet except for birds, and I went to the car. Despite the strangeness I was hungry as a bear. So I sneaked half a sandwich and a warm stalk of celery, both dry as chalk. That kept me from worrying for three or four minutes. But then, as quick as Gaston had left, I asked myself "Why on earth am I here?" It's a question that's struck me more than once in my life, and generally I've answered it in some hot way that made me stand up and bolt for the firedoor. But this was the first time, so it came unexpected and strong as voltage.

With what love had done to my family and me—just in my short life—what was I doing, a certified woman with a monthly chance, hanging at the end of this one boy's string? I craved the fact that he'd turned to me—the first human ever—and asked for big gifts. And I liked the tricks his body could do, though they never seemed *him*, no big part of him. Never seemed worth fighting or killing for, which he said they were once when another boy named Tom Ball asked me if I was ever free on a weekend night. "I need to be gone" was the next thing I thought, which I guess meant *free*. And then the next true thing dawned on me hard—"A child *can't* go." I remember clearly thinking *child*, not *girl*. (One small thing I'm proud of—not one time, in all I've done, have I ever asked mercy for being a girl. I've meant to be strong. Strength just comes in one brand—you stand up at sunrise and meet what they send you and keep your hair combed.) By the time I'd worked my way through that, I was halfway to being Amelia Earhart, tasting the cold wind through my white scarf. But a noise brought me back.

Gaston had found a long wide board and was laying it down from the house to the ground as a steep gangway—for *him*; he needn't think I meant to climb it. He stood at the top awhile, looking straight at me. And I met his look but didn't budge. So he came on down the plank with arms out and leaned in the window on the driver's side. He said "I found the room she died in."

I said "Did you get a lock of her hair? How did you know? They put up a sign?"

He said "I could tell. It's little but high." He was calm as a sensible older man.

I was mad by then. I said "With all the dead people I know, I think you might have picked some place but this."

Gaston got in and sat and faced the windshield. Then he said "You name it."

I said "Where's your baby?"

He said "Name a place you'd rather be."

I said "Just something with no graves in it."

"That would be the planet Venus," he said. He laughed and cranked the engine and drove on deeper down the narrow dirt road—not a house in sight—till we came to a big field of brush with pines behind it. He stopped in the road and looked it over slowly. "This live enough for you?"

I said "It's O.K."

He said "Course I can't give a signed guarantee that it's not some Indian burial-ground. Or a squirrel cemetery."

"It'll be *my* cemetery soon," I said, "if I don't eat dinner." I've always relished three meals a day and distrust anybody lowrating food.

Halfway through eating, it dawned on me that this was the first time we'd ever had a whole meal together by ourselves. Back then people didn't eat out like now—it insulted your mother or wife's reputation as a satisfying cook. The realization didn't make me want to weep or break into rhyme; but it did seem soothing, after our bad start. Gaston seemed calm too so I thought I'd mention it. We were at the absolute edge of the pines, on the field's far side, on bone-dry ground. I extended my arms, still white from winter; and the sun lapped them up. I said "What *first thing* are we doing now?" I've never believed people think like me.

But, right off, Gaston said "Eating dinner with no spectators. It was my idea."

I was happy as quick as I'd been sad and mad before. Up to that instant, I honestly believe, I hadn't ever thought of a whole life with

Gaston. Or anybody else but me-myself-and-I. Girls in my grade were already talking marriage; in another two or three years most of them would be. What else was there but college, that almost nobody went to, or living with your parents and drying up faster than a pressed corsage? But I'd listened to them from a long deep distance—rings, houses, babies. Not that I thought of living at home or alone in a room like a paid schoolteacher. I just didn't open any doors on the future. But here this Sunday, with my arms warm, I thought I'd settle next to Gaston Stegall for the next sixty years (give or take a few minutes). I sat still and tried to think of some polite way to say as much. The sun moved up and took the rest of me, then started on Gaston.

He said "I joined the Marines last week."

I knew he had driven his daddy to Raleigh to get new glasses but— join the Marines? Had he had time for that? Was it easy as that? I was too stunned to make any intelligent answer. I cut him a wide slice of lemon-chess pie and handed it over.

He set it on the ground and shook his head, over and over slowly.

I said "It's good. Noony made all the pie."

Gaston still watched the ground. He said "I'll eat it. I was begging your pardon."

I said "It's O.K. I've seen a lot of graves."

"I meant the Marines," he said. "I'm sorry."

I said "No you're not."

He had to face me then, to check if I was crazy. I must have looked tame. Anyhow he said "Kate, I'll come back soon and be better for it. This is bound not to last."

I've never earned any kind of prophecy prize, so I don't know why I said what came next. Maybe the fact that, just that month, we and the British had mopped up North Africa; everybody knew Europe had to come next, bloody inch by inch. Or maybe it was just the blank cold meanness that seizes my mouth when I least want it to. I told it toward his eyes anyhow, gray eyes so light they looked big as plates—"You won't be back. They'll fight this thing for the rest of my life." Both sentences were right.

But I'm glad to say he laughed, then ate the pie.

I chewed along with him and recovered from the shock enough to know I'd heard, for the second time now, news that left me no way to think. Past and future were absolutely shut. And I wasn't too clear about this present day—would I get through it whole? Who would I be by dark? Would I ever know Gaston after this moment here?

We'd never had a word for making love. We knew the rough words of course but didn't use them, and we'd never got round to the private language that can work so well. I sat there dumb then, wanting nothing else but Gaston Stegall naked against me.

He finally said "We're through eating, aren't we?"

I could nod yes to that.

Quick and quiet, he cleaned up the mess and repacked the basket. Then he stood behind me, touched the crown of my head, and said "You too full to hunt down some moss?"

I said "I'm empty as a chimney flue."

Gaston said "Not for long."

In another two hours he'd taken me home. That night I went with Caroline and Holt to Commencement Exercises and saw him get his rolled-up diploma and a medal for penmanship (he wrote a fine hand; I can see it in my mind, though I burned his notes). At the end the principal asked all the boys who were headed to war to stand and be seen; it was almost everybody. Gaston's parents were there, and I'd said my goodbye back in those woods. So after the recessional when Holt tried to find him for congratulations, I told Caroline I'd walk home alone. I'd already told her Gaston had joined. She may have understood some little part of it, and she let me leave. Nobody tried to stop me; Macon in the pitchdark spring was safe as Heaven. It was just a mile walk.

A good while before, we'd given up leaving notes in a jar in the railroad bank. But the jar was still there. And toward the end of that next week—Gaston had to leave Sunday—I climbed down and left him a message that said good luck and I hoped he learned a trade. I waited till Sunday evening to check. My note was gone and nothing was waiting in its place but a beetle that reared up to fight me. So I never knew if anybody read the note, much less Gaston Stegall. He'd gone to Parris Island for Marine bootcamp and had already told me they wouldn't let him write any letters or cards for the first month at least—too busy tramping all night through snaky hot sand.

Don't let any human being ever tell you that a female child, just turned sixteen, can't hurt as hard and deep at a crossroads in eastern Carolina as a one-eyed leper in the dust of Judah. She can; I did. I'll leave it at that, I'm sure you're glad to hear.

With school being out, I tried to keep busy. At first I thought that the natural thing to do was head back to Fob's and ride Roz hell-for-leather to ease me. It was going on four years since Fob gave her to me, and lately I'd left her alone weeks on end. Mostly because of Gaston but partly too because of the bad luck that waits for all children's pets. As long as Roz was the main thing alive I could cherish and talk to—and that talked back plainly in her own way—I could organize whole days around her eyes and mane. But now I'd found a tame creature from my own breed, that God knows wanted big slabs of my heart and would sometimes talk the exact perfect words my bones longed to hear.

So Roz had become just a gentle old horse. She seemed glad to see me, though she didn't prance for joy. And the exercise probably did her good—she'd put on pounds with my neglect and Tot in the Army. But after a week I knew I was getting nothing better than sore legs and more empty silence than I wanted or could use. Even nature'd gone dead. The trees and rocks that had watched me before and heard my problems were strange now as celluloid furniture from Mars.

I'd sit with Fob in his low hot kitchen and let him run through his family tales. He had miles of them. They all were good and he'd tell them like a company of actors, all the voices—his mother with a rifle when the Yankees passed through, his own trip north (Philadelphia) as a boy and the women on the train taking leaks in the aisle, his baby sister's death from some high fever that shook her like a panther and had her singing love songs all the last night. Once I'd heard Fob's whole stock—and then he started over—to keep up my interest, I'd listen for the reason he'd wound up here like this (old and lonesome, though rich as the king of a profitable country). If he knew any clues and hid them in his memories, I never could find them. And one day— half-earnest, half to flush him out—I said "Fob, you've had a grand life. I want one like it."

He waited till he'd shelled another three pods of peas. Then he faced me, serious, and said "I have. I'm glad you notice. But Kate, you're a girl. Your chances are slimmer than a newt's in the fire."

I smiled but asked if he had any help to offer the newt.

Fob said "Not a drop. You're doing all you can."

I said "You know about Gaston and me?"

He said "Very little. Better not tell me more."

I said "What if I'm choking to tell?"

He said "Swallow hard. You're way too thin."

I still spotted airplanes with him after that, and we laughed a lot. But now he was one more broad locked door, and most days I would just brush Roz down and head back to Caroline's without even trying to speak again.

I was waiting for mail, you can well understand. Though Gaston had said they wouldn't let him write, I thought he'd find some way to slip me word. Even that many guns wouldn't make him so happy he'd forget how kindly we'd tended each other. So every morning I'd rise to meet Noony as she came with the first letters off the dawn train. After several days of nothing for me, Noony finally said "You sleep on, Katie. You're streaking your looks. I'll bring you any secret letter you get and not tell a soul."

The only mail that came though was on my birthday—a card with five dollars from Dan's folks in Henderson and fifteen dollars from Walter in Norfolk. He hadn't been to visit since the Thanksgiving trip more than three years ago, but he'd written to Caroline every month or so. How he knew my birthday, I couldn't imagine. Caroline flatly denied ever telling him. Maybe he owned some baby announcement that Frances had sent sixteen years before; that would have been like him. Anyhow he said sixteen was *grown*, that his own grandmother was married by then, and for me not to let any Macon honeysuckle entwine my feet and trap me down. I showed it to Noony.

She read it slowly, then spat on the ground, and said "I told you Walter Porter was trouble long years ago."

I said "No you didn't. You said you'd heard some mess."

Noony nodded. "Don't *mess* always turn to *trouble?*" She tore Walter's letter in two, gave me the pieces, and walked toward the kitchen.

I was too shocked to yell. And all that day—mad as I was—I knew if I griped, Caroline would catch on and ask a thousand questions. So I had another secret, and the hot pressure hurt.

Then four weeks after I last touched Gaston, a letter finally came. It was just half a page on wartime paper so thin you could take spy photographs through it from miles above ground. But it said every word I'd prayed to hear; and through all my adventures, I've kept it in reach.

Dear Kay,

They've given us five minutes off, first time this month, and I need to say I'm sorry. I thought this new life was going to be better. I had got scared at home, of where we were headed. I felt too young. But this place is nothing but screaming and meanness from two-legged dogs too rotten to drown. I've been sick since the second day—inside, don't worry, nobody knows.

I'm mainly sick for you. You've been better to me than anybody else in my whole life or than I ever had any call to expect or will ever meet again. I want to say thank you, I remember all the times from the river till the afternoon in Annie Lee's woods. In two weeks when this childish bootcamp is through, I'll come home and see you for three long days. You may not know me, I'm so thin and bareheaded, but I hope you care enough still to be ready—whoever I am. I am ready, I'll swear.

> *Yours truly,*
> *Gaston Stegall*

I was so ready—not knowing what for—that, after I'd ridden Roz maybe ten miles in blistering heat, I caught Noony out in the garden picking beans and showed her the letter. All I said was "You tear this one up and I'll skin you alive."

But Noony said "Burn that thing right now." She pointed to the kitchen. "The cookstove's lit."

I said "You don't believe what he says?"

Noony took up the heavy pan of string beans and handed them to me like I'd asked to own them. Then she said "I believe every word. He out to *steal* you."

"Let him," I said. "I'm ready as the Citizens Bank after dark."

Noony said "It'd kill Miss Caroline dead."

I said "What is to be, will be."

And she slapped me. When the little noise had bumped off the trees beyond us, she stepped back and rubbed her hand hard on her leg.

We didn't have the Ku Klux or anything that mean in Macon back then, but I stood there knowing I could cause a small stink—maybe get Noony fired—if I mentioned she hit me. But I'd have to say why, and I wouldn't do that. I thought "Dumb nigger" but kept it in my head. She never heard me say it, I'm glad to report; nobody else has in any year since. Black people as a rule have been better to me than any other brand. So we sat on the back steps and strung every bean in silence like the grave.

The whole next week I was happier than I had been since Dan and Frances died. The only hitch was, there was no one to tell. And then, tell *what*? What had Gaston really said except *Please be ready*? I was ready for anything from eating walls of fire to midnight elopement. Being what I was and where, I leaned toward elopement. If you weren't young during World War II, you may not ever know how romance can taste. It came at us stronger than any white drug, and it seemed free (or cheap) and endless as water. Nobody but your parents and guardians or some wild Baptist ever so much as frowned at people plunging through twelve states on trains packed to bursting just for love in a coldwater tourist-court through one weekend maybe followed by death.

My sensible side had realized a wedding was out of the question. Unless I meant to spit on Caroline and Holt and slam out forever, I'd need permission which they'd never give. And Gaston was no doubt soon bound for hand-to-hand meetings with Japs. Where would that leave me? Well, scared as a rabbit and half-blind with dread of the danger before him but also drunk on his words and the certainty of seeing him soon and feeling the warm back of his broad neck (he had a better neck than any perfect statue).

You'd have thought a child with my background would know not to lean on human words. But I did, like a ton of mountain granite, for eight more days. To outside eyes I acted like a model industrious daughter. I dreamed up whole new ways to help—in the garden, in the kitchen, walking timber with Holt.

Holt mentioned it first. Midway through the first week, he said one night after Charlie McCarthy "Kate, I was wrong to ever want sons."

I thought I understood and said "Thank you."

Caroline said "You've still got two sons; they'll be taken from you if you talk like that."

Holt said "*You* like her. You've told me you do." It was the first time since Frances's funeral that I thought he was drinking.

But Caroline stayed as calm as a book. She said "I'd walk through coals of fire for her—I have already—but I love my sons too."

Excited as I was, secretly inside, I heard something click in my heart. *Don't forget this.* I knew, for whatever curious reason, that two more people were honoring me. I knew I should save the words, as they said them, for rainy days to come. I think my eyes watered. Holt was back at the radio, listening in.

But Caroline faced me and smiled at last and said "Haven't I told you how much you mean?"

I nodded and smiled but knew she hadn't, not directly. And by lying I'd stopped her. Now she maybe never would. In a minute they were back at the radio again.

Gaston hadn't named a day for coming here, and I wasn't about to ask his mother (she'd given no sign of cherishing me!). So within ten days of getting his letter, I was spending the nights lying wide awake and the days mostly taking long walks up the road or riding Roz. I was trying to make myself easy to find. I'd figured he was bound to come on Saturday or Sunday and most likely by bus. Buses had recently discovered Macon, and the station was "Rattling" Charlie Harris's garage across from the depot. I couldn't wait there—too many men, white and black, hanging round the little side yard, paved with bottle caps.

Saturday morning I'd promised Fob to spot planes with him. But I broke my word. I got up and bathed, intending to meet him. At breakfast though, when Noony and I were alone, she whispered "That dream of yours, coming true today." She hadn't breathed a word on the subject since the letter.

I said "How do you know?" Blacks knew everything back then, days before us.

But Noony just said "Letter said two weeks. Two weeks is up."

So I realized I wanted to be alone. The last thing I wanted, or guessed I could handle, was for Gaston to surprise me in other people's presence. I knew Fob had left his house by then and was watching the sky, so I put on my britches and went down to Roz and saddled her up.

I rode her a wide slow circle through woods and fields out from town, every place where Gaston and I'd ever met locally. The hot spell had broken, and we were just having a fine cloudless day with moving dry air—what Holt used to call a "June sweetener," though it was July (what could that have meant?—a day to sweeten fruits on the tree and wild bush-berries?). In the past I'd sometimes seen scuttling creatures that later I couldn't find named in any book (one was big as a bear but was striped white and gray). And once I'd stumbled on a lonesome boy with his pants half-down, consoling himself.

But this day the whole place might have been a desert, and no Arabs. All I remember was thinking I hoped we'd live in a city, if *we* ever lived. Greensboro had still not faded from mind, and what I missed from my days there was strangers. In a place like Macon you know everybody and his shirt-and-hat-size, so you know the chance of surprise is nil—except for the odd screaming breakdown or killing. If you plan to be healthy, you can't let yourself do a whole lot of dreaming since everybody's spoke-for till Judgment Day. But a city's *all* chances, coming at you round the clock. It's finally what kills you. I didn't know that then; I was green as Ireland. I thought we would thrive.

By twelve o'clock I'd worked back to Fob's and figured I'd leave Roz and go home for lunch. I thought Fob would still be downtown, spotting. But as Roz climbed the last little rise in the pasture and stopped where she always did for a snack, I saw Fob's black pickup by the oak. I thought "Oh croak! What lie can I tell?" I'd have to say I flat forgot to meet him. He wouldn't believe me but wouldn't say so. I couldn't see him; he'd be in the kitchen scaring up something like cold pork-and-beans and week-old biscuits. So I nudged Roz on toward the stable through the same light that had stroked us all morning.

The door of the pickup squeaked open suddenly. Fob fumbled out and took the sun.

I waved and rode on like a normal day.

But he didn't wave back or yell a single word. He stood by the door with his mail in his right hand, shading his eyes and watching me.

So I left Roz almost at the stable and walked toward Fob. It was fifty yards but seemed more like a million miles with each step. When I finally got to him, I said "I forgot."

He nodded. "Know you did." Then he dropped the hand that had covered his brow, and the eyes seemed five shades lighter than before—the color of sky that's trying to kill you with happiness.

I said "Did you spot any Messerschmitts?" They were a brand of German plane we always joked about reporting ("Let's call up and say we got a Messerschmitt over Macon, N. C. See how quick they faint.").

Fob smiled and said "Maybe one. I didn't call em. With you not there, I couldn't have laughed."

I said "I'm sorry."

Fob said "It's a whole lot more than that." He leafed back through his mail.

I thought he was saying he was mad at me. He had that right; back then I thought everybody did. But I said "I'll make it up to you soon."

He said "Katie, you don't understand this."

I said "Maybe not." But I thought I did. I was so used to adults blackmailing me with sulks and pouts.

We were still standing there in the yard like statues. Fob said "You tried to speak to me about Gaston." He pointed toward the Stegall place—"Gaston Stegall."

I thought that meant Fob had seen him just now, and my face went hotter than the sun had made it.

But he said "Gaston's been dead since Thursday afternoon."

At first I thought "Thursday—where was I this Thursday?" My mind just would not hear the main word.

Fob shut the truck door and said "Let's go in."

I said "I've still got to tend to Roz."

He said "That saddle won't hurt her for a while. She knows she's home."

I looked back and she was standing where I'd left her, ten feet from the stable in cool leafshade with her right rear hoof tipped up, barely touching the ground, like the lady she was. I thought "I've got *her*," and that helped for a second. But then I had to face Fob and say "Tell it here."

He took off his hat and sailed it gently to a small patch of grass beyond the truck. "This Thursday he had his last test to pass. Had to crawl on his belly under live machine-gun fire not six inches over his back. A hundred yards of that. Right near the finish Gaston just stood up. Nobody knows why. He had been doing fine. Four shots in his back. They didn't tell his family till ten this morning when the telegram came. It had got missent to Macon, Georgia and spent the night there. His daddy came to find me at the little shack downtown, and we called the base at Parris Island. They said yes and told us how. The body'll be here Sunday morning early."

"That's tomorrow," I said.

Fob said, "Yes, Jesus." Then I think he drove me home; but that's mostly dark to me, the one big thing I ever blanked out. I sometimes think I remember Fob saying "This won't kill *you*. You've been through worse." But I don't remember telling him how wrong he was. I'd have surely said that much for Gaston, even then.

* * *

The funeral was Thursday. That's as clear as today. I went with Caroline and Holt but sat with girls from my class, the few that lived near enough to town to get there. What was left of his baseball team were pallbearers, and the clearest picture of all is two Marines in starched dress-uniform that outshined the flowers. But would they have spared two whole strong boys to bring Gaston home, with the war like it was? Maybe I dreamed that. Anyhow he was buried in sight of my mother and in cool walking-distance of that mossy trench we'd started up in. If there really were Marines, wouldn't they have played Taps? But the sound I remember is a billion crickets conversing in the weeds. At the end we girls filed past his family and tried to smile. The family had never sent me any message through the long weekend, but I straightened my back and shook their hands now. His older brother was already overseas; so except for one old aunt, lean as a walking stick, there were just his parents. His mother looked down at the flag in her lap and barely nodded her head at me. But his father stood up and trapped my hand in both of his. He had these deep farmer-trenches in his face, and they all were full of tears. He said "You meant the world to him, Kay." At least he knew what name Gaston called me.

The girl behind me—a short Taylor girl that later made good in Latin grammar at Chapel Hill—said "She certainly did." It seemed like the loudest noise of the year but nobody heard her. Or showed they had.

By the end Holt had vanished and taken his car; he'd had more funerals than his nerves would take. So Caroline and I rode home with Swift. I'd have walked if they'd let me—if it wouldn't have shown I was wild as a bear in a chickenwire cage at a crossroads junkyard, smelling the woods.

The fact is, I was. I wouldn't know a true way to tell you how I grieved, and I doubt Shakespeare would. In the years since then, the whole world has noticed what it hadn't before—that children suffer worse pain than adults. But in 1943, with half the world in flames, a sixteen-year-old girl who'd lost a sweetheart couldn't expect much nursing care. Especially when barely three people alive even knew she'd been in love. I remember staring at the ceiling in my bedroom and wishing we were poor. Then I'd have to work. Children were still taught the virtues of work—it kept off the Devil, was the general claim—but in Macon, N. C. if you were a girl, and unless your people farmed, you had as much chance of useful work as a Luna moth. I went to the length of hauling out my bead loom and rigging it up, but Noony saw me and went into an imitation Indian-dance (like a lot of proud blacks, she claimed Indian blood). That finished that.

I kept on spotting planes with Fob and taking Roz out two or three times a week. But mainly I stayed in my room and slept—ten hours at night, long afternoon naps.

One evening when Noony had to wake me for supper, Caroline said "Kate, you think you need a doctor? Is it maybe sleeping sickness?"

But Holt said "Hush. It's growing pains." And they never mentioned my health again.

So I stayed on asleep as much as I could, and the dreams I'd feared just never came. Not once did Gaston, in any shape or form, ever pass through my rest. What did was my father, time after time. Not in any awful way, mad or bleeding, but alive and well. I'd walk in the store and ask for a comb or five pounds of flour, and then I'd hear somebody say "Dan." I'd turn and there Dan would be, playing checkers, with Marvin Thompson's hand on his shoulder to prove he was real. I'd think "Now wait. Did I get this wrong? Dan Vaiden is dead." But I'd ease over there and stand by the game; and after some brilliant move where he'd jump six other men and win hands-down, he'd look up and meet my eyes but not speak. It was always that—Dan rescued and active but maybe not recognizing me anymore.

Maybe that was the reason why, when I was awake, I started accepting the blame for it all. I had surely been what came between Dan and Frances and set them off. Now I'd driven Gaston to leave his home and rise up into a flood of live bullets, from his own country's guns, no nearer an enemy than South Carolina. Who would be the next ones I ruined? I thought through that a thousand times in those summer days, never breathing it to any soul likely to answer. Some minutes I was calm enough to think I was crazy—imagining that *I* mattered so much in the world. But then I'd remember something Frances used to say in her own blue moods, to cheer herself up, "If you *think* you're crazy, you're not. Crazy people don't know it."

The main question was, what was Gaston doing? Was he in his right mind? Did he mean to kill himself? How long did he plan it? Could anybody, knowing he planned to die, write the letter he wrote me? What had I ever done to earn such cruelty from somebody gentle as a fine down-quilt? At least I had company in asking most of that. You couldn't meet any two people in town without them finally wondering about Gaston. The main public answer seemed to be that he had snapped, just the instant he stood up—no advance warning. All the old men would say "That Marine camp is mean. They *try* to break you." I could hope that was it. But then that would mean the idea of me—seeing Kay soon and maybe for life—had not been strong enough to pull him through.

One afternoon when Fob and I were spotting and no planes had passed, Gaston's father stopped by and sat on a stool. He and Fob talked awhile. There'd been a short hailstorm; they'd lost some tobacco. Then Mr. Stegall picked up our airplane-silhouette book and studied that quietly. I saw he didn't really care, was just passing time; and I saw his face was somehow younger now and showed signs of Gaston (I guess he'd lost weight). So I suddenly said "Mr. Stegall, what happened?"

Fob laughed and said "To what?"

But Mr. Stegall knew. He kept on turning pages carefully—the way men used to do who never read books but honored them still. And he never met my eyes, but he finally said "The captain I talked to said they were mystified; he'd been a model boy. His mama tries to say Gaston's time had just come and how much better it was here than overseas or in some prison camp in a foreign tongue, hungry. I don't believe that. It's eating me up."

So I said "Me too"—the first time I said it.

Fob said "I'm older than all of you together. It'll happen again."

He wasn't that old but he wasn't wrong either. I knew he meant it as a promise to help us. Most people over forty say it every day, knowing full well it seldom changes anything. It somehow changed me.

By then we were down near the end of August—summer almost gone, though the heat got worse. That month was the first time heat ever bothered me, and that was another sign I was grown and faced my own life. (Children, if you notice, never think about heat. They'll run and swelter, happy as Eskimoes. Or sit in schoolrooms hot as steelmills and think they're lucky not to be at home.)

School was two weeks away, the eleventh grade for me. That Thursday night we were out on the dark porch, fanning our necks and looking for stars. Then Caroline said "Kate, it's time to buy clothes." Every August she'd take me to buy my school blouses and a skirt and some shoes.

I said "Oh Lord" (I've never loved clothes).

She said "This Saturday."

Holt said "Kate's old enough to pick her own duds." He didn't sound mad; it was just a sudden fact.

That was what set me off. I didn't see any big door yawn open. I didn't have a big plan. I thought "Holt's right. I'll get my own clothes." Till then I'd barely bought a pair of shoelaces without my mother or Caroline present. So I said "I'll ride in with Swift tomorow." Swift clerked in the only department store.

Caroline said "Take your savings book then." I knew she'd be hurt, but I'd never heard her threaten to cut me off.

Still I had a nest-egg, and I said "Yes ma'm."

For minutes after that you'd have needed a hacksaw to part the air. The only good thing was, we couldn't see each other.

Holt finally stood up and faced my chair. Then he almost whispered "I'll buy every stitch you want, all my life. Don't worry one instant." He went down the steps, on out through the yard, and seemed to turn left toward more dark and woods.

The thought of Holt taking a walk—any exercise—came as the first funny thing all month. Caroline and I both laughed the same moment.

But early next morning I called Swift's house and asked could I catch a ride in to town with him. He sounded enthused and said he'd come get me. I gritted my teeth but said I'd be ready. Since my parents died I'd shunned Swift Porter every chance I got, without acting mean. And even though he and his scared-squirrel wife lived in sight of our house, he seldom came by. Sometimes weeks would pass before Holt would say "Anybody seen Swift?" And Caroline would call him to stop by for breakfast. So I knew that morning I was hell-bent on something if I'd stooped to call Swift.

Swift was usually asleep till noon. He'd rise and drive to work but be sluggish till everybody else was fine. So on the way to town, I barely had to speak. Yes, I'd turned a new corner, shopping alone. Yes, I'd go to the show that afternoon. Then I'd meet him at five o'clock to head on home. Otherwise we were quiet. Back then nobody that far from a city ever had to warn you of any human danger. The place wasn't Heaven. There were killings and rapes but never by strangers, always family members. A sixteen-year-old girl like me—no stunner but nothing to ruin your lunch—could drift through the streets and never pass a thing more harmful than wishes.

Holt had given me four five-dollar bills; and I bought the clothes first, everything as dark as possible except a white blouse. That was partly in mourning and partly because I'd already seen how much finer everybody looks in deep blue. Then I bought some school shoes and had my feet X-rayed to prove they fit (everybody my age took hours of sizzling foot-rays, but we're mostly still upright). I left those boxes in Swift's department and figured I'd wander.

Warrenton then was a one-street town, far as sights were concerned. Down at one end were the grocery stores and clothiers—high dim old places where an ancient clerk would hand you every can from closed shelves behind him or a lady with a goiter could make you a hat to match your shape and color exactly. Then the bank and the courthouse square with the library. Then the one white cafe and theater, then the Hotel Warren with salesmen on the porch, and then just houses. On a Saturday morning the sidewalks would be chocked solid with black people in from the country. The county was seventy-percent black in those days, and a stranger driving through might well have thought he'd stumbled on Africa—dressed-up blacks all swapping the news. That was well before the local whites had heard blacks were miserable, and even now I'll have to say nothing ever gave a better imitation of relishing life than those shining faces.

But this was Friday and, though a few farmers were already lined up with trucks of tobacco ready to sell, I cut a clear path to the library door. In the years right after my parents died, that one bright room of worn shellacked books had been a real rescue-ship for me. Miss Mabel Davis, the spinster librarian, was deaf as a biscuit but had the knack of knowing what book you needed on any given day and leading you to it, with no grins or cooing. Right as she always was in her choice, her face and tight body also served notice that this long job of improving your mind and bracing your soul against oncoming life was no daisy hunt for rich white sissies but rough steady labor. (I recall her with even more gratitude now whenever I see a television culture-host, all oiled and alluring, promising easy profit from books. No wonder nobody reads more than drug labels or whore's revelations.)

That day when she saw me, Miss Mabel just said "I thought you'd quit" and turned back to mending torn pages with tape that her long tongue licked in slow frowning stripes.

In the years with Gaston, I'd slacked off here and at the bookmobile. You didn't abandon Miss Mabel but once. I was on my own now, to find my cure like a dog in the woods. So I went toward *Fiction*, the dangerous aisle. Miss Mabel was liable to veto you there. *Forever Amber* was still a few years down the road, but there were already plenty of novels you'd better not try to check out until you were married. She'd refused *Grapes of Wrath* to a girl in my grade the year before. I searched the historical novels first but had read most of those more than once already. In a few more minutes, I'd begun to believe I could never sit still long enough to read again. Just the sour-milk smell of old paper and glue made me think books were one more comfort ruined by Gaston. I turned to leave and there was Miss Mabel, bearing down on me fast with a big green book.

She held it out in both hands. "You've never had this" (she always spoke of *having* a book). Her eyes were bright as icepicks.

I took it—*Moll Flanders* by Daniel Defoe. I'd had *Robinson Crusoe* half a dozen times but had never known of this. I said "No ma'm" and checked it out to please her. It was still by my bed unopened when I left. Not till twenty years later did I find another copy, and by then it was too late to ask Miss Mabel if she'd offered me consolation or a warning that hot clear day.

There was no way to linger after that. Her books were never intended for browsing, and I was back out in the sun with nearly two hours to pass before the movie. My appetite was one thing that hadn't suffered; so I thought I'd walk on to the cafe for lunch and talk to Mr. Papageorge, who'd once tried to teach me the Greek alphabet. As I was passing a bench full of men just before the street, a voice said "Kay." I went cold and stopped. In the five old faces grinning up at me, I knew nobody and took another step. But one of them raised a big hand and then stood.

It was Fob, shaved clean and dressed for town in clothes stiff as icing. To my knowledge he'd never called me Kay in his life, and I almost asked him not to again. But he had a kind of blue mischief in his eyes like he knew a grand secret. I held my ground by the water fountain; and he came within two steps of me, then studied my face. Finally he said "You here on your own?"

He knew I didn't have a driving license yet, so I thought there must be something in my face to make him see me as bigger than before or maybe more cut off. I said "Yes sir, I'm testing my wings." I hadn't known I was till the words were out.

Fob seldom touched a human (I'd noticed before); but he reached out then for both my wrists, and raised my arms straight out at ear-level. When he turned me loose, I kept my arms out. Both hands were in sunlight. Fob said "*See* you are." Then he said "Well, good. Wings are always handy."

I thought we were playing, and I wanted to stop. I said "I'd better be heading along." I didn't mention food; I thought he'd want to join me.

But Fob said "You want your tobacco money now?"

I said "I didn't know I owned a farm."

Fob said "You don't but I own eight. I named three rows of tobacco for you, and they came on nice."

I've mentioned that I once asked him for money; and through the years when I least expected (never at Christmas or Easter or birthdays), he'd slip me ten or fifteen dollars wadded small as a bullet and always say "Don't tell Tot, hear? He'd just get sad." Since Tot was in New Caledonia now—palm trees and crabs, or so his letters said—I figured this tobacco-tale was just a new way to cover Fob's awkwardness at any small gift. I said "I've always had a green thumb" (a lie—to this day I can't even grow wild onions, much less money crops).

Fob looked behind at the bench where he'd been. Two old men were watching us, grinning like dogs. So he said "Come on to the truck with me, Kay."

I went. It was parked back behind the Farm Agent's, and we didn't speak in the hundred-yard walk. Fob didn't open my door for me either. We both got ourselves in the best we could (Fob was breathing hard). Then we sat looking out at a ragged string of boys flinging each other in a game of Crack-the-Whip down the road toward the bottom. Finally Fob said "They'll be dead soon enough. They ought to be careful." He leaned to the glove compartment, unlocked it—years of old mess. But on the top was a clean white envelope with *Miss Kate Vaiden* in Fob's round hand. Whatever this was, it was planned anyhow. He sat back and pointed. "Ain't that your name?"

I said "Most days" and reached to take the envelope. Once I pressed its thickness, I felt cold fright. What in the world would Fob want from me? Understand, this was well before girls assumed every man thought of nothing but seduction or rape. It came to my mind Fob would somehow ask me to live at his place, now Tot was gone; and I thought "I can't even cook cornbread." I prayed he wouldn't make me open it here.

But he said "Count it now. I don't want to cheat you."

So looking only down, I opened it neatly and drew out the bills—stiff as new straw hats. They were fifty-dollar notes; and Fob counted with me, one to ten. Five hundred dollars then was a big raft of money. It would buy you a whole house from Sears, Roebuck. I thought "I'm rich" and I guessed that meant I was stronger than I'd been. But I didn't believe it; it didn't sink in. I did say thank you and tuck the money deep in my library book. Then I looked toward the street, and the boys had vanished, but one or two yelling voices still reached me. I hoped Fob would say we were finished now.

He just said "Kay, *make* something of yourself."

I said "Yes sir. I'll do what I can"—a miserable answer to that much openhanded loneliness and hope. Then he opened his door and climbed back out. Not one other time did he ever call me Kay.

So I had my lunch on a stool at the counter of the Puritan Cafe and talked to Mr. Papageorge about his whole family. They were outside Athens in one small house. Or so he hoped. The Germans still had Greece firmly in hand; and he'd only had word once in eighteen months—from the Greek Red Cross—when his son disappeared. He told me he was worried and showed me their pictures and made me learn to pronounce their names, but he didn't seem all that downcast about them. He smiled more than not. That was why I decided to mention Gaston. Till then I hadn't asked for anyone's pity. I didn't tell everything about the early stages, but I let him know we had cherished each other, and I said all I knew about that last letter and the mystifying death.

Mr. Papageorge heard me out, between supervising waitresses and joking with men. Then after I'd described the funeral, he brought me a cup of hot tea in his own small hands (the first *hot* tea I'd had in my life and on such a warm day). He stood half-behind me—he'd never sit down in his own place of business—and said "Nothing worse will happen to you."

Some days he seemed not to know my name and I wouldn't mind; but today he'd given me such a welcome answer, with such a strong promise, that I wanted to hear him say who I was and make the words private. I said "Mr. Papageorge, please call me Kate."

He moved round to meet my face head-on. Then he said "Kate Vaiden." He'd known all along.

I was sorely tempted to show him my money, but I thought how far five-hundred dollars would go in Greece, and I kept that secret. But when I left him and headed to the show, I had one more prop under the platform something was building for me to leave here on—God or the Devil or good or bad luck.

The movie was good—*The Moon Is Down*, Germans in Norway— but I've seldom seen a movie I didn't like. I generally feel that if that many people have gone to that trouble, in costumes and makeup, to help me kill two hours of life (for less than the cost of a breaded veal-cutlet) then the least I can do is lean back and watch and hand them my troubles for the time they've volunteered to move in my presence. I sat through this one twice, then knew it was time to make my way on back toward Swift and our ride home.

It was not till the moment daylight struck me and blinded my eyes that I saw what maybe I was meant to do, what the whole of this sum-mer and especially today were saying to me—*Get up and go*. But where to and why? And who to, for what? I could stay on here and finish school and pray some other boy would look my way, outlast the war, and want my hand for ten years of babies and fifty of cooking. I could splurge my savings, and maybe more from Fob, and buy a one-year business course in Raleigh and then type letters, answer phones, and polish nails till they wheeled my blue hair west toward sunset. A gen-uine college never crossed my mind. Nobody on either side of my family had ever gone to college; and even if they had, there was slim money now to cover the pearls and sweaters and gloves a girl's college called for.

I sound bitter maybe but I didn't feel it then. I was still too sad from Gaston's death to feel anything but trapped by one particular loss. And coming just five years after my parents' vanishing, I felt like the place itself was ruined. Something in the ground here, something you breathed, was out to club me down to my knees till my back teeth crumbled and I called quits.

So I tried to hate the poor old heaved-up sidewalk, the far box-bushes by Emmanuel Church, and Miles's Hardware (with one of every item ever made by man). But something deep in me refused the feeling. Only lately I've wondered if it wasn't just Frances—my mother's blood in me, working for pleasure in the here and now (nobody under forty can believe how nearly *everything's* inherited).

Whatever, by the time I got back to Swift—the men's depart-ment— and waited for him to flatter an old gent plain as a turnip in a new sport-coat, I was fairly calm again. Still the new secret money was warming my hand through all the pages of that thick book. I won-dered why I hadn't walked straight from Fob to the Citizen's Bank and put it in my savings. I told myself I wanted the actual crisp paper near me a few more days, and that thought made me hungry for supper.

But it turned out Swift had promised to deliver an altered one-legged suit to a cripple out past Inez; and I was in for a long ride home, more time with Swift than I'd meant to have. The first half went easy. We sped up to cool off the broiling car, then listened to news on the radio—we'd conquered Sicily the week before; and everybody knew we'd be invading Italy any minute now, more thousands lost. In a way I still don't understand, war news had come to be a consola-tion for me. With Gaston killed and my father long gone, there was no man dear to me in present danger. I don't mean I wished harm on anybody else; but I do remember how peaceful I'd feel, hearing those regular evening stories of distant trouble and thinking I'd already had my share of possible harm.

We delivered the suit and spent twenty minutes fending off the crip-pled man's invitations to eat his good supper, spend the night, live with him forever, and share his grapevine and homemade jellies. Then we drove on again. For all the riding I'd done with Gaston, I didn't recognize this part of the county—emptier even than up around Macon. But it was still broad hot August daylight, so I didn't think anything strange was due.

Swift had always been the quiet man in the family. The weak eyes seemed to have made him unsure of his general knowledge, and he wouldn't risk much in the way of small talk. In the years I'd lived with his mother and father, he'd barely said more to me than "Merry Christmas"; he'd seemed scared of me or sad and respectful, either one of which was fine. But this day, once we left the cripple, Swift talked a red streak—and all about himself. How plugged up his life was with regrets, how bad his luck had been, and how he'd spoiled his few good chances through being too careful and always thinking of his mother and daddy—staying near to help out as they got old.

I knew how seldom he darkened their door and how rude he could be to Caroline, but I saw no need to poison the day and mention any of it. And I'd long since given up blaming him in my parents' death. My own taste for Gaston convinced me early that Dan had gone wild and mean with love and that nobody shared in that but him and Frances.

Suddenly Swift seemed tired and shut up. But I'd thought of Frances and how she chose him from all her kin to feel sorry for. I even tried watching the side of his face, trying to imagine *I* was Frances, and wondering what she could have liked in him. In quick clear glances I concentrated on Swift Porter then for maybe five minutes while he drove in silence. The shock was in seeing how much older he looked. His hair was still its natural curious cinnamon-brown, and it bristled on his collar. But the kind of hunger that had lit his face like a high gas lamp seemed gone out now. He was thirty-three and his strong jaw had slackened already and would slide. His eyes had always been his best feature, weak as they were. But he held them firm on the road as we moved; so I had to guess how green they were and how they could reach you from ten yards' distance, strong as a hand. We stopped at a crossroads I recognized; we'd cut left and be at Caroline's in ten minutes.

But Swift stayed in place for maybe twenty seconds—long enough anyhow to hear crickets cranking up, now the heat was breaking. Then he looked square at me—eyes slant as a Tartar's but emerald green.

c cp. 1

I'd been wrong in one thing; his eyes had survived. He said "Fan used to ride and watch me like that."

It had never crossed my mind he'd notice. And one of the last things I'd ever have wanted was to hear my mother's name again in his mouth.

I looked away as quick as I could but not before I saw at least the blunt edge of his power to hold my mother and gangs of other girls. It lived in his eyes, up toward his thick brows. He looked either startled, like he'd run if you breathed, or ready to take the last step toward you and lay down his life for your perfect care. I couldn't speak a word.

He never moved his hands from the top of the wheel, and after a while he faced the road, but we still didn't roll.

Finally I said "My lunch is thinning out. It's feeding time, Swift."

He said "That's one more thing you get from Fan. She never got full but she never gained flesh."

I thought if he said *Fan* one more time, I would bolt and run. I said "Your daddy'll peel a strip off me if I'm not home soon."

Swift said "No he won't, not while Mother's alive."

"Then *she'll* skin us both," I said. I was mad. And when I faced his profile again, I knew for the first time plainly one thing that has never left me since. I was *Kate*—*Kate* Vaiden not *Frances* or any other soul, live or dead. I would do my own will.

Swift may have seen it too. Anyhow we rolled. Once the air started moving past my neck, I could feel it was cooler. But every nerve in me was frying like a fuse. We'd gone half a mile before I realized he'd turned the wrong way. We were heading back into deeper country. None of it looked peculiar or bad, just new. I didn't feel scared but, for the first time since Gaston's death, I managed to pray—that I be strong, that the car turn now with no word from me. It didn't of course. I got calmer though and, once I saw the next Stop sign coming, I managed to say "Please turn around up there or I'm getting out."

Swift said "Where's your parachute?"

I said "In my head. I've got a hard head."

The car slowed a little. We passed a church with two old black women standing in the yard under blue parasols, though the sun was low. They were facing the road, separate as trees like they'd never met. Swift's foot tapped the brake. Then he suddenly turned right, wallowed in sand, and stopped ten yards from the staring women. I'd never seen either one of them, but I knew I could get out and stand beside them if the need arose.

Swift opened his door and stood up quick. He didn't grin and they didn't grin back. He said "I'm lost. Can you point me to Macon?" I knew he was no more lost than Eisenhower aimed at Hitler's heart.

The older woman raised a finger so black I could see purple in it. Then she pointed true, directly behind us. She said "Four miles, straight as you can go."

Swift thanked her and said "I'm a stranger here."

I almost believed him for that one instant till the same woman laughed and said "No you ain't—you Walter Porter."

"*Swift* Porter," he said. "Walter used to be my brother."

The woman said "Then I don't know about you." She still hadn't smiled but she took a step toward him, and the other woman followed.

Swift ducked back in, slammed the door, and spun us around and back the right way.

By then we were maybe an hour overdue. I told myself to sit quiet and get my alibi straight—just the crippled man; I wouldn't tell the rest. I faced my side of the road, all woods.

After a mile Swift faced me again. I could feel him turn, but I didn't meet him. He studied me longer than was safe, even on a back-country road at dusk. Then he said "I understood you didn't mind riding with Gaston Stegall—or walking or resting on the cool moss either."

It had been bad enough that he mentioned my mother. But in five years her name had cooled off enough to help me bear it. Gaston was still a hot open cut. The car had speeded up, but my first thought was *Jump.* If Dan could choose to leave for good, then so could I—I had his example, which is always half the battle.

I had my hand out to open the door when I thought the next thing— *Who told him that?* Anger and curiosity froze me. Who knew that much about me and Gaston? Nobody but Noony and she disliked Swift as much as me. Fob might have guessed but would he have told? And surely Mr. Papageorge hadn't already had a chance to pass on the little he knew. Then I thought the worst—Gaston. Gaston had told Swift or told somebody who scuttled to Swift. Who else but him and me knew about the moss? I didn't face Swift but by then I had to speak. I said "Some liar's been wasting your time."

He smiled at the road, then lifted both hands from the wheel long enough to rake his fingers over both his eyes. Then he said "These eyes may not be strong enough for General Mark Clark, but they know what they've *seen*."

I said "Thank Jesus you're not *at* war then—we'd all be dead: you seeing false worries behind every tree."

Swift said "Nothing I saw you and Gaston do ever worried me. I'm progressive, Katie. I'm *swift*, understand?"

I was calm enough to know he was lying—he'd never *seen* us, whatever he'd heard. But again either God or something worse struck me. My mind saw two words printed clear before me—*Walter Porter*. I'd take Walter's offer and go to him. Now I had strong reason, the means in my hand, and a warm destination five hours up the tracks. I was sick in the mouth—a taste like brass—but in my thoughts I was still as the ground. I held my book and my secret money tight and swore not to speak another word in that car.

Swift said "Understand?" one more time slowly.

But I kept my vow and just watched trees in absolute silence till we turned into Caroline's yard and stopped.

There was Holt stood up like a handpainted statue at the foot of the steps, looking our way with a face grim as flu.

Swift said to me "You're safe. I did my part. Don't upset him."

I nodded and reached to the backseat to get my new wardrobe. Then I got out fast.

Holt had already walked more than halfway to meet us.

I smiled across the roof of the car and prayed he wouldn't start asking us where we'd been so long.

He drew out his watch and tilted it to Swift. "Your mother was scared you'd had a wreck."

Swift said "No sir, just tending the sick. Had to take a new one-legged suit to a saint down near Inez. He tried to save us."

Holt faced me then—I had almost reached him—and said "Good, I'm glad somebody's on the job."

I said "*I'm* saved." I was in dead earnest. I felt like dropping those bags of junk and rising, on just my good white arms, through oak leaves to Heaven or some cleaner place.

Holt said "I always hoped you were." Then he smiled and stretched out his hands to help me.

Riled as I was even after I washed, it never crossed my mind not to sit down with Caroline and Holt and eat the big supper Noony had fixed and waited to serve. At the time, I knew it was nothing grand—a clean white tablecloth, worn plated-cutlery, worn plates with cabbage roses, cutglass saltcellars, and plain perfect food in warm abundance—but I also knew how much I would miss it, if and when I left.

The *if* had started creeping in from the minute Holt met me, helped me indoors, and Caroline had no word of reproach. And it got a strong brace as we finished the lemon pie when Holt said "Now go put on your clothes." He always wanted a fashion show after any buying trip, not because he'd paid for every stitch (sometimes he hadn't) but because he liked familiar things in fresh strange settings. Most times it seemed like a dumb chore to me, but that night I seized it like the last straw afloat.

There was still light enough outside, so they waited on the front porch for me to dress and join them. Lipstick and rouge were the only makeup south of Baltimore in those days; and being naturally high-colored and a loyal churchgoer, I used very little. But that night, once I had on the blue skirt and white longsleeved blouse, something made me go to the mirror and paint myself like a grown woman headed to a summer dance. I had everything I needed but perfume. As I combed my hair, I thought I looked good but also funny. I told myself I meant it as a joke and that Holt and Caroline would see it that way.

Neither one of them did. When I stepped out and gave them a slow deep curtsey, I expected them to laugh and then say "Wash your face."

But they sat still, though their eyes never left me. I turned around a time or two; then stepped up close to Caroline, knowing she always liked to feel the cloth.

Her hands stayed flat on the arms of her chair; and when she looked up to meet my face, she was clearly as near to tears as she got.

It scared me. I laughed and said "If it's that bad, we can take it back" (I meant the outfit, exchanging the outfit).

She just shook her head.

It was Holt that spoke. He finally said "You look good, Kate. You look first-rate. You just look more like your mother tonight than ever before. That caught us by surprise."

He seldom spoke for the two of them, but this time Caroline nodded and was quiet and faced the road.

I've already mentioned how, that afternoon, it was maybe my mother's traits working in me that calmed me down when I thought I hated life here and ought to run. And in general the memory of Frances had come to seem sweet and peaceful in all my actions. Odd as it sounds in light of her end, I could think of Frances and cool my nerves in almost any crisis (Dan was something I hardly dared to touch). But tonight with them seeing Frances in me, I was suddenly scared. Even Gaston's death hadn't hit me this way; nothing had since the last night my family lived together, that night when I sat up in my dark bed and heard Dan's voice smashing us up like glass. Was there some part of Frances growing in me now—shining through my face—that would soon break out and hurt these harmless souls and God-knew-who-else?

I could see Caroline was still in pain; so I stepped back behind Holt's chair, rocked him gently, and then asked the thing I'd never asked before—"What caused her to die?"

Neither one answered at first, and Holt didn't look at Caroline (he always checked with her). I had almost decided to go in and put on old clothes again when Holt cleared his throat. I wanted to stop him (he'd keep us half the night now, and still we wouldn't know). But he said one word and stopped—"Herself."

Before I could ask for more or deny him, Caroline said "Somebody's coming, Kate. Better go wash your face."

Gaston's car—his father's car at least—was turning in. No Stegall had ever driven up to this house till I knew Gaston. But before I could think I was faced with a ghost, I saw his father's snow-white head upright at the steering wheel.

Holt said "John Stegall, poor fellow—"

And Caroline said "What on earth can he want?"

I said "Not me" and thought I'd run; but when I saw Gaston's mother crouched low in the passenger seat, I stayed in place. She'd never had three kind words for me, and I didn't want to give her the right to shy me.

Holt struggled to his feet, walked to the top of the porch steps, and waited. I sat down by Caroline and looked out through the scraggly spirea bushes.

At first it seemed the Stegalls were wrong. Their engine was running and they stayed inside. They even backed up five yards. But finally they stopped and Mr. Stegall stepped out and stood.

Holt said "John, let me sell you some hay." He waved at the sandy waste around us (one of the standing jokes in Macon was Holt's long effort to grow grass in oakshade).

Mr. Stegall took him seriously. "Mr. Porter, I haven't kept a cow in four years." Then he said "I was hoping Kate was home."

Holt said "She is" and pointed behind him. He'd squared his shoulders the best he could, a kind of polite but earnest guard.

That was when dread hit me. I knew some broad black boxcar was rolling down the tracks, aimed for Kate. I knew it had to have some connection with Gaston.

Caroline touched my left arm and whispered "Go see what he wants. Don't make him come in."

I stood up, walked to Holt's side, and stopped there.

It was nearer dark now, and Mr. Stegall's hair was the one bright thing. He leaned back into the car, then came forward.

Holt said "Go meet him."

I said "Go with me."

Holt said "He wants you."

I thought of the night Caroline left me in the dark by Frances's

Penny Show. *People would leave you.* I'd tried to forget that; time kept flinging me regular reminders. Nothing I'd done up till now even slowed it. So I went down the steps and walked a little way and waited in the flat dry spot by Caroline's century plant.

There were only twelve steps between me and the car, but it seemed to take him a week to reach me. I watched his face so steadily that I failed to notice what was in his hip pocket.

He came right to me but didn't reach out. Those eyes never smiled but never left me either. You couldn't have guessed whether he was about to scream or whisper. He said "I been meaning to come see you."

I said "All right."

He said "A whole month after we buried Gaston, a buddy of his from training camp sent us a letter Gaston had give him in case anything went wrong like it did. I don't know why the fellow waited so long, but he did and now so have I. I been so busy I couldn't show it to you, and then I mislaid it. But today Christine she found it somewhere, so I'm up here to let you read it." He reached a hand to the pocket of his shirt and took out an airmail letter, folded triple. With the same one hand, he opened it out and offered it to me.

Just the sight of Gaston's writing on the envelope was awful—pale blue ink like he'd watered it down to make it last longer. Well, longer than him.

I took a step back and looked toward the house. Holt was back in his chair by Caroline, both watching like God's own eyes at Judgment. I said "Mr. Stegall, does he say he killed himself?"

He thought about that; then said "No, he wrote it two days before they say he died." The letter was still in his hand, still near me.

I made what I knew was the kind of choice you pick at in dreams the rest of your life. I said "I believe I better not see it."

His eyes broke their hold then and studied the letter. He said "It don't say one mean word."

"I'm glad of that," I said.

He looked up again. "He speaks about you."

I couldn't answer that.

"He says if anything happens to him for me to give you this old foxhorn." Either he smiled or showed such surprise it looked like a smile. He folded the letter, put it back in his shirt, and finally reached to his right hip-pocket. Then he held out Gaston's stubby brown fox-horn—the one made out of some dead local steer, that Gaston had used the first day I knew him in the sun by the river.

I said "Thank you, sir."

"You're welcome," he said. "You aim to keep it, don't you?"

I said "Yes sir." But sad as I was, I saw a funny side. I said "I'm not sure a fox'll ever hear it."

Mr. Stegall smiled, no mistake, at last. "That'll suit them fine." For the first time he turned back to check his wife. All the car windows were still shut tight; and she was staring back toward her house, way out of sight. Then he said "You and Mr. Fob and me—we'll go hunting once we get a good frost."

I said "All right" but knew, then and there, I'd never break through those same woods again. I asked if his wife would like to come in.

He said "No thank you. She left her teeth." He took another long dead-level look deep into my eyes (I was tall as him). Then he gave a slow wave, with both hands before him like he meant to prove he had never been armed. His palms were yellow and smooth but as tough as the horn I held. I was not old enough to think how someday, if Gaston had lived and come back here, he'd have looked and moved very much like this. But some little thread of all I'd felt for Gaston Stegall snagged on his tired father's hands and face. With everybody watch-ing, I touched his arm just above the wrist—a touch not a grip.

His eyes didn't water, I'm almost sure; but they did open wider. Then he shook my hand like a friend he'd met in town or in a field. But he said "You'd have give him your whole life, Kay—am I right about that?"

I nodded yes.

"Did Gaston know that?"

I said "I told him time and again"—in *deeds,* I meant; the only way we told each other anything but the news.

Mr. Stegall said "Good." He waved at the house and took two steps toward the car and his wife. Then he stopped and faced me again and said "It's nothing but a goddamned shame he's gone. Find you somebody else."

I thanked him again, not knowing he'd changed my life that instant or thrown me the final freedom I needed, like a new clean ball that burst into flames as it touched my thumbs.

T W O

THE TRAIN WAS A LOCAL and stopped at every pig path between home and Norfolk; but the car I was in had a few vacant seats till, of all places, Gumberry. For some reason half a boatload of sailors climbed aboard there. The one that flopped down right beside me was so plump I doubted he'd float if torpedoed. When he was rearranging luggage overhead to make room enough for his long sea-bag, he asked how many of the bags were mine. I said "Not a one" and showed him my purse—truly all I had with me when I walked out of church and climbed aboard—and he fell asleep in under ten seconds. His arm puddled over my shoulder for an hour. The day was hot as the doorknobs of Hell, but I figured he'd be sailing out Monday morning for something worse than heat and damp, so I let him be. One unex-pected blessing was, he smelled like celery, washed and crisp. He'd almost got soothing—something I needed badly—when we slowed again and stopped at Boykins. First stop in Virginia, Southampton County.

One woman got on. The first thing I noticed was, she wore my size. But once she had stopped at the head of the aisle and seen no seat, I saw we also looked alike.

The plump boy beside me had waked up by then. He said "You and that girl bound to be kin."

Before I could say no, he lurched upright and waved her to the seat.

She was Daphne Baxter from a farm near Boykins; and when she had thanked the boy and was settled, she turned to my face and said "I always dreamed of a sister."

I said "Me too," which was not really so, and told her my entire story before she'd breathed deep again.

At the end she said "I can lend you a dress that has won blue ribbons. My husband'll love you." Her husband was Cliff, her age—nineteen—and due to sail right back out on his battleship any minute now for dangerous duty. I regretted I'd already mentioned Gaston's death, but I thanked her and said I'd be going straight to Walter's and would buy clothes Monday.

Then a sailor sitting near us, not five feet tall, brought out a pearl-plated autoharp and played hymns all through the last miles to Norfolk. The whole car joined in, singing the words, and by the time we could smell city air—and the ocean behind it—I suspected I'd live now and bury old pain.

Glad as they were to see each other, Daphne and Cliff waited with me in line for a telephone booth. By then it was almost suppertime; but Walter didn't answer, though I tried three separate scary times. That risk had never crossed my mind. I turned to the Baxters and pretended I was brave—he had just stepped out but was such a homebody he'd be back soon and I'd be safe.

Cliff said "You're safe as a hand near a shark"; and while I could see it ruined his plans, he said we would just eat here in the station and then call again.

Despite war shortages, stations in those days served fine food; serious travelers wouldn't stand for less. And by dusk I was starving, so I ate as much as Cliff—two salmon croquettes, three vegetables, and tea, then Boston cream-pie (a novelty for me). Daphne barely touched hers. I got the impression she regretted having met me. But she stayed polite; and when after an hour Walter still hadn't answered, it was Daphne that turned to Cliff and said "Is there any other place in that room to sleep?"

Cliff said "A big rocker" and stood up to pay the whole check and lead us. By then I was far too scared not to follow.

*   *   *

It was my first taxi since leaving Greensboro, and it seemed like a
longer ride than the train. We passed through districts solid with sailors, then sailors and women, then lovely brick homes, then a lot of
marsh grass. It turned out Cliff had rented a tepee at the Arrowhead
Tourist Court at Willoughby Beach, and the final fare came to nearly
six dollars—a day's pay then for many strong men. I thought I'd offer
to pay my share but decided not to flash my riches (like a fool I had my
whole bankroll in a white church-purse).

The tepee was lifesize but painted cast-iron; and its round inside
was divided three ways—bedroom, kitchenette, bath. Cliff had told
the truth; there was only one bed and one stiff rocking-chair. He said
we could set it back in the kitchen, and I could sleep there if Walter
didn't answer by normal bedtime. But by then Daphne'd had time to
calm her nerves; so she said "No, let's you and me dress like sisters;
and Cliff can tell the manager that blood-kin's turned up unexpectedly,
and we need a cot."

I said "All right" and Cliff went out while we rinsed off the train
soot. Then Daphne sat me down and—with nothing but a comb,
three bobbypins, and lipstick—made me her sister in under ten
minutes. Even Cliff was amazed and he'd been strafed in the winter
Atlantic.

It was when I saw my face in the manager's-office mirror that I first
realized how I'd hurt Holt and Caroline. That strange painted girl,
pretty for the first time and grown, had struck two people who loved
her more than any. They'd have surely called the sheriff, and men
would be out now—Fob chief among them and maybe Gaston's father—hunting the woods for my remains. (I didn't think anyone had
seen me board the train; you could buy your ticket once you found a
seat.) But the thought didn't stop me. I figured that, once I was safe
with Walter, I would write and thank them and halfway explain and
say I would hope to see them Thanksgiving. So I kept calling Walter
every hour till bedtime with still no luck.

Between tries I'd walk on the beach in the dark. I stumbled on
more than one toiling couple; but I hadn't seen the ocean since I was

five, when Dan and Frances took me to Kitty Hawk; and I concentrated on it, not the lovers. No need by now to describe my thoughts. The only one that surprised me was a kind of cold thrill. The breeze was warm but my scalp was cold with this new taste of freedom. I saw I'd been free since Dan fired his shots—free but a child. Now I could pass as a real married woman with serious plans, a will to work, and a taste for travel.

A sailor came toward me just past ten o'clock. His suit was glowing in the night like silver. He stopped and said "I was hunting for you."

I laughed and said "Men older than you are hunting for me all up and down the coast."

He said "In that case I won't wait in line" and vanished like he came, a shining thing.

I told his back goodbye and that I'd pray for him. He didn't speak again but I've occasionally wondered if he died at sea or is somewhere dry now, watching TV and waiting to retire after decades of recapping tires or pruning trees.

The next surprise was, I *did* pray for him. When I knocked at the tepee door, Cliff and Daphne were still fully dressed with the radio on. They'd wedged my cot in between the midget gas-range and the rusty sink. And when I'd lied and said Walter's roommate had finally answered and said he would be back early tomorrow, they were plainly relieved—for me and them—and we turned in at once. The only thing between us was a cotton draw-curtain. As I switched off my light, I could smell stove gas; and I added suffocation to my list of dangers. But once I was praying, I just begged life for the boy on the beach that had left me alone. I didn't even mention poor absent Walter or anyone at home or my own self, wild as the blind sandfiddlers I'd just now seen—tan ghosts at my heels.

Then we all seemed to sleep, after Cliff had told us one long funny tale of how an older sailor on his ship brought a thirty-pound ape safe home from Gibraltar, on a human Navy diet, and not one officer ever found out. By the time they were home, the ape knew the multiplication tables, at least through six. I halfway suspect I woke near dawn and heard Cliff breathing in cadence and Daphne saying his name one time. If so it would be the only time in my life I heard any two others agreeing that deeply. I *know* that well after light I dreamed Cliff was trapped underwater in barnacled chains and that Daphne and I were swimming toward him with our lips trailing blood through thick seaweed.

I paid for the three of us to eat a big breakfast—corned-beef hash and fresh poached-eggs, a Yankee dish Cliff had found in the Navy that I've liked ever since. Then to save my lie about Walter's return, I called a taxi and hugged them goodbye. Cliff asked was I absolutely sure I'd be met in Norfolk and told the driver not to turn me loose till a grown white man had me well in tow. Daphne gave me her address in the country and said I was welcome there, rain or shine.

When we saw the first phonebooth, I asked the driver to let me use it. Still no Walter, nobody but silence. I'd already given the driver Walter's street address, but now I broke down and told him the truth— I was sixteen and lost.

At first he said "You ain't alone in *Norfolk.*" But then he said he had a daughter loose somewhere in Texas, and would I listen to his good advice?

I said "Please sir."

He said "What brand of Christian are you?"

I said "Methodist."

He said "Then let me drive you straight to a Methodist preacher."

Something in me coiled like a spring at that. If I needed help—and I'd started to wonder—then I'd only take it from Walter or a kind girl roughly my age. I said "Is there some kind of U.S.O. for women?" The U.S.O. was a string of aid-centers for servicemen, with doughnuts and dartboards.

He said "You ain't a WAVE."

"I may be soon. You want me to walk?"

He didn't say no but he took me downtown to a U.S.O. near a tattoo parlor that was just throwing up its shades for business—wonderful drawings pasted to the walls that you could have transferred to your hide and a young-man manager already lilac from head to toe with his own handiwork (he was smiling barechested at the street as I passed).

The lady at the door of the U.S.O. saw right away I was nothing but a high-school civilian from the sticks, but she did let me use her free telephone—by then I'd spent a good dollar in nickels. It was ten a.m. and a woman's voice answered "Mr. Walter Porter's residence"—so plainly middleaged and black that, the first time in weeks, my eyes made tears. I quickly explained who and where I was, expecting she'd at least have heard my name.

But she said "Mr. Walter and them still out at the beach. Won't be here till dark." Not a word about, come on and wait in cool safety.

For some strange reason I told her not to let Walter know I was here. Maybe I saw the chance to surprise him as also a test; his instant reaction would show where I stood.

When I stepped back onto the street, I thought "I'll price a tattoo"— a redbird right in the crease of my arm. I'd seen one tattooed woman in my life, an old missionary that spoke at our school and had been tattooed more or less against her will years earlier in Fiji.

My driver had waited though, there by the curb. He said "You enlist?"

I laughed and said yes, I'd be seasick by sundown. Then I told him my cousin would be home tonight, and I guessed I was safe.

He took out his watch. "You got ten hours. Girls stronger than you have been ruined in less time."

I said "Tell me your name."

He said "Tim Slaughter."

That somehow made me trust him even more than I had. I said "Then where must I spend the day?"

Tim studied my face. "Ever heard of Yorktown? I don't mean the ship."

I gave a little school-recitation on the subject of Washington accepting Cornwallis's sword on the fields of Yorktown.

"Breastworks," he said. "It's all breastworks now—just up the road here." He pointed northwest (I can always tell directions like a soul with perfect pitch).

I said "I've never seen a battlefield," then remembered the creek where Dan and Frances died.

Tim checked his watch again. "Let me drive you there."

I was lost for a second and thought he meant Macon. I said "I'm an unemployed orphan; can't afford it."

But he said "Stand still" and studied me again. Then he came right to me, two feet from my face, and said "You never even told your name, but I'll dedicate this whole day to you and guarantee you safe in your cousin's house by dark tonight—not a flyspeck on you nor my fingerprints."

I said "What you plan to do? What about your job?"

Tim said "The cab's mine. I can quit when I want. Ain't got a wife to stop me. Let's see Yorktown."

I said "How old are you?"

He grinned. "Fifty-six."

That seemed trustworthy enough to me; and I said "Well, thank you."

Yorktown, Jamestown, Williamsburg, an oyster dinner, Old Point Comfort, and four ferry rides—I'd never known the world was so old and big. Not a cloud crossed the sky, the actual sky; and Tim made me sit on the backseat the whole time, a chauffeured lady (though my clothes were wilting). He was from Cape Henry, so he knew it all backwards. And if proud old Virginia ever made a truer gentleman than Tim, I never met him. More than once through the years, I've said to myself "What a pity Tim Slaughter didn't ask you to marry him that fine day." He'd be in his nineties now, but he might have saved Kate Vaiden whole worlds of waste.

By six in the evening, we were back in Norfolk. It was still far from dark; and though my clothes had ripened by then, I took Tim's offer of a second meal—a big fish-platter. I ate more seafood that one day than in my entire previous life. Anybody living out of sight of the ocean was scared of fish back then, with good reason.

After dessert Tim finally mentioned what we hadn't breathed about since morning—his guarantee to take me safe to Walter. He said "You still plan to call your cousin?"

Before I thought, I said "Yes—who else but God in flames?"

Tim laughed but said "Then use your own nickel." He'd paid out every other penny all day.

I'm glad to say I told him I'd had the best day of my life, till then at least. I doubt I was lying.

Then he gave me his business card, the first I'd ever seen; and he said "Any hour of the day or night."

A man's voice answered, deeper than Walter's. But Walter was there. When I said it was me, not two miles away, Walter gave a long hoot that I first thought was pain. I said "I can head back to Macon right now," though I knew I'd crawl on my hands to Hell first.

Walter said "Hush up. This is better news than peace. I'll be there in a jiffy."

I told him I had a ride, if that was all right.

And he said "Anything you want, Baby Child." That was what Frances called me in early years; I'd forgot till then.

So Tim drove me straight there—Bruges Avenue—and climbed the steps with me and delivered me like a small chandelier he'd been hired to guard. Walter asked him in, offered him supper, and tried to pay him. Tim solemnly refused but shook our hands.

As he left I told him I'd keep his card forever.

Tim nodded. "You'll need it."

I said "We'll see."

Walter tugged the back of my damp belt and said "Come in here now and tell the whole story."

It turned out Walter would sit still for any *story* on earth, long as the teller claimed it was true. He never judged whether it was good or bad. I kept mine true—Gaston's life and death and Swift's dirty meanness.

By the end Walter's eyes were swimming again; but when he could speak, what he said was "Where's your trunk?"

I reminded him I'd walked straight from church to the train.

He said "Tomorrow I'll dress you, skin-out. You'll look like a million. Got your shoe ration-book?"

I did have that.

Then he said "Now we need to send Mother a wire."

I said "Please don't"—the idea spoiled my happiness, my notion of rescue.

Walter said "You want her to die tonight? May already be too late."

I said "You promise you won't send me back?"

He turned to face me, serious as a surgeon, and raised his plump right hand to swear. "You won't leave here till you need to go."

It was the second guarantee I'd had from men since early that morning, and I chose to believe it.

The telephone was on the far side of the living room; and while Walter was composing the wire, I tried not to hear him. I was scared he would somehow sell me out. So I concentrated on the furniture. It was all bleached oak and modernistic—the kind I'd only seen in Ginger Rogers movies—with white upholstery that, in any other apartment on earth, would have been coal-black inside a week but was spotless here (and stayed that way). And all the pictures were real oil-paintings, each one an excellent likeness of a tree. I recognized the pine and the pink mimosa.

The wire said simply *Kate with me. No bones broken. Letter follows. Love, Walter.* When he put down the phone, I stood up and went more than halfway to meet him. I gave him a silent bear-hug.

He took it calmly with his own arms down and said "Thank you deeply. You must be exhausted."

I thought "In another minute he's bound to call me Frances." Then I knew he was right. I was numb, standing up.

I said "Do you mind if I sleep in my slip?"

Walter backed away, smiled, and said "Sleep in your *hoopskirt,* far as I'm concerned. But Baby Child, one other person lives with us. He'll be back directly so wear my pajamas."

I wore a white silk pair, with Chinese-red piping, but was long since dead as a chloroformed dog when the other person came back.

* * *

Their voices woke me early though, from back in the kitchen; I couldn't hear words. So I lay on, drowsing and saying short prayers of strong thanksgiving. At half-past seven a light knock woke me—Walter in his bathrobe and a younger man, sandy-haired and dressed for work. I thought "He's not exactly handsome but his smile'd grow roses on rusty barbed-wire." I was partly right.

Walter said "You ready to spend all my money?"

I said "No, mine." I'd shown him mine.

Walter said "We're banking Fob's money first-pop—government bonds. Sit up, smile now, and meet Douglas Lee." He reached back and drew the dressed man a step forward.

Douglas Lee was a name I'd heard, but I couldn't think where. I sat up and said "Hope this isn't your bed."

He said "You needed it far more, I hear." Then he said he shouldn't delay the war effort and would see us this evening.

Even after I'd bathed and put my dirty church-dress back on, I could smell his trail all through the room like new spring leaves or one of those living-room pictures, alive.

Walter had a whole week of vacation left (he was chief of rolling freight for the Norfolk and Western Railroad). He and Douglas and some friends had taken a cottage at the beach for one week, but now Douglas had to work (a civilian Navy clerk), so Walter was loose to stay with me. I accepted, partly because I couldn't imagine having the gall to ask Caroline to ship me my things and partly because it seemed to thrill Walter, dressing me nicely as a Christmas doll. He also bought me a Chinese dinner with lychee nuts at the end, weird as sheep eyes. When I'd swallowed one I thought "Well, now I can stand anything." I was more than dead wrong, but the last few weeks had seemed like a long vaccination that gave me strength. So when Walter had asked a few gentle questions about my story—Gaston and Swift and my hopes for life—I felt old enough to say "Who is Douglas Lee?"

Walter took up the chopsticks he'd never used. "From *Macon*—Simp and Sue Lee's son but of course they were gone way before you were born. Sue keeled over when Douglas was ten, and Simp had vanished on the midnight train two years before that. They were very distant kin of *my* father's, and I'd known Douglas from the week he was born. But once he was left alone in the world—there was no close kin—the church had to send him to Oxford Orphanage. I'd been his Sunday-school teacher till he left and had practiced with him in the children's choir, so he and I kept up a thick correspondence. And that first Easter I went down to Oxford to visit him. They led me toward him through a dim dormitory, with more orphans watching like starved-out squirrels. And there he sat on the foot of his cot, dressed in all-brown clothes and third-hand shoes. I fought back the tears and gave him his present—a silent piano keyboard for practice. He didn't say 'Thank you' or even my name but laid out the keyboard and tested it a minute, then played and sang 'Love Lifted Me.' I all but died to think the world was built like that—the fact had escaped me up till then. The whole trip home, I worked on plans. I was seventeen years old and had a good job as late-night telegrapher in Warren Plains, more money than I could possibly spend. In under an hour I'd decided to spring Douglas Lee out of there. I want you to know I *did*, a year later. It took me that long, every minute hard as fits. My father wouldn't agree to adopt him—Tas and Swift were younger than me—so I just slowly persuaded the orphanage to let me take him. It wasn't true adoption but a complicated loan that they could revoke anytime Douglas yelled. And it might have been easier to dam the Roanoke River singlehanded than try to help a miserable child, age eleven—even then when they barely had laws for orphans. I *did* it though, as I said, and it lasted. I only had to tell one lie—let them think we'd be living with adults. But I'd already moved out from home and rented us a three-room house in a cotton field two miles from my job. We kept it two years and were happy as if we had good sense, eating mostly out of cans and paying old Aunt Sloe Wilton to wash our clothes and sweep. It was school that ruined it. Teachers couldn't stand the idea of Douglas *free*, though he always rose to the head of his class. Finally one of them wrote to my father, said it was his duty to take a stand—

either bring us both home or send Douglas back where he'd have a woman's care. He paid us a call that Sunday afternoon. We'd visited him and Mother every week or so, but neither one of them had darkened our door. I was reading a book on how to raise goats—we planned to start that—and Douglas was back in the kitchen boiling sugar to make pull-candy. We tried to welcome him, show him the place. But he said he had urgent business with me and for Douglas to run outside and play, like Douglas wasn't thirteen and wiser than thirty. The business of course was that Douglas had to leave—back to the orphanage till he was independent, two or three more years. I took the news calmly but said to myself in the first five seconds 'Just act obedient; then you and Douglas *run.*' So while Douglas was still outside, I said I would recommit him a week from today; and Father drove off satisfied. We left Monday, soon as I'd drawn out my savings—just took what our two little grips would hold and abandoned the rest. I'd been to Norfolk once years before on a church excursion and had loved the water. We headed straight here. I paid my Macon debts by mail, wrote my mother a letter of explanation; and here we've been ever since, sixteen years. At first I dreaded the orphanage would track us down—I still dream about it—but if they ever knew, they never objected. And nobody else did, not up here. That's the reason for cities. But you know that."

By then I had swallowed my last lychee and decided I liked them. I had a hundred questions; and I knew that today, maybe never again, I could ask them all and get true answers. But I didn't see the need or was still too tired or was happy for the first time since Gaston graduated.

That whole first week Walter never mentioned school. One of the secrets I'd ponder at night was whether or not to bring up school and say I'd like to finish. I was old enough to quit, on my own free will. In one more year I'd finish the eleventh grade; and that was the end, for most Virginia schools (not in North Carolina). Like so much else I just let it ride and spent the entire week touring round with Walter—

the town and the beach and the huge rollercoaster at Ocean View. Evenings we'd get back to find Douglas cooking enough for eight, though no company joined us for weeks to come.

Saturday the three of us toured the Navy base and went to the P.X. where Douglas could buy any product made, except ladies' drawers, for under half-price. They bought me a wristwatch, and we were outside eating ice-cream sandwiches when Douglas—Douglas now, not Walter at all—tapped my wrist and said "You'll be on time for school."

With no prior warning they'd made arrangements for my next school—St. Rose of Lima, Catholic, for girls. It opened in a week, and I'd need more clothes—blue skirts and longsleeved snow-white blouses. I thought "I'll finish this ice cream first, then make up my mind." They watched me like hawks but let me decide. And when I'd wiped my mouth clean again, I said "You won't be ashamed of my work."

And they never were, long as it lasted. I enjoyed the school, especially religion class and most of the nuns. Catholics were scarce as tigers in the South then—strange as Eskimoes and far more subject to wild suspicions. Most of the rumors centered on Mary Blessed Virgin. It was generally thought they worshipped her and shortchanged Jesus or at least that her pull with the men in her family was overwhelming and could be bought or begged by kissing her statue, fingering beads, or crawling the length of church on your knees. (My limited personal time with the nuns confirmed more than part of the Mary rumors, back then anyhow. But that was what I loved most—a mother who could face you through anything you said and not blink once and still help you afterwards. In the long years since, when I've paid rare visits to Protestant churches, the main thing I've missed is a chance to see Mary—though most of them mention her name in the creed—and to think of the long test she had to bear.)

However strange, the nuns were kind to me, even the two I suspected were crazy or headed there fast. The other girls were surely no worse than girls anywhere, not to mention boys. The main difference was, they were hipped on sex. I heard more talk about bodies that term than in any other stretch before or since—most of it wrong, I happened to know.

It had to come from the nuns discussing impurity as much as they did. Few classes went by without at least a shudder for *impurity*. That fascinated me. From what I could tell—and I wasn't sure they knew— I thought they were warning against body-touch, ourselves or others. Touching myself has never meant much to me, as I said; but God (if nobody else alive) knew I'd touched Gaston Stegall many glad times. *Glad* for me. Maybe it had struck Gaston some other way and helped cause his death. Maybe God really did agree with the nuns, and naked bodies used for anything but babies infuriated Him and set His arms flinging like scythes in hay.

I puzzled through that more than any nun guessed and came to the near point, more than once, of begging forgiveness for what we'd done—the touching at least. But God (or the Devil or my parents' blood in me) kept me loyal to the past, which was mainly the memory of Gaston's neck on the meat of my wrists when I pressed him close.

The memory was fading though. And bitter as that was, it was also a blessing. I'd never asked Gaston for any kind of picture; and once he was dead, I couldn't ask his mother; so I didn't even have his shadow to remind me. I could do other things. The school work of course took hours every night. But it turned out Macon High School had prepared me for bigger things. I read Latin better than all but the nuns, and nothing really hurt but plane geometry. I saw how clean it was and how, in the right hands, it marched like music; it wouldn't budge for me.

That was why I turned to Douglas. I tried Walter first but he begged off as being a "numerical nitwit" and said "Try Douglas. *He* can think that way." Douglas spent most evenings reading detective stories or going to movies, apparently alone. And he'd never studied geometry in school. But once Walter said "Come rescue Kate," he walked in and learned the whole hard subject with me—though faster and better. Every night we'd sit at the breakfast-room table and independently work each problem, then compare results. I'd never watched a grown person learn anything, but soon I knew I was watching Douglas. And little by little the daily sight of his serious face struggling to win—still an orphan's face—was what I lived for.

I think Walter noticed but he didn't seem to mind. Sometimes he'd sit at the table with us and nibble away at a crossword puzzle or write long birthday-greetings on cards to the thousand friends he claimed but never saw. He sometimes bet us a dollar who would solve the next problem first; a dollar was something worth winning then. And always he'd call time on us at eleven—"You scholars shut down. This fool's got to *rest*."

That would be the signal for ice cream. Walter wanted dessert last thing before bed but wouldn't eat a mouthful unless we joined him. We usually did. Then we'd take turns using the one bathroom. They'd sleep in Walter's old room (twin beds with quilted headboards), and I'd sleep in what had been Douglas's room with his ship pictures on the walls above me—every ship he had ever boarded in his work. Dozens, all gray.

That was pretty much how we lived for four months. Excitement consisted of trips to the movies every second weekend, church with Walter on Sundays (a different church every week, for the music), and the mail from Macon. Who could ever have guessed that neither Holt nor Caroline would be mad or hurt? They waited a week or so after Walter's wire; then wrote me separate letters, calm as bread dough, telling me the local news and hoping I was well. I was shocked at first and maybe disappointed—were they glad I was gone? But after a while I noticed neither one of them mentioned my clothes, shipping me my clothes. So I thought of those few little skirts and blouses as hostages of their lasting love for me. I figured we'd go down and get them Thanksgiving and renew our ties.

But in late October when I said as much to Walter and Douglas after chocolate ice-cream, Douglas simply walked out—not mad but silent. Walter sat me back down at the table and said "Douglas hates every rock in the road to Macon, and rightly so. I can't ask him to go, and I can't go without him. When I went that once, after Frances died, he vanished from here and was gone three weeks—I never knew where, just walked in one evening and took up where he'd left."

I said "Isn't that just a little bit crazy?"

Walter said "I think you and I are two of the people with no right left to call anybody wild." Then he laughed and touched my geometry book and, from memory, recited the Pythagorean theorem. He'd known it thirty years.

I liked him more than ever and said I'd stay here with them.

Walter wrote to Caroline and said I could visit them once I'd finished school or had a vacation but that now I needed to sit still and study. When Thanksgiving came, I saw he was making an extra effort to cheer me up. Pauline (the maid who cleaned two days a week but hated to talk) stayed late Wednesday night and cooked the side dishes—yams, macaroni and cheese, snap beans. And Thursday morning he and Douglas were up by dawn with the turkey, ambrosia, and rolls. I polished the silver, set the table; and before we ate at two o'clock, I tasted the first alcohol of my life. Douglas went to their bedroom and brought out sherry. With no jokes about my age or innocence, they poured me a big glass, toasted my future; and I slugged it down in one long gulp (still the only way I can bear the taste). Walter laughed—"Whoa, Sadie!" Then we had the grand meal.

Walter and Douglas never said grace. But by the time we got to the end of Thanksgiving dinner, I felt it was time somebody prayed a little. So when they stood to start clearing, I said "Please wait. How about a benediction now?"

Walter looked to Douglas, who said "Go to it."

By then I'd embarrassed myself but went on and named my causes for thanks—Walter Porter, Douglas Lee, and the turkey. When I said "A-*men*," Walter gave my mother's old response—"Brother *Ben*; shot a rooster, killed a *hen!*" But when I looked, both he and Douglas had full eyes. For some reason I thought "I can't stand this."

And reading my mind, Douglas said "Get dressed. We're going to the beach."

I said "We'll die."

Walter said "No, you won't. It's gorgeous out there."

So I went for my coat. When I got back, Douglas was ready and waiting in his camel's-hair jacket and red-plaid scarf; but Walter had on his butcher's apron. He said "My nerves need to wash these dishes" (*nerves* were everybody's big problem back then, and washing dishes was Walter's drug). "You chillun run on. Turkey sandwiches at eight."

I thought "Don't go. Kate, stay here in safety."

But Douglas said "Hash—turkey hash and we'll be here."

I hadn't seen the beach since my night with the Baxters, my day with Tim Slaughter. And like most inlanders, I hadn't really thought of the ocean existing except in summer. There were so few cars that we parked Walter's Studebaker almost in the surf, way on up past the Cavalier Hotel that was nothing but officers' quarters now—the empty swank part. The sky was gray but the air was gentle. We locked our shoes in the car and walked. The water was not much cooler than the day—one more surprise—so I walked in its fringe, me and twelve zillion creatures (not one of them human). Douglas stayed nearby but in the dry sand, stopping every few yards to check the trash. We must have gone three or four miles at least and passed nobody. I began to imagine the war had ended but with everybody else in America dead (this was more than a year before Hiroshima). Soon there was one high dune with tall grass. I turned back to Douglas and said "We need to stop."

We sat on the ridge. Douglas laid out his harvest of treasures at our feet—polished glass, one huge prehistoric shark's tooth (coal-black), and a good-looking fountain pen with no brandname stamped on it anywhere (we decided it was German, washed up from a sub—submarines were far the best mysteries in this war). Then he said "You're a serious *walker*, aren't you? I'm worn flat out."

I said "That's all right. We're searching for home."

He said "We've got a dry home—and cold yams."

"No," I said. "We're the last two alive in Virginia—in the U.S.A.—in maybe the world." I thought he would anyhow ask what I meant.

But he said "That's not the worst thing that could be."

I said "Make a suggestion."

Like he had planned it far in advance, Douglas said "Being you and me as children, back when." He grinned but it looked like the grin on a corpse.

He'd never said a word about his past or mine. And being locked up all fall in my own cares, I'd failed to notice what we had in common, a secret awful as a poisoned well—orphans, both of us. Not good enough magnets to hold even *parents*. I suddenly thought "Lord, I was right—we're alone in this." There was some little grain of truth buried in that, but otherwise it proved one of my worst thoughts. It was something I hadn't known I needed to believe. But once Douglas Lee had flung it my way, I seized onto it like a starved bitch-dog. I finally faced him and said "Tell me this. How bad would it be if we left here now?"

"You cold?" Douglas said.

"No," I said. "I mean *leave*."

He waited, then laughed. "Cruel," he said. "Lowdown and wrong."

I'd known that of course. And we left it at that.

In the car, headed home, it was nearly dark. The road was lined with sailors hitching back from one-day passes. Douglas said "Do we want to help one of these boys?"

I said "Suit yourself." I was already tired.

So he never slowed down but, on the edge of town, began to talk slowly. "Katie, be thankful you're kin to Walter Porter. He's the one person I ever knew in my life who couldn't say a mean word or do a mean thing."

I said "I know it. There's one more though—his mother, my aunt."

Douglas said "So I've heard. But she never so much as flicked a finger to save me from perishing when my mother died."

"You lived," I said.

"Yes ma'm—because of *Walter*. You know about that?"

I said I'd heard Walter's version.

"Then you heard the truth." We drove in silence the rest of the way and were almost there when he spoke again. "One thing I doubt

Walter told you, I'll tell. I tried to kill him, the time he went to Macon—four years ago today."

Somehow I was calm. "Does Walter know that?"

Douglas waited, then laughed. "I'm pretty sure, yes. The kitchen *door* knows. The knife stuck there—just missed Walter's neck."

I told him no, I hadn't heard that. In a minute I said "I wish I still hadn't."

Douglas said "I like you staying here with us; but you and I—being as wild as we are—need to know each other real well, every step. Walter Porter has simply meant life to me." By then he was signaling to turn for our place.

I said "That's something I already knew."

Douglas said "Good."

But two weeks later on a Wednesday night, we were out alone again. Walter had gone overnight to Lynchburg, to Ringling Brothers' Circus (they'd bought a new big-as-a-house gorilla, and Walter had to make the final decision on whether it could travel on his company's tracks). I cooked a quick supper, and we went to the show—*Lady of Burlesque* with Barbara Stanwyck. Afterwards, although it was a school night and cold, Douglas headed us out toward Ocean View, not asking my advice, to eat ice cream. There was one place open he knew about. In the midst of a small dish of buttered pecan (and a ring of glazed sailors), I thought "He's going to want us to walk on the beach, and we'll hurt Walter badly." I was wrong about the walk.

The hurting took place in the car—ten o'clock, parked farther south by a boarded-up cottage but in sound of the sea. And Walter, after all, was the only thing hurt.

Halfway home Douglas took my hand—we still sat far apart as ever—and said "I want you to know I'm happy."

I didn't move but I said "Me too," and then he turned me loose. The whole night long I kept waking up and searching my soul like the nuns prescribed. I thought there ought to be a small stain at least—black, plain to see, and threatening to spread. But no, in my mind I was clear as a June day with no cloud foretold. And through my door I could hear peaceful breaths from Douglas's sleep. We'd agreed in silence, like deaf-and-dumb murderers, to sleep in our own beds and not touch once under Walter Porter's roof.

Once he got back, Walter spent the next few days laying out all the stories from his circus trip. He had not been content just to do his one chore but had taken advantage of his time and position—meeting some of the freaks and riding an elephant, his lifelong ambition. The gorilla was a full-grown male behind bars and bulletproof glass in a cage the size of a bungalow. They advertised him as a bloodthirsty terror—posters showed him dismembering a feathered native. But privately to Walter the circus officials claimed he was a sissie and eager to please. Finally though Walter had to ask to see him. He said "They looked a little pale but led me to the cage, painted white like the thing was in a private hospital. It was back in the corner on a milking stool. When it saw us there, it gave us a minute; then came up slow on its knuckles to the bars. It was black as a hot night—arms like the whole hindquarters of a horse and eyes more human than any of ours, except they didn't blink. I'd have sworn it was a sad swarthy man in a suit if it hadn't suddenly turned its back on me and walked straight over to the toy they had for it—a tractor-tire hung from the roof by a chain, the kind of swing for children you see in farmyards. He didn't sit in it though. He walked to the far side and stared back at me, exclusively *me*. Then with his gray hands, he seized that tire and turned it inside-out as easy as you'd skin a fig—no six men could have done it. The manager was paler still when I faced him, but he said 'That's an old weak tire, Mr. Porter.' I could see he was lying, but I felt so rewarded that I gave full permission to roll that cage on the N & W's tracks."

Douglas asked him why—think of all the mountaineers torn limb-from-limb if the train should wreck and the ape break out.

Walter laughed. "*Exactly.* I gave him the chance—freedom up there in the Shenandoah."

That was the time I felt ashamed. Shame bore down on me hard for a while. The Christmas season had cranked up around us. Walter was as thrilled as a four-year-old, bringing home boxes to hide from me and Douglas. And at school the nuns were stressing the necessity of purging our souls to receive Baby Jesus. I was one of nine non-Catholic girls in my grade, but I craved the chance to beg a priest's pardon and be clean again. I even asked Sister Jeanne d'Arc if I could (she was my science teacher and a tall lean beauty). She said the rules wouldn't stretch that far, but was there anything I wanted *her* to hear? I thanked her, no.

I was already planning a letter to Caroline, saying I hoped to see them Christmas, when Walter changed it all at one blow. He and I mostly got home before Douglas and listened to war news together in the kitchen. On a Thursday evening, word came through that—for the first time—we and the British had sunk more German submarines last month than they'd sunk ships of ours. I thought it was good news but nothing too special. Walter, though, spun around and yelled "Praise God!" By the time Douglas walked in, Walter had the sherry out and poured us all drinks. Then he said "I'm treating us to Christmas at the beach."

Douglas said "Me included?"

Walter said "Bet your boots! You're out of danger now."

Neither one of them asked if I liked the idea, but I knew I did and right away planned how to tell Caroline I'd be here till spring at least. All I said though was "Douglas, what danger were you in?"

Walter said "The *draft*."

Douglas said "I had a touch of T.B. as a child—never knew it till the Army X-rayed my chest. But it's kept me provisional 4-F till now. That could change any day."

Walter said "Hush. They're winning this war—and without your gimp lungs and my asthmatic heart."

In spite of Gaston, I hadn't thought to worry that anybody else might go to the war. Now I realized Walter was too old but Douglas wasn't. And I'm sorry to say that, late in the night, I woke up in my narrow bed and prayed to the dark, "Let Douglas go and not come home—not soon anyhow." I knew as I said it how wrong it was, but I didn't take it back. I was fighting for myself.

* * *

One of the few things I saved from that wreck is a letter of Caroline's—

December 19th

Dear Kate,

We are having a hard freeze here. Bluejays were sitting on the back porch at dawn, hoping for a handout. Only time I ever saw them show any manners, and lucky I had old biscuits to throw them. We did not get to go to the store last week. Holt was down in the back. This freeze has helped him though. He is outdoors now strowing hay so the birds can make warm nests tonight. I asked him how he had lived this long not knowing birds nested to breed, not to sleep. But he said they would learn when they got cold enough. I said that would be after Judgment Day.

Hope it is warmer up there by the water. Holt listened this morning for the Norfolk weather on the radio but they never gave it. I know you are not ten thousand miles off. It just seems like it.

I am sending your Christmas herewith, a white fruitcake. Share it with Walter and Douglas if he is there. I have never understood why everybody loves it but they swear they do. So I made two this year although I doubt anybody will be here to try ours but Holt and Noony (it gives me the headache). Noony said to say hey. Swift and Essie have moved to Littleton closer to her mother. She has always wanted that.

Merry Christmas then. We know how you look and we miss your smile.

Love,
Caroline

She's somebody else I don't have a picture of; but anytime I feel a need to see her face, I read that last line. Nobody else in all my acquaintance would have said *love* by saying *we know how you look.* Again though, I noticed nobody was howling for my actual presence. So by the time school shut down for a week, I was glad to think Walter had made beach plans.

*   *   *

What we had was more like a shack than a cottage. Walter's boss kept it as a duck-hunting place in sight of Back Bay. It was one big room, two dwarf bedrooms, a woodstove, a two-burner hotplate, an outdoor johnny, and a mean-tasting well—all hid in the grass, low to the ground but an easy ten minutes on foot to the ocean. And we had it four days and nights, Christmas weekend. You'd have thought we were going to the North Pole for life, all the stuff Walter brought—everybody's gifts, enough canned goods to last out a siege, towels and sheets. But not enough blankets. I froze at night.

Still it was one of the best times I've had, and in spite of my fears. Strange to say but I've always suspected the goodness was owing to one of my gifts. I've mentioned how much Walter loved dressing me—picking and buying me clothes. When we exchanged packages Christmas Eve night, one of the many things he gave me was a pair of slacks, dark brown. That was years before women (except Katharine Hepburn) wore pants for anything but climbing ladders. So I was thrilled enough to run to my room and put them on by lantern light. There were no mirrors anywhere, and I could see they'd need a little trimming in the seat, but I wore them the rest of the evening. By midnight when Walter lit the eggnog, I had unexpectedly remembered my last train-ride with Frances—the day I changed myself to a boy and felt safe briefly. This time I didn't choose a name or picture myself with red hair. But as Walter toasted us three where we sat on the floor by the stove, I thought "Now I'm something that can never hurt them. I will be a good soul." I felt as lean as a good ladder-round. And I felt we three would celebrate Christmases all our lives, together like this—the parts of one thing, all pulling one way.

Well past midnight I asked a question I'd always wondered. "Was Baby Jesus born in the dark of Christmas morning or on Christmas night?"

Not blinking an eye, Walter looked at his watch and said "This minute. Here he comes. Look hard."

I guess it says a lot about how we were raised, but all three of us went still as wax and *watched*. I was facing the woodstove. Down where the draft was open, there were live coals; and while we were quiet, I had a vision.

I don't mean I dreamed or imagined a sight. It simply took place in the room there beyond me. Mary was lying on strong-smelling straw. Her long dress was bunched around her waist. Her bare knees were up, and the Baby's head was coming out slow as cold used oil—his wet hair was black. The only noise was her hard breathing, and nobody else was nearby to help her. But once I could see the Baby's face—that it was not deformed or bruised—I held my own right hand out toward them. Then they faded off.

Walter said "Bedtime! Santy Claus comes next."

So we broke apart and tried to sleep. I know I was much too calm and pleased to do more than doze in snatches till dawn. And cold as it was, I knew that something bigger than Walter, Douglas, Holt or Caroline—something present but hid—wished me well in this life and offered to help.

The rest of the weekend was also fine. We went everywhere together but the johnny, and no cross word was said that I recall. Long walks on the beach and, on Christmas night, artillery practice from the Norfolk base—Walter reciting poems to the waves (like Holt he knew scads of poems by heart)—Douglas singing all the national anthems of the Allied Powers by a fire we built on the beach the last evening (Walter said "They'll surely arrest us as spies, for flashing facts to Nazi subs")—and more canned corned-beef and cold fig-newtons than I hope to eat again. But I never complained. I thought we were proving how long we could last—together, the whole other world shut out.

Then I almost ruined it the morning we left. We had walked across to the bay to see ducks. Douglas had brought his binoculars, but what we needed was more like a broom—to sweep ducks away. They were there by the thousand, with cranes and geese. And while the cranes were so dignified they looked like statues on a white-trash yard, the ducks mostly made big fools of themselves—climbing aboard each other's rear ends, pumping away, then plowing through the water in wide fast curves like lost torpedoes. But soon Douglas spotted a flock of swans and gave a little speech on their lifelong loyalty as mates and kin. When he'd lent me his glasses and I'd spotted them too, I just said "—Like we plan to be."

Douglas held out his hand.

I thought he meant me and Walter to shake it.

But he said "Let me have my fieldglasses please."

I handed them over.

And then he walked away from us fast, toward the shack.

Walter called his name once. When Douglas didn't turn, Walter stood on with me and the ducks a minute. Then he said "Douglas Lee can't stand to talk *family*."

"He found those swans," I said, "not I."

Then Walter said what had never dawned on me. "Few people on earth are as strong as Kate Vaiden."

The pleasure hit me slowly like a seed set deep in my legs blooming upwards. Then when one more duck did his comedy, I touched Walter's back—"You want me to protect you?" I was halfway confused, halfway a child joking.

But Walter took it straight. He faced me level and said "Please ma'm."

That threw me and I laughed.

So Walter turned too and headed back.

I let him walk ten yards ahead the whole way. It gave me room to get scared again, not about what Douglas and I had done but *orphan* scared—that they'd found my secret (I was stronger than them; I could last alone) and they'd leave me now.

They didn't, not then. We got through the worst of winter in fair shape, everybody working hard and calmed by the season. I'm a lot like something with natural fur. I hibernate most of the dark part of winter, into late February when the days draw out. I'd be better off curled up in a cave. But being half-human I stay upright and pretend I'm awake. Douglas was the same way. He even got to looking like something asleep for eight or ten weeks. Walter kept after him to get a haircut, but Douglas would just say "The first warm week."

That was the third week in February—five straight days as sunny as Spain (I've never seen Spain) and air you'd have paid good money to breathe. On the Wednesday I got home from school as usual in time to start the vegetables for supper (that was still when everybody south of Philadelphia cooked any green thing at least three hours).

On the kitchen counter, waiting, was a note from Walter. It said he had rushed home at one p.m. to get his pajamas. There had been a big trainwreck up in the mountains—a top-secret freight—and he was headed up there to supervise the cleanup, two men known dead. He'd phone or wire us when to expect him. Meanwhile, stay *fed*. Walter always thought that Douglas and I would starve without him; we hated to cook anything but desserts.

I got the vegetables underway. Then I went to my room and locked the door—only time ever—and prayed as hard as a saint in the ring with a lion bearing down. My Christmas vision had stayed strong and clear, though I'd never mentioned it to one living soul (least of all, the nuns). And now I leaned on it. *Lead me through this, the way I should go.* I meant Jesus Christ and maybe His mother—any powers that wanted me safe.

I was led, all right, like a fish on the line (though I never knew who by and never pulled back). Walter had phoned Douglas at work, so Douglas was calm when he got home at six. I'd thought he might say "Save the vegetables; we can eat out." But he just washed his hands and dozed in his chair while I finished cooking macaroni and cheese. I had never cooked an entire meal for a man. It went on smoothly though and Douglas liked it. (One of the lacks of my present life is not having any one person to cook supper for at least four nights a week. There's no nicer means to knit love and trust.)

Then we did my homework. I'd got better at geometry; so I asked Douglas to help me write a theme—two hundred words for Sister Jeanne d'Arc on a Deadly Sin. Being born a Methodist, he didn't know what the Deadly Sins were. When I reeled them off, he said we should each pick one in secret, write a theme, then criticize each other. I'd already picked Glutton, for no reason I understood. And I started work at the breakfast-room table. Douglas got a tablet, wrote down the names of all seven, and went to the living room.

In forty-five minutes I hollered I was ready. He'd finished well before me, and we drew straws to see who read first. I lost and began. I'd written about how sad it was that there were still so many fat people in America, especially children, when half of humanity was starving from the war. Douglas corrected a comma here and there, then laughed and said he'd picked Glutton too. He barely had to look at his tablet when he read.

I wish I still had it or knew it by heart. It was just a little story, called "The Growing Boy." A boy named Carl was put in an orphanage at five years old. Food was scarce and bad, and the rooms were cold. When they let him out at sixteen to make his own way, he ate everything that stood in his path or came too close. Nobody saw him do it; but things disappeared—doors on houses, privet hedges, a red-headed girl that tried to help him, the desk next to him at his place of work. He never got fat but he never got full, and nobody caught him till he died of old age with a big bank-account. The autopsy found all the stuff in him still, dead and shrunk but plain to see. When Douglas finished he said "I think you should hand mine in."

I said "That's cheating."

He said "Mine's true."

"And dumb," I said. "Sister would laugh, then flunk my butt."

Douglas balled up his paper and threw it toward the kitchen floor. His face was blank; it always was when he had strong feelings.

But I was mad too—no reason on earth for any grown man to act that childish, and more than once now. I stepped to the kitchen, picked up his theme, and threw it in the trash. Then I finished cleaning up. Walter didn't call and Douglas never came in and offered to help. When the last dish was dried, I called out "You ready for your ice cream now?" Douglas didn't answer so I served myself, enjoyed it as always, then went to the living room. No sign of Douglas. A gentle breeze would have left more trace. It hit me hard—*You're here, flat alone.*

I'd never spent a whole night alone in my life, with no other human in reach of my voice. I was back in Holt and Caroline's yard in the pitchdark, crouched by my mother's Penny Show. I thought "I can try to call Tim Slaughter," and I went toward my room to find his card. From the hall I could see that the door to Douglas's room was shut—Douglas and Walter's. No light showed though and not a sound came. I turned back to the kitchen and shamed myself by hiding the butcher knife deep in the pantry and taking the paring knife with me to my room (now it seems like good sense, no shame at all). Then calm as I could, I washed myself, shut my own door, and stretched out in the dark.

At first I was scared—not just of Douglas, if he was still there, but of all that hollow space above me and all that quiet. I knew I hadn't deserved my life, but I didn't pray again. I've always thought you can wear God out—ask hard but ask once. So I did the next calmest thing. I named the humans who would fight for me against any foe—Caroline, Walter, Fob, and Holt. Despite the fact they were miles away, I repeated the list several hundred times; and then I was out. Young as I was, I slept like a cinder-block wall in the moonlight. And if I dreamed, God helped me forget it.

But who gave permission for what happened next? Weak gray daylight woke me up at six—still no noise. I must have lain on my back five minutes, thanking my stars I'd come through the night, before I suspected my door was open. I looked and it was, on the dim empty hall. So not really thinking, I spoke to the air like I often did. I said the word "Help"—not loud, just a statement I wanted to make. Never dawned on me it would travel past the door, and I was too sleepy to wonder who'd opened it. But before my mouth was halfway shut, I could hear bare footsteps. That finally woke me but my heart was calm (what I did, I did calmly).

It was Douglas, in lemon-yellow pajamas. He was the only man I ever knew who could sleep a long night and still have pressed pajamas at dawn; he rested that deeply. So here he stood now with his face all hazy but dressed fresh as jonquils.

He said "You in pain?"

"Not yet," I said. "You just wake up?"

Douglas nodded yes.

"Who opened my door?"

He said "Not I."

"Is Walter back?" I knew he wasn't; Walter loose in a room was as quiet as a gander.

Douglas said "Praise God, not to my knowledge, no." Then he turned to leave.

It was me that stopped him. I've never known why. I was still being led, I can swear that much. To this day I've never felt sorry for a second. I said "Help" again.

Douglas stopped where he was, down the hall toward the toilet. He said "You in pain?"

I said "Not yet."

So he came on back and, this time, never even paused in the door.

But I'd shucked my nightgown well before he reached me.

He said "Is this your idea of help?" His knees were skimming the side of the bed.

I said "Don't it seem like help to you?" I remember making the grammatical error.

Douglas said "No ma'm."

"Then shave," I said. I was naked as a newt but under the cover. One thing I can do is stop on a dime, whoever is leading.

He stood there a minute, then knelt where he'd stood.

I thought "All right. He just wants to pray."

But he faced me frank as a month-old boy. He said "Can you unbutton this coat?" He meant his pajamas.

"You crippled?" I said.

Douglas nodded and smiled. "Need help anyhow."

I gave it freely, from that instant on. He had never seemed old to me—a little short of thirty—but he got a lot younger the longer we worked. And within half an hour, he seemed no older than me or Gaston (he'd got his haircut). The same things pleased him and made him laugh. I was the one though that watched the clock. Finally I had to say "It's quarter-past seven"—it was get up now or forget school and work. I wanted him to choose.

He said "We both could call in sick."

"We could," I said. "What if Walter gets back?"

Douglas by then was facing the window, and the sun was on him. He said "Fine by me."

I spent a whole minute watching his face. He looked very nearly as good as the light, but he never met my eyes. So it slid out of me, natural as birdsong. "You planning to try to kill him again?"

"Say *we*," Douglas said.

"Sir?" I said.

"There's two people lying here, both of them grown."

I'd been propped on my elbows beside him. I fell back, kept myself apart, and tried to think how awful I'd been—here in Walter's place, in the world in general. But shame wouldn't come. Whatever had got me through my life—God, I had to believe—still wished me well, since Christmas at least. And young as I was, I guessed that day what one main trait would set me apart from here on out and make me an outlaw of sorts forever—I could seldom feel shame.

Understand me now. I couldn't lie there and risk hurting Walter's feelings if he suddenly appeared. I'd yet to meet anything I wanted to hurt, even poor Swift Porter. But also I'd do every last thing I needed to—do it and be glad. I said "Well, me—I'm going to school."

Douglas didn't answer that. He lay on, facing my one high window, through the time it took me to dress and eat. When I came back to get my coat and leave, he was still there; his eyes had still never shut. I said "I guess I'll see you this evening."

At last he faced me and said "Beg your pardon."

I said "For what?" and was really sincere.

Douglas said "Just say you pardon me please."

"Righto," I said (because of the war, British slang was popular). Then I left, not knowing whether he would get up. I even wondered if he might kill himself. But it took me something like forty-five minutes—we were singing a hymn at morning chapel—before I suddenly knew I was pregnant. I don't mean I wondered or guessed or dreaded; I *knew*. No voice spoke to me. No statue in the church leaned down with the news. I just felt a child in the base of my belly, about the size of a dry grain of rice. And I thought "This is going to change more lives than you ever changed before." At first that thrilled me. But as we marched back behind Sister Margaret to civics class, I went cold as ice. I had to grind down on my strong back-teeth to hold my head still and work through the day.

Stuck in the door when I got home was a telegram. Because of all the war casualties, the sight of one of those yellow envelopes was always bad. This one of course was from Walter to say he was still detained and would phone us that night at nine. I stood in the living room and thought how awful I should feel. All I really felt was tired. But before I lay down, I decided one sure thing—Douglas and I were eating out tonight, and I would pay the check.

He'd been back half an hour, and outside it was dark, before I woke up. I could hear him reading the paper down the hall. I washed my eyes and walked in to meet him. You'd have thought we ran a little knit-goods shop on a deadend street and were just home, waiting for our model children to show up loaded with gifts they'd made us at school—bookends, placemats.

Douglas said "Hungry yet? I see the stove's cold."

"You're the growing boy," I said. "I'm taking us out." Something in me was howling to hurt him again.

But he smiled. "Has Walter called?"

It turned out Douglas hadn't seen the telegram though I'd left it on a table right inside the door. Once he heard the news, he slowed down a little but still seemed nicer than he'd been since Christmas. I could no more imagine him naked in my bed, rooting deep in my body, than I could have foretold the atom bomb (which was already warming up, next-door in Oak Ridge, Tennessee). So I said "I'm buying us a bait of chow mein. Get your glad rags on."

Douglas never minded using anybody else's cash, but he did change into his dark blue suit.

The Shanghai Garden had wonderful booths. They didn't have private doors, but the way-in was a baffle, so nobody passing could stare in at you. Douglas and I were both starved as bears, and we ate our way through a hill of chicken chow mein with very little talk but frequent smiles. It took us so long that, once we'd finished (I passed up the lychees), I said we'd better get home for Walter's call.

Douglas said "He'll keep on trying till he gets us."

I said I had a lot of homework to do.

He said "I don't plan to kidnap you, Kate. We're in no big rush."

So I poured our fiftieth cups of tea and sat back to wait. At first Douglas watched our lantern in silence like the red silk tassels might burst into song, and I suddenly thought I'd speak my mind. I'd say I knew I was pregnant; what now? But facing him there—that real and that strange—I figured I was more than half-crazy so I held off.

That was when Douglas said "Ask me anything you need to."

For the first time with him, I felt like a child—a big world of secrets he knew and I didn't. Anything I asked would show my ignorance. So I laughed. "Will Judgment Day come in our lifetime?" (Since the war began, every radio preacher was forecasting Judgment; I'd sometimes sit still and listen for trumpets.)

He said "I gave up on God years ago."

I'd heard of atheists but hadn't known I knew one. I had a quick chill, like hearing my best friend was really a spy. I said "I doubt that ruined God's day"—I meant to be pleasant and change the tune.

Douglas said "He sure as hell tried to ruin me."

I said "But then He sent Walter to save you."

Douglas said "Thank Him for me, if you migrate to Heaven."

I hadn't heard that much meanness in a voice since I last saw Swift. I said "I thought you truly loved Walter."

Douglas said "Is that your question?"

I hadn't thought it was, but I said "All right."

He went back to watching the lantern again and sent his whole speech in that direction. "Walter thinks he loves me. It's the main thing he thinks. I think I'm thankful to Walter for my life—I'd have died long ago—but I also think I've about paid him off. He's had all but eleven years of me. I think now it's *time*."

I knew he meant me to ask "Time for what?" But I'd just been slammed broadside by the guess that he meant *time to marry* and that *I'd be the bride*. It didn't quite scare me, but it stunned my mind. I said the first fool thing my tongue could manage—"No time like the present."

And Douglas said "For what?"

So I laughed. "Whatever a growing boy craves." I ought to have been drawn and quartered on the spot.

He waited awhile—by then he was facing me—and finally said "I doubt you understand the whole story here."

I said "You sure I need to understand?" I halfway knew men could love each other and share whole lives—I'd watched Fob and Tot—but no one had drawn me a plain picture of it, and I drew back from that. (In general I was acting like most people then, very different from now. We halfway knew everything people did and didn't really mind and left them free. Now everybody wants a satellite photo of everybody else's private actions, then broadcasts the news.)

Douglas sat far forward; I could feel his clean breath. He said "Tell me when you need to."

I thought "I'll be needing to know a lot soon—and not about Walter." I meant, about having and raising a child. But all I did was look at my new watch and say we should get back to take Walter's call.

He called on the absolute stroke of nine, and Douglas made me answer. The wreck had been worse than even he expected. War secrets were strewn all up and down the valley.

I asked were any gorillas loose?

He said "Several dozen" and that he wouldn't be home till late tomorrow; were we fat and sassy?

I said "Let Douglas tell you."

He and Douglas laughed through another five minutes, which calmed me enough to start my Latin. By half-past ten I'd finished and was too tired to want ice cream. So Douglas ate without me; and I turned in, passing out in two minutes. The last ten bombs of the war could have gone off right at my door and not touched my rest, not the first three hours.

But then I woke up, fully alert and not knowing why. I checked first thing and my door was still shut. So I knew I'd waked myself. Or that something not human had called my name. I lay on peacefully and waited a good while. No voice spoke though, in my head or out. The next thing I wondered was, could a baby call me—just a one-day-old? I knew that was foolish; but I pressed my whole belly gently, in hopes some contact would start. And there, exactly on the center line just under my navel, I found a hard spot that was bound to be him, still small as a grain (I was that convinced and I knew it was a boy).

Next thing, the whole dark world fell on me. The chill I had felt at school wasn't fear, more like a huge surprise. But now all the facts—me being sixteen, unwed, no parents (in a time when unwed mothers weren't showered with gifts on TV)—they all piled on me so I could barely breathe. To save myself I thought "Kate, you're crazy. You're no more pregnant than Admiral 'Bull' Halsey." That didn't work long. Next I tried to pray. For the first time ever, my words were blocked by the plain plaster ceiling. So I shivered again a few hard minutes, hoping for tears. I thought tears would tire me back down to sleep. I was dry as a stove; I had to seek help. So next I stood up and walked in to Douglas.

The instant my foot touched the sill, he said "Kate."

I've already told how I enjoyed Gaston, and I told the flat truth. Maybe since he and I were so close in age, I felt good knowing I was being used (and gently enough) by something like a school friend that had a big problem with his actual health and needed just me, every last bit of me. To be sure, touching somebody strong as Gaston Stegall—with eyes like a lion—all down his skin and bearing his weight was no pain either, whatever any part of my own body felt.

But Douglas Lee was a different story. Despite him seeming to grow younger sometimes, I knew he was thirteen years my senior. So right off, there was that fence between us—me thinking he knew much more than me and was testing my mind and body each instant for things it lacked. *Testing* not *using*. He took a polite and quiet care not to hurt me or leave me stranded and cold. And that last night, in his quilted bed, he said worlds more about what we were doing than Gaston did in years—how he'd dreamed of this so long and how I'd been sent (since Douglas was an atheist, I wondered *Who by?*). But he never said he wanted more than one part of me.

And looking back now, I can *see* Gaston—feel Gaston on me, in me like sun on my hide through days and nights. Douglas seems more like a light cotton-spread thrown over my legs for a short nap, then folded forever—or a shovel of coals.

Still we worked through most of the rest of that night. We didn't sleep again till first light raked across Walter's bed beside us. We were facing it by then; and without speaking of it, we stretched on our backs towards the black ceiling and slept till time for school and his job. At breakfast we spoke like brother and sister. I couldn't have sworn we'd ever touched anywhere much below the neck. And all Douglas said about future time was "We'll make Walter feel extra welcome tonight."

I said "I thought you were breaking free from Walter."

Douglas ate one whole strip of bacon, then said "I say a whole lot I mean *at the time*; then the time moves on." He smiled like he might have just made me a present of the secret of life.

And I smiled back.

It was perfect weather by the time I really knew, by the time I had full proof from my body that a child was working. In the weeks before, things had pretty much settled to normal again. We all came and went on our own little rounds and gathered at night like a clutch of birds. Walter kept on remembering new tales of the wreck and the tough mountaineers who had hindered a rescue. Douglas was quiet as usual, reading mostly.

I was caught up at school in the long days of Lent. I had given up Baby Ruth candybars and romance movies and was reading, over and over, the stories of Jesus's last days in all four gospels. They can still flat shiver my timbers to the sockets, and then I was even more sensitive than now. (You go read the story in Mark 14—Him alone in the garden that last night, begging to live—and see if your own problems don't shrink a notch.)

We spent the last part of Good Friday in church; and everything beautiful was wrapped up in purple, to mourn the crucifixion happening there just over the altar before our eyes. The nuns had advised us to see through the eyes of the holy women at the foot of the cross, and some of the girls said they managed that. But I stayed on the kneeler three hours; and what I keep the memory of, deep in my palms and the soles of my feet, is how iron nails would feel in your skin.

I don't mean I came out bruised or bleeding or got a second vision, but I gave it my all and have never been sorry. I knew it was what had set me free to live on earth and hunt a better life than my sad parents or the rest of my kin. I also know—saying that much now—how nearly crazy, or at least self-struck, that makes me sound. I had after all so far deceived my cousin with his closest friend and was growing a bastard right under my lungs. But I told him first—Walter, once I was sure.

That was Easter Sunday and, like I said, a glorious day. I had begged Walter not to buy me any new clothes (he pouted but agreed). And I'd asked him to take me to a Catholic church but not the one at school. He said "Baby Child, they have the worst *music*," but he picked Sacred Name in a rich neighborhood, and we drove there—no Douglas of course. The place was packed with families dressed to kill. The music had no more tune than a hinge, and Walter didn't know when to stand or kneel. Still, there in the priest's hands, they had the resurrection—real flesh and blood. I explained that to Walter as we left at the end.

He already knew and said he believed it. "I was baptized a Methodist, but Protestants are pitiful—they've missed the real boat and are out in rafts in all this storm. If I had good sense, I'd join the Catholics quick."

That was one of my favorite things he'd said. And as I thought about it, riding through the sun, it freed my tongue; so I told him the truth. We had paused at a Stop sign for two black women, handsome as orchids. As we moved on forward, I turned to Walter and heard my voice say "I'm bound to be pregnant—me and Douglas." Then I thought we might wreck or the car blow up or Walter just die at the wheel of heart failure.

But he looked dead-ahead and shifted down to turn a corner and, once we were safe, said "I thought maybe so."

"Why's that?" I said.

"You been looking so good." (People used to believe women looked better pregnant; I've always thought they looked like wash-ups from a drowned rowboat.)

That was almost worse than the car exploding. I streamed sudden tears.

For once Walter didn't. He still didn't face me, but he said "Don't worry. How long has Douglas known?"

I said "He hasn't got the least idea."

Walter said "When is it?"

"November, I guess—near next Thanksgiving." I'd begun to feel like we had cut loose from standard human guywires and were rising too fast where the air was too thin. I said what I thought would bring us back down. "You don't want me to go through with this, do you?"

Walter said "Who'd stop you?"

I'd thought it out before, from what I'd heard at school. "The biggest navy town on earth has got ways and means."

Walter just said "Hush" and drove on in silence till we got nearly home. Then he touched me at last, his knuckles on my knee, and met my eyes an instant. "Can I tell Douglas?"

"Today?" I said.

He nodded. "After dinner. Let me take him to ride. You can say you're sleepy."

I knew we were still ripping up through clouds, way past Earth now. But I told myself Walter Porter was grown, thirty-six years old, and had got this far still able to move. I said *"That's the truth"*— I was tired as a wheel.

Walter and Douglas, when they first got to Norfolk, had roomed with an old widow. She'd died before the war, and they took lillies to her grave every Easter. So when they stood up after dinner to do that, I begged off exhausted (it was three o'clock). Douglas asked was I sick. Walter said "Sick of school," and they left without me.

Strange as it sounds, I did go to sleep—not a minute of worry. I'd meant to step out and walk in the good light, but nothing woke me till nearly dark. Then the doorbell rang. I sat up, thinking the men were back and would answer; but no, the air was still. So I smoothed my hair and trudged to the front (that was years before anybody hesitated to open a solid door on the world).

An elderly man in a black suit and tie was standing there, holding a huge potted lily. He looked like an undertaker and my flesh crawled.

I asked could I help him?

He grinned. "I'm years past help, Kate. But happy Easter still." He held out the lily.

I stepped back, baffled and a little spooked. But the lily kept coming, so I had to take it.

He said "Tim Slaughter, your taxi man—you forgot me already?"

I all but melted; he was that good to see. I begged his pardon, saying I'd been asleep, and asked him in.

He said "Where's your folks?" (the place was dim behind us).

"At the cemetery but they should have been back. Come in and sit down."

Tim thought awhile. "No, I go on at six. I just found the flower at a sale down the road, and I thought about you."

Suddenly I felt I couldn't stay there alone. I said "You don't plan to work in that suit. You're lying to me, Tim."

He waited again, then took a step back. "I couldn't trust myself, locked up indoors with you." He laughed. "Understand—I don't mean to brag. I'm no Easter biddy but you look too good."

Nobody had mentioned my looks in so long, I welcomed the lie. So I smiled. "We could leave the door cracked open."

Tim said "You've grown too much since summer."

I hadn't grown an inch, not yet anyhow. But I almost told him the whole story there—just how much I might have to spread by fall—

but something in his sharp face and thin wide shoulders told me he'd turn and vanish for good. I said "I've got a long way still to go."

He wanted to know were they good to me here.

I said "No complaints."

"But you ain't thrilled to death?"

"What makes you think that?"

Tim said "—You asking an old codger in."

I said "You look fine."

"I aimed to," he said.

By then I knew I would either have to beg him to sit with me or send him off. So I took him at his word and started goodbye. "I've still got your card."

Tim nodded. "I told you you'd need it—remember?" Then he grinned, looked back toward the weak ceiling light, and tapped a front tooth. It was new since summer—gold. He said it was his Christmas present to himself.

I said "My aunt's got a mouthful; I feel right at home."

He said "Then Tim Slaughter don't work in vain."

I had lit-up the place and, on faith, made a lot of batter for waffles before anybody else turned up to join me. Walter and Douglas walked in at six, not a word about where they had been for so long. And not one reference to my big news or Douglas's reaction. All of us acted a little damped-down, but that was just normal for a Sunday night.

So when Douglas sat down by the radio and Walter drew dishwater, I went to my bed again and stretched out. With them back near me, I'd stopped being scared. I was tireder though than I'd ever been before (I'd thought adults wouldn't get so tired), and I dozed right off. My door was half-shut, but my lamp was on.

In a while Walter tapped and said my name. He was in his bathrobe.

I said "Ice cream?"

He touched a finger to his lips for quiet. "Too late. I called you an hour ago; now Douglas is asleep" (Walter and I had Easter Monday off, but Douglas had to work). Then he stepped inside and shut the door.

I moved to make him a space on my bed.

He sat by my feet; then slipped my shoes off and kneaded my toes, which he knew I liked.

I finally had to say "Where was that cemetery? I thought you had died."

Walter smiled "Oh no, but it is out a ways." He took up my toes again like nothing else mattered in the present world.

I said "You going to make me beg?"

"For what?"

"For Douglas—what he said about me. Did you tell him?"

Walter took the time to cover my feet with a black wool afghan. Then he went to the chair. "We took a long ride, as you probably guessed—the ferry to Portsmouth and back more than once. Douglas asked first thing how you were so sure."

I said "I'm a girl. I'm trained to know." My voice sounded mad.

Walter said "Whoa now. We don't doubt your word. But you need to see a doctor. I'll take you tomorrow."

I said "You both hope I'm wrong, I know."

He said "That *would* iron out a few wrinkles."

"But I'm not wrong," I said, "and *if* I'm not?"

He was calmer than I'd ever seen him before. "Douglas Lee wants to marry you."

That idea really hadn't crossed my mind—more than once anyhow and then in a hurry. So I laughed automatically, in Walter's face. "And we'd live with you?"

Walter waited a good while. "I'm a neat soul, sure. We could find a bigger place."

I knew I'd hurt him, but I forged right on. "Why is Douglas asleep now and you here talking?"

He knew a quick answer. "I'm your cousin, Kate. I caused you to come here."

"You didn't," I said. "I've caused myself for some years now—me and God Almighty. You don't owe me the next *meal*, Walter, much less a home and husband." Then I thought "Well, listen to me run on. I'm Dan Vaiden's child." But I couldn't say that.

And Walter didn't think it, or blame me at least. He stood, came back, and sat on the bed. This time he didn't touch me, but he managed to smile. "I may be wrong—I usually am—but I thought we'd settled one thing at Christmas. *We loved each other.* You, Douglas, and me."

I nodded, though I also recalled Douglas leaving the family of swans.

"Then what good reason could anybody give against the plan of us three spending our whole lives together? We're nothing but a family; they're common as beds."

I said "My reason is, nobody asked *me*."

"I'm sorry. I thought you expressed your feelings Christmas, and Thanksgiving too. You blessed us three; I took you at your word."

He had me there. I knew every word of mine was ruining some hope he'd cherished all afternoon, or maybe for years. Had he come to Macon more than three years ago—and urged me ever since, to join him here—with some such plan? Had he made Douglas do what Douglas did? Once I'd run through that, I saw it was crazy. But I knew I'd better not talk again tonight. I said "I'm old enough to make this child. I'm sixteen though, not sixty-five. I'm mixed-up and tired, and I need to be quiet."

He nodded. "You trust I love you, Kate?"

God knew I didn't but I said "Thank you, Walter."

He stood up and then said the best thing I'd heard since Gaston's last letter—"Don't ever thank me. You're a lovable child."

I almost believed it.

Dr. Wilburn said yes, I seemed to be right (they didn't have dead-certain tests back then). He'd been Walter's doctor for many years, and he called Walter in once he'd finished checking me. He said "Your niece is expecting a child; and it's due next November, around Thanksgiving. She ought to see a doctor every two or three weeks. Will she be living here?"

Walter said "She's my cousin. But yes, she'll be here—she's in school till June, at St. Rose of Lima."

Dr. Wilburn faced me, which he'd barely done before, and said "The baby will be showing by then. Will the nuns let you stay?"

I clearly remember not liking "*the* baby." I said "*My* baby. No sir, they won't"—though for all their talk about purity, it hadn't dawned on me till that bad minute how this would strike the nuns.

Walter said "I'll get her a correspondence course; she'll graduate."

Dr. Wilburn said "Is that the way she wants it?"

Walter said "We think this is how it's going to go." He didn't say a word about who *we* was, and neither one of them had looked at me again.

I thought "They are solving this, step by step like the F.B.I. But I'm not a crime, and I doubt I love Douglas." Still I kept my mouth shut, accepted the diet charts and vitamin samples; and once we'd stepped back out into daylight, I felt like I'd felt more than one time before—an arrow shot from somebody else's bow, flinging away with no other aim than to go far, far.

That evening I was in my room with the door shut when Douglas got home. I'd had a long nap and by then was darning a tear in my school skirt. My mind had somehow decided I'd walk on to school every day till a sister met me in the door and said "Stop"; I'd lasted through worse. I was also running through the names of girls my age and guessing which one would notice my belly first and ask the big question and what would I say? Douglas and Walter talked in the kitchen—I could just hear voices—and at six twenty-five, Douglas knocked on my door. I can still see the hands on my loud alarm-clock. I said "All right."

And then he was there. I knew it was Douglas by his hair and his tie, but everything else about him was changed. He looked ten pounds lighter, and his eyes had grown till they seemed like things that could start brushfires if the sun struck through them. His long lips were parted, but he stood and didn't speak.

So I didn't either. I kept on darning.

Finally he said "Let's ride to the beach."

"For what?" I said. "It's suppertime. I'm hungry."

"We could eat out there."

I said "The beach never did much for me."

Douglas laughed and looked even stranger. And better, like something *sent* bearing precious gifts. But he stayed in the door.

I thought I loved him, for the first sure time. I thought "All right. I'll have a life with him."

He said "You think we're too close kin to be man and wife?"

I said "You're kin to the Porters, not *my* side. You and I don't share one corpuscle."

"We seem to now," he said.

I guessed he meant the baby—us meeting in the baby. I said "All right."

He said "Is that your answer?"

"To what?"

"My question. Kate, I asked could we marry."

I'd sewed so long my seam was stiff. I stuck my needle back into the spool, and then I said "Is this your idea?"

Douglas waited. "It is now."

I said "When and where?"

"I'll have to find out. Walter's going to get all the answers tomorrow—whose consent we need, blood tests, all that. Maybe somewhere nice like Williamsburg."

"That's also the state crazy-house," I said.

He laughed again.

So I said "All right." I was numb but not sad. I thought "In a few days this will seem happy."

The next fact is, Douglas turned round and left—just back to the kitchen, for now at least.

I lay down again and listed a dozen things I wished he had said. The only one that could really have helped was some natural form of *Till death do us part*. What I've wanted all my life is the earnest sound of that from somebody.

But at supper we all said normal things. And from then on till bedtime, a witness would have thought nothing big had happened

here since Walter and Douglas ran away as young boys. I kept thinking Walter at least would start planning, but it wasn't till after my
light was out that he opened my door and said "Baby Child, I'll start
in tomorrow on all our details." I told him "Good" but I felt otherwise. They were *my* details or Douglas's and mine; and since Douglas showed so little intention to do the work that was his and mine,
then I'd take over. Of course I didn't think it through that clearly;
but before I slept I knew I was just Kate Vaiden again, a thing people
took up and then put down. It made me almost happy in the dark.

By morning I still didn't know what that meant or where it would
lead. I was in sight of school before it hit me. And what brought it
on was the sight of a telephone booth ahead. I had the money and I
had Tim Slaughter's card in my purse. Calmly as if I was praying for
naturally curly hair, I stepped in and called him—sure he wouldn't
answer. What I got was a woman, and that set me back. But she
turned out just to be the dispatcher and said Tim was driving up at
that same instant. I thought "This is fate" and waited two minutes.
Girls that knew me were stopping outside the booth and asking in
signs if I was O.K. I told them all yes and almost believed myself
when Tim answered.

He said "Yes ma'm?"

"Tim, it's me," I said.

"I hoped it was. Where you standing at?"

I said "How'd you know I was *standing* anywhere?"

"Your voice is weak."

"Then I need you," I said. "How busy are you now?"

Tim said "At your service."

So I gave him an address three streets away, to avoid more girls,
and walked straight toward it. He was there in five minutes. I still
didn't know where I wanted to go. But when Tim had told me to sit
up front, I had the first idea. I asked to go to Walter's.

Tim said "You sick?"

Then I had the second idea. "No, I need to get a few duds
together."

Tim said "Wash day?"

"Train day," I said. It had just come to me.

"Where to this time?"

I saw I didn't know, and I let a few blocks of houses go by. They were already baking in beautiful light—healing, I thought (though I didn't think *from what?*). So I said the truth. "I wish I knew."

He'd stopped at a light and was studying me; I didn't turn to face him. Then he moved on and said "You will. Don't worry."

I suddenly filled up with thanks like a rain. I said "Tim, please take over again—just today, till I know. I can pay for your time." I'd still barely touched my savings from Fob, and since leaving Macon I always kept ten dollars with me.

Tim laughed. "My time is too precious to buy." But from that instant on, he calmly took over.

He wouldn't come inside Walter's with me but waited at the curb. I still had no suitcase of my own, but at Christmas Walter had lent me the Gladstone bag he brought to Norfolk with him. I half-filled that with a change of clothes, the vitamin samples, and my Latin book; then I took a fast look through all the rooms for anything else of mine that mattered. When I couldn't find one single urgent thing, I thought of Gaston's foxhorn I'd left in Macon; and I craved to touch that. But then I left, with no note or signal.

Tim stepped out and stood when he saw me at the door. He let me bring my bag through the yard and down the brick steps. Once I was on the public sidewalk, he offered to help me. I guess I was free by then, in his eyes.

The house was little and low as a hut in *Hansel and Gretel*, but it hid on an unpaved alley toward Portsmouth, and Tim owned it outright since his wife's death (it had been her birthplace). I figured what it was before the cab stopped, but I went on and said "Who on earth lives here?"

Tim said "You do now—for an hour or for life."

I was too young to feel the ache in that, but I'd been well-raised enough to say "Many thanks."

He said "You recollect what I told you Sunday?"

"Yes," I said. "You aren't safe cooped-up."

"With you," Tim said, "indoors with you."

I wasn't disgusted or scared, either one. But I thought I owed him the truth, or half of it. "I'm waiting on a baby."

He sat a good while, then said "*That's* some news."

"I can go right on to the station," I said. I didn't sound mad.

Tim said "How come you didn't bring your flower?"

I didn't understand.

"Your Easter lily. We could plant it out back." He pointed to a backyard big as a Jeep and high in bamboo.

I said "I wouldn't plant *Hitler* there."

Tim said "Well, I hope you like it better by dark." He opened his door.

It'd never once crossed my mind to spend a night. I thought I'd say as much.

But Tim was out, opening my door and giving a schoolboy-bow of welcome.

So what I said was "I need to send a wire." I didn't know *to who?*

There were two dark rooms, a kitchen, a bath, and a fourteen-year-old English setter named Lindy that was three-fourths human (she was named for Lindbergh because she lived solo). Everywhere was clean and bare as porcelain. The first thing I said was "You've got a good maid."

Tim said "Me. I can't stand junk. When my old woman died after Pearl Harbor, I shipped her clothes and the two pictures of her to my daughter in Texas. Then I cooked up a big bonfire out back with everything else I'd never use again—cardtables, a lifetime collection of shoes, feather pillows. Hope you don't use pillows?"

I said they were something I could take or leave, but had he burned the phone?

He hadn't, though it looked like a piece of the Ark and was lost back under the front-room daybed. He told me to call any place in the world.

I still had no idea where to go but I said "Yokohama."

Tim said "Fine, if you know a kind Jap."

A girl in my grade had made me a present of a green address-book, and I'd recorded the ten names I knew. I fished it out then and prayed for inspiration. My thumb went straight to the Bs—Daphne Baxter. She'd have to be back with her parents by now on the farm near Boykins; and she'd saved me once (or her husband had but he'd be at sea, if not beneath it). So she would be it. I sent her a wire— *Can I come down for a short visit now? Need answer today.* I gave Tim's address, charged it to his phone, then hung up and tried to pay him on the spot.

He said "Just work it off. Fix me my dinner."

It wasn't ten o'clock, but I had to wait somewhere. I went to the icebox and checked for supplies. He had enough bologna for a team of starved huskies, a load of light bread, and a big jar of mustard. That was absolutely all; it looked like Oklahoma. But I made us four sandwiches and Tim boiled coffee.

When we'd eaten he said "Your friend won't answer for a long time, Kate—Boykins is *country*. They'll reach her on muleback tomorrow at the soonest. You want to wait here?"

I hadn't thought of that. I was suddenly tired enough to die, upright. I said "I'd thank you. You go on to work. I bet Daphne answers in plenty of time for the six-thirty train" (I still knew the trains).

To my surprise Tim nodded agreement. He stepped to the bathroom, left the door open, and rinsed his mouth. Then I heard little clicks as he trimmed his fingernails. Then he came back silent as a cat in velvet. I was washing the plates. He touched my back between my shoulders and I jumped hard. He said "Steady now."

I repeated I was tired.

He stepped back and said "I understand that. I'm leaving you awhile. Just tell me one thing—you're sixteen, ain't you?"

"Seventeen in two months."

"You ain't in trouble?"

"What kind?" I said.

He was serious as a senator. "—Hurt anybody, stole anything big."

"No sir," I said.

He smiled then, welcome as a dogwood bud. "Understand—I could be in jail for this. Hiding a thief, kidnaping a child, statutory any-thing-you-want-to-name."

I thought through that. "You're safe," I said. "I'm an innocent girl." The relief in Tim Slaughter's pale-blue eyes all but convinced me I hadn't lied.

He hadn't cranked the cab before I was out—deep asleep on the front-room daybed under a quilt with the phone nearby. If I dreamed, it was nothing punishing or true; so I slept till a little past three o'clock, nearly school-closing time. When I woke, the main thing I felt was the scary thrill of playing hooky. I got up, washed my face, and made a sandwich (my third of the day).

Then I went to the bedroom and searched Tim's bureau. I wasn't ashamed. He'd trusted me here and I wanted to know him. The drawers weren't much help with that—just neat low stacks of under-wear, tan socks, and four white shirts. Under the shirts were two worn magazines with pictures of women. Titles like *Midnight Cat* or *Pink Lace* with healthy grown girls in fur stoles and pumps, tame compared to the teenaged slabs of sockeye salmon boys buy at any crossroads today. I'd known they existed but had never seen any, so I studied them slowly till I saw they were harmless.

But when I re-hid them, it suddenly struck me—Western Union hadn't called with Daphne's answer. I wanted to phone them and check. Then I suspected Walter might have found out I was missing, called the police, and they'd be watching the wires and trains. So I waited in misery but not sitting still—I mopped Tim's kitchen and bathroom floors and oiled his one nice thing, an old oak rocker. Near four-thirty the telephone rang; I lost two pounds in the rush to answer.

It was Tim, in a booth at Hampton Roads. "Need a ride anywhere?"

I said "Not yet. My wire hasn't come."

"What you want for supper?"

I admitted eating another sandwich and said I wasn't hungry.

"But you'll starve by morning," he said. "Like steak?"

"Yes," I said and wondered what blackmarket meat he'd found. Then I knew I was spending a night at Tim's.

I spent thirteen. Daphne wired next morning to say her father was deathly sick; could I please wait? Tim was there when the word came and saw me break down. All I could say was "Now I don't know." I'd been so sure Daphne meant good luck, that I could spend a few days with her on the farm and watch my troubles dissolve in the light—I hadn't thought *how*? I'd still felt led. Now in Tim's front room, with the phone in my hands, I doubted there was any next step to take.

Tim waited and then said "What don't you know?"

"What happens now."

He said "You go right on. You're strong."

I said "Go where?" and thought I knew his answer.

But he said "Anywhere your smart brain takes you."

I said "Will I get you in any trouble here?"

Tim said "You tell me the truth yesterday?—no warrants out on you?"

"Lord, no," I said. "But I may be missing."

"You can't call your cousin and say you're safe? Whatever he's done, he'll be sick by now."

I said "What he's done is try to be kind."

"You saying he ain't laid a mean finger on you?"

I said he'd rather fall down and eat dirt.

"Weren't there two men there?"

"Yes," I said, "—both harmless as leaves."

Tim said "Then call up the one you've hurt the most. I'll go while you do it. Then I'll come back at noon. If you're still waiting I'll do what you say."

It was laugh or cry again. So I tried a smile. "Tim, how long you plan to put up with my mess?"

"Till Judgment," he said. He took out a card and pencil from his shirt and signed his name laboriously—"*Timothy Slaughter*" with quotation marks. Then he handed it over.

I finally laughed. "This your autograph?"

"No, my oath," he said. He pointed to the card. "That swears me to you."

I said "Oh Tim, I never asked for this."

"You got it," he said. "One man'll stay true."

When he'd left I telephoned Walter's on the chance he might still be there, waiting for news. And he answered at once. I said "Walter, this is Kate Vaiden and I'm safe."

"Thank Jesus," he said. "I haven't shut an eye. Where are you, Baby?"

I said "I'm sitting down, warm and dry."

"In Norfolk? At the beach?" (He knew I was local—long distance back then sounded like the sea floor).

I said "You tell the Law I was gone?"

"I was giving you a whole day to turn back up. No, I just told Douglas."

"And what did he say?"

"He knows you've been nervous—"

I said "He's wrong. I'm calm as the pavement."

Walter said "I'm glad. Now tell me where you are."

"I can't," I said. "I need quiet to think."

Walter said "Sit quiet and think yourself *bald*, but keep yourself *well*." He stopped and then said "I know where you are."

"I doubt you do."

"With your taxi driver. Well, he's got kind eyes."

I said "You don't know his name or address, but I guess you could hunt us down pretty fast."

"You want me to?"

I wondered for three seconds. "No. Thank you, no."

Walter said "You know *I* ran away once. Want to say why?"

I thought "The reason is, nobody there wants me." But I couldn't say that. I just said "I'm grown and I like this friend."

So Walter said "You know all my numbers. Call me soon as you need me, day or night—you'll be welcome, Kate. And think about what a fine life we can have. We've all been blessed, if we reach out and take what's in front of our eyes."

I said "What *is*?—all I see's a green wall" (Tim's whole house was green).

Walter laughed. "The chance to make something last."

I had to laugh too. "Something *new* at least. The Porter quadruplets—two strapping boys, a teenage girl, and a howling baby. Maybe Carnation Milk would sponsor our bills and hang our picture in grocery stores." It came out meaner than I intended.

Walter said "You can call me if you ever get ready. You're acting for more than one person now."

"Yes sir," I said, "—mine and Douglas Lee's child. Get Douglas to act a little more grown." But I still didn't volunteer Tim's phone number or my whereabouts and Walter didn't ask.

When Tim came back at noon, I told him two things. "My cousin knows I'm safe and will leave me alone" and that we had to buy more groceries than bologna or I'd die-off.

Tim said "I don't wish many people harm." Then he took me to a store and bought us groceries enough for a week, though I'd left my ration books at Walter's. They'd got in a case of pineapple that morning; Tim knew the manager and got six cans, which cheered us both up.

I spent a good part of the afternoon making upside-down cake, alone in the house. Then I took another long nap and, this time, dreamed an entire life. It included Tim and, as we moved on through places and years, he kept getting young till he equaled me. Then I told him about the baby I'd hidden from him, and he asked to see it.

I woke up calmer than I'd been since Easter and baked a hen, with rice and peas. (I've never loved to cook; but I learned how early, from watching Noony and helping Walter, and reading cookbooks. Anybody that can read, and move, can cook.)

Tim ate like a boy and—after the dishes—hauled out a shoebox of Navy pictures, brought them to the table, and explained his boyhood. He'd been in the First War and seen the world, which somehow surprised me (he seemed so alone). But he didn't say a word about his adult life and I didn't ask. When he finished explaining the pictures, I prayed he would just dive in and force my hand—make me tell my troubles.

But all he said was "That daybed suit you?" And when I said "Yes," he went to his room.

Something woke me up in the dark hours later. I cleared my mind enough to know it was creaks from the rocking chair (so it couldn't be the dog), but I was too dazed to know who was present. I wasn't scared though and I lay on still and tried to imagine who it might be, who I hoped had arrived. I started with ghosts. Dan—no, too late. Gaston—no, too many hard questions to ask. So I thought about Douglas; should this be Douglas? I named over all his likable traits (which were mostly his looks and his early adventures). Finally I thought "If it's Douglas, all right. I can go with Douglas, if he's tracked me down." Then I raised myself up and said "Who's there?"

A man's voice said "Just me. You rest."

In the pitch-dark and still confused by sleep, I didn't recognize him. I said "I may have had enough rest for now."

He said "Not yet. You're sleeping for two."

"Two of what?" I said.

"A baby and you."

I didn't answer that.

So he said "Am I wrong?"

I said "No sir."

He said "That won't cause any trouble here."

I said "Then it's Tim?"

"In person," he said. And fully dressed. When he came to the daybed and sat by my knees, I could smell his clothes—a world of clean starch.

I said "Can't you sleep?"

"No, but that's normal. I slept in the Navy."

"You worried about this baby then?"

He said "Not if you ain't."

I said "Not yet" and that was true. I wondered why not and guessed I was too young to know enough to worry. Then I said "How's your back?" (he had lumbago; all cabdrivers do).

"Awful," he said, "but it's my cross to bear."

"Stretch out," I said and rolled as close to the wall as I could.

He waited till I was almost asleep. Then he stretched on his back, just touching the length of my side through the cover.

I did go to sleep; I felt that safe. But maybe because I'd napped through the day, I woke up at dawn completely rested. I'd stayed in place and Tim had too. I didn't look over but he seemed to be dozing (most people with insomnia sleep like buckets).

So I tried to find my baby again—gently with my fingers, below my navel. And again I thought I did. It wasn't like a knot or an actual voice but a hum, high and thin and strong as a wire. I thought "Now there's one thing that won't ever leave me," and happiness seeped all through me like a stain. Never crossed my mind that I would leave *him*.

Tim finally said "Can I speak to you now?"

I said I was awake.

He said "Understand—I know it's your business, but how far gone are you?"

"Not quite two months."

"You been to a doctor?"

I said I had. I looked at him then.

He didn't face me but reached up and buttoned the collar of his shirt. "You tell the daddy?"

I said "He knows" and told Tim the story as true as I could. It lasted five minutes, and by the end he had dozed off again. At first I was mad but then really grateful—any story you can sleep through can't be evil. So I rolled to face him and laid my left hand over his chest.

It took him awhile to accept the idea and start his reply. And it *was* a reply. I didn't understand I'd asked a question, and I still don't think I could ask it in words. But he answered me fully, to my heart's content, for then at least—answered *me*, Kate Vaiden, not some dream-plan of freedom or fun. He stayed fully dressed (his collar stayed buttoned); and he used just touch, his kind gentle hand.

We went on that way for nearly two weeks. By day I stayed home, learned to cook from a book that had been Tim's mother's, and learned more Latin than in all my school years. I'd read Cicero, listen to the radio, wash my few clothes, and sit in the backyard with all the bamboo. Lindy the dog was my main company, and she didn't like me more than she had to to get her neck scratched. Still I never got terribly bored or blue. It was like the air in that part of town had a secret drug intended for me, to cause strength and patience.

By night I'd still turn in on the daybed; and always before dawn, Tim would come to me. He was always dressed and I never asked him to be otherwise. In fact, I never asked for one thing more than the roof and the meals; and we took those for granted since I cleaned and cooked. We talked about nothing more pressing than the weather or customers of Tim's or shows I'd heard on the radio (but never the war—Tim ignored the Second War and even seemed to grudge it being bigger than his).

After his first hints about me staying there till the end of time, he dropped the subject; and I never took it up. These many years later—me older than him—I think I can guess how he dreaded to ruin a hopeful setup by talking too hard. But then I thought he had just relaxed, was liking what we had, and hiding no dreams. I thought we were happy and could stay that way—or not unhappy (I was easy to please). The peacefulness of it was what I liked. Surprises were my main fear, with good reason.

The second Sunday morning after Easter, we were in Tim's backyard in clean hot sun. I was drying my hair, and Tim was sanding a new wood biscuit-bowl for me to use. With all the bamboo, no neighbors could see us. And it seemed like we might be on an island; even the heat was salty to taste. We hadn't said a word in maybe an hour and hadn't felt the need. Almost all of my really good times have been silent but have had to end.

So right before noon Tim finally stopped his work and said "Here comes a taxi." Lindy barked once. We couldn't see the street, but Tim knew a taxi if it passed a mile off. Then he said "It's stopping," and he stood up to check.

I said "You're hearing things. Sit down and finish." I planned to make biscuits for supper that night.

But he walked past me round the side of the house.

I thought it was just some friend of Tim's and only hoped it wasn't somebody asking him to work. I may even have dozed. But the next thing I knew, Tim was back in sight with a stout man behind him. It took me awhile to see it was Walter. I pulled my hot hair back the best I could.

He was ashy and drawn, and his right hand was bandaged up big as a dollpillow. When he saw me, he passed Tim quick to reach me. But he stopped well short. He said "I'm sorry; I just had to see you." He held up the hand.

I said "How'd you find me?"

Walter looked to Tim. "Just called a cab, described Mr. Slaughter, and said 'Take me to him.' "

Tim said to me "You want me to leave?"

"It's your place," I said.

So Tim came on, stood behind my chair, and beckoned Walter to the other seat.

Walter shook his head. "This'll take two seconds. Kate, I've got to know—have you heard from Douglas?"

"Not a quack," I said. "Douglas speaks through you."

Walter said "Not today." Again he showed his hand.

Tim said "He stabbed you." It snatched my breath and I thought "That's crazy."

But Walter smiled. "I stopped an icepick—self-defense."

Tim said "Need a doctor?"

"Thank you, no. I've seen one—nice clean hole right through my palm. Too late for Easter."

I said "Where is he?"

Tim said "Jail, I hope."

I looked back to shame him; he was hot as a boiler. When he touched my shoulder, I could face Walter finally and say "I'm sorry." I knew I'd caused it, and I still think I had.

He said "Hush your mouth. This has gone on forever."

Tim said "You hungry?"

Walter looked amazed like peace had struck. Then to everyone's surprise, he laughed and said "Famished!"

I made a big salad of lettuce, ham, and hardboiled eggs (that was years before salads hit the South—one of my best inventions, though I got no credit); and we ate it out back with oysterette crackers and ginger ale. It took us nearly an hour to finish, and no other words had been said about Douglas.

Walter finally said "Kate, your cooking's improved."

I said I'd been practicing, and he should come back one night soon for supper.

Tim stood up and said "Mr. Porter, my shift starts now. I'll drive you home free."

I knew it was a lie—Tim was off all day—and I suddenly hated to make Walter leave. But I didn't speak up, though Walter waited through one long instant to see if I would.

Then he stood too, stepped over and kissed me. "I'm your family, Kate. You know where I live."

I said "That I do."

He said "Douglas Lee is nobody's enemy but his poor self's, so don't be scared if he shows up or calls. Just let me know."

"He's gone?" I said.

Walter nodded. "Or dead."

Tim's throat made an awful sound like disgust.

But I had to ask "What makes you think that? He's lived through worse."

Walter said "No he hasn't. I told him so."

"Tell *me*," I said. I meant *Reassure me*.

Walter said "I told him what he'd done to you, a child. I finally told him what he'd done to me. I'd kept my mouth shut too many years, and I guess it swamped him."

The idea of Walter keeping silent for years swamped me. But then I thought how little I knew of him and Douglas, what they'd given each other. I said "I'm grown and don't you worry. Douglas won't come here."

Tim said "Better not."

But he did—Douglas—the very next day. That morning Tim had tried to make me ride with him (some drivers had girls with them more days than not). I told him the bumps might harm the baby, which was all it took.

He said "Lock up and don't answer the door."

I told him I'd smother—we were in a hot spell—but would take extra care.

And I did. Our regular Jehovah's Witness knocked for two minutes to sell me *The Watchtower*, but I played possum in the kitchen closet. Then I tackled a cleanup on Tim's filthy oven and was black to the elbows when I heard a car door. I crept to the frontroom and peeped round the shade.

Another cab was waiting at the curb, and Douglas Lee was coming up the walk. He was neatly dressed and his necktie was straight, but he seemed like something that had run all night through woods for his life. Something strong and goodlooking as a horse but outmatched now.

I thought "Oh Lord, he's skipping work. I caused all this." I didn't feel bad.

He climbed the stoop and stood at the door.

I knew I wouldn't answer.

But he didn't knock once. He just waited, still as a post in water.

So I had to open.

Douglas smiled but didn't speak. Then Lindy the dog walked past me and welcomed him. I'd never seen her do that much for anybody;

she kept her own counsel. So Douglas knelt down and scratched her. Then he looked up at me and said "Let's go."

I said "Where?"

"To Raleigh. I've called an old friend from orphanage days. He's got his own shoestore, and he offered me a job."

I'd liked Raleigh ever since Dan took me there when I was nine—the Hall of History and the snake museum. I said "All right." The idea surprised me a lot more than Douglas; I thought I'd be a Virginian for good.

He just looked back at his taxi. "We're late. Run grab your nightshirt."

"It's at Walter's," I said.

Douglas reached for my hand. "Then you're ready," he said.

I knew I was. I didn't feel happy exactly, more like *cleared*—a train with cleared tracks and a named destination. The man here touching me was part of my body now, part of my child. Everybody else with any claim to say that—Dan and Frances, even Gaston somehow—was long since gone. But I couldn't just cut. I pulled my hand loose and said "You wait. Cabs'll wait all day. I got a note to write."

Douglas said "Don't. You'll raise false hopes."

I thought "Douglas Lee shouldn't talk about hope," but I just said "Wait."

And for once he did. He went to the cab and sat by the driver, that I'd never seen (though he must have known Tim). I packed my few scraps in under three minutes; then got my notebook and wrote out what I thought was the actual truth, something like

Tim, I'll remember you thankfully and hope you know why I've got to leave now with my baby's daddy. Don't think hard of me please. We've got the promise of a job elsewhere, so I'll still be cooking and you can visit soon. I'll write more once we've settled in.

As I left it on the rug inside the front door, I thought "Tim Slaughter won't want to see your hand ever again. This is his lucky day." But I took a last minute, found his shoebox of old Navy pictures, and stole the good one—Tim standing on a French beach with fog all behind him, and blurred doughboys, but his own grin plain and white as dried bone.

*   *   *

He was nowhere in sight at the station, thank God, and our train was the noon Seaboard local for Raleigh. I knew one thing that Douglas maybe didn't—that it stopped in Macon—so when we got aboard, I chose the south side. Douglas said "Let's sit over here in the shade." But I held my ground with no explanation (Caroline and Holt's house would pass on the north; I didn't want to see it). And Douglas grumbled awhile but joined me. I don't know why he cared. We'd barely rolled before he fell asleep and stayed two hours. He looked up once or twice and begged my pardon for falling against me. But he never volunteered why he was that exhausted. Anyhow it gave me time to think.

What I thought then and what I'd think now are two different things. As usual I'd more or less amazed myself—leaving one more set of familiar things and knowing I'd strewn more pain behind me— but I didn't feel wrong. I still felt cleared and, again, led or carried.

Here forty years later, I can well wonder if I was carried by anything but my selfish hope and steady fear—*Leave people before they can plan to leave you.* I'm still not ready though to wear sackcloth. I recall too strongly how young Kate felt, beside sleeping Douglas—*I'm finally having my own grown chance. I'll sit still now.* I was glad to be me, no thought of turning into anything else—man, woman, or beast.

With my own little money, I even bought myself a roast-beef sandwich and an Orange Crush from the strolling salesman, a ruddy old man with gold-wire earrings (the first I ever saw on a live man till soldiers got back from Vietnam). I asked him who had pierced his ears; and he said "My mother, the week I was born." I thought he was an Indian, another cause for cheer. And so was the sandwich (train sandwiches then were made on the best bread the world ever cooked; it's vanished of course).

So by the time we crossed the line and were in Carolina, I was feeling like *home.* I didn't look forward to the minutes in Macon, and I wondered how Douglas would feel when he saw it, but I fixed my mind down the track on Raleigh and tried to guess if we had any plans—a room to sleep in, our own air to breathe.

Douglas eventually woke up, not talking but smiling.

I said "Are we sleeping in a hotel tonight?" I hoped we were.

Douglas smiled and shrugged to show he didn't know.

Maybe I'd taken my risk for the day, but I suddenly wanted a firm goal ahead. "Will your orphanage-friend be meeting the train?"

Douglas smiled again.

So I said "God strike you dumb in your sleep?"

And he laughed. "No, I was talking all night—just resting now."

"To Walter?" I said.

"No, I had to say goodbye to several old friends."

I'd never known Douglas had a living friend but Walter and me; still I didn't ask for news.

I said "You know I saw Walter on Sunday?"

Douglas smiled. "No, Walter's *your* business now."

"I've hurt him, if that's what you mean. So have you—I saw his punctured hand."

Douglas said "He tried to stop me. But I'd paid him my debt."

"I haven't," I said. "I hope I get to."

"Walter Porter's rich. He won't need us."

I said "Cash money was the last thing I meant."

Douglas faced me and smiled like sunrise in Kansas. He said "I'll just say this much more about our Cousin Walter; then we'll black him out. He has been repaid—in the finest gold I had to give, gold I'll never get back—for all he gave me. Now I'm starting my life at thirty years old with eighty-five dollars and you and a child. So sure, thank Walter—but just by postcard and not for me."

I said "You don't have to pay for me. I've got my savings."

Douglas nodded. "Send for them."

I've generally known what money is for, though I've had little of it and have not worshipped that, so maybe his words made me ask the next thing. I let two miles of fields go by—blacks planting tobacco and watching our steam—and then I said "What am I here for?"

Douglas laughed. "For *fun*—asking questions like that."

"I'm serious. Tell me." I don't think I had a clear answer in mind, such as *I love you*. But I did want the truth, and I hoped it was gentle.

He waited long enough to tie both his shoes (fine two-toned wing-tips, brown and white). Then he spoke to the back of the next seat forward. "I hate to be lonesome. You've helped in the past—" He seemed to hunt for more but didn't find it.

So I said "Look here."

He obeyed and was solemn.

I searched his eyes and mouth and chin. No Spanish conqueror ever searched Ecuador harder than I pressed Douglas Lee's face—from a distance, with my eyes. And I saw what was fine, what good he had to offer. But I didn't see one cell I wanted for life, or for that minute then. It scared me cold in the hot close car and I didn't speak.

Douglas wouldn't look away though; he stared on at me.

And I had to break it finally by saying "You know what station we'll be stopping at soon?" I was already recognizing actual trees I'd known all my life.

Douglas nodded. "Yes."

"Will that upset you?"

He looked down and smiled. "What makes you think that?"

"Macon treated you bad."

"You too," he said.

"I forgave it though."

Douglas said "You'd have to—a dues-paying Christian like you, no grudges."

I smiled. "That's why—the pride of the nuns." Then I knew I'd hurt myself worse than Douglas. I also knew love had not been mentioned ever between us, or any long promise. So I sat on quiet through the next quarter-hour and tried to memorize Tim's whole house—how everything looked and where it stood, how grim Lindy looked when I shut the last door. I hardly noticed when the whistle blew for the cemetery-crossing just outside Macon (where Frances lay and where I met Gaston that first time in the moss). But the old conductor passed through and called the stop.

Douglas stood upright, said "I'm going to the toilet," and walked forward fast.

Right at the moment I didn't think *why?* Back then the conductors would lock all toilets before a big station (not to foul the tracks), but at country stops sometimes they wouldn't bother. Douglas must have known that—and also that train toilets had no windows you could see out of. He'd be spared what he hated, what he thought hated him.

So I was alone in the seat I'd chosen to avoid Caroline's. What I hadn't planned on was the sight of Fob's. There it was though, slowly, as we slid into town—tall, painted yellow with the awful green trim—and it struck me hard. If Fob had been in his swing on the porch, or Roz anywhere in sight in the clover, I might have broke down and resented the tears. But I suddenly felt as good as I'd felt since before Gaston died, like opening a message on cheap tan paper and finding it swore you a cloudless existence, loyal children, and painless death.

Then we stopped at the depot; behind was the post office, Mr. Russell's store, "Rattling" Charlie's garage, and the shack where Fob and I spotted airplanes. Plain as day, I could see Tommy Rowan seated in there and talking on the phone to announce some bomber (and he blind as bricks). Not thinking a word, I stood up, hauled down the Gladstone bag, and walked toward the back of the car— the door. I'd left the Raleigh part of my ticket on the seat behind me. Douglas could redeem it.

I was on the ground in a bunch of dressed blacks, waiting to board, before I thought the next words—*Now where?* No chance on earth I'd reboard the train. No chance I could walk back down the road to Fob's without being seen by five or six people that would tell Caroline. The Methodist church was fifty feet ahead; it was never locked. I'd walk in there then and cool off and plan.

I'd taken three steps when a woman's voice said "God-in-the-grapevine! Kate, is that you?" It was Noony Patrick hugging a tall beige man in khakis with eyelashes long enough to plait in braids and a duffel bag. She was in a green dress; and except for eyeglasses (which she'd never worn before), she hadn't aged or changed a hair.

I'd taken a swan-dive, on faith, into space; and I'd landed in water. I went straight to her.

She hugged me hard. "Mr. Holt liable to *die* when he see you!"

I said "You off for Easter still?"

"Just an hour, to tell my cousin goodbye. Then I'll fix our supper. Wait for me a minute."

It dawned on me Douglas might somehow try to stop me. I said "I'll wait in the church. Come get me."

Noony laughed. "You got *religion*, ain't you?"

I laughed too, ducked my head for disguise, and walked to the church. It was empty of all but white dogwood on the communion table. I sat in a back pew and tried to pray. But I couldn't even think of God's first name. It wasn't from being scared or ashamed. I honestly think I had just used up my last watt of strength to choose or move. I wondered if I'd sapped my baby or marked it. So I spoke about that. To the blank plaster-wall behind the pulpit, I said "Don't let this child pay for me, any wrong of mine."

Then Noony was beside me, standing in the aisle. I hadn't heard the train leave, but she said "He gone. I hope he go to China—wore me out."

I could smile. "We're in church."

She grabbed her elbows and gave a long shiver. "Let's get in the light."

I said "I can't go up home, Noony."

"Why not? They forgive you."

"Let me go to your place. Is Emlen there?" (her sick old husband).

"Kate, Emlen *dead*. Ain't nobody wrote you?"

I said "I'm sorry."

"He ain't," Noony said. "He begged to die—got the sugar on top of everything else and swole up twice his natural size. Dropped dead in the yard, and the dog come to tell me."

I stood up. "Just let me go there."

Noony waited. "Miss Caroline kill me; you know it."

"I'm in trouble," I said. I hadn't said it before, even to Tim, because I hadn't known it.

Noony said "You been in trouble since I known you. Trouble's your *place*."

I said "This time I'm pregnant."

"In Norfolk?"

"No, here," I said.

Noony said "I know where you are, Miss Smart. Where's the daddy at?"

"—That train." I pointed south toward Raleigh.

She shook her head hard. "Who know you're here?"

"Just you. I was headed to live in Raleigh."

"Hide yourself," Noony said. "What you got in that grip?"

I had a white rayon scarf Tim had bought me from a surplus store (the only thing he bought, besides all the food). Noony wrapped my hand up in that like a turban. I said "Now every eye in Macon'll see me."

Noony stepped back and said "You want help?—hush." She laid her dry palm over my mouth.

Then we went to her place.

It was down in the bottom behind my old school; and when we passed that, every window was open. The schoolday had ended but teachers would still be in there, grading. I tried to look as foreign as I could, sucking in my cheeks. But no face showed and we passed by safely.

In those days you'd very seldom seen your cook's house, unless she lived on a kept-up road; and I'd never seen Noony's. She lived in a jungle of honeysuckle, though thank God it hadn't got its full summer growth. Still the first word she said as we stepped inside was "Saw a snake under that stove last night. Keep both your shoes on."

It was one tall room with dark pine walls and a johnny out back, one big bed, a cot, a big woodstove, two straight chairs, a slop jar, and dime-store brass frames with pictures of General Oveta Culp

Hobby (the inventor of the WACs), Joe Louis, and Marian Anderson. We'd said almost nothing on the half-mile walk. But once we were in the midst of her room, Noony said "Set your grip down and tell me quick; Miss Caroline waiting."

I asked could I sit down.

She sat on one of the chairs and said "Take the cot."

I didn't know why she was sparing the second chair but I didn't ask. I unwound my turban and sat down and told her the whole busy truth. When I finished—with Douglas shut in the toilet, me leaving the train—Noony kept her eyes on me and didn't frown but didn't speak either. So to fill up the air that seemed too empty, I said "What's wrong with your extra chair?"

That broke whatever spell I'd cast. She said "That's Emlen's favorite chair."

I said "He still use it?"

"When he want to," she said.

I'd seen Emlen years before but just from a distance, in a rust-red wagon, so that didn't scare me. I said "You got any good advice?"

Noony said "How big a hurry you in?"

"The baby won't show for another six weeks."

Noony shook her head. "I knew when I saw you, when your foot touched the ground."

"How?"

Then she frowned. "Ain't I known you since you had flat titties? Ain't I warned you what bad trouble was, how to keep your hand clean?"

I had to say yes. "But now it's happened."

She nodded to that and never so much as mentioned a change, like stopping the child. She stood up and said "You bound to be hungry."

I agreed I was.

"Ain't so much as a stale biscuit here; that boy eat it all. Suck your tongue then till dark. I'll see can I bring you Miss Caroline's scraps." She walked to the door and took a step down, then looked back again. "Don't show your face, hear?"

It seemed so grim I had to laugh.

Noony said "What's funny?"

"That boy," I said, "—your cousin at the train? How close kin is he?"

"Right close," Noony said, then touched her butt. "Close enough to bruise me up right bad." She laughed and was gone.

That was a Monday. I spent two nights. The first night Noony came back in the dark (I'd lit a lantern) with plenty of food. Before she served it out on plates, she made me swear that whatever happened I'd never admit I'd darkened her door. She said "The Klu Klux'd boil my ass," but I knew there was no Ku Klux in reach—she respected my aunt and was scared for her job. I swore and we ate. Then she went to the johnny and came straight back with a battery radio Emlen kept hid there.

We listened to that till midnight, barely speaking between programs. Then Noony stood up, scalded our dishes in a galvanized tub; and I helped dry them. It gave me a close chance to study her face.

She was twenty-five now; I'd known her six years. What had changed was that somehow her face had crouched. Her full cheeks and neck had drawn in tight on themselves, like some creature planning to jump any instant. On her smooth right cheek was a two-inch dark scar, new to me.

In a while I wondered if we'd lost the right of speech, so finally I said "Any mention of me from Caroline or Holt?" (I thought Walter might have wired them by now, if he knew I was gone.)

Noony seemed not to hear me, then swung round and said "They ain't studying you."

I could stand most anybody's meanness but hers; she knew me too well. I fought to stay still, and then I said "My aunt loves me."

"She don't *know* you."

I said "Since when did that stop love?"

Noony said "Every minute of the day and night."

"If I believed you, I'd kill myself."

Noony said "Step outside then, not here. I scrubbed this floor three days ago."

"You didn't use to be this mean. What hit you?"

By then she was washing a stoneware pitcher. I thought she was going to break it on my face; she looked that mad. We waited awhile with neither one moving. Then she laughed. "Just old age, tired old age," she said.

"You're not but eight years older than me."

Noony said "Look at you; you breaking," but she was still grinning.

So I laughed too and said "And I'm white." I think it was the first time I'd thought such a thing, really felt the difference; and I guessed it might hurt her.

But she handed me the pitcher to dry. "If you ain't dead-tired, I don't want to hear it. I slept about fourteen minutes last night."

Sometime before day I woke up in the dark again, a habit by now. I thought I could hear Noony sleeping on the bed; so I lay neat on the cot, a little chilly, and tried not to think. I managed fairly well for maybe three minutes. Then I heard a loud creak from the midst of the room. Noony had mentioned seeing a snake, and that seemed all I needed at the time—a cold snake beside me. So I spoke out. "Noony, you hear anything?"

"I hear *you*," she said. Her voice was nearby.

"That creaking," I said.

She said "The chair" and was even closer.

I recalled Em's empty chair. "Where are you?"

"Sitting up," she said. "Couldn't sleep too good."

"You in Em's chair?"

"How'd you know?" she said.

"I guessed."

"You right. I sit here sometimes to keep Em out."

I said "You scared?"

"Of what?"

"Em—anything."

She said "Not Em. I just like to spare him—sights he too weak to watch."

"Like me?" I said. I wanted to laugh but couldn't make it work.

"I never said that, Kate. I'm scared for you though."

Then I knew I'd dreaded her fear most of all. Anything above ground that scared Noony Patrick was a powerful foe. But I had to ask why?

"You white," she said, "—no husband, no folks, no job to do. You can't live here in no cold nigger shack, not you and no baby. I'm no sister for you; I'm mean as a jay."

We stayed quiet through maybe two minutes. I may have been worse off at some other point in the years after that—praise God, I don't remember. The worst thing was, I knew I couldn't speak. I didn't know one more question to ask.

Finally Noony stood up, fumbled for matches, and lit the lantern. Then the radio—some station in Panama coming in clear as the wind in the trees (which was breaking limbs behind us in the woods), the farm news in Spanish. Noony was tall in her blue flannel nightgown and came back toward me. She stopped by my head. "Go home," she said. It was halfway whispered.

"Where on earth's that?"

"You know," she said, "—the only one'll have you now and not club you dead. I'll lead you there for breakfast."

I thanked her and felt like the blindest beggar, chopped off at the knees. Then I actually waited till she'd gone at seven. I ate a bait of last-night's biscuits and syrup, cleaned myself up the best I could, and sat in Noony's chair planning my story. When I heard the bell for the ten-thirty train, I took my grip and walked past the school again—no turban now—and on toward Caroline's. I couldn't think *home.*

But there it was. I'd been gone eight months, so I don't know why I thought it would have changed. Like Noony, it hadn't. Outside under my bedroom window, there was still the red-dirt handprint I'd put there the week Frances died. Holt had made me scrub at it with a wire brush, but the ghost of it stayed and was clear that morning as I trudged up the road. Again nobody had passed or waved. And I knew that, for three minutes more, I was free. I could turn and go to the depot and leave. Or stand on the highway with my face blank till some man stopped and took me on or shanghaied me to East Chicago and a dark yellow room.

A screendoor slammed, the sideporch at Caroline's. I couldn't see her but it had to be Caroline, out to sweep down spiderwebs from last night. Everything I had learned and done in Norfolk since summer—all of it flew to my mouth. I thought I'd drown. And I knew I'd drown her.

So I turned in my tracks and faced the station. Which train came next, I couldn't remember—northbound or south. I'd take either one. And I'd gone halfway when the first car showed, black, coming toward me. Nine out of ten cars were black in those days, but I recognized this one and hoped to die. It was Gaston's father, Mr. John Stegall. I pleaded for somebody else to be driving, even Gaston's mother (though I knew she couldn't drive). And I shot to the side of the road on the chance I wouldn't be seen.

But the car slowed down some fifty yards ahead and eased on toward me. And of course Gaston's father was at the wheel. He rarely smiled but was smiling when he stopped. He was quiet so long I thought he didn't know me till he finally said "I prayed for this." He had the kind of face that could say the word *prayer* and not make you hold on tighter to your purse.

I smiled and said "What?" and stepped nearer to him (my grip was behind me). The car itself was a place I'd been happy, and how could I not move in on Gaston's eyes?

He said "You—home. The sight of you, Kay. I prayed most nights."

"Thank you," I said. "I *guess* it's Kay. Early train wore me out."

"You come on number seven?"

I nodded yes.

"Where you aimed at now?"

I found a quick lie. "The depot. I need to send a wire to Walter Porter, saying I arrived safe. So tired I forgot."

"And nobody met you?"

"Nobody knows," I said, "—a spring surprise."

"I know," he said. "Yes ma'm, it's spring. Be summer any day."

Then he stepped out, found my grip in the weeds, and drove me the last hundred yards to the house—no more mention of a wire to Norfolk.

Caroline stood there, holding her broom—still as a perfect child—and watched me come toward her. Her eyes were better some days than others. The gale in the night had blown the sky clear; and the sun was so bright over my shoulder, I thought she might be blind and confused. Maybe I was some woman selling soap or brushes with my sample case. I could show you right now though the actual spot my feet were crossing when she knew my name. She shied away from me and looked northeast past the Baptist church, like all of Norfolk might have chased down after me with blood in their eye. So I went to the front steps, not the side, to give her an extra minute to choose.

I'd passed out of sight before she moved. Then she showed at the corner, not smiling, and said "Holt told me you'd do it exactly this way."

"What way?" I said.

"Like a bolt."

"—From the blue." I pointed at the sky, so blue it seemed almost in reach.

"You look good," she said.

I thanked her.

"You've grown." She stepped on closer. "You pausing awhile?"

"If you'll let me," I said.

She nodded. "I'll let you—and let out your clothes." Then she called indoors for Holt and Noony. Holt was the only one that cried.

So that same night he was who I told. I guess that might amaze some women now, and I can't explain my choice. Maybe because Holt had been so hard on Walter and Douglas and had seemed to love me. Maybe because I was partial to men. Maybe because Caroline was so good and I couldn't imagine slamming down on her with crushing news (I'd seen it as crushing the minute I spied her sweeping the porch; up till then it had just been a strange prospect, partly a dream).

Anyhow we got through the first day with very few questions. My room had been kept the way I left it. My clothes were practically trembling on hangers to leap on my back; and after the two weeks at Tim's in one change, I was more than ready (though they were a little short). Caroline asked after Walter and Douglas; Holt heard my lying answers but didn't press on. Neither one of them said a word about school. By suppertime I realized they saw me as somebody still at a distance—and wanted me that way, in case I exploded or told them something they were silently begging not to hear (like what Gaston Stegall had truly meant to me or meant by dying or how Swift had hurt me). They were kind and polite, and they knew me better than anybody else except maybe Noony, but now they were trying to show themselves something I'd already learned—they could outlast me; I'd outlasted them. They neither one wanted to be alone with me the whole long day, and after supper we all sat in the living room and played hands of Rummy till Noony finished.

I'd never known Holt to drive her home, except in ice; but that night he put down his cards and said "Noony asked me for a ride, said her back was out."

I thought "Now's my first time alone with Caroline."

But Caroline said "You go keep him company."

When we stopped as close as the road went to Noony's, she thanked Holt and said "Kate, step in with me. I got you a little welcome-home souvenir."

I figured she had some secret to tell, and I followed her flashlight down the dark path.

But once we were inside, she walked to the far wall, reached up high to a nail, and caught something. When she got back to me, she laid it in my palm—a fine gold chain and a gold dogwood-bloom the size of an eye.

I studied it by lantern light and couldn't understand (had it been there before? I surely hadn't seen it). I said "Not for me?"

"Me neither." She laughed. "But you may need to sell it."

"Where'd it come from?" I said.

"He said the P.X.—I'm scared he stole it. Don't want the sheriff swooping down on me."

"He wouldn't," I said. "It's pretty; you keep it."

Noony shook her head, shut my hand, and stepped back. "No, you. You and that poor baby. Run on."

I said "I love you."

"You can't," she said. "Nobody has yet. But thank you for trying." Then she stepped to the bed like I wasn't there and fell back hard.

I said "You sticking by me?"

Noony said "Can't tell."

I tried to laugh. "When you think you'll know?"

She lay on flat and mostly dark till I thought she was out. Then she suddenly bolted up on her elbows. "—When *you* know where you're dropping this baby. If it's Macon, I'm here. I got a job here."

I laughed. "I love you."

Noony looked away. "Go tell Mr. Holt—he the one need love."

And he did seem to. When I'd scrambled back up the black bank to his car, he was slumped at the wheel like a shrunk ragdoll of himself, flung down. I got in and sat before he seemed to notice, and then it dawned on me he might have been drinking (he kept a pint locked in the glove compartment). So I leaned close to kiss his cheek and smell for liquor. He smelled clean as grass.

Finally he rallied. "What's your souvenir?"

"A little gold chain and a dogwood bloom." It was still in my hand, but I didn't want to show it for fear he would laugh.

"Good," he said. "Noony's rich—glad she's generous. We may all need it."

That chilled me a little. "Since when is she rich?"

"Emlen made hills of money. Sold firewood ever since slavery times and saved his pennies."

I said "Noony hasn't got but two straight chairs."

"She's got money buried all around, if she can find it. Em was scared of banks—buried money in jars."

I said "Who told you?"

"I saw him," Holt said, "—once when I was a boy. He swore me to silence or he'd put a spell on me; he could conjure bad trouble on his enemies."

"But you've told me."

"Em's dead as a plow."

"Noony doesn't think so. She waits for visits from his spirit in the night."

Holt said "Then tell her to ask him next time for a map—all his treasure spots."

"Are we that broke?" I said.

"Been a right lean year. I've borrowed a lot; Caroline doesn't know."

I said "I could lend you five hundred dollars" (I had nearly seven).

He faced me then, the first time fully. "You'll need it soon."

I saw he wasn't speaking idly or lightly, and I had to know why. "For what?" I said.

Holt said "You tell me."

So I said "This baby."

And he said "I thought so."

Holt had never so much as breathed on me about the facts of life, and I'd never even heard him tell a risqué joke. Imagine how stunned I was by his bullseye—and my confession. I couldn't think of words.

He started the car and rolled off slowly; a turtle could make the trip in ten minutes. He said "You want to tell me anything else?"

I shook my head no.

"Can I ask one thing?"

I said "Help yourself."

"Is it Douglas Lee?"

I said "Yes sir."

Holt took a long breath and said "Well, I'm punished. Nobody escapes." He seemed to be smiling at the windshield and the night.

So I said "Can I ask one thing now?"

He said "Just one."

"Can I stay on here?"

He actually drove through a full long minute—we could see the house—before he said "My half of everything is yours, yes ma'm."

"What will Caroline say?"

He said "It'll almost kill her but it won't."

He was right again. That night we'd surprised ourselves so hard that we didn't even mention when to tell Caroline or who would or how. So another whole day went by like a dream with no sounds or smells—still no word about school and no more questions about life in Norfolk. Then on Wednesday morning I was on the porch in my old bathrobe, smelling clean air, when Noony walked up with the early mail.

She whispered "Here's a letter from Virginia, and it ain't for you. So get ready quick." She walked on in.

But I'd seen Walter's hand on the envelope—to Caroline. I waited five minutes, counting cars on the road; and then I knew I would have to go inside or head for the highway and flaunt my thumb.

Caroline and Holt were both in the front room, and she had the letter lying open on her lap.

I sat on the hassock near Holt's feet and didn't say a word.

Caroline smiled; it was startling as a scream. "Walter says you're lost."

I said "Maybe so."

Holt said "That's funny—I saw her here somewhere." He shut his eyes and rummaged in the air with his hands.

I reached up, caught his left hand, and held it.

He kissed my knuckles.

And Caroline said "Walter wants us to wire if you turn up here."

I said "I'm writing him a note today."

"Please do," she said. "He sounds upset."

Holt said "Walter's always been fragile as a cup."

That caught me wrong; Walter had only one weakness I'd ever

seen. I said "Walter's got every right to be worried. I've done him bad harm."

Holt sat back; this was new to him.

But Caroline said "I doubt he deserved it."

"No, he didn't," I said.

Caroline stood up; it was time she swept the porch and watered the plants. "You know how to spell the word *sorry*, I trust?"

I said "Yes ma'm." Then I stood up too. There were three yards between her eyes and mine. I said "Caroline, now I've got to harm *you*." But then I went silent.

"Go on," she said. "You never stopped before."

Next I prayed Holt would step in and tell her, but he stayed in his chair and reached for the newspaper. So I had no hope but to tell the plain truth. "I'm expecting a baby next fall. I'm not married yet and I'm not going to be."

She was already standing by the open hall-door. She turned and put her right hand on the frame; her back was to me. I thought she hadn't heard. I said "It's the reason I'm here. Can I stay?"

She didn't look back but she said "Ask your uncle."

I didn't want to tell her he already knew, and again he didn't budge. So I said "You're my only blood-kin here."

She looked around then. She hadn't turned pale or flushed or trembled. She was just the person I'd known all my life; that one thing hadn't changed. She said "Don't you guess it's got a blood-father?"

"Ma'm?" I said.

"This child you're claiming."

"Yes ma'm," I said. "But the father doesn't care."

She said "The world seldom stops for that." And then she walked on to her and Holt's room and shut the door, a new fact almost as strange as a child.

Holt just said "This will cool down, Kate" and left in the car to estimate timber.

I knew that, short of dying, no baby *cooled down*. And I stayed in the front room half an hour, waiting for Caroline. When she didn't come I dressed and put my feet in the dirt road and walked to the cemetery—my mother's grave. I've never been big on mooning around graves, laying wreaths on Mother's Day and holly at Christmas. But that day it seemed like I had to try Frances. Every other known human had slammed me out or been slammed out by me. I wasn't really sure dead people would listen, even if they heard. But I knew I had to speak to somebody now; and a corpse is generally there, where you left it.

Frances would have been thirty-six that year—the same age as Walter, six years older than Douglas. So when I stood there at her feet on the new grass, I wondered—if she could claw her way up—what she and I would do that day. I'd tell her what I had told Caroline and Holt, and what would she do? She and Dan both had had wild streaks down their backs broad as prairie fires. Would that help her sympathize with my trouble now or turn her howling crazy against me or cold as glass? (I didn't think of Dan then; I couldn't have stood it.) What would she want me to do about Douglas? (She must have known Douglas when Walter first claimed him, if not before; and she'd stayed with them in Norfolk.) Or what about both of us drawing my savings and finding some doctor in Raleigh or Norfolk or Kalamazoo to scrape my womb out and start me over?

I wondered all that, and a whole lot else. But of course she didn't answer, no way I could hear. I'd pretty well gathered I was on my own, from the night she died. So I wasn't surprised that the only noise was birds—male cardinals fighting their own old war. "All right," I thought. "I'll walk back and eat Noony's dinner, if they let me, and face Caroline. Whatever's been leading me has hold of her too." But then I asked what had led Dan Vaiden—through this same grass—to shoot my mother and his own good self. I had never asked that before, never even thought it. And it burned my skull every step of the way back toward what my aunt had decided to give or fling at my teeth.

Holt's car was still gone—he'd be gone till dark—and I sat on the front steps among flower pots and waited to see if I'd be called to eat. My watch was still keeping perfect time; and on the stroke of one, Noony rang her dinner bell (a loud hand-bell) at the kitchen door. I didn't see anybody waiting but me, so I stood up and smoothed myself and walked in.

Two places were set at the dining-room table, in mine and Caroline's usual spots. She was not in sight, but I sat down and ate grains of salt from a glass saltcellar, thinking "This baby craves salt; he'll be a strong man." That was years before science knew salt could kill you; athletes wolfed it down. The food had already been laid out—ham, corn pudding, stewed tomatoes, baked apples.

Two minutes passed and Noony's voice spoke out firmly in the hall. "Miss Caroline, all my work going to waste?"

In a few more seconds, Caroline's door opened. "No it's not," she said. Her voice was still calm. But I knew she could burn through bulletproof glass in a tone calm as cream. She had changed her dress—nothing fancy, just clean—and I thought that might mean a lot else had changed. She walked right in though without looking at me, sat down neatly, and said "Bless it please."

Holt generally blessed it—and in whatever words came to him on the spot, never in a form. So I'd never learned a form and had nothing easy handy. The silence seemed long as *Gone with the Wind*, till Caroline looked up and met my eyes. Then I said it to her. "Lord, help this food make us strong for what's coming."

She said "Amen" and passed me the ham. We'd each served our plates before she spoke again. With a little quick smile, she said "Kate, I'm scared."

I said "You don't scare."

She said "Feel this" and held out a hand.

It was cold and damp, and it jerked when I touched it. I said "Scared of what?"

"This new thing," she said. "I've watched people marry, I've watched babies born, and the angels know I've watched people die. But I've never watched somebody bring a whole child to life with no husband near."

"Negroes," I said.

"You know what I mean; let's don't trip each other."

I said "Yes ma'm" and we both ate awhile. Then when it seemed like she wouldn't speak again, I said "Well, one thing—it's not against the law, the baby at least" (I'd asked Tim that).

Caroline said "Maybe not. But the law is for crooks."

"You think I'm a crook?"

She pushed her plate forward and said "All I think is, I don't understand."

"Which parts?"

"Every one—why you ever left here, why you loved Douglas Lee, why you're back here now, what I ought to do, why your mother and father crushed your life." By then she had changed and was chalky pale. Her lips had dried too and cringed on the teeth. She closed them with her fingers.

I tried to remember and answer in order, as true as I could. "I left in August because Swift Porter hurt me badly after Gaston died. I know I never loved Douglas Lee—he has his good points, and I got close to him because we're both orphans, but I've seen his hard side. I hope you'll love me like you did before. And I don't know where my parents *are*, except maybe Hell, much less what they meant." At the end I thought of a thing she hadn't asked—what I had against *her*—but I left that alone.

She took her plate back and ate at the apples. Noony had baked them with a topping of cinnamon candy-hearts you could buy at Valentine's, small as peas and red as fire. The heart shapes had melted, but that left red splotches. Finally Caroline swallowed and faced me. She said "I hope I can love you again, in some new way, and love your child—if God lets it live. I can't promise that. If you don't plan to marry Douglas Lee, then none of us have any other choice, do we? You're sixteen years old. You live here or die or walk the cold streets."

I said "Oh Caroline, we're halfway to summer."

She said "I'm back at the North Pole now."

That made four recent people who had been good to me and were worse for the wear—Tim, Walter, Douglas, and now Caroline. She was the one near enough to forgive me, but I didn't ask for that.

And she didn't wait. She rose up, cleared her own place, and left.

In five seconds Noony was grumbling at her. "You cooking these beans? I can't stand to smell em."

I knew I had a roof then, and that fact freed me to show my face. The person I wanted to see was Fob. I took my own plate on to the kitchen, told Noony I'd enjoyed it, and asked Caroline if she needed me.

She said "Not a bit" (she was washing navy beans).

I asked if she knew whether Fob was at home.

When Caroline didn't speak at once, Noony said "Most people don't never need to *leave* home."

She was right, about Fob. He was there, asleep on his own back-porch, looking ten years older than when I'd left (his teeth were in his pocket). I stopped well short of his chair, not to scare him; and then I sang a bar of "Pal o' Mine."

He kept his eyes shut, but he said "Don't stop."

I said "I can't remember the words," but I finished the tune.

And then Fob looked. "I heard some had seen you, all smothered in a turban. Thought it couldn't be true; thought you'd let me know."

"I have," I said, "—in person, right now."

"And several days late."

I said "Fob, I had to get the train dust off."

He looked and nodded. "You must be broke."

That hurt but I said "I've got every penny you gave me, in war bonds."

He said "Sit down. You've stoutened right up."

"Four pounds," I said. I sat on the steps. Not till then did I look toward the barn and the pasture for signs of Roz. All I saw was the mule.

Fob said "She's gone too."

I knew he meant Roz. "I thought she was mine."

"So did she," Fob said. "You went off and left her. With Tot gone too, she was pining bad; I gave her away."

"Where to?"

"Dude Wicker's—he's got kind children."

That was eight miles away. I smiled and said "Let's ride down to see her."

Fob said "She's started over again, a whole new place. You forget her."

"She wouldn't know me."

He said "Hell she wouldn't."

"Let's ride anyhow. We'll stay in the truck. Might see her from the road."

Fob said "I'm about two hundred years too old for that brand of mess. She's a dumb damned beast."

But once we had pulled to the side of the road by Dude Wicker's pasture, Roz turned and saw the truck. She walked on forward another ten yards, leaned down and nipped at a thick patch of grass, then faced us squarely as God on a throne. She was still not close, but a blind girl could see that the Wicker children were plainly kind. Her coat was clean and took the sun like tightwoven cloth. Fob's window was toward her, and he cranked it down.

I said "Please don't."

"This was your idea." He opened his door.

I said "I'm punished. Let's leave her be." I had looked down by then.

"She sees you," Fob said.

I said "All right but still let's go."

We were back in sight of his own house in Macon—having barely talked through the long eight miles—when Fob said "What have you done to us, Kate?"

"Not to you," I said.

Fob said "Then your self."

I said "Don't ask me. Just stay close and watch."

He said "You couldn't run me off with fire."

I felt like a high blaze was roaring up through me, with smoke and the power to eat every bone, and that I wouldn't be there to touch cool ground when Fob's truck stopped in its place in the yard. But I was—all of me, a girl strong as most good arms you've held.

THREE

THE MIRACLE IS, you can last through time. You pray to die when you pass a calendar—all those separate days stacked before you, each one the same length and built from steel. But then you butt on through them somehow, or they through you. However many days I doubted I'd make it, I got through the rest of spring, summer, and fall on Holt and Caroline's quiet baffled trust, Noony's rough concern, the news of the Normandy invasion in June, and a good many more long rides with Fob, my own wits, and possibly the hand of God (also possibly not; He can leave for long stretches, I seem to have found).

At first I spent a lot of time in my room, stretched out on the walnut bed Dan had bought me—the one with the carving of my young face up at the head. I'd stare at the ceiling, reach back and feel the face with my fingers, and try to guess how the human that had got through my life till now could walk on forward through the seen and unseen for maybe one more year, not to mention forty (I've had forty more).

Hours could pass doing no more than that, and I know it sounds like a fatal case of purple self-pity at a time when in Europe and Asia people younger than me were tortured and torn with no bed beneath them, no roof, no food. Back then though what I felt was more like pure curiosity than actual pain. The question seemed to be *What was this girl* for *and would she be missed, if she vanished or died?*

(I'd noticed how nobody ever really missed me, but subsequent years have shown the same thing, and it's yet to kill a soul.)

I didn't ever say the question out loud. I also barely touched on it in prayers. I've said several times how—in Norfolk, after Christmas at least—I felt *led on*, planned for and protected. In my room in Macon, I felt like a creature on the flattest widest plain with nothing but skyline, a trillion ways to go, and the choice up to me—no volunteer guide.

I also hauled out my Indian bead-loom and made a beautiful belt for Douglas. Don't ask me *why him?* Till Halloween week I never had so much as a postcard from Douglas. Walter wrote to me faithfully (and tried to send money, which I sent back with thanks); and every time he'd add "No word of our friend." I didn't tell that to anybody—I knew they'd laugh. But somehow, to me too, Douglas still seemed a friend. I couldn't wish harm on his memory or his whereabouts. I even kept thinking that the baby, as he grew, was a shared thing Douglas was helping to make by remote control (and before you yell at my ignorance, wait and see what he did). Once the belt was finished, I of course had to keep it. I had no idea if Douglas was alive, much less where he lived. I thought about making it half-again longer and giving it to Fob, but I knew he wouldn't wear it and would joke about Tonto or fancy-boys.

Fob stood by me though. Even after he could see I was pregnant, he'd stop at the house every two or three days and take me out for a long country-ride or to one of his farms where all we'd see was a sunbaked tenant who didn't know me from Adam's back-teeth. Fob never asked me a single painful question, and he never tried to show me off in public where people could watch.

I *was* a sight. Through early summer I was still thin enough to walk downtown to the store or post office (downtown was mostly men; you seldom saw women). Occasionally old men would stop and ask was I Frances's child and hadn't I been up living in Norfolk? I'd smile and answer and that would satisfy them. In a place that small, which people seldom left, you were always being confused with your mother or a dead third-cousin—whoever you looked like, and you looked like half the town. I welcomed the confusion; you could hide behind it. By July though I was big as a carload of green watermelons, and swaybacked from it. So I kept to the house and porch and back yard.

After the day I stepped off the train, I never attempted church again. Church was too full of women who'd known you forever and were still clearheaded enough to know you were *Kate*, not *Frances*, and that *Kate* wasn't married; so who'd set her working on this huge child? Church anyway is an optional thing I can take or leave. When God or whoever wants touch with me, I find myself sending prayers up the line. Many times He and I go our ways in silence.

Macon was not a social town; but in that many months, we had a few visitors—neighbors and kin. At first I'd go to my room and avoid them, but finally Caroline said "You're welcome all over this house. Our friends have survived worse shocks than you." After that I'd show up more times than not. And nobody said a hurtful word, not in my presence anyhow. Still I could see how hard they strained not to look below my face or to mention Norfolk. Sometimes when they'd left I'd go to my mirror and check *was I there?* and laugh at the answer (*yes, or the Macy's balloon of me*).

But mainly I realized how strange it was. Here was plainly a well-raised healthy white girl with no signs of being a moron or crook; and a baby was hatching due-south of her chest that nobody understood, spoke of, or stopped (I'd personally known of two abortions in my years in Macon, both paid for and suffered in Richmond, Virginia).

Even Dr. Hunter in Warrenton, that Holt took me to once a month, might as well have treated me for housemaid's knee. He was bound to have noticed I didn't wear a ring; but maybe he thought I'd married in haste and had a teenaged husband fighting overseas, missing or dead (maybe I did, though no teenager—maybe Douglas had enlisted). Sometimes I'd want to yell "Let's just *discuss* it. It's a fair-to-good story," but I never quite did. I already saw it was probably a mercy—I'd turned to clear glass. You could see right through me.

Another mercy was, I didn't have girlfriends to pass by and stare. In the Macon town-limits there were literally none, not white anyhow. All eligible candidates lived in the country and rode the schoolbus. To see them, I'd have had to haunt the schoolgrounds. I'd have rather haunted Hell.

Speaking of which, Swift finally showed up. They'd moved, as I said, after I went to Norfolk. And though they'd gone less than twenty miles, their visits were scarce (*Swift's* visits—his wife Elba never showed her face; she resented his people). Holt and Caroline had mentioned him occasionally early in the summer. He'd got a new job, new glasses for his weak eyes, but still seemed to grieve at being too blind to fight in the war. Nobody spoke of inviting him home. Still one Sunday afternoon in July he showed up.

I was on the sideporch by myself and recognized his car in time to go hide. But for some cold reason, I held my ground. I'd been reading Willa Cather, *Sapphira and the Slave Girl*; I kept on at it as he climbed the steps toward me. Then something told me "You speak the first word or live to regret it." So over the open book I said "I seem to remember you from somewhere, stranger. But your eyes have changed." I went back to reading (he did look better, less startled and shifty).

He paused on the top step and said "We were kin in a previous life."

"Were we friends?" I said.

"Good friends."

I said "Then I don't remember."

Swift smiled much better than he'd ever done before. "Keep trying; you will. I thought the world of you."

I'd stayed in the chair, so I suddenly wondered if he'd noticed my belly (by then I was wearing those awful smocks that were all the maternity clothes yet invented). I decided, on the spot, to hold nothing back. I said "I'm in no position right now to forget old friends."

Swift waited, then nodded. "I heard you weren't."

"Heard from who?"

Swift said "The air—it's a general fact."

He and Elba had never had children, though we knew she'd tried. I said "A little new blood in the family might not be amiss."

"Might not," Swift said. "You're the one picked to bleed it."

Whatever he meant, I hadn't meant that. My mind wiped clean and my mouth shut down. Pain and death hadn't been real dangers till he laid them out on the steps like fabric.

He went in the house and talked to his mother; and when he left half an hour later, he just said "Write me when the going gets rough."

It never truly did. I had a lot of boredom. And I went through the miseries of the last two months when you waddle like a duck in a fast getaway and are so off-balance that tying your shoes or rolling over in bed at night are problems like spanning the Rockies with a bridge or hauling Lake Erie cross-country in your arms, not spilling a drop. But my mind held up, a lucky kind of blindness.

I just didn't try to see far ahead—where I'd be in one year, not to mention forty. There'd be this baby (a boy, I still knew). I'd be fed by my family and could then feed him. Ravens would likely supply the rest. What was the rest? Time, years of time. I didn't think of asking for love or touch.

He came a week early, November 16th. And though he'd been rambunctious in the ninth month, he slid into life as calm and easy as an underwater swimmer with breath to spare. Holt and I stayed up for the late news—MacArthur was back in the Philippines, and the Japs were sorry. Then Holt went with me back to my room and built me a fire to take off the chill (it was not really cold). When he said "Good night," he pointed to the little bell on my table. Despite the metal shortage, he'd found it at a country store and set it beside me in case I was needy but speechless some night. I said "Never fear."

Once Holt was gone, I stretched out fully clothed on top of my bed; something told me not to strip. I read half an hour in *The Reader's Digest*—how to keep your chin high in all grades of weather. Then I pulled my quilt up and dozed awhile with the light still on. At ten to one I came to slowly. It seemed like a low wave had just passed through me.

Nowadays of course girls all but get master's degrees in pregnancy and labor. Back then you never heard anything but jokes on the pain involved ("like peeing a baby-grand piano, bench and all"), the dangers of mishaps; the only advice was "Bear-down and pray." Still I knew right off that the big thing had started. The wave was not pain; but when I reached downward, my skirt was wet. First I listened for any sign of life in the house—pure black silence. Then I opened my bedside-table drawer and found the letter I'd got two weeks before. I've long since lost it, but it said something like

Dear Kate,

That train ride got lonesome fast. But I made it to Raleigh and tried three jobs before finding one that I think is the ticket. Not much money but a cheerful boss and a good place to stay. I wonder if you've got any news for me? Like I said, I'll stand still to hear it any time. And I'll do my part if you say what it is.

Love anyhow from
Douglas

That had come Halloween, delivered by Noony, so I knew it was a secret from Caroline and Holt; and I kept it that way. I also knew it was maybe a tunnel towards better times. Douglas gave an address on Person Street, but I didn't rush to use it. I thought I would wait and have the child; then if it was strong with a full set of features, I'd let Douglas know the fact and the name.

When I'd hid it deeper back in the drawer, I composed myself and called "Caroline." She didn't seem to hear, so I rang the bell.

In less than a minute, she was there—Holt behind her. She said "Lord, you're dressed."

I smiled, not to scare her. "I never undressed and now my bed's wet."

Caroline said to Holt "You stand here and wait." Then she came over, raised the quilt, and checked slowly. She looked back to Holt and said "It's not blood."

"What does that mean?" he said.

"It means we all get dressed and head out. Kate's having this child."

I knew she was right. I felt warm and more or less safe in their presence. Before I stood up, I'm glad to say, I thanked them both.

Holt said "You're welcome."

I had changed my clothes and packed a bag (and Holt and Caroline had come back to get me) when I looked to the bedroom door and saw my mother's straight back six years ago—following Swift to the graves, the creek, her own quick death. It froze me long enough for Caroline to frown, but I didn't speak of it.

Dr. Hunter's clinic was a twenty-minute drive. We were all so quiet; and my pains were so light, it gave me time to settle finally on the baby's name. I'd started out months before with names from books, movies, or the war—Balfour, Anthony, Cordell, or Coventry. But in the last week, I came round to thinking that a name ought to be a kind of private owning up—own-up for the baby, who he is and why, unless it's so bad it brands him for life. As we passed the Warrenton jail that night and turned toward the clinic, I said "In case anything goes wrong, this baby's name is Daniel Lee Vaiden—called *Lee*, not *Daniel*."

Caroline didn't speak but Holt said "What if it comes here a girl?"

"It won't," I said.

Holt laughed. "You hope."

Caroline said "Just drive. She's right."

I was—nine pounds-eight ounces worth, named Daniel Lee Vaiden with my own voice the instant I saw him. That was when he was maybe four minutes old. Back then in America "natural childbirth" was reserved for people too poor to buy ether. White girls like me, with grownups behind them, got anesthesia for every yell. What surprised me was, how little it hurt—more like passing a streamlined spinet than a full-sized grand. Even Caroline, who'd stood hails of pain, had warned me to pray it wouldn't last long. *Long?*—the nurse had no more than got me undressed, hitched in the stirrups, and slightly dazed when Dr. Hunter walked in sleepy in street clothes and started to scrub.

It took him awhile and he tried to chat with me till finally I felt a hard wave coming. I said to him "Man, you're missing this baby" (I've mentioned I was dazed, a big whiff of gas). Then I thought "Oh, I'm wrong; my bowels are moving"—I know I blushed. They weren't. The baby was three-fourths born, and the nurse had to catch him so he didn't hit the floor. By the time they'd spanked him, washed out his eyes, and showed him to me, I'd waked up enough to say his name, though I didn't try to hold him.

The nurse said "Danny Boy, poor little Dan."

I heard the *poor* and decided to ignore it; but I did say "*Lee*, he'll be called *Lee*."

By then she was already taking him off to the crib in my room and Caroline.

Dr. Hunter said "Kate, how old are you?"

I said "A hundred-seventeen last June the third." And I felt every minute of it that morning.

He'd finished his scrubbing and put on his gloves, so he walked toward the table to close me down. First though he met my eyes and waited. Then he said "Old as that, you may not have more babies ahead. Be glad now you got you a beauty." He smiled like he meant it, like it all was true.

It was, especially the beauty part. I stayed in the clinic exactly ten days. Since breast-feeding hadn't come back into style and doctors assumed you'd lose your organs if you stood up and walked before the eighth day, Lee was mostly in other people's hands. I saw him for maybe thirty minutes a day. He still looked more like a parboiled old-man midget than a boy, but he would stare at me—I remember that. What he saw I can't guess. He wouldn't smile or frown, but he'd choose a spot between my eyes and watch it like a sunflower eating the light. Being an only child myself, I thought that was normal till Caroline said "He's a scholar, this child. He's *studying* us." That made him seem, more than ever, like something else I could hurt.

But the beauty showed when we got him home. He seemed to

know he was there and safe when we turned in the drive. I was on the front seat with him in my lap, the longest I'd held him. And when Holt drove the car right up to the steps, I raised Lee high and said "You live here." The sun was strong and the trees were bare, but could he have seen a low white house with eyes that young? He laughed anyhow.

Holt saw him first and said "*He* knows."

Then I looked. Ten days old, he was grinning wide and flushed as a rose. I held him sideways for Caroline to see.

She said "It's wind. He's too young to smile." But she smiled back at him.

And he kept that up. Not the grin (he waited weeks longer for that) but the kind good-nature, the grateful ease he met life with. He'd cry at bottle time; and once every few days, he'd have a bad dream. But when he was full and belched and dry, you could count on as friendly a pet as any feist. So everybody liked him and the word got out.

Fob was the first to visit of course. He brought Lee a present of old gold-money he'd kept when Roosevelt confiscated gold—three ten-dollar coins with Liberty's head. I thanked Fob and offered him Lee to hold.

He said "I'd break him. I'll wait till he walks." But then he said "You give him his horn?"

I said "What horn? He's got a good yell."

Fob said "Gaston's foxhorn. We'll be hunting him soon."

I hadn't understood and hadn't really thought of the foxhorn in months. How did Fob know about it? Before I went to Norfolk, I'd hid it far back on my wardrobe shelf; and once I was home, I couldn't bear to see it. I wondered now if Fob thought Gaston was the father, but even Fob couldn't be that dumb (Gaston had been dead sixteen months). Still it made me wish I could change Lee's name—*Gaston Lee Vaiden* or just *Gaston Vaiden*. I knew it would be a name I could love, the name I'd hoped to give children to. But I also knew, in a place small as Macon, it would start brushfires I couldn't control, not to mention the boy.

Considering how I was soon to behave, I have to wonder if I ever

really loved him. I'd shown most other human instincts till then.
Why did mothering fail me? In the months I knew him, I can honestly say I enjoyed his company. Nobody gets a long-term kick out
of dirty diapers and spit-up milk, but Lee Vaiden more than made
up for his faults. I've mentioned his peaceful knowing nature; but
I've seen other good babies, though they're scarce.

What Lee offered extra was quick good-looks. By three weeks old
he'd lost his boiled skin and straight dark hair. From then on he
seemed like a big pearl growing in front of my face—a hundred colors
of brown, pink, blue and eyes that just got deeper by the day and
gladder to see me whenever I stopped.

But awhile before Christmas I saw I'd slacked off in tending to
him. He had a bout of colic while I had a cold, and Caroline moved
his crib to the hall outside her room so I could rest. We never moved
it back. She didn't volunteer to and I didn't ask. I'd tend him all day,
bathe, feed him, enjoy him. Then about sundown I'd start feeling like
he was Caroline and Holt's—and Noony's (she liked him more than
I would have guessed). They were glad to take over, in perfect
silence.

Maybe it was lonesomeness, the reason I failed. I didn't have anybody my age near me. I'd got used to fun at Walter's and Tim's.
Most of all though—and worst of all—I'd started to worry that no
man would want me, no decent man with a regular job. A teenaged
mother with a needy bastard-baby and no big skills, no big nest egg
or moviestar looks. From my room in Macon, it looked like a long
one-lane road ahead with a boy to raise, like a cast-iron sidecar
hitched to my bike. Holt and Caroline were in their early sixties.
They couldn't last forever and anyhow I couldn't ask them to support us once I was on my feet. Walter was nowhere I meant to revisit permanently. I'd walked out on Tim. Also I was hungry, not
for food or love.

There's no true way for me to say it—what I felt as that hard
winter came down. With Gaston and Douglas I'd used my body
more ways than any white girl my age I'd read about or known. And

for all the harm I'd caused the world, nothing convinced me my body was wrong and ought to be curbed. It was all I absolutely knew I had; everything else in sight could vanish—parents, kin, love—and in my case already had, more than once. My own strong head and limbs had lasted and kept me happy maybe half the time (a more-than-fair average). I couldn't just maim that much of myself by bolting doors on the wide green world and camping-down forever in a house with no man near me under sixty years old.

So on December 21st I wrote to Douglas Lee. I told him the child was born and strong and was named for him. I said I was sorry I'd left the train with no explanation, that I'd been confused. I said I bore him no grudge whatever and didn't want money; but if he was curious to see me or Lee, I'd meet him anywhere in reason. I'd planned to ask Noony to mail the letter.

But once it was sealed, I had the courage to walk downtown on my own—first time since the baby. I was almost there before I thought "Somebody will say something spiteful to me." But I forged on anyway and nobody did. Miss Lula Harris, when I bought my stamp, said "Noony keeps me posted; that boy sounds *pretty*. Bring him down here to see me." I almost fainted but told her I would, the first warm day.

It stayed cold through the whole next week. And Christmas was calmer than I'd ever known it. Christmas Eve we sat up late to hear the last news on the radio. The Allies had rallied in the Battle of the Bulge, and it looked again like we might beat the Germans (people now forget that was ever in question). Then we dressed the little fat cedar-tree Holt had brought in; and I laid out Lee's first Santa Claus presents—dresses, caps, and a Dopey-doll from Disney's *Snow White*. Caroline brought in hot spiced tea. Before we drank it, I made a short speech. I begged their pardon for what I'd caused and thanked their patience and their generous hearts.

Caroline smiled. "It has been a year."

Holt said "If soldier boys stand it, so can we."

Then we went to bed. But I lay wide awake for hours longer, thinking of last year's Christmas Eve (my vision in the fire with Walter and Douglas) and hunting the cold black dark of my room

for any new sight or sign of guidance. I might as well have been Helen
Keller in a barrel. So I told God in that case I couldn't be responsible
for my next mistakes—not all of them anyhow, being so hungry. Then
I slept till dawn.

It was New Year's Eve before Douglas answered, and Noony delivered the letter in the kitchen where I was feeding Lee with Caroline and Holt. The envelope didn't show his name and address (his
letters never did, like spy reports); but of course I knew his hand. I
stuck it in the pocket of my robe right away, though I knew Caroline
would rather die than ask about it.

Still Holt said "Who's the mystery correspondent?"

I couldn't lie to him. I said "I very much suspect it's Lee's father."

"Where's he living now?" Holt smiled but was genuinely ignorant.
I'd never explained why Douglas left Norfolk or where he'd gone.

Caroline stood up and left the room fast. She wouldn't hush Holt,
but she wouldn't stay to hear.

We stayed quiet long enough to honor her wish. Then I said
"Raleigh, the last I heard."

Holt said "Without Walter?"

"To the best of my knowledge."

"Who supports him then?"

"He can work," I said. "He's got a good mind."

"An orphan's mind."

I said "What's that?"

"A bottomless well," Holt said. "—*dry* well."

"You forget I'm an orphan?"

That stopped him a second, and over at the sink Noony gave a
deep grunt. But then he said "You never lacked love, Kate—not for
one hour."

Holt had been more than good to me, and I took his claim seriously. I tried to remember some strong exception while I went on
feeding Lee in my arms.

Finally Holt said "Was I wrong?"

So I said "No sir." To be fair, I hadn't come up with an hour when the whole world actually turned its back. At the worst, he and Caroline had always been here, ready to serve.

Noony said "Ask *me*. I'll fill up your day. I got my bill of complaints wrote out."

Holt decided to laugh. Then he asked for the baby.

I went to my room, took a short sponge-bath, dressed warmly, and sat by the window with the letter.

He said my news was more of a shock than he'd planned it to be. It had made him sure he couldn't launch one more orphan on the world, even half an orphan. He was still far from settled and still had debts, but would I bring the baby to Raleigh and let him see it and he and I talk about all our futures and what seemed right? He stressed that he wanted to see me with the baby. He enclosed five dollars, not as small a sum as it sounds today.

Something in it scared me, something hid between the lines. I halfway suspected he had plans for Lee—kidnapping him, killing him, God knew what. I guessed I was almost certainly wrong, but anyhow I wrote to him then and there. I said, in light of the weather and Lee's age, I didn't feel safe on the train right yet; we could wait till spring or the February thaw. It didn't hurt all that much to say.

Ten days passed and Douglas didn't answer. But late that Saturday when Noony had come back to fix our supper, she found me changing Lee in the hall (Holt was gone; Caroline was in the kitchen). She touched Lee's navel and said "Your daddy back in town."

He grinned and stretched out.

I went blue-cold.

Noony looked me square in the eye and frowned and whispered the rest. "Mr. Douglas at my house, waiting for you. Come in by train and asked some nigger at the depot for me; found me too. I'd have known him anywhere—this child got his color. He said he got to see you, Kate; come running right now."

I didn't think long. I finished with Lee, then said to Noony "I'm going. Tell Caroline the truth or a lie." When I'd got my coat from the rack by the door and buttoned it tight, I said "Is he wild?" I guess I had to mean was he drunk? (I'd barely seen him drink).

Noony said "Wild as a horse in fire." She folded an extra blanket over Lee. Then she said "You ever mean to see us again?"

"I hope so," I said. I couldn't guarantee it.

The big surprise was, Douglas was calm as water in a glass—standing water in clean cutglass; he looked that fine. Even in the dark of Noony's house, he burned his own light. He was in Emlen's chair. And when I walked in, it shocked me so bad I said "That chair belongs to a ghost." But I laughed.

Douglas said "It's welcome to sit on my lap."

"It's an old man," I said.

Douglas said "Then I've had my share of that." He stood in place and watched me awhile. Then he came on forward and kissed me once.

My skin had forgot how good that felt. I said "Go on and sit down; I was joking." I went to my old cot and sat at the foot. Douglas still watched me (he could outstare an owl). So I said "I thought you hated this place."

"I do," he said, "but I had to see you."

"Shall I thank you or run hell-for-leather to the Law?" In the long cold silence (Noony's stove was out), I laughed again.

Douglas said "I've asked you to marry me. Remember that?"

I said "Eighty years ago, on Mars or Venus—it seems even farther."

He finally smiled. "I'll repeat it. Kate, marry me."

I know it sounds crazy; but for one weird instant I couldn't understand him, couldn't think what his words meant. Eventually I said what first came to mind. "How would we live?"

Douglas laughed. "Your fortune. No, it wouldn't be Norfolk; but we'd make it someway. I've got new friends."

I said "You and I tend to lose friends, Douglas. Who've you got now?"

"Whitfield Eller, a blind piano-tuner. Don't laugh yet. He's saved four cents of every nickel he's made, thinks I'm his main light, and can play sweet music till morning breaks."

"You working for him?"

"Lord no," Douglas said, "—couldn't stand the monotony. He lives near my rooming house. I've chauffeured him some; he owns a car."

I said "I hope he won't drive a lot once I get there."

He said "Then you're coming?" He stood up again and started toward me.

My right hand stopped him, flat in the air. I said "The bank is shut today." I hated myself; my meanness had said it. But I knew it was a test.

Douglas passed it cold. "To hell with the bank. Save it for the baby." He came on over to the cot and sat by me.

I said "We're sitting in a field of gold."

He touched the back of my neck. "How's that?"

"The ghost—old Emlen Patrick, Noony's husband—buried his money in jars outside. Holt says it's still here."

Douglas said "Good for Noony" and pressed me downward.

When our faces were touching, I said "It's cold and it's time to feed Lee."

Douglas said "I can remedy the first complaint."

I said "All right" and he did, on Noony's narrow cot—room enough for what I knew I'd missed, a clean man wanting and using my services. Noony's clock ticked through it like a tin drumstick.

When Douglas had finished but stayed on with me, I started to count the seconds. At ninety I said "When you want us to leave?"

He waited so long I thought he had dozed. But his eyes were open, and he finally said "If *us* means you and me, the six-thirty train."

I shook my head. "It means us *three* and I won't tear Lee out of Caroline's arms—not tonight. I've hurt her enough."

He said "I figured Lee was more mine than hers."

That stopped the sweetness he'd sent all through me. I said "You ought to have said that last summer."

Douglas rolled to his back, then propped on his elbows, and faced the door. At first I thought he'd heard a noise, and I wondered if Holt might have come to get me. But we spent a long silence, and then Douglas said "I was with you, Kate, on a real train—remember?—headed somewhere real, where people can live. It was you that quit."

No denying that. I could mention how wild he'd seemed that day, and what Walter told me, but it was me that quit. I sat upright on the side of the cot and assembled my clothes.

When I bent to tie my shoes, Douglas said "You're quitting again."

Every other time I'd quit, I always knew it. Nobody else had ever just said it out flat before me, the truth. I was quitting the one person still in reach who was asking for me. I opened my mouth to say "Let's go"; but I thought "Lee'd ask for me, if he could." My eyes didn't water; my throat didn't close, but I knew I was right. And I thought of Noony—how she'd taken me in, and now Douglas Lee, and how much mischief I'd cause her by running. I stood up and said "What's so grand about me that you need me this minute?"

Douglas stayed on the cot, more than half-bare. In the chilly house he seemed at ease. He said "Your voice."

"My *voice?*" I hadn't expected a quick short answer; and nobody ever claimed my voice was special, though people understood it.

"You could talk your way through granite rock."

Years later, having balked at a million more rocks, I knew he was wrong. Still at seventeen, in a drafty shack with nowhere else to turn but the place that had driven my father wild and killed my mother, it sounded true. I could taste the pledge of a whole fresh life—the life people want with a warm companion and chances to mend the world by giving it well-trained courteous healthy children. I turned back to Douglas and said "Would you want me now, without the baby?"

He said "I just proved that."

"We'd leave now and then come back for Lee?"

Douglas nodded. "Fine. You and I settle in; then you come get Lee."

"How soon?" I said.

"When the spirit moves you—a few days, a month, the first good weather."

"Can we stop by the house now and say what we're doing?"

Douglas said "I wouldn't pour cold cat-piss down Holt Porter's throat if his heart was on fire. Anyhow they'll know. By now Noony's told them."

I said "If she has, she's lost her job."

"She'll live." He grinned. "She can dig for gold."

I took a long moment to study his eyes. Was there any plain reason why he'd come this far, to a town he hated, to harm or deceive me? Apparently not—the eyes never flinched. I thought "One growing boy is *grown*." And I said "All right."

At the depot I took a blank telegraph-form and wrote to Holt and Caroline. I said Lee's father had a good job in Raleigh and had come to get me. I'd write again in the next day or so and let them know when I'd come for Lee.

Black Pap Somerville was out on the platform to catch the mail. I gave him a dime I'd borrowed from Douglas to take the message straight to the house. They'd have it by supper.

It was long-since dark and frozen as the Pole. When I raised my foot to board the train, I saw a face hung in the air before me, real as mine. It should have been Lee's, I know—that trustful. But it was my mother one more bad time—young and ready and lovely, screaming. I stepped back and looked at Douglas behind me. There were no lights anywhere near us; but I saw him, pale from the cold.

He nodded. "Go on."

I shook my head. "I'm going to Lee—just a few more days. We'll come to you soon. Let's do this right."

His face was so blank I thought he might strike me. But he suddenly smiled. "You're hell on train trips."

I laughed. "It saves money."

The conductor, beside me, was saying "All aboard." No other humans but us were in sight.

So I told him "This gentleman's going, not me." I stepped aside.

And—not touching me—Douglas moved on forward, skipped the mounting stool, and climbed the steps. Then he turned back toward me.

The conductor blew his whistle and signaled the engine; then he boarded too.

I wanted to speak, something like *I'm sorry. But soon—I promise.*

The engine lurched though and Douglas staggered, then saved his balance.

I've always thought his mouth said "Promise," but I didn't hear his voice.

One more lurch and his face was gone.

I went to find Pap and reclaim my note. He offered me the dime, but I couldn't take it. I said "Celebrate."

Pap said "Tell me *what.*"

I said "World peace. The war's ending soon."

Pap said "Don't believe it." He'd been in the trenches for months, and gassed; and he'd never accepted the armistice.

Caroline and Holt had finished supper and were back in the kitchen. She was scraping plates for Noony to wash, and he had Lee asleep in his arms. When I opened the door, nobody moved but Noony. She looked back and said "You nearly too late."

"For what?" I said.

"Your something-to-eat."

I said "I'll probably live awhile longer."

Caroline faced me and went to the warming oven for my plate. She set it on the table at her own clean place—chicken pie, carrots, and little boiled onions. Then she said "Noony, it looks good as new" and beckoned me toward it.

Holt said "Damned nearly *better* than new."

Lee gave a low sigh from the almost endless dream he lived in.

I thought "They were gambling on me" and it burned. I said "That was Douglas Lee just now. He's gone back to Raleigh, but he wants his son. Lee and I'll be moving on with him soon."

Not one of them said so much as a word or met my eyes.

I wondered if I'd actually made the sounds, but I didn't try again. I sat down and ate like a harmless famished girl. And in a few minutes, we were talking together like a peaceful family that's never known any pain harsher than toothache.

Later I asked Holt to help move Lee's crib back to my room; and Caroline joined us, with no objections. Lee woke up and watched through it all, very solemn. When we had him settled in his old place, down at the foot of my bed, he took another long rolling look around; then shut his eyes and slept.

Caroline said "There may have been better children in history, but I never knew them." Neither she nor Holt though said one more word to acknowledge my announcement of moving to Raleigh.

So all night long I kept waking up between good dreams of life with Douglas and asking myself again if I'd said my plan out loud and if I meant to keep it.

By morning Lee had answered the second question. When Caroline came in at daylight to help me with his feeding, she said he felt hot. By seven he was hotter still and coughing. By ten when Dr. Hunter came, he was trapped in long spells of coughs and cries. The doctor said it was just a chest cold, but it turned out to be a severe strep-throat. And even with medicines invented for the war, it was nearly a month before we could see he was out of danger. Then he reacted to sulfa drugs with a body rash that got so raw we had to pin his sleeves to the sheet to keep him from gouging great holes in his skin.

Lee stayed in my room, and I stayed right with him till I was the one he trusted most. Some nights Caroline would sit up with me when he couldn't sleep. But that one month was my real motherhood, and I can't say I look back on it with anything but regret and pity. *Regret* that the germs must have come from me and *pity* that he had to suffer in a world I'd brought him into, unasked. To be fair, I can also say I admired him. He was my kind of person, a scrapper and cheerful when he had little cause.

*   *   *

Once we knew how sick Lee was, I'd written to Douglas to say we'd be delayed in our trip. I also said we still meant to come; did he still want us? He wrote straight back with much concern—keep him posted on Lee; was Dr. Hunter good enough? And yes, by all means, he wanted us there. Enclosed was a money order, fifty dollars. I hadn't imagined he was that far ahead, but I cashed it the same day and paid doctor bills.

We exchanged letters two or three more times thereafter. I'd tell our slim news—Lee's inch-worm progress—and Douglas would report on his business trips. By then he was fulltime chauffeur for the blind man. They'd work out in eastward circles from Raleigh, tuning pianos as far off as Smithfield and mending church organs. He seemed fascinated at being the eyes for two grown men (himself and the tuner). It made me think what he'd been for Walter—not the eyes but the *sight*, the thing Walter saw wherever he looked. Douglas also mentioned that his only contact with Norfolk had been the draft board. He'd sent them his new address and the news that he was the main help to a helpless person. Their reply made him think he wouldn't be needed in the war after all.

Hard as it was, locked in with a sick baby and no real company, I began to notice that Douglas was fading again—in my memory and my hopes. I'd spent so few private minutes beside him. And he was somebody who needed to be *present* before you; otherwise he'd melt off toward the edges of your mind. *My* mind anyhow. I knew what problems would be solved if I married him. I knew the new troubles that would certainly follow. I could feel and smell his body still on me. But he faded as I say.

And by the time Lee's throat was strong and his skin mostly clear, I was drifting in a lazy dream of freedom. I'd stay in Macon, finish high school by mail; then Lee and I would live our lives somewhere down the highway with rooms and jobs and men who wouldn't give a damn about history. It seemed that easy. It seemed crazy too. But so did the whole weight of my short life (which felt about as short as U.S. 1 from Maine to Miami).

* * *

Douglas seemed to read the drift in my letters, and his own slacked off. I didn't much mind. As I mentioned, I was dreaming and fooling myself. That isn't to say I've turned against dreams—hopes and plans for life and peace. I've just come to wish I'd had some wise soul near me right then, a soul I trusted, who could shoot down all my dumb clay-pigeons and make me like it and start dreaming things that stood some chance of lasting longer. Of course there was Caroline, Holt, and Noony. They weren't exactly swimming in rose-colored light; they knew what would work (in their world at least). But they didn't speak up, and I couldn't have listened.

There was also Fob. He'd kept stopping by, while Lee was sick, with kind little gifts—hard candy, new pencils, some *Life* magazines, and the latest news on Tot in the Army (Tot was being rushed through the Panama Canal from England toward Japan, where they needed him more).

Then on the sixteenth of March we had a grand day, warm at dawn and cloudless thereafter. Lee was four months old exactly and stronger still. I'd already planned to take him out, knowing full well I'd have to fight to do it.

But Fob turned up at ten o'clock and eased my way. When Caroline met him at the door, he said "I've come for Lee. Time we opened his eyes."

She laughed. "Fob, he can't go out till late April. It could snow by noon."

Fob said "It could quake but Lee needs light."

So we got Lee ready. Moving a baby in winter in those days was more work than moving the Pope to Utah—caps, flannel suits, stomach bands, wool blankets, and food for six. Still we did it and Caroline waved us off with the face of a widow on the stormy sands.

Fob said "Say where."

And I said "Raleigh," without really thinking.

He slowed down but looked dead-ahead. "I'll let you out here then; you're free to walk on. I won't be part of you tucking your tail and hauling to Douglas—as slick a snake as ever licked dirt."

It made me mad that he'd misunderstood me, so I said the opposite of what I meant. "Douglas Lee will marry me the minute I say."

"Then Douglas'll get a bigger fool than he deserves."

I thought "In a second Fob will beg my pardon."

But no, the truck stopped; and he looked down at Lee. "I'll take you, old boy, if she's hell-bent to lose you."

I said "He's with me, from now on out."

Fob said "I could say two things, both true."

"Say both," I said.

"—*Lucky boy* or *poor bastard.*"

I had to laugh; he'd hit it so close.

Lee grinned and thrust his legs out against me.

So Fob rolled on and we drove a whole hour past fields and trees as ready for spring as I surely was.

When we got back home, Fob stroked Lee's forehead—he was still awake—and said "Tell your mama the war's most over. There'll be men again, a big selection. Tell her, just hold on."

Lee's eyes went serious and switched to me.

I told him "Tell Fob, men are my last concern—all of them but you."

But once we were safe indoors, I saw the late-morning mail on the mantel—a letter from Douglas, the first in a while.

Caroline followed us to the bedroom and helped unswaddle Lee. She asked him how he'd enjoyed the world. "You didn't know the world *was* so big, did you?"

When he seemed to agree, I said "Lord, Caroline. Macon's not the world." It came out a good deal harder than I meant.

She said "It's taught me what I know." She started changing Lee and she finished up neatly. But then she left, with him uncovered in the midst of the bed. That meant she was madder than I'd ever known.

I called out to her "I'm sorry. Come back."

She never broke step but said "Read your mail—fresh news from the world."

Poor old world. The letter was one short page. The writing was

steady and carefully curled as ever, but the message was trouble. It's
one more thing I've lost but still know.

Dear Kate,

 *I'm glad our boy is better. This boy is worse. Somebody in Norfolk—
bound to be Walter—has given my whereabouts to several people I
thought I'd shook. They're howling for money, a few small debts. One
of them has even called in the Law and they want me too.*

 *I can't satisfy them. My blind man is well-fixed (three bank-
accounts) but he won't help. He pays my wage and not a cent more,
though I button his britches everytime he craps. When I mentioned
my latest problems just now, he said "Only way to profit is to suffer."
I was suffering in a dormitory room of wormy orphans before he was
born blind; and I don't brag about it, even when he mentions eyes
for the two-millionth time since I landed in his life.*

 *Walter would bail me out but I'd drink hot lead before I'd let him
know.*

 *I need you now, Kate. I say so again—I'm not ashamed to say it.
With you not here, and Lee (who is us), I seem not to feel any safe
ground beneath me. It will be warm soon now, so no reason left not
to keep your promise and join me here with the boy in tow. Then we'll
head for better places, which will mean better things.*

Love from,
Douglas

 I think my memory of all he wrote is fair, give or take a word. He
never referred to my little savings. He said what he needed was me and
his son; he called in a promise I'd plainly made, and he signed it *Love*.
Lee was his blood-son (no shadow of doubt), and more than once I'd
felt like I loved him. But the words didn't turn me the way he intended.

 When Lee was asleep I went in to dinner. Caroline and Holt were
there; and we talked in civil tongues, no mention of the letter. Holt
asked about the ride with Fob, and Caroline refrained from dire pre-
dictions of the harm to Lee. Soon as we'd finished she had to get
dressed for a missionary meeting. I took over and helped Noony clear
and scrape. Then when the last fork was dry, I asked Holt to listen

for Lee while I walked with Noony as far as the post office. I didn't have even a card to send, but I wanted ten minutes of Noony's hard sense.

She was ready as ever, having already recognized Douglas's hand on the envelope. But she waited for me to ask her opinion. We'd almost got to the Methodist Church (and her turnoff) when I said "He's calling for me and Lee, Noony."

She laughed. "I'm calling for *rest*; where is it?" She turned round one whole time, arms out.

I caught her hands and stopped her. "Should we go?"

She craned her neck to see behind me. Then she stepped back and said "Your *butt's* smoking, Kate. Sure, run on and see can you drown the fire."

I smiled and said "That's not what I meant."

"You sure-God meant it that cold day at my house—I found your leavings; had to boil that blanket."

I said I was sorry but my question was serious. I said "I'm not as young as I was, and I've got that child. I can't let Holt Porter own my life; he's paying for it now."

Noony took another two steps back to see me. The sun was still bright, and it loved her face—not a seam or line in it, like strong dark glove-leather stretched on a fist. She said "He been right good to you."

"Douglas or Holt?"

She was ready to spit. "I don't know Douglas but I heard some mess. And I saw him that day at my house, wild as foxes."

I said "He was calm when I got there."

Noony said "Maybe so. And he may be again. But ask one thing—what he want with you? What he want with a baby? Way he living now, he got *spending* money."

I already knew not to mention his debts. I said "Some people like a little warm company."

Noony said "*Heard* they did." She turned aside, hid her mouth, and finally spat.

"Help me please."

Her face clouded up, though the light still struck her. She looked down and came back all the way. For a second I thought she was planning to bow. But she bent from the waist, limber as a whip, and tapped both my feet. When I stepped back she said "Two feet, good shoes—walk on em yourself."

"I have been," I said.

Noony laughed. "Been *bouncing*—Greensboro, up here, then off to Norfolk, back here, now Raleigh. You're seeing the world."

"It hasn't all been exactly by choice."

She said "Sure it has. People *choose* everything, grown people anyhow." She turned then and left.

I said "I'll see you at five o'clock."

Noony didn't look back but she laughed and said "If I *want* you to." She looked fifteen as she went, that strong, though I hadn't known her then and though she was bound for a dark empty shack.

For three more days I held off answering Douglas. I hadn't discussed it with another soul, except maybe Lee. By which I mean that, on the third night, as I fed him his bottle while the house was asleep, I whispered the facts of the case near his eyes. "Your father is broke and calling for us. We've got a little money, you and I, in savings. If we take it and go to Raleigh, he'll spend it in a matter of days; I couldn't keep it from him. But if we stay here and bide our time a year or so, I'll get my diploma. Then we can live—us two, like we want—anywhere on earth."

Lee really turned to listen; his eyes barely blinked. But when I held a finger toward his hand, he didn't reach to take it. Then he looked away.

Even I wasn't fool enough to think he understood and had cast a No vote. Still, all these years later, I won't deny that I thought he'd turned away from me at a big crossroads. It left me with feelings that played some part in what I did.

* * *

Next morning after breakfast, when Lee was bathed and back asleep and Holt had left, I went to the living room to read the paper. Our nearest daily was the Raleigh *News and Observer*; and most days I paid it no notice, except for maybe the serial story and Major Hoople. But that day, the minute I touched dry newsprint, I thought "My name is somewhere inside" (I'd never been mentioned in a city paper). My next thought was, Douglas might have bought an ad to catch my eye. And I combed two pages of classifieds—nothing but strange men disclaiming the debts of reckless ex-wives. The hunch stayed with me though; so I kept reading, page one straight forward. For someone who's never had two minutes' fame, I've possessed an odd gift—I can spot my name in less than a second anywhere it appears.

It was nowhere in that day's *News and Observer*. But tucked down low in the local news was this brief item—"Man Injured In Fracas On Person Street." That was Douglas's street. A man named Whitfield Eller had been treated at Rex Hospital for minor hand-wounds received while shielding his face last evening from an unknown intruder who had left the scene. No property was missing and no charges filed. The street address was close to Douglas. And while there was nothing said about the victim's blindness, I remembered Douglas calling his blind man Whitfield. It had to be him.

The first thing I did was turn stone-cold. Douglas had cut his blind piano-tuner. Then I thought how he'd never raised his voice at me and how his best side had to be present here in Lee's good nature. Then I thought I'd caused it. Douglas called on me for help I could give. I held back on him and drove him wild. From forty years' distance I can estimate I was three-fourths wrong—Douglas Lee was stove-in years before I met him, maybe even from birth.

But one-fourth was right and it seemed big as Detroit. That was all I needed. I'd done enough harm in eighteen years (I was nearly eighteen). I thought I knew how to help the one person that had said he needed me and had no other help. And I'd do it in daylight. Then I felt important, for the first time maybe since my mother's funeral; and that had its thrill.

I went in the house and found Caroline. She was in her room, crocheting on a bedspread she'd worked at for years. As calm as I could, I told her I'd need to go to Raleigh today; would she please watch Lee for a night or two?

She watched my face for maybe half a minute. Then she went back to work and said "Wish all jobs were that nice to do."

I thanked her and said "Douglas Lee needs help."

"That may take more than a few nights, Kate. Douglas Lee needed help well before you were born."

I said "You remember him clearly, back then?"

Caroline looked up. I barely recognized her, her eyes were so pleased. She said "Sweetest child I knew till Lee came."

So I knew I was right. I was being led again. I said "I'll be back here in two days. The time may come when I go for good, but not today. Bet money on that."

Caroline was still smiling. "I've learned not to bet—I'd have lost several fortunes. But I'll be glad to see you."

I knew I'd have to go, that instant or never. I packed one change of clothes, two fifty-dollar war bonds, the beaded belt I'd made for Douglas, and (at the last minute) the seahorse-paperweight my teacher had given me when I left Greensboro seven years before.

Lee slept through it soundly. And when I bent to kiss him, his skin was cool as wax.

The bus got in at four o'clock. I didn't know Raleigh from Cincinnati, but one thing a girl can count on in stations is volunteers-to-help. My cash was scarce so I knew right off I couldn't take a taxi. Still I walked up to one old kiln-dried fellow who was leaning on his cab and asked him was Person Street in walking distance?

He said "All depends. It's five miles long."

So I told the first intentional lie of the day. "Look, my daddy drives a cab in Norfolk; please help me out. Is there some cheap way to get to Person Street?" It had crossed my mind he might take me free or at least trim the fare.

But no, this was Raleigh, a capital city. He said "Take the city bus, three blocks ahead."

I laughed in surprise but I liked him assuming I could walk, see, and read. In twenty more minutes I'd passed the Governor's Mansion and Fred Olds School, and then I climbed down with my grip in hand.

The houses were old frame two-story white, but they mostly were clean. Several had *Rooms for Rent* signs out on the street. At Douglas's though there was just a handlettered sign in the window— *Room for Gentleman*, all but hid by a lineup of ferns like the Congo woods on the wide front-porch. I walked up and rang the old crank-doorbell. Then I heard slow footsteps for what seemed an hour, coming toward me.

Finally a woman maybe fifty years old appeared at the door in a purple dress with a gold-knot brooch at bosom level. She studied my face, then my own bosom, and suddenly said "I never saw one in gold before."

I said "Excuse me?"

"Those dogwood pendants. My cook has one but it's silverplate."

I smiled. "They're scarce. This came from overseas"—my second lie.

She smiled too, on teeth as long as thumbs; but she shook her gray head. "Dogwood won't grow outside this state."

I thought "All right, she wants to swap lies." I said "No ma'm, it's all over Palestine. This pin itself's from Calvary, sent to me by a soldier."

She studied it again and seemed to surrender. But then she said "I'm Elmira Peebles. What would your name be?"

For the first and only time in my life, I said "Kate Lee, Mrs. Douglas Lee." I still don't regret it.

She nodded. "I knew. He had your picture, in a school uniform. But I see he stole your ring."

I said "No, I leave it at home when I travel."

She said "True or not, you owe me twelve dollars." She began to scrub at her hands like Pilate.

I said "You're barking up a bare tree, lady."

Her hands worked on but she said "So I see. Mr. Eller will pay me; he guaranteed him to me."

I said "Is Mr. Eller doing all right?"

"You'd have to ask his doctor; he's still at Rex."

"Where's Mr. Lee then?"

Her hands stopped abruptly (she'd wrung them blue) and waved out beside her. "Dissolved into air, I pray the sweet Lord!—in the night, last night."

"Did he leave anything?"

She said "Not a button. Left it clean as he found it, I'll give him that much. I was sound asleep till the police came."

"Came here?"

"Mr. Eller's—" She pointed across the street and down. "The Law has never had to darken my door."

"I know you're proud," I said. "I'll pay the twelve dollars once I get to a bank. But now please tell me how to find the hospital."

She waited awhile, then pointed to my chest. "I'll take that necklace—full payment. Then I'll tell you."

"I'm sorry," I said. "You'll have to call the Law. This is my main treasure." I cupped the gold with my warm hand. Then I saw her look past me, so I followed her eyes.

A taxi had stopped across the street, and the driver was helping a tall man out.

By the way the man's left hand towed at the air, I knew he was blind. His right hand was bandaged and held a cane. In a clear voice he told the driver "I'm home. You go on, thank you."

I didn't look back at Miss Peebles, but I said "I'll pay you." Then I got to the blind man before his porch steps.

The first surprise was, he looked so young. I remembered Douglas saying he'd been born before Whitfield, but this man tapping his way up the walk was fresh in the face as a rainwashed rose. And his eyes, though blank, seemed much more ready for fun than grief. I went to his left, six feet away, and said "Mr. Eller?"

He stopped in place and turned toward me, "I *was*," he said, "till early last night; then I lost a little ground."

I said "You look fine."

"So would you," he said. "I'm glad to meet you."

"I'm Kate—Douglas Lee's friend Kate, from Macon."

"I knew you," he said. "Doug described your voice."

I'd never heard Douglas called Doug before, but I thought how he'd said he liked my voice. It made me shy to speak; I might spoil the hopes of someone who lived on voice alone. Still I said "It's nothing but a homegrown voice. When have you seen Douglas?" (with blind people, most of us flaunt the word *see*).

He didn't correct me. He said "Step ahead; let's sit on the porch."

I knew not to try to touch him and lead him; but I went on ahead up eight high steps, humming the only tune I could think of— "Blessed Assurance" (I'd forgot the words). At the top I set my grip down and waited.

He came on slowly but sure as a cat. Then he motioned me toward a green rocker and said "These chairs aren't mine but I pay to use them." So both of us sat, and he breathed fast for a minute or so. Then he thought to hide his bandaged palm. Then he faced me. "Train that voice, child, and *sing*." He was almost ready to smile, not quite.

I said "Too late. I'm an unemployed mother."

He waited, still watching till I thought "He can see me; he's faking those eyes." Then he said "Can you drive?"

"Yes sir"—lies were stacking up—"but I don't have a license" (Walter had let me drive a few Sundays, very much against the law; so at least I knew the gears and the general location of radio and brakes).

He said "You drive up here to join Doug?"

"On the bus," I said. "I don't own a car."

"Do you know he's gone?"

I said "I spoke to Miss Peebles just now. Mr. Eller, gone where?"

He smiled at last and looked even younger. "*Whitfield*," he said. "I'm just three years your senior."

I laughed. "Whitfield—I've aged a lot lately."

His eyes kept smiling but he said "—With cause. I can guess you've suffered."

"Thank you. Life numbed me a few years back."

"Life won't do that," he said. "That's *all* it won't do. They teach you that the first week at Blind School. Then you choose one other thing to learn—mattress-making, chair-caning, or tuning pianos." He sat, staring at me, till the air calmed a little. Then he smiled again. "No forwarding address."

I said "Beg your pardon?"

"Doug left in the night. Didn't give much notice."

"But he hurt you, I heard."

"Not from me, you didn't."

"I guessed it from the piece in *The News and Observer*—he's hurt other people."

Whitfield rocked a little. Then he said to the shrubbery "*Unknown intruder*, the paper said. A nurse read it to me."

"The paper can lie."

He waited again. "It was dark and I'm blind."

"You heard him and felt him."

Whitfield shook his head. "It never made a sound."

"And nothing was stolen?"

"Not a penny, no." He suddenly stood up, smiling again. "Let me show you my place."

Something made me say "Is the whole house yours?"

"The whole downstairs; I pay big rent. Mr. Dod Jackson owns it. He's a widower with no kin and travels for the state, four nights a week—roosts upstairs on most weekends. Otherwise, it's mine." He left his cane on the floor by his chair and moved surefooted toward the shut front door.

So I followed him in, with no real fears. As I crossed the sill, I did think Douglas might be hid inside; but Douglas had never said a harsh word to me. Whitfield led the way, naming off the five rooms— living room, kitchen, bedroom, bath, and the old dining room which he used for music. They all were empty as the heart of a bell. There were no rugs anywhere, and the few sticks of furniture were pushed to the walls. But the walls were covered with scads of framed pictures, each room a different subject—birds, waterfalls, storms at sea, com- posers, pianists, and grand-opera singers (it would be some time before I guessed their meaning to him).

We'd only paused at the bedroom door, but I got a look in—no nun's could have been neater. So when he stopped in the music room and motioned me down on a noisy wicker-sofa, I said "Somebody sure cleaned up the fracas."

Whitfield pulled out the piano bench and sat. Maybe being that close to a keyboard, he was tempted (he played a few silent chords across his strong knees). Then he said "Kate, I want very much to count you a friend and know you for life. But understand this—the paper was wrong. Here's the whole gospel truth. About nine last night I was on this bench, playing "To a Wild Rose" with a lot of soft pedal not to bother the neighbors. My hearing's right keen, but I heard no footsteps or any voice near me. When I'd finished the piece though, I felt something near me—at my left shoulder. I turned and said 'Doug'—I'll grant you that much; I thought it was Doug—but no voice answered. I'm good at stillness and I sat here still. Then after a minute I waved my right hand slow out before me. Nothing was there. I honestly thought so; I still nearly do. Then my feeling washed out, and I seemed scot-alone. I thought I'd play one more soft piece, but something made me smell this hand—warm and rusty. So I tasted it carefully and found a clean gash deep through my palm. I had to call help. I knew Doug was gone—he'd failed me that morning, just didn't show up—so I called the police; they've helped me before." Whitfield stopped there and shut his eyes (I suddenly wondered if he'd so much as blinked in the time I'd known him). Then he opened them, faced me, and snapped his good finger and thumb, loud as gunfire. "The end—true story—every word I know. Set your mind at ease."

It may have been true (I could see he nearly believed it by then), but it did very little to ease my mind. I said "Can you still play, bandaged like that?"

He said "Haven't tried" and turned to the keys. He played a child's version of Brahms' "Lullaby," mostly with his left hand. Short as it was, it gave time enough for a low black cloud to stop overhead; the room dimmed down like early evening. His eyes must have had some awareness of light. At the end, when I clapped, he stood up and said "Let's see how you drive."

"Lord, no," I said.

"Why not? See the town." He was moving toward the door.

"Whitfield," I said, "we'd end up in jail."

He walked straight onward toward the front door and his cane. He laughed. "Every cop not at war is too old to catch us, Kate." He couldn't be stopped.

And he turned out right. The hard part was starting and backing his car out of that slim garage and into the street. From then on, give or take a few bucks and stalls, we drove like experts back past the Capitol and on out Hillsboro Street to State College and then Pullen Park. He wanted me to see Andrew Johnson's birthplace and the indoor merry-go-round with horses carved "by a master hand."

In the process I learned how he liked to be guided—just stay at his elbow and make clear noise (talk or hum) that he could follow. We'd seen the park, got ammonia Cokes at a drugstore big enough to dope a division, dodged the end-of-day traffic, and were back on his porch, upright and unbruised, without me touching Whitfield or him me (for guidance, I mean)—an impressive feat that fascinated me.

When he got out his keys to open the house, I said "I'd better go on while it's light" (the sky had cleared but it was almost dark).

He said "Go where? Miss Peebles won't have you."

"The station," I said, "—train or bus."

"You won't get home tonight, not alive."

"Then I'll sit up," I said. "I'm lucky in stations."

Whitfield made a shocked look, then laughed and sat down. "You don't know Raleigh, N. C., sweet lady."

"I navigated Norfolk with my hair in place."

"That's Norfolk," he said. "Sit up in *our* stations, and they'll be mailing scraps of your skin and gristle back to Macon all month. Let's fix our supper." He motioned me over to my previous chair.

I felt like obeying and presently did.

When I was settled and gazing at the street, Whitfield bent and said to the floor "What on earth is our life now, Katie?"

At first I wondered what he meant but then knew. "It's *simpler*, I guess."

He thought that over, then shook his head hard. "Not for me. Doug Lee was the best friend I had. Now I'll prowl this house and grounds like a pet till I've put one more want-ad in the paper, interviewed six or eight ex-cons and winos, then laid my life in one of their hands to chauffeur me out of here to work again." He'd said it calmly with no frown or whine—the end, true story.

So I said "I've never spent a minute in jail and have never drunk more than two glasses of sherry. What if I apply?" It surprised me more than Whitfield.

At least he took it in a business-like way. He had a row of questions—how soon could I get my license? where would I live? how much pay would I expect?

I said that I'd walk in tomorrow, get the license-instruction book, memorize it, and apply the next day. I said if he advanced me a week's worth of what he thought was fair wages, I'd look for a room.

He nodded but was silent.

Then three things hit me like crows in the face and I got scared. First, I'd torn off again with no careful plan and no thought of any-body's life but mine. Second, I'd promised Caroline to be back the next day. Third, since Whitfield hadn't mentioned Lee, I could be fairly sure he didn't know about him—one more of Douglas's secrets. So I said "You know Douglas left me a baby?"

He faced straight ahead. "No ma'm, I didn't."

"Then who did he say Kate Vaiden was?"

"His fiancée."

I said "That's something like two-thirds true; I was promised to him. But Daniel Lee Vaiden, four months old in Macon—Douglas never mentioned him?"

"I said he didn't, no." Whitfield still hadn't faced me, but I couldn't see signs he was hurt or mad. He straightened the crease in his shark-skin trousers.

"Well, it's true. He's real and he's all mine now, far as I can see."

"You can't work then."

"I've got to," I said. "Babies can't eat air. Douglas Lee contributed fifty dollars, period; it all went for doctor bills."

"Who's tending him now?"

"The aunt that raised me."

That shook Whitfield's face loose; he turned it toward me. "I was raised by an aunt, when my mother died."

"In Raleigh?"

"No, the mountains—out from Asheville, up a valley in hemlock trees."

It was all but dark by then. Even Elmira Peebles had turned on her lights, and cars in the street were scarce and slow. I said "I'll be glad to fix you some supper, then I'll call me a cab and head on back."

Whitfield reached for his cane and stood up again. "I'd rather you did something else, since you offered."

I said "All right." Then I thought "Lord God, he may need the bathroom and help with his clothes." But I stood up too and followed him in.

The whole place was dark, and Whitfield didn't touch a light till he heard me nearly stumble at the turn in the hall. His hand felt out for a wall switch and lit a dim ceiling-bulb; then he lit the music room. When he'd sat at the piano, he said "Step here and get that big blue book in the corner."

In the corner on a low round table was *Beloved Poems of the Human Race*. I wondered what other race loved poems—bees? whales? But I brought the book forward and held it out.

Whitfield said "Page eighty-six, lower left." He struck three wide bass-chords and waited.

I said " 'Success' by Emily Dickinson"—she was news to me.

He said "Read it slowly in your natural voice; I'll play soft beneath you."

I told him of course I didn't know the tune.

He struck a new chord. "*Read*, not *sing*."

So I tried to oblige. I don't have a copy of it near me now; but Whitfield put me through it many times in the days we had, and I almost recall it.

> *"Success is counted sweetest*
> *By those who ne'er succeed.*
> *To comprehend a nectar*
> *Requires sorest need.*

> *Not one of all the purple host*
> *Who took the flag today*
> *Can tell the definition,*
> *So clear, of victory*
>
> *As he—defeated, dying—*
> *On whose forbidden ear*
> *The distant strains of triumph*
> *Break agonized and clear."*

Somewhere in the middle Whitfield's chords stopped; and I finished alone, not knowing what I'd said. I read back through it silently.

Whitfield knew to wait. Then he said "You agree?"

I thought I understood him; I still think I did. I thought he meant how he and I had lost till we'd turned into experts. And yes, I agreed (though I wondered who had *won* and though it didn't make me proud). But I didn't answer, not directly right then. What stopped me was a high run of happiness, all through me. This room felt ready to fold me in. This blind man, all but helpless as Lee, felt like a deep port or a tough wondrous creature I should learn to touch. One more time I thought I'd found a place where green leaves would grow. I said "I've never met a poem I didn't like."

Whitfield said "I can tell. If you'd started earlier, and I knew enough, we could have you singing on big-time stages before you vote— Madame Butterfly!"

I sang a high line in imitation-French.

Whitfield stood up and grinned. "Lady, you've got *gifts*. Sit still and recover, I'll cook you a western omelet with cheese."

He did, singlehanded, and I've seldom had better. I cleaned up behind him and phoned in a telegram to Caroline—I was safe and would be there day-after-tomorrow. I slept on the sofa in the music room; and creaky as it was, I was tired enough to sleep till seven when I heard Whitfield stir. After breakfast I walked down to Capitol Square, found the license bureau, and asked for the rule book.

The grayhaired patrolman said "How old are you?"

I told him I'd be eighteen in June.

He said "Any proof?"

I pointed to my face.

He checked and nodded and tapped my near hand. "The rules are common sense—don't kill a child. You got your car here?"

I told him no, but I could get one fast.

He said "—And somebody to drive you till you're legal."

I laughed "A blind man owns the car."

He looked around him; nobody was watching. So he said "This is all against the rules. But it's wartime, ain't it?" He took up his clipboard, put on his hat, and said "Follow me in a minute." Then he went out the door.

I thought "I'm in for a Swedish massage." But I waited and went.

In forty-five minutes I'd seen more of Raleigh than I've seen since (with me at the wheel). I'd had the massage, though just of my knee; and I had the receipt that would let me drive till they mailed the license. I gave my address as Macon, N.C.

Whitfield and I were on the road by eleven o'clock. He had three customers in Henderson, that he'd postponed for weeks. So I left him there and drove on to Macon. I knew the road of course, from trips with Dan and Frances and rides with Gaston. But the feeling, that warm day, of making the road myself as I went—really *building* it beneath me—was new as cool water to a perishing child.

When I turned in at Holt and Caroline's, there was Noony in the side yard, hanging out wash. She didn't know the car (a light-tan Crosley), but she held her ground. When I got out I went toward her first. It seemed like the three days had changed me completely; she watched me come like a total stranger till I was no more than ten feet away. Then she bent double, laughing, and said "You a *sport*! Leave here, trucking pitiful in this old dust, and come wheeling back in a rich man's car. I taught you right."

I laughed too. "You did."

Then she whispered "Where you hid him?"

I knew she meant Douglas, and I'd decided to protect him. I told her I'd left him in Henderson with his piano-tuner.

"And that's his car?"

"The blind man's," I said.

"Safer you driving than them, I guess."

I said "We thought so." And somehow that was it. The lie about Douglas had shut us both up. I said "You're looking good."

Noony nodded and took a long look at my face. Then she pointed to the house. "That baby in yonder."

"He doing all right?"

"He waiting," she said.

And he was, on his back, in the midst of his bed. Just being away that short time made him partly new. For instance, I saw how his skin was still splotched with the remains of winter eczema. His eyes seemed definitely larger, so big they might well speak before his mouth did; and his smile (when he knew me) was slower than before but so strong it seemed to hurt him.

Holt and Caroline both were beside me. I'd already repeated my claim that Douglas was working in Henderson till late afternoon; but I hadn't said a word about my own plans, not to mention Lee's. Holt dived in though. He tapped Lee's covered knee and said "You ready?"

I didn't face Holt but I knew he meant Lee. I said "For what?"

"A traveling life."

I looked to Caroline but she didn't speak. So I said "Can we go in the living room and talk?" They went on ahead while I settled Lee, in hopes he'd sleep. He was serious again and wide awake, but he didn't complain when I finally went.

Then I told them the truth—Douglas Lee had vanished; his old employer had offered me a job; I meant to stand on my own with Lee; would they just watch him a little while longer till I'd dug in in Raleigh?

They were both bowled over but Holt spoke first. "Who's the man and what's the job?"

I explained that too, far as I understood. I stressed Whitfield's blindness and his present need, though I didn't mention his cut right-hand. I showed them my driver's-license receipt.

Holt studied it and said "Hell, you could join the Army—drive a tank for the WACs."

Even Caroline smiled but she said "Who'd watch Lee, once he got to Raleigh?"

"Me. He could ride with Whitfield and me. All I do is drive and wait."

She didn't try to answer, but Holt said "Gypsies have thrived on less; course I never knew a gypsy."

They hadn't condemned me and they hadn't yet said they wouldn't keep Lee. Looking back, I can see how normal that was—and how completely strange. I might as well have been a young widow in olden days, kissing their foreheads and striking out alone through the Cumberland Gap at the mercy of redskins, floods, and rattlers—no postal service to keep us in touch. So I forced their hand. "Can you keep Lee awhile?"

They looked at each other. And though I'd known them all my life, I couldn't see any signals passed. Finally Holt said "I don't doubt your word, Kate; you've never lied to me. I do need to know one more thing please—is Douglas really gone?"

"Vanished, yes sir."

"Douglas will hurt you if you've hurt him—"

Caroline said "Holt, you haven't seen Douglas in eighteen years."

Holt smiled. "In that one respect, I'm blessed."

I said "I think I know what you mean. Douglas can't be crossed, not when he's drawn his own deep line in the dust. But no, I haven't hurt him and don't plan to."

"This child hurts him bad." Holt pointed toward my room, where Lee was still quiet.

"I doubt it," I said. "I doubt anything hurts Douglas but Douglas."

So Holt looked at Caroline and, this time, nodded.

She made a slow gather in the thigh of her dress. Then she said "Lee's very little trouble. You go."

"With your blessing?" I said

She didn't answer that.

But Holt said "Caroline blesses all but houseflies."

I settled for that, went back to the bedroom, and packed two grocery bags full of clothes. The only thing I added was my papers—my birth certificate, school report-cards, and my parents' letters. Lee was quiet right through it; but when I looked down to say goodbye, his eyes were so involved in following every move I made that I didn't try to touch him. I did speak though. I said "Any day now, you and your mother will start this life we're meaning to have." I know I believed it.

And through the next six weeks, I had no serious doubts that Lee and I would wind up together. I didn't dwell on it in my private thoughts, and I didn't pine for him. But I saved every penny I possibly could and kept my eye out for some place he and I could live and know each other in peace. I also wrote to Caroline frequently, enclosing notes Lee could read someday—just short descriptions of the trips with Whitfield, funny things we did.

I was rooming upstairs at Whitfield's temporarily. His landlord, Mr. Jackson, let me have the back bedroom with bathroom privileges for almost no rent. I barely ever saw him. As Whitfield had said, he was gone all week; and on weekends he stayed in his own room, polite and quiet but knee-walking drunk. I knew it was no place to bring Lee to. Still after a day on the road with Whitfield, it served me fine for clean deep rest. And since Whitfield never attempted the stairs, I could be all alone for hours on end (the first time ever); and soon I liked it—I was fairly good company, compared to some I've had. The room had been Mr. Jackson's son's before the war—a high single-bed, a rifle on the wall, an Indian rug. And I tried not to mark it with my little mess, just kept it as-was in hopes the son could return alive from mainland Japan (Mr. Jackson thought he was already on a boat bound for Japan; he was twenty years old).

Four or five days a week, I was bound with Whitfield to tune pianos in homes and churches. If we worked in the country, I'd wait on the lady's porch, lie to her questions, and read a book (I got through Mr. Jackson's whole set of Emerson and started Bulwer-Lytton). In towns I'd stroll through shady streets, count the gold-star-mother flags in windows, eat a sandwich in the diner, and strike up talks with middleaged men who'd tell me identical tales of marriage—all bleak as Nebraska. Any place, the work-day would always end with Whitfield testing his job one last time by strumming harmony to my recitation of some new poem (I always brought the book and he chose). The more poems you know, the more you suspect they're all saying one thing in slightly different ways—*Stand up and be counted before they bat you down.* Still I memorized dozens and they've mostly stayed with me till now, useful games I can haul out at night to see me through.

It would always be on the long drives home that Whitfield would open up and tell me his life. He never once alluded to blindness or affliction; and if he complained about anything small, I don't recall it. But he did have one big grief he'd harp on. He felt that being single was an insult to God and nature, maybe even a crime. He'd remind me of all the great Bible couples—Adam and Eve, Jacob and Rachel, how they'd started mankind and blessed its future.

I'd tease him with Samson and Delilah, David and Bathsheba, and remind him of Jesus's bachelorhood. He'd laugh—my pairs were not legally married and Jesus might well have had a wife back home (read the Gospels again and you won't say me nay). I'd laugh and say "Nobody's stopping you. Take a want-ad tomorrow; you'll be hitched by dark." He'd never laid a tender finger on me, so it never crossed my mind he was thinking of Kate. I'm sorry to say it was only because his blindness made me see him like some kind of saint, a thing that had caught God's special attention (which seems to cause pain).

A very small part of my mind still thought Douglas might reappear. It didn't scare me much. I was fool enough to think what had happened in my past life was customary, not all that awful, and would likely continue—Douglas or Lee or both or neither.

Anyhow late in April (which had been a full month with Roosevelt's death and his long slow funeral, where they buried more than they've ever had since), we were almost back from a trip to Goldsboro. It was hot and I was dazed; and since Whitfield was silent, I hummed old songs. I thought he might be dozing. But as I began to hum "Deep Purple," he began to recite.

It was one of the Emily Dickinson poems I'd learned by heart; and he said the first verse in a low clear voice, "*This is my letter to the world—*"

I waited for the rest, but he stopped right there.

So I finished my tune and said the next verse, "*That never wrote to me.*"

He didn't quite let me get to the "*me*" but pressed his cool palm hard on my wrist. "I remember," he said. He gave us maybe ten seconds of quiet; then he said "I could spend my whole life with you."

I answered too quick. "You certainly could." I must have meant I was loyal and strong (I still thought I was).

Whitfield faced the road and almost frowned. Finally he said "Is it settled then?"

And I saw what he'd meant. He'd simply asked what I'd begged to hear since I was a girl—an honest offer from a man my age. I paused, in respect, to think it through. I even said a quick prayer to be led. No answer came though, not from my heart. My mind said "Safe. Kate, take this now." But I drove on quiet—he didn't turn toward me—and when we had passed the modernistic cemetery east of Raleigh (with no tombstones), I heard my voice say "Whitfield, *thank* you. I'll stay close by long as my life lets me; but no, not for good."

"Would you tell me why?"

I thought he'd earned it; so I went on and told him—my whole life-story, that I'd kept back till then. It lasted till we were home and supper was ready, and every word was true.

Whitfield didn't generally say grace at meals. But that night we sat down to creamed chip-beef; and he said "You mind if I bless this, Kate?"

I said "It could use it."

He smiled but bowed his head and asked that this food heal our bodies and souls. Then he found his buttered roll and chewed a big bite. Then he said "I think we're both waiting for Doug."

I laughed. "To do what?"

"Come back here or die."

I said "Douglas Lee is either in Norfolk, where he knows the ropes, or he's joined the Navy. The Japs may kill him but otherwise, no—he's lasted through far worse than you or me."

Whitfield said "You still think I made him cut me, don't you?"

"He cut you, sure—he cut my cousin Walter."

Whitfield said "I was kind to Doug."

"But he asked you for money?"

"A good deal, yes."

"And you turned him down?" I could hear the know-it-all chime in my voice, and I bit my lip.

But it didn't faze Whitfield. "I told him I never lent money to friends; I'd give him what he needed."

"How much was that?"

"He said he'd have to think."

"When was it?" I said.

"Two days before he left; he didn't ask again."

"He wouldn't," I said. "He hates a gift."

"I noticed that—the saddest thing about him. I'd have given Doug Lee a big share of my life."

"Relax," I said. "There's plenty good drivers."

Whitfield faced me and, once more, I thought he could suddenly see—his eyes were that focused. He said "You of all people shouldn't mock love."

I took his rebuke and said I was sorry. But when his eyes had calmed down again, I said "What would anybody love in Douglas?"

He waited, then gave a long genuine laugh. "I choose who to love, Kate; I couldn't *see* Jesus if he skipped through the door."

I looked at the open door, said "Well, he hasn't"; and we both laughed again. But through the years since, I've recalled his answer and gradually realized how serious he was and how much I agree. Love or take-it-or-leave-it or hate—from the day I was born till this cool minute, I've *chosen* which feeling I have for each face. And I've got nobody but me, Kate Vaiden, to thank or blame. In many other trips I know I've been led but not in love; I've flown that solo—pilot, navigator, wrecking crew. I don't ask one other soul to applaud. I will say, though, it's let me travel light.

*   *   *

Whitfield was right in another thing too—I was waiting paralyzed, though not for Douglas. If you weren't young then and living in America (safe as Mount Shasta but surrounded by war), you can't imagine how everything waited for the war to end. Long-range plans, new stockings, deep *breaths*—all snagged on the war and marked slow time. I was as hypnotized as everybody else, especially in those early spring weeks in Raleigh. People were saying the Japs would fight till the last baby died, but the Germans were plainly losing fast.

I'd promised myself that, the day the Germans quit, I'd make plans for Lee—where we'd live and how. It was one vow I kept. Whitfield and I had taken the day off to get the car fixed. I was washing windows; he was working on his watch, and neither one of us had listened to the radio. Then in the still warm midafternoon, sirens went off in the heart of town. Cars shot by with blaring horns. Even Elmira Peebles was out in her yard, in bedroom slippers.

Whitfield found me in the music room. And while I was thinking it might be an air raid, he sat down somber on the piano stool and played straight through "Praise God from Whom All Blessings Flow." He paused, faced my way, gave a wide grin, and charged feet-first into "Columbia, the Gem of the Ocean."

Finally I said "You rehearsing a show?"

"Show's over," he said.

And then I understood. We walked down to Capitol Square, to Christ Church, and said private prayers on our knees on velvet benches. The sexton told us there'd be a full thanksgiving service that evening. But neither one of us was strong on crowds. So we walked back home and, on the way, I stopped at the house of a gold-star wife I'd been noticing for weeks.

I've forgot her name now but can see her like a drawing—tall and thin, dark and white. She was maybe twenty-five, with two little children; and she had a place big enough for several more. I guessed she'd be feeling more lonely than ever on that glad day. I was probably right. In under ten minutes she said she'd been thinking she'd rent two rooms, for the money and the company; and no, she wouldn't object to a baby. Did I have any references? I introduced Whitfield as my employer. He said he'd guarantee my honesty and neatness, though he didn't know the baby so couldn't speak for him. She asked if I'd also lost my husband; and I said yes, but not in the war. She left it there and I said I'd move in on the first of June (I was paid-up at Mr. Jackson's till then).

All through the evening Whitfield seemed blue. I thought it was just his response to the day—the surrender, everybody kissing in the streets in spite of many thousand dead boys' ghosts. And I left him alone. But at bedtime when I headed off upstairs, he said "Will it mean you're gone completely?"

Again I understood. I said "Whitfield, I've given up on meanings. But no, I haven't gone anywhere yet and don't plan to—just down the street. I'm your chauffeur and friend till fate says *Stop*."

He said "Fate stops me the instant I wake up, every last morning."

"Tries to," I said. "You've mostly disobeyed."

He didn't smile but he thought it out and nodded. Then he went to his own room, slow but straight as any trained birddog.

Upstairs I sat at the small student's-desk, with the gooseneck lamp as hot as a broiler, and wrote to Caroline and Holt. I said my job was going fine, that I'd found good rooms with a clean war-widow for Lee and me, and that I'd be up there the end of May to move our things. I thanked them in advance for the last few weeks—and most of my life—and then at the end I surprised myself. I mentioned that Whitfield and I had gone to church now that half the war was over. Then I said that the bitter part for me was Gaston, how I couldn't forgive the world for Gaston. I knew I'd never said such a thing before, but I didn't strike it out, and I sealed the letter.

And all night long, when street noises woke me, I'd lie on my back and try to see Gaston in the pitchblack above me. I guess I was building my own war monument from scraps of one good dead boy's face. He'd been a real boy though, not a Rebel marksman on a courthouse column. And I built to last. As recently as now, I can say "Gaston Stegall," shut my eyes, and have Gaston near me—warm and clear in every hair and vein. In that way anyhow, he'll live long as me.

*　*　*

Next morning Whitfield wondered if we ought to make our trip (a short one, to Cary). Maybe people wouldn't want a piano tuned on such a grand day. I said "If work stops everytime a war ends, then mankind'll make no headway at all." So we kept our appointments and were welcomed at each, though one lady had a brand-new black-eye.

The mail hadn't come when we left that morning, and I'd dropped my Macon letter in the corner box. That evening there was Whitfield's usual crop of letters. I always told him who they were from and read him the few not typed in Braille, and he never failed to ask me if I'd received any and would I care to share? I'd never lied to him and had generally passed on Caroline's news of Lee and the garden and clouds in the sky. But that day the one thing for me was from Walter. He hadn't been in touch since I moved to Raleigh; so I was surprised, said as much to Whitfield, then bit my tongue. He'd want to hear it now.

But he didn't push. He sat on the porch; and as soon as I could, I slipped upstairs. If I'd ever thought Douglas meant nothing to me, my hands disproved it. I knew his name was somewhere in the letter, and my fingers shook hard as I eased it open. The first page said he'd heard from his mother that I had a job. He wanted me to know I was welcome—I and Lee—with him any day. He also said, if I stayed in Raleigh, he'd support me and Lee while I finished school, went to business college, or took any training to better myself. He said he had put me square in harm's way, and he prayed I'd give him a second chance. The last page said he'd finally heard from Douglas Lee two days before, that Douglas was in Durham keeping books for Liggett and Myers but was broke again, and that he'd just sent him a substantial check. I remember, at the end, Walter said "If a hundred dollars buys *any* of us peace, it's the one sound investment I've made in my life."

So there was real news. Douglas hadn't gone farther than twenty-five miles. Tomorrow morning I could pick up the phone, call Liggett and Myers, and hear his voice. Would he stand still to listen, and what would I say? I know I sat still in my rented chair for a long quarter-hour and asked myself old questions again. Did any cell in

my mind or body need Douglas now? Did I owe it to Lee, to find his
father and do what it took to calm and feed a soul as restless as a tree
in flames? Again I couldn't feel any fear of Douglas (he'd only hurt
men), and I had little pockets of pleasant memory and the sizable
fact of a child we'd made. But no, I couldn't want him anymore than
the nearest face hid in the dim street below.

Whitfield called up from the foot of the stairs. "Could you help
me a minute?"

He seldom asked for help, and his voice sounded strange.

I went down at once.

He was upright and still by the railing post; he'd gone a lot paler
in the last half-hour. He said "Do you smell anything strange?"

I could see he'd made a quick trip to the toilet (his fly was buttoned
crooked), but I sniffed and said "No—a bus just passed."

"It's not that, Kate. Step in here with me." He turned and led the
way to his toilet at the end of the hall. The door was open. He stopped
outside and said "I seem to smell blood."

I'd noticed before that, despite the blindness, his sense of smell
was nothing special. And I wondered "How does blood smell?" (even
now I can't remember). But I stepped through the door and took a
short breath. He kept his bowl and tile spotless, so the smell was clean.
But yes, there was something strange in the air. I said "You got any
new medicine?"

"For what?" he said. "I'm well and you know it."

"Then I don't see anything. Let's start supper."

Whitfield touched the back of my arm, something he almost never
did. "Whatever's wrong, it's in the tub." His tub was deep porcelain
with a canvas shower-curtain, and the curtain was shut.

I thought "He's making me look," but it didn't scare me. I switched
on the basin light and drew back the curtain. There's no way to say
the rest and not make it sound like the last dream you hoped for. I
managed not to yell or faint. But I did sit down hard on the commode.
Then I said "God help us, Whitfield—Doug is here dead." It was the
only time I ever called him Doug. He looked that young and finally at
ease.

Whitfield turned and walked fast toward the kitchen. After a few steps though, he came back and quietly found me with his hands. He said "You sure it's him?"

I'd watched Douglas Lee asleep more than once and I was certain. Since Whitfield's right hand was still on the crown of my head, I just nodded. "His face is all here. He's shot through the heart." I guessed it was his heart. He had on a white shirt, still buttoned at the neck, and his dark blue tie, tan slacks I'd never seen before and—in his breast pocket—a hole the size of a dime. Most of the blood was under him.

Whitfield said "Is the pistol there?"

"A little silver one."

Whitfield said "I know when he bought it."

"Then you think he killed himself?"

Whitfield said "No doubt on earth. Nobody else despised him enough."

I knew I didn't. The years since haven't shown me a lot of reasons to thank Douglas Lee; but when I finally bent forward out of Whitfield's reach and laid four fingers on Douglas's forehead, I knew that his heart (which was all but gone) had taken too much of Kate Vaiden with it, wherever it was bound.

That was early evening, still not dark. By nine o'clock the undertaker and the police and the few neighbors had left. Nobody turned up who'd seen Douglas enter (he'd kept a key), and nobody claimed to have heard a shot. Whitfield had run it like General Mark Clark. Before he called the police, he'd calmly asked me to search the house for any note or letter. When I came back with nothing, he'd said "That's as kind a thing as Doug ever did." Then he said "Wait in your room. Nobody knows you knew him."

"Elmira Peebles does."

He thought about that. "I doubt she'll harm us. Let me try to run this."

So I climbed upstairs again and shut my door. I changed clothes, skin-out, and fixed my face. Then I sat in the one lean easy-chair and watched my hands for longer than I thought any human could watch.

Nobody that's ever touched anyone in happiness, and then really lost them, will need a list of what I felt. At once I realized I'd now lost four—Dan, Frances, Gaston, Douglas—and of course I came back time and time to the worst chance of all. *I'd caused their deaths.*

The thought of that chance hung on me long years. As lately as ten or twelve years ago, I could wake up sweating at three a.m. with the pure conviction that *Yes, I did it*—any one of them or all. But eventually you live; your body wants to live. Nobody comes to charge you (though angels may be waiting). You offer to pay but the world looks puzzled and asks little more than a well-wishing face, clean nails and hair.

I heard every car that came to the house, every time the door opened. I heard the hearse leave, and I heard men's voices but no clear words. Finally it was quiet—and quiet for so long I thought "They've arrested Whitfield and I'm here alone." Then I felt the last ton of the day fall on me. For once I couldn't think where to go.

But before I could move, Whitfield spoke from somewhere downstairs—not the foot of the steps.

He said "All right," in a normal voice.

And I had to go find him.

He was in the music room, on the piano stool but turned toward the door, not the keyboard. He looked thinned-down like he'd run a long race, with poor results. But when I'd walked to the sofa and sat, he said "Have we got enough gas to drive up home?"

"Whose home, Whitfield?"

It seemed to surprise him that there was more than one. He finally said "Mine, you know—near Asheville."

I said "If Faircloth will sell us the stamps." (Faircloth Phipps owned the nearest gas-station and sold Whitfield blackmarket ration-stamps.)

Whitfield nodded. "I've sat here thinking and I hope I've planned it right. We pack a light bag each and strike out for home."

"Right now?"

"Yes ma'm. The trees'll be out and I want you to see it."

I said "You've got two jobs tomorrow."

"I can cancel them."

"Are we free?" I said.

"—As we've ever been, yes."

"The police took your word?"

"Had to," he said. "I told them the truth."

"Tell me then please."

He stood up in place; and for a few seconds, he seemed confused—the first time ever in my weeks with him. But then he held out the palm of his right hand. The scar was still red, though neat as a seam. Then he sat down and faced me. "I said he was Doug Lee from Norfolk, Virginia. I said his nearest kin was Mr. Walter Porter of the N & W Railroad. I said he'd come down here last year to better his lot, that he'd been my driver in the winter and spring but had left me, worried about old debts. I said I'd heard he had a history of trouble, but he'd been kind to me like nobody else and faithful till the minute he walked away. I said I couldn't even try to fathom what turned him wild. And I said I was sorry from the depths of my heart but no, not surprised."

"They walked off with that?"

"That and Douglas's cold body—they washed out the tub."

I couldn't believe it could end that quickly (even now I have to remind myself how innocent the Law used to be back then). Still I didn't question anything Whitfield had done. What I really meant to ask was, had my name been mentioned; but I said "—The whole truth?"

Whitfield said "Nearly. I left out I loved him."

We stayed downstairs the balance of the night, like we'd silently decided not to sleep that near Douglas Lee's restless spirit till we knew it was gone. I sorted the pantry, where Whitfield had hoarded half the canned goods made since 1941. He framed more pictures that he'd recently got—a crying baby from *Look* magazine, Helen Traubel in a helmet, an elephant charging. Neither one of us turned on the radio; Whitfield didn't play a note, though I almost asked him to. And when we heard the paper hit the porch before dawn, he said "Can you see now?" (he was scared for me to drive in the dark).

I said "I'll get the paper and check on the sky."

He said "Throw that paper far as you can."

I'd never known him to litter the world with so much as a chewing-gum wrapper, so I took him at his word. And we were on the road as soon as the world started pumping gas.

Back then traveling west in North Carolina was only a little easier than it was for Daniel Boone. You gritted your teeth and curved and climbed and prayed your radiator didn't explode. It was by far the longest I'd driven, and of course I did it on my own with nothing but gas and pee stops (we'd packed a small lunch). For the first time since I'd known him, Whitfield slept most of the way. Every half-hour he'd jerk awake, say *Excuse* me," then sink again.

Once we'd passed Winston-Salem, traffic slacked off; and I got a lot of opportunities to watch him. I could no more guess what he thought or dreamed than I could with a swan, but I knew we had literally not mentioned Douglas since early in the night. And I came up with long rows of questions to ask—the way he'd known Douglas, the reasons he'd loved him, and what that had meant to either one of them.

But when we began to slow for the foothills and he finally woke up, I couldn't speak a word—not a question at least. They all seemed ways to risk having Douglas spring back plain beside us, fine on the eyes but way too famished to fill or ease. I said to myself the one thing Douglas Lee actually taught me—"Never *dream* you *know* a person." Then I took a silent pledge not to be the first to name him. And we never did again—not Whitfield and I, in the time we had left.

His home was out from Asheville, near Weaverville. In his childhood stories he'd made it all sound like hamhock poverty and hillbillies that wouldn't speak for days and then not in English. But when we got to his aunt's place in the shank of the afternoon, it looked clean and open. The house was two-story, unpainted boards; and everything seemed kept-up—clean stunted chickens, a swept dirt yard, and plants by the porch. I remember thinking "Some of the meanest women on earth raise houseplants." But by then I'd stopped the car, and a short woman with coal-black hair and a bone-white face had appeared at the front door. I said to Whitfield "How old is your aunt?"

He said "Sixty-three."

"Then it's not her—a blackhaired lady's barring the door."

"It's her; she claims her hair is part-crow."

"Get out then," I said. "Let her see who's landed."

Whitfield got out slowly and stood by the car. The woman stayed in place; and if a word was said, I didn't hear it. Finally he leaned down and said "Please walk in with me," the one and only time he asked me for guidance.

I climbed out, nodded to the lady, went to Whitfield, and led him forward. It seemed about a month till we got to the steps. If a kind blind creature hadn't asked for help, I'd have run like a rat on a blistering road.

As we started up toward her, the lady said "Corbett."

I thought "Thank God—we're at the wrong place."

But Whitfield said "How are you, Aunt Rio?" (Corbett turned out to be his middle name.)

Then the lady turned to me, and a smile good as Whitfield's spread out across her. If she'd moulted peacock feathers on the porch, it couldn't have shocked me more. She said "Who would you be?" but the smile survived.

I waited for Whitfield to introduce me but he stayed still. So I said "Kate Vaiden. I'm Mr. Eller's driver."

"Prettiest man I ever saw," she said.

I didn't know whether she was crazy, joking, or mean as a snake.

Whitfield said "If you ever get the chance, trade any three men you know for this Kate."

Miss Rio said "I haven't known three men, Corbett. You step in and rest."

In spite of her smile, the invitation was addressed just to Whitfield. But he said "Both of us could use good beds."

Miss Rio said "I've got them" and stood aside, and Whitfield led me on through the door. As we passed her Miss Rio said—to herself, I think—"Greatest crime on earth."

*   *   *

Before sundown Whitfield led me out to see the sights. They were limited naturally to mountains and trees. Until that day I'd never seen a mountain, so they came as a surprise. I'd expected to admire them. But after an hour of Whitfield praising their beauty and strength, which of course he'd never seen, I began to think they'd crush me flat if I stayed here long. The trees were better—high dark hemlocks and worlds of laurel.

Still I asked Whitfield to take me back to where he'd played as a child. That turned out to be Miss Rio's yard and a set of cedar poles. She'd strung wire between them in a long network that ran to the backdoor. With a hand on that, he'd been able to fetch firewood and fresh bantam-eggs. And when chores were done, he could feel his way out again and play in a roped-in ring by the fig bush. The wire was gone by the time I was there, but Whitfield walked me from pole to pole with perfect aim. When we stopped in his play ring, I asked what he'd played.

He said "Mostly war. That may surprise you. I had a lot of meanness in me back then though, and Rio's husband had been in the Army. So I learned it from his stories and his hard hand on me. I'd lie in the dirt on the edge of this ring—always on the *edge*—and cut down whole divisions of men that poured in at me, after my life. No toy gun either, just my long finger. I believed they were there, bunched there in the ring. I knew my hope was to kill every one. I managed to— till now—and I never made a sound, so nobody's known I was that redhanded."

I said "Well, you won."

It took him a good while but finally he grinned. "Maybe so. *Hope* so." Then Miss Rio came to the door and called us.

When we'd finished eating her fairly slim pickings (corn bread, potato cakes, and hard porkchops), I volunteered to wash the dishes. Miss Rio accepted, showed me how (she still heated her own water), and then went toward the front room with Whitfield. I figured they had some catching-up to do.

But before I'd finished she was back beside me, mixing the hydrochloric acid she drank to dissolve her food inside her.

I'd seen a piano in the front of the house, so I said "Maybe Whitfield'll play us a tune."

"In his sleep then," she said. "He's flat-dead asleep. I took him to his room, and he fell right off."

Before I thought, I told her neither one of us had slept in two days.

At first that didn't seem to register on her. She put away dishes and wiped the place down like an operating room. Then she got the kettle, made two cups of Postum, set them at the table, and motioned me down.

It was the first time I'd ever been offered hot liquid *after* a meal, so I sat down near her and felt a little ease in the quiet between us.

Then Miss Rio faced me like a cold creature trapped in a tunnel. Her lips spread open well before she spoke, and the acid had leached her front teeth upward in a grinning curve. "Corbett's been *struck*."

"Not by me," I said.

"But struck—am I wrong?"

I knew she'd known him too long to take a lie. So I sat there, drank my drink, and told her what I knew he'd told the police—that he'd hired a man to drive him, they'd quarreled over money, the man had vanished, then come back yesterday and shot himself dead in Whitfield's toilet while we were at work.

She took every word like a card played at her in an earnest game. And when I finished by saying he'd headed home soon as trouble struck, she said "Where are you?"

I said "Beg your pardon?"

"—In that little story."

I knew I'd lost. I said "Near the middle. I was almost his wife."

"The dead man's?"

"Yes ma'm. His name was Douglas Lee."

She frowned and said "I'm sorry you told me."

I said "You might have liked him; he mainly harmed himself."

"Who cut Corbett's hand?"

"That's a mystery," I said.

She studied me carefully. "He sure harmed you."

At first I thought she meant my looks (I was tired and drawn, and my hair was dirty). But then I thought *"She's* the one means harm." I wanted to say he's blessed me with a son—Whitfield had told me she never had a child—till I thought "I've got to save back something here. Things are *leaving* again." So I said "Miss Rio, I'm tired is all. When you see me rested, I'll be strong and ready for anything you got."

She said "Where's your baby?"

I begged her pardon.

She said "Corbett wrote me his driver had a baby."

I nodded "Six months old, a smart peaceful boy. He lives with my aunt; I'm claiming him soon."

Miss Rio drank in a mouthful of Postum, rinsed her teeth, and swallowed. Then she reached out and touched my left shoulder lightly. "Your church don't believe in wedding rings?"

I said "Oh yes, the more gold the better. But I turned down the chance."

"Is it him?—the man that killed himself?"

"It was," I said, "till yesterday evening."

"You understand Corbett was a bastard too, don't you?"

I'd never heard the word used literally before (though I'd thought it many times when Lee was on the way). I said "He's been a kind life-saver to me."

She nodded so hard her neck gave a pop. "Don't doubt it—*never.* Even when he lived here, before the Blind School, he used to pay children to play with him. I was talking about his mother though. She was my baby sister, and she no more had a husband than I've got fleas. But she had a blind son, that was hungry and could scream; and she gave him to me."

"Whitfield said you raised him."

"*Begged* to raise him," she said, "and still thank Jesus in the night for the chance."

I asked how long ago her husband had died.

Miss Rio said "Too recently—mean as a cold axe but I stuck by him. It was stick or starve up here back then. He had a big forge, and his customers paid him—always in money; he wouldn't take eggs or butter or cloth. So he kept me and Corbett—but hard, like I said."

"Whitfield said he beat him."

She said "Yes, God. I hoped he'd forgot—I've managed to, myself. But I saw a whole lot. It saved Corbett though; I can see that now. If I hadn't known he had to clear out of here, I never would have thought about the State Blind School—or any place else beyond this yard. I asked around though and wrote all the letters. And when they wrote back and said 'Send him on,' I figured God just might forgive me now for some of the meanness I'd stood by and watched."

"He's strong," I said. "It all made him strong."

Miss Rio said "He's done fairly well. But glad as I am, I miss him to death. I won't try to tell you how I felt the morning I led him out of here and down to Asheville and put him on the train to Raleigh— far as Asia. My husband wouldn't let me make the trip with him, so I turned him over to the old conductor. When they climbed aboard, I knew he was *gone*. He'd either come back in a pine box or never."

"He's back right now."

She stood up and walked to the one tall window. Beyond it was a green ridgeline in the dusk. I thought "I haven't seen a better sight since Gaston died." But Miss Rio didn't see it, I thought—her eyes were glazed. Then she fooled me. She reached out one knobby finger and traced the line of the mountain exactly on the pane. Then she looked back and said "He brought you, girl, right to my front door. That's nowhere near the same thing as coming back." I might have thought I'd been struck one more time, but she broke out smiling and asked to play cards.

I stayed downstairs in her husband's old room; she and Whitfield were upstairs. And all of us were out by nine o'clock. For three or four hours, I slept like limestone. But then something shook me, a noise in the woods uphill from the house. I've always thought it was a panther's cry; I'd already read how they mock human babies and lure you to death. So I woke up cold in the cold mountain air. The only light was a ceiling bulb, and the switch was by the door, so I stayed in the dark and listened for the next cry. But nothing else came, just a few night birds.

In less than five minutes, I was in deep trouble. It started in the form of a sudden thought—Douglas Lee's body should have been sent to me; *I* was his next-of-kin, in more ways than one. And I'd failed him there too. Then I plunged on downward through dark and pain to the fear I'd discovered the night before—I'd caused the death of every man that touched me, really *touched* me in need. Dan, Gaston, now Douglas. All I'd done in repentance was to give birth to Lee, another frail man. Could I kill him too?

I've mentioned how that fear stuck with me through the years. It was never as bad though as that mountain night, with the picture of Douglas's body so clear—just past my reach. Most people I've met have gone through minutes when they dropped their hands and begged to die. That night was the time I called on death—and *meant* it with every cell in my blood. I wasn't prepared to creep to the kitchen and find a knife or break a window and saw at my wrist. But I lay still the better part of an hour and strained to *cease*.

Of course I didn't. Still I tired myself and by the time daylight started its climb, I was twitching back and forth from sleep to distress. Every time I'd wake I'd see some part of a deer in the room— his startled head, stuffed, on the mantel wall; his feet as a gunrack, his tail on the bureau beside my comb. I'd think he'd somehow exploded in the dark; then I'd have to shut my eyes.

Finally I heard my door creak open. Since I hadn't heard footsteps, I thought it was Whitfield (he could move with less noise than any down-feather). But when I raised up, it was Miss Rio in her nightgown and braids. I said "I'll be glad to help out with breakfast."

She put a finger to her lips for silence. Then she stepped to the bed— her long feet were bare—and sat by my knees. She took real pains not to touch me through the sheets, but she met my eyes. When she'd studied me a long time, she said "I spoke some hard words to you—"

I noticed her eyes had changed in the night. Now they were pitiful and skittish as the deer's. Still I didn't want to spare her too fast. I said "Yes, you did."

"But I want you to know what I've thought all night; I barely shut an eye. I know I've lost all my rights to Corbett. I sent him to Raleigh and he changed his name, but I am his one kin-person left on the earth, and I give him to you." She shut her eyes finally and swallowed hard.

I said "I doubt I understand you."

Miss Rio waited, then said "Maybe not. I doubt I can explain." She tugged at her ring. "But I had a kind of vision, deep into last night. You were tending to Corbett in a clean dry house. He seemed all at ease, for the first time ever. I wanted to bless you."

I said "Thank you ma'm. I've tried to help him; he needs so little."

But she said "—A life. He could use your whole life."

I thought I understood but I said "How's that?"

"Be his wife, for good."

I said "Miss Rio, did he tell you he'd asked me?"

"He's still fast asleep. No, he didn't mention that."

I said "Well, he asked me."

"You answered him yet?"

"I had to say no."

Miss Rio finally touched my knee, just her knuckles through the cover. "What stands in your path?"

I quickly said "Nothing," then saw it was true—nothing stronger than a feeling; who was I to trust *feelings*? But I said "I can't burden him with a child."

"Corbett Eller loves children like Jesus himself."

I knew that wasn't entirely true. I said "My feelings are all numb now."

Her eyes were calming down at last. "I think you'll find feelings don't count for much—through the years anyhow. I'm dying soon."

I said "You look strong."

"I guess I am. But I'm seventy-three (I've lied to Corbett); and I hurt all over, every inch of my bones."

"You been to a doctor?"

She finally smiled. "Oh no, I enjoy myself too much. Doctors killed half the people I've known up till now. Talk about *blind*."

I smiled. "Then you're still good for decades."

Miss Rio nodded. "Or minutes or seconds." She stood up fast and went to the door. With her hand on the black latch, she said "Tell him yes."

She must have thought I nodded—she smiled as she left—and maybe my face did seem to accept her. But before her steps had started upstairs, I knew it was sweeping me off again—whatever thing seized me in corners and led me.

As blank as any child in the Blind School night, I stood up and dressed and rubbed my teeth on the hem of a sheet. Then I closed my bag and took it to the front hall. Still no sound from Whitfield, though Miss Rio was gargling.

I hadn't thought of the name of my plan, if there was any plan, or a destination. I didn't even think of the name *Lee Vaiden*. I was treading my cloudy luck again, like a warm deep pond that could float my weight. I set the car keys on a stand by the door. My eyes were hazy but I saw one last thing—framed on the wall, Whitfield's school picture, maybe thirty blind boys all facing the sun in identical gray shirts and black neckties. That steadied me some. So calm as a last breath, I let myself out. I recall one thought—when my feet struck the road, I said to myself "I still owe Elmira Peebles twelve dollars for Douglas Lee."

The end—true story—every word I know (as Whitfield said to finish the tale of his cut hand). My life stopped there, my old life as Kate, a girl people thought they knew and could lean on. Pictures of course do show the same face, scraping forward through the years. And I never changed my name but I gradually vanished. That turns out to be the easiest trick—in America anyhow, if nobody's hunting you.

Not that I ever intended to vanish or was scared of being caught. I walked the three miles from Miss Rio's to the main road and stuck out my thumb (a first time for me, and for the whole country practically—women in general didn't beg car rides for another twenty years). When I held out my thumb and four cars passed me, I knew my first stop. I'd go on to Raleigh, pay Douglas's debt, pack my few things, and plan from there (Whitfield wouldn't be back fast as me, he'd need a new driver, what mountaineer would help him?).

The fifth car stopped, an elderly man from Tennessee who was headed to his mother's hundredth birthday near Kitty Hawk. He said very little; I slept several hours. And when he left me in Raleigh, I still barely knew him (though he gave me his card, a roofing salesman). It was midafternoon.

The house of course was empty. It took me less than twenty minutes to pack. I left the beaded belt on Whitfield's bed; he wouldn't see the colors, but he'd feel my neatness. I also left a check on Mr. Jackson's bed, my last week's rent. On the back, where he'd endorse it, I wrote how I thanked him and how much I hoped his son would be home by fall.

As I went down the steps, I realized I wanted a souvenir of Whitfield, like the snapshot I'd stolen from Tim in Norfolk. But he'd already told me there were no pictures of him (he'd forgot the only one—his Blind School class). I thought of taking just one of the hundred frames off the wall—all those loud subjects; I'd seen they were *loud*—but I knew he'd eventually find out, miss it, and think even harder of me than now. So I left emptyhanded (of Whitfield at least), though my mind was full.

I'd already put Elmira Peebles's money in an envelope, in case she was out. She was, or at least never answered my knocks; so I put it in her mailbox. As I picked up my bag and turned to go, something made me think of my dogwood necklace—the gold one from Noony and her soldier friend. I stopped, took it off, and laid it in the envelope. I've since wondered why—Miss Peebles had never said a civil word to me. All I know however is that once I surrendered it, I had a clear destination before me. It wasn't Macon either or my son Lee.

I took the train to Norfolk. It got there at two in the morning, but I went straight to Walter's. Tim never drove that late, and the driver I got didn't know me. He talked about Moses all the way, how Moses had misunderstood God's voice. I still had my key; but I rang the bell first, not to startle Walter.

He hadn't gone to bed and was nearly dressed, in his easy chair, reading *Strange Fruit*. He hadn't really changed—a pound or two thinner—and he seemed to think me showing up that late, with no word of warning, was a natural pleasure. He kept his seat but said "Your room's waiting, Kate. I cleaned it tonight."

It turned out he had been telephoning Whitfield's the past two days and getting more frantic but praying I'd appear. The coroner in Raleigh had kept the body an extra day, and Walter hadn't got it till suppertime the night I got there. (It seemed that the coroner's hobby was tattoos; he had a collection of tattoo pictures. He'd found one on Douglas and had to photograph it. Walter said it was on Douglas's left shoulder-blade—the one word *Star*, with streaming rays, all but too small to see. It had looked like the homemade kind you find on reform-school boys, *Born To Lose*. Neither one of us had known it, one last secret kept.) The body was downtown now, in a funeral parlor. Walter had seen it, to check the face. Then he'd ordered the coffin to be locked. He told me of course it could be reopened, if that was my wish. It wasn't. I'd seen it as Douglas intended, fresh as killed beef. I'd come just to finish my half of the deal, whatever deal there was or ever had been.

Walter asked me questions till nearly dawn. I answered as truly as I knew how. Finally I said "I accept a lot of blame."

Walter didn't contradict me but said "Me too."

Then we slept three hours.

In the morning we drove way out of town to the cemetery where Walter and Douglas's landlady was buried. In her will she'd left them space in her plot of sandy ground. Walter had asked a Presbyterian minister to lead the short service. And he did it very neatly in a quick clear voice, not one of those Protestant holy-Joe drags. But was I the only one there who recalled Douglas's atheism and how much he'd have hated St. Paul being read out over his helpless body? Maybe so—there were only five or six more mourners (mostly Navy friends, one or two old strangers).

In present-day funerals the coffin isn't lowered in the ground till the family are well out of sight. The idea apparently is to help you think your loved one has been wrapped safely, blessed for the trip, and will now be borne off by express mail to celestial bliss, all moisture-proof. But in 1945 you stood on an artificial grass footmat by the star-

ing hole and watched your friend sink down—last time. They had
progressed though in one respect—you were no longer asked to watch
the dirt shoveled or throw in a handful. I remember watching Douglas
sink and saying to myself "You've done your last duty; now forget all
this." I believed I could.

Walter said "We did everything in our power." He faced me and
pressed for confirmation.

I knew it was a lie, for me at least. But I said "All right. Let's go on
home."

He thought I meant his place; and maybe I did, still that close to
Douglas. But after another long night of talk—Douglas and my
mother and the early days—I could see there was nothing at Walter's
but the past. And the past had never done anything for me. I eventually nodded agreeable answers to most of his visions of our future;
nobody but a lunatic or a criminal could have openly objected. Lee and
I would live with him; I'd get my diploma and keep house. That would
solve all *our* problems, if not the world's. By bedtime, sad as he was
about Douglas, Walter was excited and shining at the prospect. So I
was smiling too when we said goodnight and went to our rooms.

But when I fished in my suitcase for slippers, I found my old schoolteacher's seahorse—Miss Rosalind Limer, Greensboro, N. C., "eighteen
years a teacher." I hadn't seen Greensboro since 1938; so if she was
still alive, she'd have been teaching twenty-five years. I still loved her.
In my mind she was still a tall thing, giving light, streaming hope
like Douglas's star.

In person too. When I got to Greensboro two afternoons later, I
walked straight on to my old school. I knew the way perfectly, like
home in a dream. Even the cracks in the buckled sidewalk were pre-
dictible, but it was nearly three-thirty (closing time) when I walked
in the door. Going back to any school you've attended is a dangerous
trip. Nothing else acts as such a harsh time-mark. The place itself
seems shrunk of course from what you remembered. But strangest
of all is finding your own body, pieces of yourself in the new generation of children underfoot—your braids on that knock-kneed girl

there, your oversized wristwatch on that thin arm; your eyes everywhere, nervous but steady, not missing a trick. It can make you feel older than you'll ever be again, or already dead and brought back in scraps.

For all I knew Miss Limer was dead, but I went toward her room-door and waited awhile. Not a word seeped out—then suddenly the cry of thirty-odd voices, shutting down one more day with the Marines' Hymn. The final bell rang; children streamed out past me. And there I stood, bag in hand, feeling foolish. If this turned out to be some young war-bride with an Illinois accent, teaching for a year or so till Johnny marched home, what on earth would I say?

But it was Miss Limer at the same oak desk, a teacher for life. The only change I noticed was, she'd faded slightly. Her clothes and hair and even her eyes were three shades lighter, like she laundered daily from head to foot.

I figured I must have done the reverse—deepened in color—and I guessed she wouldn't know me. Still I walked through the door.

She held up her left hand and said "Stop a minute." Then she searched me up and down with her eyes. "I know you," she said. "You sat right *there*"—she pointed to the third row, halfway back, exactly the spot. "But your name won't come."

I set my bag on the floor, bent to open it, and held out the seahorse.

She went on searching my hand and face; then she reset the pins in the back of her hair. Finally she shook her head again. "I think that may have belonged to me; it escaped years ago."

I stepped on forward and set it on her desk. Every paper and pencil was squared off neat as a marching-ground; the blotter was fresh.

She didn't reach to touch the paperweight. Her eyes seemed wet and I thought "She's cracked." But she kept looking at it and then said "Who are you?"

I said "I used to be the girl that loved this." I stroked the seahorse. "Now I've brought him back."

She accepted it at last and took it up. "It may be a *she*; did you think about that?"

I laughed. "No ma'm. I hope it's not."

"Me too," she said. Then she said "Kate Vaiden. I know that

laugh." Then for the first time ever in my life, I saw the meaning of "dawning" on a person. I'll take to the grave my memory of the smile that lit Miss Limer's face when she knew me.

That was two weeks before my eighteenth birthday. I stayed in Greensboro till I was twenty-two. The first week I told Miss Limer all the facts, except Lee Vaiden; I never mentioned him. She responded by saying she'd seldom heard worse, but she granted all the blame didn't rest on me. She'd do what she could to strengthen my luck; she'd always regretted me leaving her class before the term ended— she wasn't *done* with me.

The first three weeks I stayed with her; she had a small apartment in a building full of teachers. I slept on a Murphy bed in her small living room and cooked our breakfast and supper most days. If you went to grade school before the Second War, you probably share the feeling I had—that teachers were not quite human beings. No movie star or president or general had the same grand air of being divine. So imagine my surprise at seeing Miss Limer in her blue nightgown, hearing her brush her teeth at night, or being waked up before day by her snore. Even the fact that she slept was amazing.

Those hours in the dark were the hardest by far. If I put aside the question of my blame for the deaths, I was still pressed raw against one sure certainty—I'd left my child. I never lied about it, to myself, in my thoughts. From the minute I'd boarded the train in Norfolk with a Greensboro ticket, I knew Lee Vaiden was Caroline and Holt's, as long as they lived. I couldn't say *why* at the time and still can't. I didn't think I'd be a worse mother than many (though I've always thought any girl wanting babies ought to have special training and pass hard tests before she's licensed; the fact that a person has ovaries and a womb is far from the minimum qualification). I didn't think his presence—a baby bastard—would scare men off me or cost too much.

All I could think then, and all I understood, was *I did not want him.* I never once doubted that those four words were awful as any a person could say. But I knew they were true. In the decades since, I've known first hand two other women who abandoned children. One discovered, after forty, that she loved another woman and rode off with her in a red Toyota—leaving two fine boys, age four and six, with no apparent pain. The other was a drunk that had ruined her mind on apricot brandy and thought the Russians were bugging her daughter.

No excuse I can offer is as good as theirs. I was strong, unashamed, and ready to work. I'd had some hard knocks—maybe more than average for American white-girls of my time and place—but I don't plead the past. Anybody leaning on the past for an alibi, don't expect my pity. Only thing in my favor is Caroline's goodness—I'd left my boy in the house of a saint. She was not his mother though, and she was too old to bear a burden I'd brought to life.

Those were my night thoughts for several months. Then even they faded. I'd realized, the day I pulled out of Norfolk, that Caroline and Holt would have seen Douglas's death in the paper and would be worried for me. So I mailed them a card from the depot platform, saying I was all right and would be in touch. But I hadn't been. Once I settled with Miss Limer, I wrote to the Warrenton bank and drew out all my savings. I had to reveal my Greensboro address, and for weeks I expected to answer the door and see Holt waiting or—God help me—Swift. It was only this year that I learned they knew where I was right along.

I'd arrived in May. Miss Limer had another month of school to teach, then three months off. Her idea of *off* was to put me through the rest of my high-school training by mail. As I said, I'd mostly enjoyed learning. When Miss Limer left the apartment, I'd sit by a window and count the adverbs in Shakespeare's *Macbeth* or draw neat figures for Solid Geometry. I'd feel like the lone pilot-navigator of a silent dirigible, floating over things. When Miss Limer was home, she would open the big envelopes as they came from the State Department of Education, read the instructions out slowly, then check back with me every hour or so—for neatness, spelling, and grammar (she freely admitted that, after all that time in primary school, most of her senior subjects were rusty). Her tall body then, at my shoulder, was no source of easy answers. But I knew it was something better—a guide.

What it guided me to was the life I was already all but set to have, one where you stayed by yourself at night but joined the other humans in daylight for work. Even Miss Limer's of course was not as plain as that. She had no nearby immediate family, and her sisters were down in Tabor City, "Yam Capital of the Universe" (the nearest thing to the moon back then). But she had more than one local circle of friends—other teachers, a few old pupils and their children, fellow members of the Professional Women's Club, some from her church, nobody close enough to meet more than once every two or three weeks. I watched how she acted in all her circles, how much she gained *and* gave, how seldom she was hurt. In the years I watched her, one old friend died of a sudden stroke—no lingering sadness. So I thought I'd try to live like that.

And I did, more or less, through the years till now. You won't want to hear the details of it all. God knows, you don't need to. It was just normal time—the kind of long story people tell you on bus-trips, illustrated with photos of their boat and dog and bolstered with timetables so precise you eventually pray for the world to end or at least a fatal wreck. The trouble with the rest of my time is not just that it would be tiresome to hear in close detail but also that it wouldn't prove anything. I've just gone on being the person I was the day my high-school diploma landed in Miss Limer's mailbox and I walked out and got my first normal fulltime job—a shelver at the Guilford College Library. If you've come this far, you're well-equipped to guess my moves through the next forty years.

Or maybe not. Maybe my girlhood, on somebody else, might have yielded a pioneer female-astronaut or pediatrician or (at the very least) a police dispatcher. Maybe you'd imagine a lot more adventure. A lot more men and running away. Meanness that kept on growing and rotting. Sorry—you'd be wrong.

With occasional spells off, I've kept up my early tendency to read when alone. Paperback books were invented about the time I lit out, and they've been my absolute steadiest companion. I'm not especially choosy. Almost anything in print can flat hypnotize me—I've missed *airplane* trips because I was waiting at the gate and happened to start reading a handout pamphlet such as "What God Thinks of Hippie Haircuts." Well, it beats drugs and drink. And few people, since Hitler anyhow, seem to have been disfigured by books. Still the main thing they've taught me is that only the wicked bear reading about. And the *busy* wicked at that, not just some spiteful old gator confined to her room with bladder trouble and prickly heat.

Take Jesus for instance. Aren't the interesting parts of His story the ones where He suddenly flies off the handle and does something scary, like curse a poor fig-tree for not bearing figs (and in early spring!) or raise a stinking dead man out of pure hot madness at death itself? — which is one more reason to skip my years from eighteen till now. I'm in no imminent danger of being declared a public saint (private either), but I can guarantee those years were as thrilling to watch as a quilting bee. Here's a fast look though.

Toward the end of that summer, I had enough money and confidence to leave Miss Limer's and strike out for my own hole-in-the-wall. Two rooms, a hotplate, and icebox privileges out near the college. In line with my uncanny nose for events, I set up independent life on the day the first atom bomb was dropped. It's talked about now as a huge surprise—mankind realizing we would someday *fry*, as had been foretold. Well, maybe a few physics teachers saw the point; but everybody I knew took it in stride the day it happened and for years to come. Just one size bigger blockbuster in stock and one that was likely to speed the surrender.

It did of course and I shared in the joy, even joined a parade through the college grounds (though the college was Quaker). But I still grieved for Gaston and so many more. Then the great change started. Like with the bomb, it took awhile before people realized that the Second War really was a *World* War. And the whole world lost, the old world we'd known since all of us were born.

My part of the globe hadn't seriously changed since white men landed in 1607 and bartered for slaves, just up the road from here. But when blacks poured home from the Second War, their tongues had been freed and their hands had been armed. The roots of the old life here were cut. It took the tree another twenty years to die. But die it did, from branch to root. Or put out a whole new species of leaf.

Not that it changed my actions much. I've said what a lot I owe black people, how much kindness I've had—and continue to have—at their strong hands. But of course I was born when and where I was. My inherited sense of how the world ought to look didn't include views of Negroes sharing in-person all we white folks had and did (it didn't occur to us how much of it they'd *done*, and all for us). And I wasn't free enough, not to mention *smart*, to recognize what dim blinders I was wearing.

To change just me it took years of Marian Anderson's voice on the *Bell Telephone Hour*—and the night I actually heard and saw her with friends in Raleigh, raised up there in the golden light like a thing God would show me on Judgment Day as he totaled my bill of right and wrong. Her and the thousands of younger voices solemnly asking for their plain due—that I'd been too dumb to know they wanted. So I changed in that, the best I could. Since I'd never been actively cruel in public, I didn't have a visible lot to reform; and there are stubborn spots I couldn't scour out however I tried. But I keep them covered the best I can. And my heart has felt lighter to that extent.

I shelved books more or less contentedly and made a few friends at the college (no boys). They eventually promoted me to a seat at the main desk, answering reference questions from the students. I didn't know *Hamlet* from *Home on the Range* when I started, but I kept at it and gradually learned a thing or two. Through my years there in fact I took pride in having found answers to all but two questions—why the sky is blue and do cats know something they just aren't telling or are they simpleminded?

The first big personal question was vacations. What would I do when everybody else went home for Thanksgiving, Christmas, Easter? The first year at Christmas I said I was going to Macon for a week. But I hauled out the atlas, traced a line due-north; then took a bus to Roanoke, Virginia and sat in a hotel room, staring out at hills and railroad tracks. The hotel was very near empty of course, so there couldn't have been any shortage of air. But more nights than one I'd come to, bolt upright in the dark, sucking hard for breath. Breath came eventually but Christmas never did, nor any new sight of the

Baby Jesus, born in my presence. Talk about lonesome—and sorry—
and lost. I begged to die.

So I never lied again. Whenever anybody asked where I'd spend a
holiday, I said "Right here. I love this place." That was close enough
to true. I never let myself walk past our old house—Dan and Frances's
and mine—and I never tried to track down any old classmates. Since
my name never showed up in any local paper, they didn't track me.
I'd sometimes be tempted to take out an ad—*Kate Vaiden is back;
all friends please respond.* Of course I didn't and time ground onward.
Otherwise Greensboro treated me kindly. And I might still be there,
a fountain of knowledge; but Miss Limer moved.

I'd gradually seen less and less of her. That was because we were
both either busy or needing to rest; we'd certainly never passed a
harsh word between us. Five or six times a year though, I'd go to her
apartment, eat one of her peculiar meals (she always said she lived on
"chocolate candy and long fast walks," and it was nearly true). Then
I'd bring her up to date on my quiet life. In all the three years, I'd
never done a thing that I couldn't tell her. Nothing, however tame,
was too boring—so long as it had *happened* and to *me*. Maybe time in
the primary grades had done it; whatever the cause, she had a tree's
patience. She'd listen to me tell how I folded my underwear or how I
cooked veal with all the close attention most people give to bonfires.
She'd made me think she would be there forever, my listening post.

But soon as school ended in 1948, she sent me a note saying come to
her Sunday for a birthday supper (I'd turned twenty-one the week
before). After we'd eaten cheese weenies, pork and beans, and chocolate sundaes—followed by my present (a stout billfold)—Miss Limer
said "Kate, I've got an announcement."

I sat up instinctively, still in her grade.

"I'm leaving town."

I thought that was my motto, not hers.

I said "You haven't held up a train, have you?"

She smiled. "No, but that would be the one other thing that could
stop me working."

"What's the first?"

"My sister, not the one you met. This is Etta, the baby. She's still in Tabor City, has never married either, and is crippled up badly—rheumatoid arthritis. Can't even feed herself."

I said "You could bring her up here; I'd help you."

"Thanks. I'm sure you would. But Etta would die; she craves country air."

Miss Limer had really seemed ageless till then, or well past a thousand. Now I sat still and guessed she was somewhere past fifty, a little slack flesh in her neck and jaws.

I said "What grade will you teach down there?"

She smiled. "I won't. I've finished all that."

I'd of course thought teaching was her lifeline and heart. I said "Won't you miss it?"

She laughed. "Not an instant! I've done my time." I must have looked hurt; she leaned out and touched me. "Kate, you gave me this—don't begrudge me now."

I nodded. "I don't. But what did I give?"

"*Success,*" she said. "You came back and let me finish with you. All a teacher needs from life is the whole chance to lead one soul. I've led you a few steps on toward the world, and now you can stride. I'll quit while I'm winning."

I thought a great deal in the next two seconds, mostly about how sadly she was wrong and how I'd deceived her. It was too late to tell her the secrets behind me. So I said "You've *won.* No doubt about that. I'll miss you a lot."

She said "I've thought about that for days. You're the main thing that was holding me here. But you've dug in now; you're safe to leave. Know this though—and I've asked my sister—you're welcome to join us there in the sticks."

I thanked her. "What would we use for money?"

"People don't need money in the country, Kate—free food and water, free roof overhead. I've saved five cents of every dime I earned."

I thought I would hurt her and that maybe I should wait and say it by mail. But her eyes stayed on me—answer right now. I said "Miss Limer, I've made a home here."

She waited so long I thought she'd blanked out (she'd done that in school—waited once you answered some question in Geography till you thought the floor was bound to fall open and you be dragged down to Dunce's Hell). But finally she smiled. "You chose right. The country's not for you."

I laughed. "Why not? I can walk, ride, and shoot."

"But you can't find a mate. Men are scarce down there—young strong smart men—as bears in town."

If she had let fly with curses and screams, it couldn't have stunned me more than it did. I'd barely heard her mention the existence of men, much less mates-for-life. When I'd caught my breath, I said "I took it you didn't plan that—not marriage, me or you."

She said "Kate, I'd marry a kind man tonight, one-legged and deaf. You used to wonder where I got the seahorse. A boy from home sent it to me from Cuba. He'd gone down there in the sugar business and wrote me letters that I thought meant *love*. But once he'd sent the seahorse—and I'd thanked him profusely—the mail slowed and stopped. The next year he married a Cuban girl, and all I had was one more paperweight. So there—I've waited these fifty-four years and never been asked."

I said "I have"—it just slipped out.

"Was he kind?"

"No ma'm. Not steadily, no."

For the first time in three years, her colors changed back; she was vivid as sun through a thin brown bottle. She leaned out near me and raked my brow, like Frances had. Then she said "I won't try to judge what I didn't get to watch. But steadiness is what men seldom have to offer—not in life anyhow, not in this green world. We're not promised that, in the Bible or any other book known to me."

Miss Rosalind Limer knew a lot of books—I recall thinking that. But I didn't say anything else worth repeating. She'd shaken me hard, down to some deep root, and on the verge of leaving me, apparently for good. I guess I wondered if she'd gone feebleminded; or would time prove her right, as she'd generally been?

*   *   *

I tested her out, her powerful claim. The summer after she left, I lived on as usual. Then with fall, and the new school year, came a big raft of vets. They stepped out of battle straight into books, and that was a sight like nothing else since. They were hungrier for learning, among other things, than young Abe Lincoln. Tall fullgrown fellows that had killed other humans in hand-to-hand fight would step up to me, tame as horses, and ask for assistance with a five-hundred-word composition they were writing in Freshman English. Most of them of course were older than me and, God knew, had passed tests grimmer than mine. I got through two months of that sort of day without feeling anything but mild gratitude that I could offer help.

Then the week before Thanksgiving, a student stepped up to my desk and asked for advice on a theme that was due next morning at nine. He'd been assigned the task of describing a *process* in less than three pages. He'd been a tailgunner over Germany, and the processes he knew had all happened too fast to tell in words. What would I suggest?

I couldn't help noticing his eyes, light gray—so light the whole eyeball seemed one color, like ancient white statues (we had some in the library). It must have been them and their pale steady stare that made me blurt out "How to kill a foe with a bayonet."

He was more than six feet tall; but he leaned on the desk, closer down toward my face. Then he said "They pay you to be this mean or you just volunteer?"

I felt like a rattler that had missed her target, and I said I was sorry.

He nodded. "All right. What's a better idea?"

I took the first peaceful notion that came. "How to fix a flat tire on a dirt road at night."

He thought, then stood up straight and laughed. "I can tell *that*," he said. "I've changed ten thousand. And if I get an A, I'll notify you."

He kept his promise (and every other promise I heard him make). He got an A-minus—too few semicolons—but he let me know. By then it was Wednesday before Thanksgiving. Till recently schools just took the one day off, no week's vacation and flights to Bermuda. I'd noticed his left hand didn't show a ring, so I said "You made your turkey plans yet?"

No, he hadn't. And before I'd sifted through my intentions, he developed his own. Could he buy the groceries and me do the cooking? I told him I didn't have an oven at my place, but that didn't faze him. His trailer had one; what time could we start?

—At ten the next morning, the way it turned out. Trailers back then were different from now—more like nice short boats with the bare bones of furnishing, nothing like the whorehouse/beauty-parlor monsters that clutter the country as "mobile homes." He'd laid in supplies—his name was Jay Mabry—and I baked him a turkey big enough for Texas, candied yams, spoonbread, and frozen broccoli (both broccoli *and* freezing were new in the South then as money and peace). I ate as much as Jay, which was quite a hill of food, and in general was happier than I'd been in years. Except for an afternoon walk in the thicket, we stayed cooped up in that blue trailer, with food and a radio and our two selves.

It was during the walk that I noticed his looks. My idea of good-looking men has never been normal. Most male moviestars touch me very little. I have to be close; and once I am, I take a long time to listen for the *sound*. The men I've loved give off a kind of bass-note, soft but steady enough to ride on. If I hear that, no temple in the moonlight looks any better. And that afternoon I heard it from Jay. We'd almost finished and were headed back in the early dusk. Jay parted the thicket two steps before me. As always I didn't know I was listening. But suddenly it came, from his straight broad back. A steady note that said "Rest here." I thought "All right; it's time I did." Maybe I was sending some harmony to his. He didn't face me, just moved on forward till we were inside. But when we were there, he turned and said "I'm almost happy." The trailer had filled up with some kind of smoke—the cool fall evening coming down fast. I said "Don't let me stand in your way. Be happy; go on." So by dark we'd joined close as two humans can, a long benediction on us and the day.

*   *   *

We kept that up through the rest of the year and on into spring. Jay was like nobody I'd known before. There were finer-built men and smarter, no doubt; there were billions worse. And he'd volunteered before me with a whole world to give. The main difference though between him and the rest was, he never asked questions—not about my life. He seemed content with the fact that I'd been there, waiting at a desk with a sensible face, when he needed help.

So I never volunteered a single memory, and he never offered me so much as one war story or the name of his hometown or whether he was born in midair, killing Germans. I still don't know how he managed the silence. Maybe the war was the cause in him; Douglas and Lee were part of *my* cause, and Dan and Frances. But the best guess now is that, there in one stroke, I'd found what Rosalind Limer prescribed. A decent man with a face you could watch and the best of intentions (he wanted a degree and a job meeting people).

The fact that our bodies fully agreed was also important. No use in recalling old feelings, old times, when the here-and-now sufficed so completely—the actual parts of young strong bodies you could touch and honor, cherish and thank.

By the end of May, without exactly planning, we'd got to the place where marriage seemed as natural a next step as drinking the next glass of sweet well-water (his trailer had a well). In the nights when we'd lie, not seeing each other, we'd flick at the notion—little jokes about honeymoons in Panama, the grand idea of Permanent Bliss or a pledge to try it.

To answer a question at work one day, I'd delved around in an old English prayerbook and found the wedding vows. One of the things the bride and groom were compelled to say was "With my body I thee worship." It shocked me then and still does now; surely that's idolatry. But I knew I could say it to Jay Mabry's face, no compulsion required. I never quite said it, though I sure tried to show him. And whatever he showed me, beyond all hopes, he didn't call it *worship* or ask the last question—should we stand up publicly and dare fate to part us? We were both too proud of what we had and were scared it would shatter if we pressed it hard.

* * *

Then somebody else pressed down, with both hands. My immediate supervisor at work was a woman not too much older than me, a missionary's daughter reared in China, the most traveled person I'd met up till then. I'd known what a sad misfortune her face was, the first day I saw her; but we'd been fairly civil in our dealings at work.

Then during final-examination week of Jay's freshman year, he spent more time than usual at my desk. We weren't meeting nights since he had to study. I was sensitive to the amount of his presence and once or twice told him to move along; others might need my wisdom. But on the last Friday we talked twenty minutes, making plans for a swimming picnic Sunday. My boss, Marianne, strode toward us hot-eyed and said "One student's getting undue attention." No one else was in line, but Jay laughed and left. That didn't help a bit. In a low cold whisper, she let me know she'd watched me like a hawk. Worse, she had an aunt that lived near Jay, and she'd heard things other than what she'd witnessed. My private morals were something she'd read of but never hoped to meet; she couldn't help that. But, sure God, she wouldn't let me rave on in public—not here in a place meant for uplift and cleanness. She regretted not having the power to fire me, but she meant to complain to the people that could.

I was struck flat dumb. I couldn't say a word. Some awful new mouth in my heart flew open and said she was right—I was foul past washing. I got through the day somehow till six; Jay never reappeared. I rushed home and waited, but the phone stayed dead. So I had long hours to ferment alone. Then at nine I called him and said we had to meet. He'd been fast asleep, exhausted from tests.

In his car on the way to the trailer, I started my true life-story. He listened, just nodding. I finished indoors, in his living-room small as a steamer trunk. Jay still didn't speak, though he looked like a frozen face ready to melt and pour out words in an unknown tongue, fit to burn down cities. Finally I had to ask what it meant to him.

He stood up and went to the sink for water, not offering me any. When he came back he stayed upright and said "This all really happened—in the actual world, not just your head?"

I told him I'd give every cent I owned if we could just lie down now and sleep and wake up, knowing it was one more dream.

Jay touched the crown of my hair and said "—Or slept on deeper till we died in peace."

I did, very nearly. Thirty-five years passed. And if you don't imagine the average human can sleep that long, let me swear I did. How else do great criminals get through their time?—child-murderers and such. Or five-star generals after glorious wars? They sleep like babies in the depths of wells—speak low; let them be. I never once thought I was any true beauty (though three or four men have mentioned the word in moments of need), but the real Sleeping Beauty never dimmed out more completely than me. Nor was waked up at last by a stranger prince.

That same June night, Jay moved off politely, with none of the hardness that might have been due. He even told me his own past story; I could hear it was true—blameless as any new dog in a box. But he said I was not what he had expected—not less, to be sure; just more than he'd planned, for life at least. He wouldn't condemn me but now he wouldn't need me; thanks for good times. Then he drove me home. As I watched him go (by then it was midnight), I knew it was urgent not to see him again. I thought I'd leave before day. But where to?

I lay on my bed and tried to choose. Every road I'd traveled seemed shut to me now. Norfolk, with Walter and Tim that I'd hurt and Douglas's grave. Miss Limer too deep in the sticks, as she'd warned. Macon with Caroline, Holt, and Lee. *They'd* have me, I knew—I was theirs forever. And they'd ask few questions, though Lee would be four years old and could ask.

I lingered on Lee—short guesses at his face now, the pitch of his voice. I didn't go soft at the center or cry, but I kept on working at a likeness of him. When I had what seemed a credible boy, out of Douglas and me, I thought I'd like him. Then for the first time ever in his life, I wanted to see him and help him grow.

It was two a.m. I went to the phone in the downstairs hall and tried to put through a call to Macon. The war had done nothing to modernize operators. It took five minutes for Information to come back with news that no Holt Porter was listed with a phone; did I have the right town? I said "No question." I'd always suspected he'd have broke down finally and bought phone service, in case I called. So I went back upstairs and finally wept.

In the next four hours of shallow sleep, I dreamed more than once of the Lee I'd imagined. Each time he and I were alone in a room. I sat on a bed. He stood in the center in a blue linen suit and talked at me steadily. His voice was clear, his eyes met mine, and his lips seemed to hover on the far side of smiling. But hard as I strained, I never understood one word he said.

The alarm went off at 6:30 as ever. In the first jagged minute, for some hot reason, I thought of my father—Dan Vaiden, a charmer. I remembered I'd never once visited his grave. Maybe his lonely spirit was afflicting me. Or drawing me towards him—in Henderson, a hundred miles from here. As I washed my face, my mind cleared a little. Still the idea lasted, *I should honor Dan's grave*. Then I'd know where next—fifteen miles to Macon or the dark side of who-knew-what lost planet.

I'd never missed a single day of work. But that day I phoned the librarian at home and told her there'd been a death in my family. I thought Marianne would have filed her complaint and that now I'd catch it. But all I heard was regrets, good wishes, and hurry back.

I packed a light bag and left at eight. At three p.m. the bus stopped in Henderson to take on passengers for Richmond and north. The station was nothing but an oily gas pump and some men on a bench. It seemed no more a part of my past than a bleached crossroads in the Argentine pampas. I sat and thought of pushing on north; I'd heard good things about Baltimore jobs. But something (Dan's need?) was still pulling hard. So I stepped down into the broiling light.

Though the cabdriver looked a lot younger than me, all he needed was the Vaiden name. He said "That'll be in the old cemetery. New

one's mainly for vets and a big copper statue of Jesus turning green."
At the place, he clearly planned to search along with me; but I asked
him to come back and get me in an hour.

The sun was the problem, harsh as a searchlight. The grave was
easy. The Vaidens had a monument taller than me—a marble obelisk
with realistic ivy twining to the top. The small headstones marked
Kate, my grandmother; Talmadge, her husband; and beyond them,
Daniel (other unknown Vaidens were sprinkled to the sides). As a
child I'd come here with Dan more than once—the two of us alone;
Frances never joined in. So I had a few memories of the general ap-
pearance. What was new of course was Dan being there. The ground
was well-acquainted with him though. Crabgrass had woven a thick
mat across him, and mowing machines had hacked at his stone—

DANIEL TALCOTT VAIDEN
1907–1938.

Then lower down in cramped script-letters—

Driven to death.

That would be from his aunts, their final word.

I had a big part of the hour to wait, and I walked twenty yards to
the nearest shade. There by a toolshed was one narrow bench, so I sat
and wondered "Driven by who?" I'd never seen the aunts again after
his death, but I had to guess that Frances was their suspect. Who else
but God or the weather or Satan? It was way beyond me and had
always been. I felt as numb as a cheek at the dentist's. I wanted at least
to feel affection or how much I missed him, his beautiful neck. But
half an hour passed, and I felt little more than my smothering dress.
I guess I'd hoped some force would be here, to guide me—back to my
job (if I still had one) or onward to Lee or Billings, Montana. Nothing, not then.

Then the cab reappeared, blessedly early. I hailed him and stood up,
bag in hand. Then I saw a water spigot by the door of the shed. I was
leaving Dan, most likely for good, without so much as a rose in a jar.
So I took my handkerchief, a sensible big one; soaked it with water
surprisingly cold, cupped it in my hand, and went back to Dan. I

wrung it out hard on the letters of his name. They darkened with the drink. Then I said "Stay with me"—the shock of the day.

My driver stood by the open door; and once I was in, he said "Look like you found him."

"Yes, no trouble."

"*He* was trouble though, won't he?"

"How so?" I said.

"Ain't you his girl?"

"His daughter," I said.

"He's *news* around here. People still tell his tale. While I waited on you, I asked in town. Several men had known you the minute you landed; said you favor him highly."

"Well, thank them," I said. Then I knew my next step.

I went back to Greensboro to get my belongings. I'd never been a saver, so I didn't have much. But I didn't need to strip myself this time, not of useful dumb objects like books and needles. By one a.m. I'd finished the job and collapsed into sleep as black as a coma. I woke up punctually and went to work.

The librarian didn't get there till ten, but I went straight to her and said I quit. She said I was taking Marianne too hard; they valued me. I appreciated that but said new conditions in my family required me; I'd work two weeks if they needed me bad. That let her loose to show how she felt. She said oh no, she wouldn't dream of standing in my chosen path. She thought the path was Jay, and I didn't correct her. In an hour I'd thrown out the trinkets from my desk and drawn my last check.

Then I tried to phone Daphne Baxter's home in Boykins, Virginia. She and Cliff, her sailor, had saved me that first long night in Norfolk. Five years had passed with no word between us, and of course I didn't know her maiden name. But she was all I had in the way of friends, and the country operator recognized her at once. Her parents, even that far out in the sticks, turned out to have a phone. And her mother answered. Yes, she'd heard about me and wondered was I safe; she recalled they'd prayed for me several times. I thanked her and told her the prayers must have worked—I was still upright, though showing my age. She then said Daphne was working in Franklin at the paper mill. She didn't mention Cliff but, after a long wait, she found the phone number. I'd have to wait till sundown.

The fact of that number, in a card in my hand, calmed me like a drug. So I passed the day by writing goodbyes to my few local friends and catching up on the recent lost sleep. At four o'clock I went outside—a cool clear day—and walked to the house where I'd lived with my parents. I'd avoided it all those past four years, and I partly hoped it had burned or vanished.

But there it stood, twice the size I recalled. It didn't seem to hurt me. A woman was out on the porch, watering plants. I walked to the foot of the steps and said I used to live there many years ago. I didn't give my name.

She said "Welcome home. This Wandering Jew is trying to croak."

I felt like she'd said the truest thing about me; here was my last home, and I was on the verge of one more journey. I said "You're drowning it; they need dry feet."

She didn't believe me and kept on pouring. But she waved at the screendoor. "Step on in. It's messy but I doubt you'll catch typhoid."

That caught me offguard so much I obeyed. The trusting soul didn't follow me in, but I took her at her word and saw every room. It *was* a mess, worse than I'd ever made (which establishes a record)—clothes stored on the floor, cold dishes in the sink. I saw signs of one man, no hint of a child. No sign of us either; even my bedroom was bigger and empty. I waited for an echo or some other message. Nothing at all. It might just as well have been a Williamsburg dummy, a rebuilt historic landmark, soul omitted. The whole place was one dead color of beige; somebody'd got a deal on ugly paint.

Back outside I thanked her and said I must run.

She said "See the baby; it's last on the tour."

At the edge of the porch, behind our old swing, was a low bassinet. I went to it slowly; and there slept a baby, too fat to be real. But it breathed and quivered when a gnat buzzed its arm.

The woman said "Brand new. We got her last Tuesday."

I started to ask "From which catalog?" but I just said "Fine."

The woman had come up beside me by then. She leaned down low and shook hands with it. It opened eyes big enough for any grown spy. She said "Arlene—I'm counting on her."

"For what?" I said.

"To brighten my life. I've had a rough ride."

"I'm sorry," I said. "I'll pray for you both."

"—And Chuck," she said. "He needs it the most—blown to pieces on Guam."

"Your husband, you mean?"

She said "Yes ma'm." And then I noticed she was younger than me. I promised her better times were ahead. It cost me nothing and it might have been true.

It was, for me. The first days in Franklin were as good as I'd had. Daphne and Cliff had separated shortly after his discharge (it was his idea). But they spent a lot of time at each other's place, and I still liked them both. The first few months I lived with Daphne—the whole second floor of a light airy house. She worked on the line at the big paper-mill; Cliff worked in the warehouse. I lived on savings for the first two weeks, till I settled in.

Then I got a nice job at the first door I tried—a lawyer's office, as filing clerk and general typist. (I'll swear to my grave, the two most useful subjects in school are Latin and typing; and I'd done fair at both.) Even in a small town, a law office gives you as much to learn as a college library. A lot of it's sad—divorce, child custody, murders, and wills—but it's every bit true, and it keeps on coming.

Daph and Cliff had friends by the dozen, from the mill—mainly country children that had left the farm to fight overseas and couldn't see going back to cotton and peanuts and twenty-hour days. They were just like the people I'd grown up with—less deceitful than blank post-cards, kind and mean, generous and wild. I've never been high-hat (or had reason to be), so I gradually fell in with their few plans—rummy and beer, the movies, the beach, radio and records, a dance now and then. We were all still young; I was maybe the youngest, though I soon guessed I'd seen more than some of the vets.

So for once I truly enjoyed myself. *I went along,* for the first time ever. A movie of it might have killed Miss Limer—I regretted that—but would barely faze a pre-teen today. Harmless loud exertion, nothing worse than that. It included men of course. I *have* liked men, no way around that. And I think I've been right. One thing about men—*you know where you are;* they can't hide a thing (unless you've run up on Jack the Ripper).

That's not to say I was loose or easy, even in the eyes of men back then. Every man I've touched in a private way has been goodhearted, quiet in public, and pleasant-looking at the very least. I thought several times that I'd fallen in love. More than one of the men felt the same and offered me rings. But at the last minute, I'd always balk.

One obstacle was, I couldn't tell my story again. I'd told it once too often already. I'd come round to seeing it was just the one tale men couldn't believe or, worse, couldn't bear. Fathers can walk out on whole nests of children every day of the year and never return, never send back a dime—that's considered sad but natural. But an outlaw mother is the black last nightmare any man can face.

Beyond my awful story though was one more problem. I'd had this vision of what *could* be—me and Gaston in the daylight, years of that—and nobody else, however strong and kind, quite promised me as much. I'd draw back and say "Kate Vaiden, wake up! You're asking for Heaven. This is Earth, *live* on it." But then I'd say no, one more hard time. And one more chance at a human team would walk on away. Nobody's fault but mine—and the dust that made me.

Still I've had worlds of fun. I think I can say—and not fool myself—that I've had more fun, clean harmless fun than any two married women I know. I can also say, and with deep regret, that I don't know two married couples I envy. Through the years, that is. The whole long haul. If I'd been God, I'd have changed that first—people's chances together. All the terrible rest would have fallen in place once I got that straight.

I've called my fun *harmless* more than once, and I know it sounds fishy. Why wasn't I harming Lee Vaiden every instant I stayed away? If you've come this far, you've got full right to fling that at me. God knows I've flung it at my own eyes and teeth a billion nights. My answer is this (and I know all its flaws)—Lee Vaiden's been lucky not to grow next to me. When they made me, they left out the mothering part. My baby-making machinery works (don't worry; it only had to work that once). But the tending rearing permanent patience and the willingness to take such slim reward as most mothers get—they left that out of my soul completely. Many times I've regretted it as my worst failing.

I've also noticed how quite a few women, as poorly equipped as me to be mothers, have gone on somehow and raised honest children that grew up and thanked them. Well, Kate Vaiden didn't. I left it to Caroline Porter, a saint. But the saint could have died and left my son to who?—Holt and Noony or Walter or Swift or the Welfare Department, all sad possibilities.

The fear of that struck me broadside many times but not hard enough to make me go home. The only comfort I gave myself was the knowledge that I'd never really *hid*. I kept my name, I paid my taxes, except for vacations I was never farther off than ninety-five miles. A blind lame bloodhound could have found me fast, not to mention the Law or a private detective. There were days I almost prayed to find a letter in the box that would say "Lee Vaiden, Box 68, Macon, N.C." on the back. But I never did. I guessed I wasn't needed. So I stuck to my path.

The path, I assure you, wasn't always lined with flowering shrubs. I was mostly healthy, the best of blessings. But more than three decades brought their natural load of troubles. Daphne and Cliff got back together in the early fifties, in time for Korea. Cliff rejoined the Navy and Daph moved to Norfolk to be near the docks (and the Navy doctors; by then she was pregnant). I couldn't follow there but, once they were gone, Franklin went dead on me.

I took my time and cast around slowly, then settled on Raleigh. I knew the street-plan and saw no objections except maybe Whitfield Eller's presence, and he couldn't spot me. Even on a file clerk's miniature salary, I had nearly two thousand dollars saved. So I pulled up stakes in 1953, moved back down, and got an apartment near Broughton High School. I looked into working at the library there, but the sight of so many young people stalled me. I was no antique yet (just twenty-six); it was maybe a feeling that so much *blood*, bursting at the seams, would swamp me eventually in my hope to be calm and not rock time's boat.

So I spent six months, taking shorthand and spelling at a business college near the Catholic cathedral. The other students there were mostly seven years younger than me. But since a lot of them were straight from the country, with city hopes, they were generally more controlled and polite—less famished for life—than the high-school rowdies.

Anyhow I kept very much to myself in those first months. I met my immediate neighbors in the apartment. They were single women too and were worked to a nub for galley wages. It hadn't much dampened their spirit or strength. But since they were at least twenty years older, we didn't have all that much to discuss. I did enjoy though cooking supper occasionally for a math teacher who knew more first-class dirty jokes than any three sailors.

Since the college stood where it did, I slowly began going back to church. At first I'd just wander in between classes and sit for short spells, steeping in the quiet and watching the candles. Then I slid back into a good many prayers. I even bought a garnet rosary and put in numerous hours on it. No tears or trembling lips but dead-earnest hopes for guidance again, personal peace, and a useful life.

That may be the reason I got the job I've had ever since—main woman in a small firm of lawyers that mainly deal in criminal cases. At first I was just the stenographer, taking reams of dictation of private statements by every kind of human from maddogs to nuns. You may well wonder (I surely did) how that represented guidance from God or performing His will.

My answer is that, as years went on, I got a strong sixth sense of truth and lies. It crept out through me like the slowest skill, like playing the violin or skating. I could sit at the edge of an office, with a pencil, and hear in three minutes if any defendant was true or false.

Good trial lawyers can do the same but only to a point. Where they leave off is where I begin. I can go a step farther and hear the last secret—does the man *know* what he's done? You'd be amazed at the simplest hardest fact of crime—most people, especially murderers, don't know what they've done. The worse the crime, the less he'll know. (I say *he* but, right down the line, all the most interesting and foolproof crimes are committed by women, around here at least. Women can plan and wait for years to do their will. Men seldom have anything like that brand of patience.) In that one way then, I may have done good. I suspect I've been the reason my firm took on some cases they at first didn't want. So with my nose for innocence, I've saved some lives.

Also of course I've worked in a men's world. The average woman in my generation didn't know any men outside her family. Through the years I've known my bosses well, and I've met every man that entered their door. A few were vicious as a hot chainsaw; a lot were cowed and pitiful, though guilty (a *good* firm's clients are generally guilty). Sooner or later I talked to each one, and I've got a box full of the letters they've sent me from prison or home or Mexico. But I've never agreed to meet one in private, though more than one asked.

The firm always has a young clerk or two. They're straight out of law school and ready to save the whole world or gas it. In the early years when I was their age, I got really close to several of them—one at a time. They're included in what I've said before, about love and rings. Right now I could be a lawyer's wife, several times over, in a rambling house with a pool and grandchildren on a shady street. The fact that I always chose against it doesn't mean that men haven't cornered a big share of my time and feelings.

That's why I've dreaded our wars so much. Korea, the long scare about Berlin, the Cuban missiles, Vietnam, Nicaragua. I can't help thinking that the purpose of war is secret but simple as a razor blade—*To kill boys fast*, at least a lot faster than God does. So because I've touched more than my share of boys, my mind has stayed clenched my whole adult life. And of course I've kept up with Lee Vaiden's age. All through Vietnam, every morning that came, I'd search the paper for dead local boys in ice-cold fear of finding Lee's name. Toward the end I subscribed to the Warrenton paper, using my real name, just to stay informed. His name never showed up, in any connection. That barely calmed me but I didn't search any closer than that.

And the time trudged by. Everybody thinks the 1960s were so exciting. I don't think I noticed. With no children near me, such events as free love, drugs, and civil rights were no closer to me than the television. I'd always loved whoever I pleased, the strongest drug I'd used was paregoric (when I cut my wisdom teeth); and for all the news of riots and bombings, I personally never heard one shot fired or an angry word.

Women's liberation also happened on Mars, far as I was concerned. I wished them well, even sent a few small checks to various causes. But my own hands had scratched my freedom out of granite rock, before I was old enough to drive (much less vote). So I couldn't get deeply riled for the sisters that had managed to grow up and still not notice where the hard laws of marriage and motherhood were gouged on the sky in mile-high letters—*Take it or leave it but don't expect improvement till babies are all manufactured in bottles and men aren't therefore raised by women.* I wish my wages fairly matched my skills, and I wish men's peters were connected to their brains. Otherwise I don't claim pity as a woman. Any woman that does—one that's been beat or starved of human food—gets my real regrets. And I hope not to die till I've seen a woman president, a woman with children. Beyond that I've got no further big hopes, except that women who work in public will get their tear glands under control. Maybe it's because tears don't come easily when I feel cornered. Still a lot of us meet all problems with water; and that's crooked dealing, no other name for it.

In the 1970s I discovered travel. Compared to most women my age, I'd been a gadabout child. But I was forty-five, just starting hot flashes, before I crossed the Mason-Dixon line. At first I always went with a friend, some girl from the office or one of my neighbors—Washington, Philadelphia, New York, Ottawa, Seattle, and Vancouver. Then I realized travel was the absolute solvent for any friendship. So I forged on alone most times after that. Several Caribbean trips on merchant steamers with small crews of seamen and even fewer passengers. Once—to Dutch Guiana and back—I was flat the one woman on the whole rusty boat. The only other traveler was an alcoholic priest that slept all the way. So I got grand attention and not a mean word, not so much as a pinch.

That gave me the courage for Italy. In March of 1984 I had some days coming, and I suddenly decided on a trip to Rome. Ever since my high-school Latin book's pictures, I'd dreamed of Rome and was always amazed when the name turned up in current news. Imagine a place enduring that long; imagine the people that *wanted* it to last (and the ones that didn't). I told the travel agent to keep me as far off the tourist track as possible. I bought some dark clothes; she handled all the rest; and I actually went, though nervous as a flea.

Nine long bright days (and though I was fifty-six, more than one pinch). Don't run; I don't plan to show my slides. The thing worth recalling is, it felt like home. More of a home than I'd been in since my parents died. Of course to my *eyes* it was utterly strange; nothing in America touches it close, nothing manmade at least. But my heart, that had been asleep so long, began to warm. I began waking up every day at dawn, impatient to get to the streets and walk. Something buried deep was calling me to find it. And new as that was, it made me happy. I tramped through the ruins I remembered from school. I saw enough fountains to last me for life. I ate like Douglas's "Growing Boy" and watched children laugh in the public street and a thousand cats. But they weren't it and the thing was still calling.

The last day I gave in and went to St. Peter's. I'd learned one rule on previous trips—*See one cathedral and you've seen them all.* But I had to admit St. Peter's was up in a class by itself, though not that lovable. Green and orange marble with space enough for every soul saved at Judgment, including the chubby.

I was leaving unsatisfied when a man in an American raincoat stopped me and asked had I been on the underground tour? I told him I'd been everywhere but underground. He said in that case his wife was sick; he had an extra ticket—it started in ten minutes. His face looked harmless and I'd barely spoken American all week so I said yes.

Underground turned out to be the bowels of the cathedral, a pagan cemetery that had been buried when the emperor went Christian and honored Peter's grave with a church on top. The pagan tombs were so spanking-new they looked suspicious, like scenery for a Roman movie—*Quo Vadis*. But I kept my mouth shut; and the guide led us on, a group of six or seven. Just as I was getting claustrophobic, the guide stopped outside another low door and said "Now one by one, look in."

I was first in line by accident. So I ducked my head, stepped through, and was staring at a scarred red wall—an obvious antique. There was barely foot-room for the guide to join me, but he wedged in and said "Here you see Peter's bones." Low down in the wall was a dug-out hole with a glass box the size of a cigarette carton. Inside I could see a few scraps of brown bone, enough to make one baby's leg. I stood there ten seconds, then yielded my place to the next in line.

I was back in my hotel, trying to nap, before I knew I was satisfied. Without ever hearing of Peter's grave, I'd been led there and allowed ten seconds in easy reach of the real leftovers of the biggest quitter in human history—the friend that denied he even knew Jesus when His cards were down. The one that didn't even wait by the cross and watch Him die, that had to see His risen body to believe his promise. In the face of that though, he did turn back and beg for pardon and get it. —Got it and came on here and died on a cross of his own, nailed upside down, and caused this church to stand on his bones. It wasn't a vision like the one I'd seen that Christmas with Walter and Douglas at the beach (visions, I've noticed, come mainly to children, a partial reward for so much pain). I didn't compare myself to St. Peter; women after all *had* stood loyal at the cross, and I guessed I might well have been among them. But I knew I'd been through something substantial, that was meant for me.

Still I was high in the air over Greenland, a whole day later, before I felt it working. It started as a powerful lonesomeness around me. I'd missed a lot of people in my life; but the hard fact was, I'd never missed what was left of my family. And even now I didn't miss *them*, not at first anyhow. It was that low house where I'd spent five years and the oaks in the yard and the shady ground that I needed to see. They'd after all sheltered my life at a time when other places failed. The first real shock was the knowledge I *could* see them. Barring fire, they'd be there now, that patient. My car could reach them in less than two hours.

Then I began to think about people. Caroline was born in 1882, a hundred and two if she'd lasted this long. Holt was even older. And Daniel Lee Vaiden would be forty in November, assuming somebody had got him this far. That I hadn't laid eyes on any of them, or sent the simplest message, seemed a brand of denial past understanding. Like forgetting your own name or failing to spot your mother's face in a small silent crowd. There was nobody else on earth, above ground, that I wanted to see. And there in the sky, with a plane-load of strangers, it seemed as easy as breath to find them, beg their pardon, and get it freely. Easy and natural and urgent to life, mine and theirs.

But back on the ground, in my old ruts, it seemed unlikely and all but crazy. Nobody could be alive except Lee and maybe Swift. What right did I have to step forward now and offer myself? And offer *as what?*—an exhibit to warn Lee's possible children, or a punching bag to receive my deserts? I'd certainly be the *answer* to nothing. And I might well shake the underpinnings of whatever house Lee'd built around himself. He wouldn't need me, this late in his day. I didn't need him. Even if I did, he was not mine to beg from. When I chose my path thirty-nine years ago, I'd forfeited that—my family rights. I couldn't rewrite the contract now and expect any other party to sign. I'd let myself get too lonely in Rome and had called it homesickness. Home was my four rented rooms in Raleigh; I'd leave it feet-first in a raw pine box and not before. No flowers please.

By early April I'd reached that point and felt at ease with it. I'd shaken off two drowsy weeks of jet lag, lost the four pounds I gained, and was feeling unusually clear and strong. Then my boss reminded me that I had a date for the annual checkup the firm always gives us— chest X-rays and such. One blessing of my life has been the absence of doctors. Except for the checkups, I hadn't seen one since Lee was delivered; and I hadn't missed the pleasure. It was one more law I'd drawn from experience—*The more you see doctors, the worse you get.*

*   *   *

But I kept the appointment, a Wednesday morning. It seemed to go smoothly; I seemed to be fine. One week later though, the nurse called up and said my Pap smear was cause for concern; come back please for a punch biopsy. I doubt many women hear that call calmly. I missed a few nights' sleep and hauled out my old neglected rosary, but I didn't cave in. I'd known my body was responding to time; but the ways seemed normal, even slower than in most women my age.

Then everything suddenly lunged downhill. And before April ended, every fiber in me had jolted awake. Cervical cancer, no possible doubt. Seventy-two hours in near-solitary in a hospital room with radium seeds planted deep inside me, bombarding the guest. Except for nurses dashing in with my meals (which, since I couldn't raise my head, I couldn't eat), the only other human I saw was a man in a long pink smock who swore he was chaplain. I thanked him but said I dealt with God alone. A fool thing to say, but the pink smock threw me. I was dealing with death.

I'd watched death at close range several times before but in other people's bodies. Like the average human, I'd assumed I'd escape. The absolute last invader I'd suspected was cancer *there*. But lying alone for two full days, with radium in me, I of course came round to the next deduction. I was punished at last in the place where I'd failed, the scene of the crime. Can you believe me if I say my first response was amusement? It seemed like a big but tidy joke.

My friends all rallied in unexpected droves, and it wasn't till I'd watched their stiff gray smiles that I saw the real picture. I'd truly been struck. They guessed I was dead. They sent plants and candy, fed my fish, did my laundry; they'd have scrubbed my floor on their bloody knees—I was genuinely touched; I believed they cared. But they loved the word *cancer*. They couldn't keep it down; it would pop up in their mouths when they least intended and fluster them badly.

Only the doctors managed to avoid it. To them it was a *tumor* or, at worst, *carcinoma* (which could after all be the pleasant name of a lake—"Lake Carcinoma, Where the Sky Meets the Shore"). And they thought my chances of another five years were better than even, all things considered. They didn't specify what the main *things* were, and the way they said "Five years" was more like a prison sentence than reprieve. Five years seemed long as a bus trip to China.

But after a week of rest at home, and three back at work, I'd begun to draw up a list of my own—*things* to consider in the time I had. If I wanted to live, I'd have to change—way-down, skin-out. That didn't mean I thoroughly repented of my past. I trust I'll be able to stand up at Judgment and at least *explain* before I'm fried. My explanation will be this story, the one told here. No alibi and no apology, just a long process—the things that happened, in order, to and through me. The choices I made once other people made their choices on me. So, no sackcloth and no excuses but a calm new path of my own making. Where else could it lead first but straight to my child?

Not *straight*, as it turned out; I swerved a good deal. Much as I now meant to be a good person, to stay awake for somebody more than myself, I had to be sure it wouldn't harm Lee to know his mother. I also had to face a mean present question—was I wanting him now just because I was down? If I'd shunned him when strong, then how could I crawl in now, stove-up? An old sick bitch with one last hope to die by the fire. Several months later I'm still not sure I could answer either question and keep my pride. But any try at goodness has to walk over pride. So yes, I've been moving.

First I tried the phone. I didn't mean to call Lee out of the blue, but at least I could make a start by finding his address. No phone listed for him in Macon or Warrenton. I even went down to the State Library one Saturday morning and searched their collection of U. S. directories. If he was in America, he didn't have a phone—not in any town bigger than Otumwah, Iowa. It made me wonder if he might have changed his name; he had good right. But to what?—Lee Porter or Daniel Lee?

Or *deceased*. That night I dreamed a long story that was so realistic I woke up believing it was simply the news. Lee Vaiden had starved to death in the mountains after Caroline died when he was a boy, age twelve or thirteen. He was hunting for me, moving always on foot. He passed me more than once on empty streets, and we knew each other on sight but were blocked by the thick air between us. Neither one of us could pierce it; though Lee tried hard, my arms went limp and could barely reach out. So finally I walked on to save myself; and he wound up in the Blue Ridge mountains, glorious weather and everybody gone—no other live humans, no unspoiled food, not a squirrel or a fox. There had been a big war. He wasted and died.

That panicked me. The next day was Sunday, and the morning was painful. I wrote a slew of checks for bills I'd neglected while sick. Then I read through the Gospel of Luke at one sitting. Several people had given me Bibles lately; and Luke used to be my favorite book, the one that could calm me when nothing else worked (Luke's partial to women in the stories he tells). But now it just somehow made me sure of death—Lee's, not mine. I'd live on for years—punished with old age, never knowing the one good thing I made.

By the middle of the day, I was driving toward Noony. My dream had not included her. But as the hours passed, she began to seem my only chance. Of everyone I'd known, surely Noony would have lasted and could help me onward. The fact that she'd always been hard on me was another encouragement. If she failed to recognize me, or turned her back, then I'd know to stop. She was that fair a judge.

My car fit the road like a train on rails. And once I'd passed Louis-burg, I knew every tree. I kept on waiting to feel a response—would the place fold me in or somehow refuse me? But the place drew back and let me pass. And my fear eased a little. Only the turnoff to Annie Lee's grave was painful to see (where I'd spent that last Sunday after-noon with Gaston).

Macon itself had shrunk even further. The depot was gone, the fertilizer warehouse, the filling station, and Mr. Russell's store. But the ground was still white, and it let me in. Without subjecting myself to the homeplace, I turned at the Methodist church and climbed on past my old brick school. It was not till then that I wondered if maybe Noony had moved—her house had seemed ready to fall on itself the last time I saw it. But I stopped by the road, where her path had been. It was still there, hardpacked and clear. I couldn't see far but nothing said *Keep Out* so down I went. The trees overhead had locked together, and the shade was thicker than I recalled. In twenty yards I'd spent more strength than I had to spare; I was already panting. More than ever I doubted the house could be here, or Noony in any shape or age.

I walked the last bend though and there it was. It had aged less than me. Somebody had put white aluminum siding on either end, and two new camellia-bushes stood by the door. Otherwise nothing had changed since the day I met Douglas here and promised to join him. Seeing his face in my mind again nearly turned me back (he was still that vivid in the air and the shade). No dog ran to meet me; even birds seemed forbidden. The silence was deep as a pond all round me. So I stepped on forward and called Noony's name.

Quicker than I planned, the tall door opened. She was plainly Noony, in a sleeveless dress. Nothing was different except her upper arms; they'd plumped up a little. Her hair was still black; and her eyes had survived, every hot kilowatt. She didn't speak but she didn't frown.

I was ten feet from her, and I said "Guess who?" I thought of the hundred things she could call me and set me running.

She took her own time, then reached out like she was cleaning her image in a dusty mirror. She said "You held up better than I guessed."

I nodded. "I've had a lot of good bed-rest."

"Bet you have," she said and stepped back in. Her right hand made a short scoop in my direction.

I followed and, once my eyes had adjusted, saw that the room had changed as little as Noony. Only the narrow cot was missing, the one I'd used. She sat on her bed and pointed in the general direction of her chairs. I couldn't remember which one belonged to Emlen's ghost, but I picked one and sat. When she didn't protest, I said "If this room could talk, child, where would we be?"

Her eyes were still solemn, and she thought out her answer. "Me—I'd be in Heaven, eating syrup." It didn't seem funny.

But I had to laugh. I said "I'll join you."

Noony said "Will they let you?"

Then I knew I'd come to the right person first. I said "That's what I'm here to find out."

Finally she smiled. "They won't ask *my* opinion."

"Have you got one though?"

She waited again. "Nobody hadn't mentioned you since Jesus was a boy."

That also hurt but I thought it was too soon to gauge her direction. I said "I see you got some aluminum siding; you must be working seven days a week."

Noony nodded. "On the ends; the ends get cold—the east and the west."

"Who you working for?"

"Ain't working," she said. "I took my retirement."

"And dug in the yard?—Emlen's buried gold."

"Ain't touched a shovel. Emlen fool enough to dig in the ground, what he buried can *stay* till he come get it."

So I had to force it. "Who's alive still, Noony?"

She waited again and then she laughed. "Not *me*."

I said "You look good as Lena Horne." (I seemed to recall she'd worshipped Lena Horne; anyhow it was true.)

Noony shook her head. "Don't *feel* it."

"What about Caroline?"

She said "You don't know? I wondered a lot."

"I don't. I'm sorry to say I don't."

"Been dead—God, how long?—fourteen years."

Nothing that had happened since I saw Douglas dead had struck me that hard. A cold shaft thrust straight through my chest. Fourteen years would be 1970. Were had I been? I doubted I could trust my voice, but I said "Remember what month?"

Noony said "Month of June, the first Thursday."

She'd apparently forgot that was my birth-week. I'd have been eating dinner at a friend's house very likely. My voice was still fragile, but I said "What killed her?"

"Her heart—heart give out one morning on the porch. I was in the back hall, heard her hit the floor. By the time I got there, I don't think she knew me."

"Had she been sick long?"

Noony said "Not a day. She was strong as me."

"Who else was home?"

She rushed to say "Me, I already told you. Lee was off in his little boat. Had to haul him out in a helicopter; we waited four days."

"What boat? Where was he?"

"That war—Vietnam, on his way to fight."

"Did he make it?" I said.

"Your memory failing? I told you—four days. We held Miss Caroline out of the ground four days till he got back and saw her body. Made me put her wedding-ring back on her hand."

I nodded. "I meant the war. Did Lee live through it?"

Noony waited so long I thought I'd lost her, or the news was too heavy for even her to bear. She looked down again. When her face came up, the eyes were wide and hot as a brand. "*You* asking *me?*"

"You're my oldest friend."

She smiled again. "Glad to hear it. I'd have been bad off if I needed you, wouldn't I? But I didn't, thank Jesus. Nobody else down here did either. Why you turning up now? We *finished* our job."

"You and Holt?" I said.

Noony pointed to the floor. "He died before her—didn't know his own name, thought I was his sister."

"Who raised Lee then?"

Her hand went up and made a slow arch. "The clouds in the sky."

"But you were still with him, at Caroline's?"

"All day, every day, till he went off."

I said "I can thank the Lord for that."

Noony said "The Lord still listening to you?"

"I hope so, yes."

"Then He's changed His ways." She stood up and walked to the west-end wall. The one window there was covered with cardboard, a single tall piece. She pulled it down and the late sun fell in across her toward me.

My feet felt the warmth, so I said "Maybe you're too hard on me.

You told me to leave, thirty-nine years ago, not a half-mile from here."
I pointed toward the church where we'd stood that day.

Noony stayed at the window. "I told you to *choose*."

"But you didn't try to stop me."

She nodded. "That's why I'm punished every day."

I said "Look here" but she didn't turn. I said "I beg your pardon
for it all. I'm sick now and feeling old age on my back. If you won't
help me, I may have to stop."

"Stop what?"

"My life." It sounded too loud in that calm air, but I knew I hadn't
lied. I couldn't see forward—from that moment, there.

Noony faced me then. Her face was still dark, but the sun lit her
hands; she kept them down. She said "You come from a right rough
bunch. You might *need* to quit, Kate—this day, now."

I said "Just forgive me."

Noony said "Too late."

"Then tell me where he is—Lee Vaiden. Can I find him?"

"You could, he's living, got a good-paying job. If you walked into
him on the road, you'd know him—your face all in him; everybody
say so."

"Poor boy," I said.

Noony said "You *right*."

The punishment had started; I understood why. But for the first
time, something rose up in me and flat refused to take it. I met her
eyes dead-level and said "Just tell me, please."

Noony said "No ma'm."

It had to be the first time she'd ever called me *ma'm*. But I let it
pass.

"You got a picture of him?"

She looked round slowly like it might be lost; then she pointed to
the back wall—her peeling mirror.

That apparently meant he was clearly mine, his face at least. And
I suddenly knew I'd waited long years for that much of a reason. I
also knew no kin or friend could stop me now, even one with rights as
powerful as Noony's. I stood straight up and walked to the door.
When I looked back to smile some kind of goodbye, she'd already

turned and was smoothing the cushion I'd just sat on. She was wiping me out of her sight and mind; I couldn't object.

Half an hour later I'd passed the homeplace—strangers in the yard and the roof rusted out. Then Fob's house, spruced up with ducks in the yard. Aimed as I was, neither sight hurt badly, though I hadn't slowed down (I was driving the limit). Then I'd found Swift Porter. The youngest boy at the Littleton gas-pump knew right away. "I heard he's parked in the old folks' home."

I asked if he had any family alive.

"He can tell you," the boy said, "He still can talk. Or could last time he drove in here; that was some while back. You might want to take an *interpreter* with you. I think the family died off."

The nursing home was stranded in the country, in an old cotton field, on a square of dead grass. It was rambling and squatty with a black-shingle roof and not a leaf of shade. On the porch old women were rocking in the glare—white and black together in thin bath-robes. They watched me like birds as I climbed the steps, and the nearest one said "I can leave this minute if you find my shoes."

I told her I'd looked but they hadn't turned up.

She sank back and said "You're a goddamned liar."

I laughed and went through the buggy screendoor. A practical nurse showed me down to the room, and there was an old man strapped to the bed with a wide canvas belt. Swift could only be seventy-three or four; this man looked a thousand—in the face and hands; the hair was still brown, no streak of gray. It crossed my mind Noony might have misled me; surely this was Holt.

But he craned his neck and said, right off, "You've stoutened up some." The eyes were Swift's, and the fine long hands.

I said "Who am I?"

"Kate Porter—I can *see*. Nothing works but my eyes."

"Kate *Vaiden*," I said. "You're the Porter; which one?"

He grinned on gums with maybe four teeth. "You choose, sweet thing. I'll be who you need."

"Well, I'm hunting Swift."

"Then I'll be him," he said. "Pull the chair up close."

I moved the one straight chair near to his side. "Why're you wearing this belt?"

He pulled at it hard. "So they can't throw me out."

I saw he was bent on telling the truth (he'd always been). So I said "Swift, who have you got left alive?"

He smiled. "Not a soul. Ain't that a damned shame?"

"You ought to have tracked Kate down; I was close."

"We knew that," he said. "They decided against it."

"Caroline and Holt?"

"—And God and His angels."

I said "Where's Lee?"

"Whoa, Katie—too fast."

"For what?" I said.

"This neck of the woods. We're slow up here; we're biding our time."

I said "Start anywhere your heart desires. Just tell me, please."

"You're the one's got the great tale to tell. We heard you were rich."

I laughed. "I am—in gifts of the spirit."

Swift frowned. "Then you can't bail me out of here."

"It looks like a nice clean home to me."

He said "It's not a *home*—don't ever let em fool you. It's nothing but a house full of heartbroken wrecks."

"I may be here any day; I'm tired."

He looked at the open door to check for passers. Then he said "Do anything—eat red *dirt*—but stay upright in your own four walls till you keel over cold."

"That may not prove as easy as it sounds."

"It ain't, I know, but take it from me—get your boy; he'll save you."

"Lee, you mean?"

"I don't meant Hitler."

"What makes you think he wants me?"

Swift studied me then, close as a map. "You're Frances's child."

"Lee never knew Frances."

"Course he doesn't," Swift said. "You owe him that much. Fan Bullock is the sweetest girl Christ ever built."

"She's gone, Swift," I said. "She'd be seventy-six."

He nodded. "I've counted every minute since she left. You're her living picture."

That all but stunned me. In my childhood, people had compared me to Frances; but I'd come round to thinking I was Dan's—his bones in my face. I said "People say I favor Dan."

Swift shook his head hard and shut both eyes. "You're Fan, to the *bone*. I know; I killed her."

I felt like crashing through the window, head-first, and flinging through space. I'd meant this trip to ease my mind, not gouge new wounds. There was nothing to say though but "Dan took the blame."

Swift's eyes stayed shut. "Dan was gone; it couldn't hurt him."

"That's wrong and you know it. It's ruined his name."

"He *shot* her, not me—get that through your head."

I said "I'm trying. But what did you do?"

Of course his eyes opened; I almost shied. He said "I loved her like nobody else."

"That night, by the creek?"

His sharp chin dug at the air like a spade. "We'd started as children; that was just the last time."

"Dan found you together?"

Swift said "Just talking. When Dan walked up, we were calm as the rocks."

"But he understood?"

"He'd wondered for years but she told him that week. So he knew he was *second*. It pushed him too far, too far and too fast."

What should I have done?—marched out, called the Law, read Swift a hot sermon? Before I began to plan my answer, I said to myself "You're the one live soul who could give him what he's earned, but you lost your license." I knew Swift knew it. I also saw he was being repaid with every breath he drew. I was wading through that when he tapped my knee.

He said "You excuse me?"

I smiled but said "You'll need to ask them."

"No, you," he said, "—what I did to you."

I thought he meant their deaths. "I've missed them a lot, but I managed to grow."

Swift's mouth twisted; then his head shook hard. "—The time I made you leave and run to Walter. That was when I *meant* harm."

The answer came quick. "Oh sure. You rest. *I* made that choice."

"I was older than you; I knew right from wrong."

"So did Kate Vaiden, then and now—rest easy." It cost a good deal less than I'd dreamed.

He lay back and waited, then smoothed his sheet. "You're going to live. I can see you've been sick."

"You said I'd *stoutened.*"

"Not your eyes," Swift said; he touched his own. "I knew your mother's eyes; you've got them exactly. I see you've been through a whole long grief."

I said "I had cancer. They caught it in time—so they say; I trust them."

Swift said "No you don't. But you can trust me; I'm mean enough to know. You'll last a good while."

Deep in my body I accepted the fact. I believed his promise. Nothing else he'd done or said earned my faith; still I knew he was right. He'd been shown the truth. I said "What for?—last for what? Do you see that?"

"Go to Lee. He'll want you."

"Does he need me though?"

Swift said "Not now, not far as I know. Sounds like he's back on his feet and running. He's bound to *like* you."

"What's been the trouble?"

He strained to recall. "The girl again—I'm just guessing that."

"Is he married?"

"He pretty much keeps his own counsel. Loves a secret much as you."

I said "Who's the girl?"

"I doubt I remember. He leans to girls in general though; they've run him near-ragged. But he sounds on the mend. Course I just heard his voice. Haven't seen him in years. He stays at sea."

"In the Navy?"

Swift nodded. "Something like that, that line anyhow." He dug at his lips.

I was scared to press him; he was going vague now. I couldn't use lies or old-man confusion, so I sat still a minute.

Then he raised up and pointed to the farthest wall. "Look in my bureau."

By the window was a low maple chest of drawers. I opened the top one. All I saw was clean underwear, socks, a white shirt. I turned back. "You want me to help you dress?"

He grinned. "When I'm dead. No, they don't let me dress; I might hitch a ride. Reach way in the back."

I found a small lockbox and held it toward him. "This what you mean?"

He hushed me with a finger. "The key's over here." He rummaged at the bed rail, then beckoned me over.

He'd taped the key up under the bed, while he still could move. I peeled it free and handed it over.

He opened the lid on a stack of papers, mostly deeds. Then he dug deep down and found two letters—one new, one yellowed. He gave me the new one. The address was to him at the nursing home, in an upright hand in dark brown ink. Swift said "Turn over." Embossed on the back in a circle it said *Commander Daniel Lee Vaiden*, with a Navy address. Swift said "You can read it."

It was just a joke get-well card—*Love, Lee*. My finger stroked the script like it might be Braille. And for one instant, I did glimpse a face—the one that had come in last night's dream, out of Douglas and me. Then I checked the postmark, *March '84*. "Is he at sea now?" I said.

"He called me last Sunday. He could be in Rumania."

"Was he well?"

"Seemed to be. A week's gone by, like I say. Who knows? The ocean's still *water*, the last I heard—*I* can't swim a stroke; course I guess they taught Lee." He shook the old envelope and passed it over. It was bare of writing, but the flap was open. He said "This is what I found forty-six years ago when we went to Greensboro to empty Fan's house—you, Mother, and me. It was there on Dan and Frances's bed, like that, unsealed. I kept it a secret."

It burned my hand and I laid it by his arm.

Swift said "I never have read it. You can."

I shook my head no.

"But keep it," he said. "It might help Lee. He's strong but he needs more help than he knows. People all think new babies need help; Hell, I need round-the-clock care every day. I pay through the nose and still can't get it." His finger scratched at the envelope.

I didn't reclaim it; it stayed by his hand. The fingers still looked like they might pick it up and play sweet music.

But of course they didn't, and he ran on through a dozen subjects in the next half-hour. How much it had altered up here since the war—all the young white people gone off into town, all the young Negro men standing round on welfare, Mexican migrants working the fields. Fob Foster's thousand acres left fallow (Fob dead and the land all deeded to Tot; Tot somewhere in Delaware, drinking cheap wine). Swift's wife dead too, his daughter in Charleston with a lawyer husband that wouldn't let her visit. Walter dead four months, left a fortune to Lee. The homeplace sold at auction last fall. His mother-in-law alive, ninety-six, with all her own teeth and a half-million dollars in fine pulpwood that she wouldn't sell to help him stay at home with a servant. How he planned to be on his feet by fall and back at work (he sold farm equipment, as far east as Weldon). He'd see me in Raleigh in his new Buick, we could eat fried shrimp at a place he knew, he'd pay the whole bill.

Finally I eased him back to the present and said I should go; I didn't want to tire him.

He said "No, *do*. I pray to get tired. I've got more strength now than I ever had. It won't let me sleep. I think all night."

I told him I'd be back soon again. Could I bring him anything?

"A *body*," he said. "This here one's quit on me. My mind's still struggling." Both hands went up and pressed his skull.

I told him I'd look, for him and me both. Then I said "If Lee calls, please don't mention me. I'll need time to think."

Swift grinned. "You're a *jumper*, Kate. Don't think long."

I laughed one last time and stood up to leave. Till then I hadn't really touched his skin, but I pressed my fingers to his cold right hand.

He accepted that and didn't ask for more. When I stepped away though, he said "—This letter." I hoped he'd forgot it. But no, it was mine—what he'd saved for Kate, knowing she'd be back.

All the way down to Raleigh that night, I worked not to *think*. Too much had flown at my face in those hours; I'd wait to think when the air had settled. But I did try to calm the shocks of the day. And as I drove through the ringing dark, Swift's addled encouragement grew stranger than Noony's just refusal. His promise that I'd last was stranger still, and I still believed him. I'd live now to deal with the news he'd left me—his past and my parents', mine and Lee's future.

Strangest of all was the big new fact—not the word on Swift and his love of my mother (I'd halfway known it, since the night itself) or all the sad deaths or Lee's present health but the fact they hadn't missed me. They'd more or less known where I was all the years; nobody had felt the need for Kate Vaiden, not strongly enough to make the half-day's hunt that would surely have found me. I understood I'd earned whatever they gave.

But facing it now made me feel like I was dead too, dead through the forty years I'd felt asleep. Was it what ghosts feel as they lounge out there on the dim edge of life?—assuming they're loved and needed still when they're long-since replaced? Maybe what I'd been was not Sleeping Beauty but a well-meaning vampire, sucking her strength from the ones she's quit, who can spare her the blood but have long since forgot her. Maybe the kindest repair I could offer was speedy death (death's always close in a moving car).

And Dan's last message. What could I do with that? Whole years I'd prayed for Dan and Frances to leave my dreams, and they all but had. Now here came Swift with hurtful *news*, from a soul I'd almost believed was at peace. I could burn it unread, but Swift had said Lee might find it helpful. Helpful for what?—directions for murder and suicide.

It lay on my round dining-table all evening; and I circled it while I fixed a cold supper—boiled chicken, lettuce, homemade mayonnaise. I hoped the paper itself would evaporate, but of course it swelled. When I'd fed myself (my appetite's healthy), I finally thought of a hopeful chance. Could one slim letter be the first bridge between me and Lee Vaiden? Maybe Swift meant that. He'd spent years grieving at the graves he'd dug; now maybe he'd seen his chance for amends.

I cleared my dishes, unplugged the phone, and sat down to read. It was one lined sheet from my old school-tablet and folded neatly. The writing was Dan's, no sign of distress, but it said

Dear Duchess,

We loved you. Remember that if things turn on me. I am hoping they don't but Frances and I are in deep water and may not make it to land, still breathing. I thought I was all she had—me and you—but I know different now. When you get grown maybe you can understand.

I hope you don't have to. But what I mean is, worshipping a person and them being worthy are two separate things. You can think you are somebody's moon and stars and then wake up to find you are just who buys the groceries. I learned that last night. I thought we had us a nice decent life. I knew I would work till I dropped to improve it. I thought you would have a safe home all your days with two people in it that would have good sense and that you could count on as long as they lived. That may yet be. I can't see how.

My eyes right now can barely see to write. I have not slept a wink. So I better get going. Whatever I do next is mainly for you. I want you to have a clear road ahead. You always claim I wanted a boy. I will say I would not have sent one back. But you have been as much help as all but my mother and she died early. You can't help this though. I am on my own.

I ask God now to guide my hand. If He takes me up we will be home

safe in time for school Monday and I can burn this. I can watch you grow up and have your own children, maybe one boy at least. If not, you will just have this from me. It comes with

> *All the love left in me*
> *from your father, Dan*

Right then at the table, I knew two things—sure as Swift knew I'd live. They dropped down into my mind, clear as roadsigns. God had heard Dan's voice and led him, whatever He meant. We never got home from that dreadful night; but what happened there was part of some plan—the start of something, not the bloody end. Then He'd guided me on to make one boy. The boy was a man now, with no help from me; the women who'd raised him were merciful but strong; and the living person who'd harmed me most was leading me to find him. Beyond that, I was still blind as Whitfield to all the rest—whether I'd moved to anybody's will except my own rank notions, needs, and fears.

I folded the letter along its old creases and thanked Dan's spirit, wherever it burned. I also saw my mother again, as she left me smiling and walked to her grave.

It all somehow had landed on me, a girl age eleven led to seize hold of fate. Maybe I had—and had not failed completely, for all my waste (Gaston and Douglas, both baffled to die, and my lost years). Then again maybe I'd gone flat crazy, since sundown today; and all my dead kin were laughing at me. At least I hadn't bored them.

I washed my supper dishes and dried them till they squeaked. I called the friend I called every night so she'd know I had lasted through one more day. She told me the menu of her big lunch (she lives to eat) and her grandchild's jokes. I got loose finally by saying I was whipped.

But once I'd bathed and turned back my sheets, I knew sleep didn't have me in mind. I own a good mattress, but it can't work wonders. I wasn't in pain; I was just alive. It felt very new, like a child's first sneeze; and I wanted to share it. By then though all my friends were asleep, or screwed to the TV, or grading homework for the sunrise class.

My hand made the choice. It literally reached out and did its own business. Before my mind caught it, it had dialed Information for eastern Virginia—Norfolk—Walter Porter's number. Swift had said Walter died four months ago. But the hand had gone forward, and by then I'd joined it.

Three long rings, four, a wait, then a hiss. I knew I'd reached some recording that would say his phone was disconnected. But a man's voice spoke up, a light baritone. "You have reached the former home of Mr. Walter Porter. I'm his nephew Lee Vaiden. I stay here now but am out for a while. If you leave your number, I'll call when I'm back."

I said "I'm the burglar and will be right over." It had slipped out of me like a cork from the deep. I hung up, ashamed. In a minute I was glad and suddenly tired as an old coalminer. Since dawn I'd worked that hard a shift, though for maybe better pay. The pay was knowledge. The boy was alive, a man with a strong voice, and no farther off than a hundred-fifty miles. Swift had promised he'd like me (for me, *like* has always been preferable to *need*). In my deepest trance, I'd somehow trusted time; time would keep me alive till I'd run my course, my lap of the plan. I could hold back now and plot this right. I bolted my doors then, lay down flat, and switched off the lamp.

Then I knew the next step. I'd keep the job I'd labored to learn; I still had my one talent to give, my ear for lies. Home would be *here*. I'd made it, unconscious, and the roots were deep. But I'd tell my story one final time, the whole thing, in writing. Not because I believed it would shake the stock market or raise the moral standards of the poor but because again it was what I'd made. It also could be my introduction—*Lee Vaiden; Kate Vaiden, your mother, her life*. I'd start tomorrow night. I could finish by fall (Norfolk's best in the fall). Then I'd make myself known. Lee would have all the facts. He would be free to choose.

REYNOLDS PRICE

Born in Macon, North Carolina in 1933, Reynolds Price attended North Carolina schools and received his Bachelor of Arts degree from Duke University. As a Rhodes Scholar he studied for three years at Merton College, Oxford, receiving the Bachelor of Letters with a thesis on Milton. In 1958 he returned to Duke where he is now James B. Duke Professor of English. His first novel *A Long and Happy Life* appeared in 1962. A volume of stories *The Names and Faces of Heroes* appeared in 1963. In the years since, he has published *A Generous Man* (a novel), *Love and Work* (a novel), *Permanent Errors* (stories), *Things Themselves* (essays and scenes), *The Surface of Earth* (a novel), *Early Dark* (a play), *A Palpable God* (translations from the Bible with an essay on the origins and life of narrative), *The Source of Light* (a novel), *Vital Provisions* (poems), and *Private Contentment* (a play). His first two novels and the story "A Chain of Love" are now collected in a single volume, *Mustian*. His books have been translated into fourteen languages.